PRAISE FOR COLLEEN HOOVER

"What a glorious and touching read, a forever keeper. The kind of book that gets handed down."

—*USA Today* on *It Ends with Us*

"*Confess* by Colleen Hoover is a beautiful and devastating story that will make you feel so much."

—*The Guardian*

"*It Ends with Us* tackles [a] difficult subject . . . with romantic tenderness and emotional heft. The relationships are portrayed with compassion and honesty, and the author's note at the end that explains Hoover's personal connection to the subject matter is a must-read. Packed with riveting drama and painful truths, this book powerfully illustrates the devastation of abuse—and the strength of the survivors."

—*Kirkus Reviews* (starred review)

"Hoover joins the ranks of such luminaries as Jennifer Weiner and Jojo Moyes, with a dash of Gillian Flynn. Sure to please a plethora of readers."

—*Library Journal* (starred review) on *November 9*

"Hoover builds a terrific new-adult world here with two people growing in their careers and discovering mature love."

—*Booklist* (starred review) on *Ugly Love*

OTHER TITLES BY COLLEEN HOOVER

Verity
All Your Perfects
Without Merit
Too Late
It Ends with Us
November 9
Confess
Ugly Love
Hopeless
Losing Hope
Finding Cinderella: A Novella

MAYBE SOMEDAY SERIES

Maybe Someday
Maybe Not: A Novella
Maybe Now

SLAMMED SERIES

Slammed
Point of Retreat
This Girl

Regretting

YOU

COLLEEN
HOOVER

Montlake

Published by Montlake, Seattle
www.apub.com

Amazon, the Amazon logo, and Montlake are trademarks of Amazon.com, Inc., or its affiliates.

ISBN-13: 9781542016421
ISBN-10: 1542016428

Cover design by David Drummond

Printed in the United States of America

This book is for the brilliant and fascinating Scarlet Reynolds. I can't wait for this world to feel your impact.

CHAPTER ONE

MORGAN

I wonder if humans are the only living creatures that ever feel hollow inside.

I don't understand how my body can be full of everything bodies are full of—bones and muscles and blood and organs—yet my chest sometimes feels vacant, as if someone could scream into my mouth and it would echo inside of me.

I've been feeling this way for a few weeks now. I was hoping it would pass because I'm beginning to worry about what's causing this emptiness. I have a great boyfriend I've been dating for almost two years now. If I don't count Chris's moments of intense teenage immaturity (mostly fueled by alcohol), he's everything I want in a boyfriend. Funny, attractive, loves his mother, has goals. I don't see how he could be the cause of this feeling.

And then there's Jenny. My little sister—my best friend. But I know she's not the source of my emptiness. She's the primary source of my happiness, even though we're complete opposites. She's outgoing, spontaneous, and loud and has a laugh I'd kill for. I'm quieter than she is, and more often than not, my laughter is forced.

It's a running joke between us that we are so different, if we weren't sisters, we would hate each other. She'd find me boring and I'd find her annoying, but *because* we're sisters, and only twelve months apart, our differences somehow work. We have our moments of tension, but we never let an argument end without a resolution. And the older we get, the less we argue and the more we hang out. Especially now that she's dating Chris's best friend, Jonah. The four of us have spent almost every waking hour together as a group since Chris and Jonah graduated high school last month.

My mother could be the source of my recent mood, but that wouldn't make sense. Her absence isn't anything new. In fact, I'm more used to it now than I used to be, so if anything, I've become more accepting of the fact that Jenny and I got the short end of the stick in the parent department. She's been inactive in our lives since our father died five years ago. I was more bitter about having to parent Jenny back then than I am now. And the older I get, the less it bothers me that she's not the type of mother to meddle in our lives, or give us a curfew, or . . . care. It's honestly kind of fun being seventeen and given the freedom most kids my age would dream of.

Nothing has changed in my life recently to explain this profound emptiness I've been feeling. *Or maybe it has, and I'm just too afraid to notice it.*

"Guess what?" Jenny says. She's in the front passenger seat. Jonah is driving, and Chris and I are in the back seat. I've been staring out the window during my bout of self-reflection, so I pause my thoughts and look at her. She's turned around in her seat, her eyes moving excitedly between me and Chris. She looks really pretty tonight. She borrowed one of my maxi dresses and kept it simple with very little makeup. It's amazing what a difference there is between fifteen-year-old Jenny and sixteen-year-old Jenny. "Hank said he can hook us up tonight."

Chris lifts a hand and high-fives Jenny. I look back out the window, not sure I like that she likes to get high. I've done it a handful of times—a by-product of having the mother that we do. But Jenny is only sixteen and partakes in whatever she can get her hands on at every party we go to. That's a big reason why I choose *not* to partake, because I've always felt a sense of responsibility for her since I'm older and our mother doesn't regulate our activities in any way.

Sometimes I feel like I'm Chris's babysitter too. The only one in this car I don't have to babysit is Jonah, but that's not because he doesn't get drunk or high. He just seems to maintain a level of maturity despite whatever substances might be running through his system. He has one of the most consistent personalities I've ever encountered. He's quiet when he's drunk. Quiet when he's high. Quiet when he's happy. And somehow even quieter when he's mad.

He's been Chris's best friend since they were kids, and they're like the male versions of me and Jenny, but opposite. Chris and Jenny are the life of every party. Jonah and I are the invisible sidekicks.

Fine by me. I'd rather blend in with the wallpaper and quietly enjoy people-watching than be the one standing on a table in the center of a room, being the one people are watching.

"How far out is this place?" Jonah asks.

"About five more miles," Chris says. "Not far."

"Maybe not far from here, but far from our houses. Who's driving home tonight?" Jonah asks.

"Not it!" Jenny and Chris both say at the same time.

Jonah glances at me in the rearview mirror. He holds my stare for a moment, and then I nod. He nods too. Without even speaking, we've both agreed we'll stay sober tonight.

I don't know how we do it—communicate without communicating—but it has always been an effortless thing between us. Maybe it's because we're a lot alike, so our minds are in sync a lot of the time. Jenny and Chris don't notice. They don't need to communicate silently with anyone because anything and everything they need to say rolls off the tips of their tongues whether it should or not.

Chris grabs my hand to get my attention. When I look at him, he kisses me. "You look pretty tonight," he whispers.

I smile at him. "Thank you. You don't look so bad yourself."

"Wanna stay at my house tonight?"

I think about that for a second, but Jenny spins around in her seat again and answers for me. "She can't leave me alone tonight. I'm a minor about to spend the next four hours ingesting a lot of alcohol and maybe an illegal substance. Who's gonna hold back my hair while I vomit in the morning if she stays at your place?"

Chris shrugs. "Jonah?"

Jenny laughs. "Jonah has typical parents who want him home by midnight. You know that."

"Jonah just graduated high school," Chris says, talking about him like he's not in the front seat listening to every word. "He should man up and stay out all night for once."

Jonah is pulling the car into a gas station when Chris says that. "Anyone need anything?" Jonah asks, ignoring the conversation being had about him.

"Yeah, I'm gonna try to buy some beer," Chris says, unbuckling his seat belt.

That actually makes me laugh. "You look every minute of eighteen. They aren't going to sell you beer."

Chris grins at me, taking that comment as a challenge. He gets out of the car to go inside, and Jonah gets out to pump gas. I reach into Jonah's console and grab one of the watermelon Jolly Ranchers he always leaves behind. Watermelon is the best flavor. I don't understand how anyone could hate it, but apparently he does.

Jenny unbuckles her seat belt and crawls into the back seat with me. She curls her legs beneath her, facing me. Her eyes are full of mischief when she says, "I think I'm gonna have sex with Jonah tonight."

For the first time in ages, my chest feels full, but not in a good way. It feels like it's being flooded with thick water. Maybe even mud. "You just turned sixteen."

"The same age you were when you had sex with Chris for the first time."

"Yeah, but we had been dating longer than two months. And I still regret it. It hurt like hell, lasted maybe a minute, and he smelled like tequila." I pause because it sounds like I just insulted my boyfriend's skills. "He got better."

Jenny laughs but then falls back against the seat in a sigh. "I feel like it's commendable that I've held out two months."

I want to laugh, because two months is nothing. I'd rather her wait an entire year. Or five.

I don't know why I'm so against this. She's right—I was younger than her when I started having sex. And if she's going to lose her virginity to someone—at least it's to someone I know is a good person. Jonah has never taken advantage of her. In fact, he's known Jenny for an entire year and never made a pass at her until she was sixteen. It was frustrating to her, but it made me respect him.

I sigh. "You lose your virginity once, Jenny. I don't want this moment to be while you're drunk in a stranger's house, having sex on someone else's bed."

Jenny moves her head from side to side like she's actually contemplating what I've said. "Then maybe we could do it in his car."

I laugh, but not because that's funny. I laugh because she's making fun of me. That's exactly how I lost my virginity to Chris. Cramped in the back seat of his father's Audi. It was absolutely unremarkable and wholly embarrassing, and even though we got better, it would be nice if our first time had been something we could look back on with fonder memories.

I don't even want to think about this. Or talk about it. It's hard being best friends with my little sister for this very reason—I want to be excited for her and hear all about it, but at the same time, I want to protect her from making the same mistakes I made. I always want better for her.

I look at her sincerely, trying my best not to seem motherly. "If it happens tonight, just stay sober, at least."

Jenny rolls her eyes at my advice and crawls back into the front seat just as Jonah opens his door.

Chris is back too. *Without* beer. He slams his door and folds his arms over his chest. "It really sucks having a baby face."

I laugh and run my hand across his cheek, pulling his focus to mine. "I like your baby face."

That makes him smile. He leans in and kisses me but pulls away as soon as his lips meet mine. He taps Jonah's seat. "You try it." Chris takes cash out of his pocket and reaches into the front, dropping it on the console.

"Won't there be plenty of alcohol there?" Jonah asks.

"It's the biggest graduation party of the year. The entire senior class will be there, and every one of us are underage. We need all the reinforcements we can get."

Jonah reluctantly grabs the cash and gets out of the car. Chris kisses me again, this time with tongue. He pulls back pretty quickly, though. "What's in your mouth?"

I crunch down on the Jolly Rancher to break it. "Candy."

"I want some," he says, bringing his mouth back to mine.

Jenny groans from the front seat. "Stop. I can hear you slurping."

Chris pulls back with a grin but also with a piece of Jolly Rancher in his mouth. He bites down on it while putting on his seat belt. "It's been six weeks since we graduated. Who has a graduation party six weeks after graduation? Not that I'm complaining. Just seems like we should be past the graduation celebrations by now."

"It hasn't been six weeks. It's only been four," I say.

"Six," he corrects. "It's July eleventh."

6

Six?

I try to keep the sudden onslaught of tension in every single muscle in my body from being visible to Chris, but I can't help but have a reaction to what he just said. Every part of me stiffens.

It hasn't been six weeks. *Has it?*

If it's been six weeks . . . that means I'm two weeks late for my period.

Shit. Shit, shit, shit.

The trunk to Jonah's car pops open. Chris and I both spin around, just as Jonah slams the trunk shut and walks to the driver's-side door. When he gets in the car, he has a smug smile on his face.

"Motherfucker," Chris mutters, shaking his head. "She didn't even card you?"

Jonah puts the car in drive and begins to pull out. "It's all in the confidence, my friend."

I watch as Jonah reaches across the seat and takes Jenny's hand.

I look out the window, my stomach in knots, my palms sweating, my heart pounding, my fingers quietly counting the days since my last period. I haven't given it any thought at all. I know it was graduation because Chris was bummed we couldn't have sex. But I've just been expecting to get it any day now, thinking it's only been a month since they graduated. The four of us have been so busy doing a ton of nothing during summer break that I haven't even thought about it.

Twelve days. I'm twelve days late.

～

It's all I've thought about all night while at this graduation party. I want to borrow Jonah's car keys, drive to a twenty-four-hour pharmacy, and buy a pregnancy test, but that would only make him ask questions. And Jenny and Chris would notice my absence. Instead, I have to spend the entire evening surrounded by music so loud I can feel it cracking in my bones. There are sweaty bodies in every part of this house, so there's nowhere I can escape to. I'm too scared to drink now, because if I am pregnant, I have no idea what that could do. I've never given pregnancy much thought, so I don't know exactly how much alcohol can harm a fetus. I won't even take that chance.

I can't believe this.

"Morgan!" Chris yells from across the room. He's standing on a table. Another guy is standing on a table next to him. They're playing a game where they balance on one leg and take turns downing shots until one of them falls. It's Chris's favorite drinking game and my least favorite time to be around him, but he's waving me over. Before I make it across the room, the guy on the other table falls, and Chris raises a victorious fist in the air. Then he jumps down just as I reach him. He wraps an arm around me, pulling me to him.

"You're being boring," he says. He brings his cup to my mouth. "Drink. Be merry."

I push the cup away. "I'm driving us all home tonight. I don't want to drink."

"No, Jonah is driving tonight. You're good." Chris tries again to give me another drink, but I push it away again.

"Jonah wanted to drink, so I told him I'd drive," I lie.

Chris looks around, spotting someone nearby. I follow his gaze to see Jonah sitting on the couch next to Jenny, whose legs are draped across his lap. "You're DD tonight, right?"

Jonah glances at me before answering Chris. It's a two-second silent conversation, but Jonah can see in my pleading expression that I need him to tell Chris he's not.

Jonah tilts his head a little in curiosity but then looks at Chris. "Nope. I'm getting hammered."

Chris slumps his shoulders and looks back at me. "Fine. I guess I'll have to have fun all alone."

I'm trying not to be insulted by his words, but it's hard not to be. "Are you saying I'm not any fun when I'm sober?"

"You are fun, but drunk Morgan is my favorite Morgan."

Wow. That kinda makes me sad. But he's drunk, so I'll excuse his insults right now, even if it's just to avoid an argument. I'm not in the mood. I've got more important things on my mind.

I pat Chris's chest with both hands. "Well, drunk Morgan won't be here tonight, so go find people you can have fun with."

Right when I say that, someone grabs Chris's arm and pulls him back to the tables. "Rematch!" the guy says.

With that, my level of sobriety is no longer Chris's concern, so I take that as an opportunity to escape from him, this noise, these people. I walk out the back door and am met with a quieter version of the party and a blast of fresh air. There's an empty chair next to the pool, and even though there's a couple in the water I'm almost certain are doing things that should be deemed unsanitary in a swimming pool, it's somehow less of a nuisance than being inside that house. I position my chair so that I can't see them, and I lean back and close my eyes. I spend the next few minutes trying not to obsess over any symptom I may or may not have had this past month.

I don't even have time to start thinking about what all of this might mean for my future when I hear a chair being dragged across the concrete behind me. I don't even want to open my eyes and see who it is. I can't take Chris and all his drunkenness right now. I can't even take Jenny and her combination of wine coolers, weed, and being sixteen.

"You okay?"

I sigh from relief when I hear Jonah's voice. I tilt my head and open my eyes, smiling at him. "Yeah. I'm fine."

I can see in his expression that he doesn't believe me, but whatever. There's no way I'm telling Jonah I'm late for my period because (a) it's none of his business and (b) I don't even know if I'm pregnant and (c) Chris is the first person I'll tell if I am.

"Thanks for lying to Chris," I say. "I just really don't feel like drinking tonight."

Jonah nods in understanding and offers me a plastic cup. I notice he's holding two, so I take one from him. "It's soda," he says. "Found a rogue can buried in one of the coolers."

I take a sip and lean my head back. Soda tastes so much better than alcohol, anyway. "Where's Jenny?"

Jonah nudges his head toward the house. "Taking table shots. I couldn't stay to watch."

I groan. "I hate that game so much."

Jonah laughs. "How did we both end up with people who are our exact opposites?"

"You know what they say. Opposites attract."

Jonah shrugs. I find it odd that he shrugs at that. He stares at me for a moment, then looks away and says, "I heard what Chris said to you. I don't know if that's why you're out here, but I hope you know he didn't mean it. He's drunk. You know how he gets at these parties."

I like that Jonah is defending Chris right now. Even though Chris can sometimes be a little insensitive, Jonah and I both know that his heart is bigger than both of ours put together. "I might be mad if he did this all the time, but it's a graduation party. I get it—he's having fun, and he wants me to have fun with him. In a way, he's right. Drunk Morgan is way better than sober Morgan."

Jonah looks at me pointedly. "I wholeheartedly disagree with that."

As soon as he says that, I pull my eyes from his and look down at my drink. I do this because I'm afraid of what's happening right now. My chest is starting to feel full again, but in a good way this time. That emptiness is being replaced with heat and flutters and heartbeats, and I hate it because it feels like I've just pinpointed what has caused me to feel so empty these past few weeks.

Jonah.

Sometimes when we're alone, he looks at me in a way that makes me feel empty when he looks away. It's a feeling I've never gotten when Chris looks at me.

This realization scares me to death.

Until lately, it seems I've gone my whole life without experiencing this feeling, but now that I have, it's as if part of me disappears when the feeling disappears.

I cover my face with my hands. Out of all the people in the world to want to be around, it's a shitty realization to know Jonah Sullivan is starting to top that list.

It's like my chest has been on a constant search for its missing piece, and Jonah is holding it in his fist.

I stand up. I need to get away from him. I'm in love with Chris, so it makes me uncomfortable and itchy when I'm alone with his best friend and having these feelings. Maybe it's the soda making me feel this way.

Or the fear that I might be pregnant.

Maybe it has nothing to do with Jonah.

I've been standing for all of five seconds when, out of nowhere, Chris appears. His arms tighten around me right before he propels us both into the pool. I'm both pissed and relieved, because I needed to get away from Jonah, but now I'm sinking into the deep end of a pool that I had no intentions of getting into fully clothed.

I surface at the same time Chris does, but before I can yell at him, he pulls me to him and kisses me. I kiss him back because it's a much-needed distraction.

"Where's Jenny?" Chris and I both look up, and Jonah is looming over us, glaring down at Chris.

"Don't know," Chris says.

Jonah rolls his eyes. "I asked you to keep an eye on her. She's drunk." Jonah walks toward the house to find Jenny.

"So am I," Chris says. "Never ask a drunk person to babysit a drunk person!" Chris moves a few feet until he can touch, and then he pulls me with him. He rests his back against the wall of the pool and positions me so that I'm holding on to his neck, facing him. "I'm sorry for what I said earlier. I don't think any version of you is boring."

I purse my lips together, relieved he noticed he was being an ass.

"I just wanted you to have fun tonight. I don't think you're having fun."

"I am now." I force a smile because I don't want him to notice the turmoil beneath my surface. But I can't help but be worried, no matter how hard I try to put it off until I know for certain. I'm worried for myself, for him, for us, for the child we might be bringing into this world way before either of us is ready. We can't afford this. We aren't prepared. I don't even know that Chris is the person I want to spend the rest of my life with. That's definitely something a person should be certain about before they go and create a human together.

"Wanna know what my favorite thing about you is?" Chris asks. My shirt keeps floating up to the surface, so he tucks the front of it into my jeans. "You're a sacrificer. I don't even know if that's a real word, but that's what you are. You do things you don't want to do to make life better for the people around you. Like being the designated driver. That doesn't make you boring. It makes you a hero."

I laugh. Chris becomes complimentary when he's drunk. Sometimes I make fun of him for it, but I secretly love it.

"You're supposed to say something you love about me now," he says.

I look up and to the left, like I'm having to think hard. He squeezes my side playfully.

"I love how much fun you are," I say. "You make me laugh, even when you frustrate me."

Chris smiles, and a dimple appears in the center of his chin. He has such a great smile. If I am pregnant and we do end up having a child together, I hope it at least has Chris's smile. That's the only positive thing I can think of that could come from this situation.

"What else?" he asks.

I reach my hand up and touch his dimple, fully prepared to tell him I love his smile, but instead, I say, "I think you'll make a great dad someday."

I don't know why I say that. Maybe I'm testing the waters. Seeing what his reaction will be.

He laughs. "Hell yeah, I will. Clara is gonna love me."

I tilt my head. "Clara?"

"My future daughter. I've already named her. Still working on a boy name, though."

I roll my eyes. "What if your future wife hates that name?"

He slides his hands up my neck and grips my cheeks. "You won't." Then he kisses me. And even though his kiss doesn't fill up my chest like Jonah's looks sometimes do, I feel a comforting reassurance in this moment. In his words. In his love for me.

Whatever happens when I finally take a pregnancy test tomorrow . . . I'm confident he'll support me. It's just who Chris is.

"Guys, we should go," Jonah says.

Chris and I separate and look up at Jonah. He's holding Jenny. Her arms are wrapped around his neck, and her face is pressed against his chest. She's groaning.

"I told her not to get on that table," Chris mutters, climbing out of the pool. He helps me out, and we squeeze as much water as we can from our clothes before heading to Jonah's car. Luckily, the seats are leather. I get in the driver's seat since Chris assumes Jonah has been drinking. Jonah gets in the back seat with Jenny. Chris is flipping through songs on the radio when we pull away from the party.

"Bohemian Rhapsody" has just started playing on one of the stations, so Chris turns it up and starts to sing. A few seconds later, Jonah is singing along.

Surprisingly, I quietly join them. There's no way any human can hear this song while driving and *not* sing along. Even if they're in the midst of a pregnancy scare at the age of seventeen while feeling things for someone in the back seat of a car that they should only be feeling for the person in the front passenger seat.

CHAPTER TWO

CLARA

Seventeen Years Later

I look at my passenger seat and cringe. As usual, there are crumbs of an unknown source caked in the crevices of the leather. I grab my backpack and toss it in the back seat, along with an old fast-food bag and two empty water bottles. I attempt to swipe the crumbs away. I think it might be pieces of banana bread that Lexie was eating last week. Or it could be the crumbs from the bagel she was eating on our way to school this morning.

Several graded papers are crumpled on my floorboard. I reach for them, swerving toward the ditch before righting the wheel and deciding to leave the papers where they are. A presentable car isn't worth dying for.

When I reach the stop sign, I pause and give this decision the contemplation it deserves. I can keep driving toward my house, where my whole family is preparing for one of our traditional birthday dinners. Or I can do a U-turn and head back toward the top of the hill, where I just passed Miller Adams standing on the side of the road.

He's avoided me for all of the last year, but I can't leave someone I even sort of know stranded in this heat no matter how awkward it might be between us. It's almost one hundred degrees outside. I have the air conditioner on, but beads of sweat are sliding down my back, being soaked up by my bra.

Lexie wears her bra for an entire week before washing it. She says she just douses it in deodorant every morning. To me, wearing a bra twice before washing it is almost as bad as wearing the same pair of underwear two days in a row.

Too bad I don't apply the same philosophy of cleanliness to my car that I apply to my bras.

I sniff the air, and my car smells of mildew. I debate spraying a bit of the deodorant I keep in my console, but if I decide to turn the car around and offer Miller a ride, my car will smell like freshly sprayed deodorant, and I'm not sure which is worse. A car that effortlessly smells like mildew or a car that purposefully smells like fresh deodorant to cover *up* the smell of mildew.

Not that I'm trying to impress Miller Adams. It's hard for me to worry about the opinion of a guy who seems to go out of his way to avoid me. *But I do, for some reason.*

I never told Lexie this because it embarrasses me, but at the beginning of this year, Miller and I were assigned lockers next to each other. That lasted all of two hours before Charlie Banks started using Miller's locker. I asked Charlie if his locker had been reassigned, and he told me Miller offered him twenty bucks to switch lockers.

Maybe it had nothing to do with me, but it felt personal. I'm not sure what I did to make him dislike me, and I try not to care about his feelings behind his avoidance of me. But I don't like that he doesn't like me, so I'll be damned if I pass him up and offer validation to his feelings, because *I'm nice, dammit!* I'm not this terrible person he seems to think I am.

I make the U-turn. I need his impression of me to change, even if it's merely for selfish reasons.

When I approach the top of the hill, Miller is standing next to a road sign, holding his cell phone. I don't know where his car is, and he certainly isn't on this road because he's out for a casual run. He's wearing a pair of faded blue jeans and a black T-shirt, each a death sentence of their own in this heat, but . . . paired together? Heatstroke is a strange way to want to go out, but to each his own.

He's watching me as I loop my car around and park behind him. He's about five feet away from the front of my car, so I can see the smirk on his face when he slides his cell phone into his back pocket and looks up at me.

I don't know if Miller realizes what his attention (or lack thereof) can do to a person. When he looks at you, he does it in such a way that it makes you feel like the most interesting thing he's ever seen. He puts his entire body into the look, somehow. He leans forward, his eyebrows draw together in curiosity, he nods his head, he listens, he laughs, he frowns. His expressions while he listens to people are captivating. Sometimes I watch him from afar as he holds conversations with people—secretly envious they're getting his rapt attention. I've always wondered what a full-on conversation would be like with him. Miller and I have never even had a conversation one-on-one, but there have been times I've caught him glancing at me in the past, and even a simple one-second graze of his attention can send a shiver through me.

I'm starting to think maybe I shouldn't have made the U-turn, but I did and I'm here, so I roll down my window and swallow my nerves. "It's at least another thirteen days before the next Greyhound. Need a ride?"

Miller stares at me a moment, then looks behind him at the empty roadway, as if he's waiting for a better option to come along. He wipes sweat from his forehead; then his focus lands on the sign he's gripping.

The anticipation swirling around in my stomach is a clear signal that I care a lot about the opinion of Miller Adams, as much as I can try and convince myself that I don't.

I hate that things are weird between us, even though nothing has happened that I'm aware of that would make them weird. But the way he avoids me makes it feel like we've had issues in the past, when really, we've had no interaction at all. It almost feels similar to breaking up with a guy and then not knowing how to navigate a friendship with him after the breakup.

As much as I wish I didn't care to know anything about him, it's hard not to want attention from him because he's unique. And cute. Especially right now, with his Rangers cap turned backward and wisps of dark hair peeking out from beneath it. He's long overdue for a haircut. He usually keeps it shorter, but I noticed when we started back to school that it got a lot longer over the summer. I like it like this. I like it short too.

Shit. I've been paying attention to his *hair*? I feel I've subconsciously betrayed myself.

He's got a sucker in his mouth, which isn't unusual. I find his addiction to suckers amusing, but it also gives off a cocky vibe. I don't feel like insecure guys would walk around eating candy as much as he does, but he always shows up to school eating a sucker and usually has one in his mouth at the end of lunch.

He pulls the sucker out of his mouth and licks his lips, and I feel every bit of the sweaty sixteen-year-old that I am right now.

"Can you come here for a sec?" he asks.

I'm willing to give him a ride, but getting back out in this heat was not part of the plan.

"No. It's hot."

He waves me over. "It'll only take a few minutes. Hurry, before I get caught."

I really don't want to get out of my car. I'm regretting turning around, even if I am finally getting the conversation with him I've always wanted.

It's a toss-up, though. Conversation with Miller comes a close second to the cold blast from my car's air conditioner, so I roll my eyes dramatically before exiting my vehicle. I need him to understand the huge sacrifice I'm making.

The fresh oil from the pavement sticks to the bottom of my flip-flops. This road has been under construction for several months, and I'm pretty sure my shoes are now ruined because of it.

I lift one of my feet and look at the bottom of my tarred shoe, groaning. "I'm sending you a bill for new shoes."

He looks at my flip-flops questionably. "Those aren't shoes."

I glance at the sign he's hanging on to. It's the city limit sign, held erect by a makeshift wooden platform. The platform is held down by two huge sandbags. Because of the road construction, none of the signs on this highway are cemented into the ground.

Miller wipes beads of sweat off his forehead and then reaches down and lifts one of the sandbags, holding it out to me. "Carry this and follow me."

I grunt when he drops the sandbag into my arms. "Follow you where?"

He nudges his head in the direction I came from. "About twenty feet." He puts his sucker back in his mouth, picks up the other sandbag and tosses it effortlessly over his shoulder, then begins to drag the sign behind him. The wooden platform scratches against the pavement, and tiny pieces of wood splinter off.

"Are you stealing the city limit sign?"

"Nope. Just moving it."

He continues walking while I stand still, staring at him as he drags the sign. The muscles in his forearms are pulled tight, and it makes me wonder what the rest of his muscles look like under this much strain.

Stop it, Clara! The sandbag is making my arms sore, and the lust is chipping away at my pride, so I reluctantly begin following him the twenty feet.

"I was only planning on offering you a ride," I say to the back of his head. "I never intended to be an accomplice in whatever this is."

Miller props the sign upright, drops his sandbag on the wooden slats, and then takes the other sandbag from my arms. He drops it in place and straightens the sign out so that it's facing the right way. He pulls the sucker back out of his mouth and smiles. "Perfect. Thank you." He wipes a hand on his jeans. "Can I catch a ride home? I swear it got ten degrees hotter on my walk here. I should have brought my truck."

I point up at the sign. "Why did we just move this sign?"

He turns his ball cap around and pulls the bill of it down to block more of the sun. "I live about a mile that way," he says, throwing a thumb over his shoulder. "My favorite pizza place won't deliver outside the city limits, so I've been moving this sign a little every week. I'm trying to get it to the other side of our driveway before they finish construction and cement it back into the ground."

"You're moving the city limit? For pizza?"

Miller begins walking toward my car. "It's just a mile."

"Isn't tampering with roadway signs illegal?"

"Maybe. I don't know."

I start following him. "Why are you moving it a little at a time? Why not just move it to the other side of your driveway right now?"

He opens the passenger door. "If I move it in small increments, it's more likely to go unnoticed."

Good point.

Once we're inside my car, I remove my tarred flip-flops and turn up the air-conditioning. My papers crumple beneath Miller's feet as he fastens his seat belt. He bends down and picks up the papers, then proceeds to flip through them and peruse my grades.

"All As," he says, moving the pile of papers to the back seat. "Does it come natural, or do you study a lot?"

"Wow, you're nosy. And it's a little of both." I start to pull the car onto the road when Miller opens the console and peeks inside. He's like a curious puppy. "What are you doing?"

He pulls out my can of deodorant. "For emergencies?" He grins and then pops open the lid, sniffing it. "Smells good." He drops it back into the console, then pulls out a pack of gum and takes a piece, then offers one to me. *He's offering me a piece of my own gum.*

I shake my head, watching as he inspects my car with rude curiosity. He doesn't eat the gum because he still has a sucker in his mouth, so he slides it into his pocket and then begins to flip through songs on my radio. "Are you always this intrusive?"

"I'm an only child." He says it like it's an excuse. "What are you listening to?"

"My playlist is on shuffle, but this particular song is by Greta Van Fleet."

He turns up the volume just as the song ends, so nothing is playing. "Is she any good?"

"It's not a *she*. It's a rock band."

The opening guitar riff from the next song blares through the speakers, and a huge smile spreads across his face. "I was expecting something a little more mellow!" he yells.

I look back at the road, wondering if this is who Miller Adams is all the time. Random, nosy, maybe even hyper. Our school isn't massive, but he's a senior, so I don't have any classes with him. But I know him well enough to recognize his avoidance of me. I've just never been in this type of situation with him. Up close and personal. I'm not sure what I was expecting, but this isn't it.

He reaches for something tucked between the console and his seat, but before I realize what it is, he already has it open. I snatch it from him and toss it in the back seat.

"What was that?" he asks.

It's a folder with all my college applications, but I don't want to discuss it because it's a huge point of contention between my parents and me. "It's nothing."

"Looked like a college application to a theater department. You're already sending in college applications?"

"You are seriously the nosiest person I've ever met. And no. I'm just collecting them because I want to be prepared." *And hiding them in my car because my parents would flip if they knew how serious I am about acting.* "Have you not applied anywhere yet?"

"Yeah. Film school." Miller's mouth curls up in a grin.

Now he's just being facetious.

He begins tapping his hands on my dash in beat to the music. I'm trying to keep my eyes on the road, but I feel pulled to him. Partly because he's enthralling, but also because I feel like he needs a babysitter.

He suddenly jolts upright, his spine straight, and it makes me tense up because I have no idea what just startled him. He pulls his phone out of his back pocket to answer a call I didn't hear come through over the music. He hits the power button on my stereo and pulls the sucker out of his mouth. There's barely anything left of it. Just a tiny little red nub.

"Hey, babe," he says into the phone.

Babe? I try not to roll my eyes.

Must be Shelby Phillips, his girlfriend. They've been dating for about a year now. She used to go to our school but graduated last year and goes to college about forty-five minutes from here. I don't have an issue with her, but I've also never interacted with her. She's two years older than me, and although two years is nothing in adult years, two years is a lot in high school years. Knowing Miller is dating a college girl makes me sink into my seat a little. I don't know why it makes me feel inferior, as if attending college automatically makes a person more intellectual and interesting than a junior in high school could ever be.

I keep my eyes on the road, even though I want to know every face he makes while on this phone call. I don't know why.

"On the way to my house." He pauses for her answer and then says, "I thought that was tomorrow night." Another pause. Then, "You just passed my driveway."

It takes me a second to realize he's talking to me. I look at him, and he's got his hand over his phone. "That was my driveway back there."

I slam on the brakes. He catches the dash with his left hand and mutters "Shit" with a laugh.

I was so caught up in eavesdropping on his conversation I forgot what I was doing.

"Nah," Miller says into the phone. "I went for a walk, and it got really hot, so I caught a ride home."

I can hear Shelby on the other end of the line say, "Who gave you a ride?"

He looks at me for a beat and then says, "Some dude. I don't know. Call you later?"

Some dude? Somebody's got trust issues.

Miller ends the call just as I'm pulling into his driveway. It's the first time I've ever seen his house. I've known whereabouts he lived, but I've never actually laid eyes on the home due to rows of trees that line the driveway, hiding what lies beyond the white gravel.

It's not what I expected.

It's an older house, very small, wood framed and in severe need of a paint job. The front porch holds the quintessential swing and two rocking chairs, which are the only things about this place that hold appeal.

There's an old blue truck in the driveway and another car—not as old but somehow in worse shape than the house—that sits to the right of the house on cinder blocks, weeds grown up the sides of it, swallowing the frame.

I'm kind of taken aback by it. I don't know why. I guess I just imagined he lived in some grandiose home with a backyard pond and a four-car garage. People at our school can be harsh and seem to judge a person's popularity on the combination of looks and money, but maybe Miller's personality makes up for his lack of money because he seems popular. I've never known anyone to talk negatively about him.

"Not what you were expecting?"

His words jar me. I put the car in park when I reach the end of the driveway and do my best at pretending nothing about his home shocks me. I change the subject entirely, looking at him with narrowed eyes.

"Some *dude?*" I ask, circling back to how he referred to me on his phone call.

"I'm not telling my girlfriend I caught a ride with you," he says. "It'll turn into a three-hour interrogation."

"Sounds like a fun and healthy relationship."

"It is, when I'm not being interrogated."

"If you hate being interrogated so much, maybe you shouldn't be tampering with the city limit."

He's out of the car when I say that, but he leans down to look at me before he closes the door. "I won't mention you were an accomplice if you promise not to mention I'm adjusting the city limit."

"Buy me new flip-flops, and I'll forget today even happened."

He grins as if I amuse him, then says, "My wallet is inside. Follow me."

I was only kidding, and based on the condition of the home he lives in, I'm not about to take cash from him. But it seems like we somehow developed this sarcastic rapport, so if I suddenly become sympathetic and refuse his money, I feel it might be insulting. I don't mind insulting him in jest, but I don't want to *actually* insult him. Besides, I can't protest because he's already walking toward his house.

I leave my flip-flops in the car, not wanting to track tar into his house, and follow him barefooted up the creaky steps, noticing the rotting wood on the second step. I skip over that step.

He notices.

When we walk into the living room, Miller discards his tarred shoes by the front door. I'm relieved to see the inside of the home fares better than the outside. It's clean and organized, but the decor is ruthlessly trapped in the sixties. The furniture is older. An orange felt couch with your standard homemade afghan draped over the back faces one wall. Two green, extremely uncomfortable-looking chairs face the other. They look midcentury, but not in a modern way. Quite the opposite, actually. I have a feeling this furniture hasn't been changed out since it was purchased, long before Miller was even born.

The only thing that looks fairly new is a recliner facing the television, but its occupant looks older than the furniture. I can only see a portion of his profile and the top of his balding, wrinkled head, but what little hair he does have is a shiny silver. He's snoring.

It's hot inside. Almost hotter than it is outside. The air I'm gently sucking in is warm and smells of bacon grease. The living room window is raised, flanked by two oscillating fans pointed at the man. Miller's grandfather, probably. He looks too old to be his father.

Miller passes through the living room and heads toward a hallway. It begins to weigh on me, the fact that I'm following him to take his money. It was only a joke. Now it feels like an extremely pathetic show of my character.

When we reach his bedroom, he pushes open the door, but I remain in the hallway. I feel a breeze sweep through his room and reach me. It lifts the hair from my shoulder, and even though the breeze is warm, I find relief in it.

My eyes scroll around Miller's room. Again, it is not reminiscent of the condition of the outside of his home. There's a bed, full-size, flush against the far wall. *He sleeps there. Right there, in that bed, tossing about in those white sheets at night.* I force myself to look away from the bed, up at a huge poster of the Beatles hanging where a headboard would normally be. I wonder if Miller is a fan of older music, or if the poster has been here since the sixties, much like the living room furniture. The house is so old I wouldn't doubt it if this was his grandfather's room as a teenager.

But what really catches my eye is the camera on his dresser. It's not a cheap camera. And there are several different-size lenses next to it. It's a setup that would make an amateur photographer envious. "You like photography?"

He follows my line of sight to the camera. "I do." He pulls open the top drawer of his dresser. "But my passion is film. I want to be a director." He glances at me. "I'd kill to go to UT, but I doubt I can get a scholarship. So community college it is."

I thought he was making fun of me in the car, but now that I'm looking around his room, it's sinking in that he really might have been telling me the truth. There's a stack of books next to his bed. One of them is by Sidney Lumet called *Making Movies*. I walk over and pick it up, flipping through it.

"You're really nosy," he mimics.

I roll my eyes and set the book down. "Does the community college even have a film department?"

He shakes his head. "No. But it could be a stepping-stone to somewhere that does." He walks closer to me, holding a ten-dollar bill between his fingers. "Those shoes are five bucks at Walmart. Go crazy."

I hesitate, no longer wanting to take the money from him. He sees my hesitation. It makes him sigh, frustrated; then he rolls his eyes and shoves the bill in the front left pocket of my jeans. "The house is shit, but I'm not broke. Take the money."

I swallow hard.

He just stuck his fingers in my pocket. And I can still feel them, even though they're no longer there.

I clear my throat and force a smile. "Pleasure doing business with you."

He tilts his head. "Was it? Because you look hella guilty for taking my money."

I'm usually a better actress than this. I'm disappointing myself.

I walk toward his doorway, even though I'd love a better look at his bedroom. "No guilt here. You ruined my shoes. You owed me." I back out of his room and begin to walk down the hallway, not expecting him to follow me, but he does. When I reach the living room, I pause. The old man is no longer in the recliner. He's in the kitchen, standing next to the refrigerator, twisting the lid off a water bottle. He eyes me with curiosity as he takes a sip.

Miller sidesteps around me. "You take your meds, Gramps?"

He calls him Gramps. It's kind of adorable.

Gramps looks at Miller with a roll of his eyes. "I've taken 'em every damn day since your grandma skipped town. I'm not an invalid."

"*Yet*," Miller quips. "And Grandma didn't skip town. She died of a heart attack."

"Either way, she left me."

Miller looks at me over his shoulder and winks. I'm not sure what the wink is for. Maybe to ease the fact that Gramps seems a little like Mr. Nebbercracker, and Miller is assuring me that he's harmless. I'm beginning to think this is where Miller gets his sarcasm from.

"You're a nag," Gramps mutters. "Twenty bucks says I outlive you *and* your entire generation of Darwin Award recipients."

Miller laughs. "Careful, Gramps. Your mean side is showing."

Gramps eyes me for a moment, then looks back at Miller. "Careful, Miller. Your infidelity is showing."

Miller laughs at that jab, but I'm kind of embarrassed by it. "Careful, Gramps. Your varicose veins are showing."

Gramps tosses the water bottle lid and hits Miller square in the cheek with it. "I'm rescinding your inheritance in my will."

"Go ahead. You always say the only thing you have worth any value is air."

Gramps shrugs. "Air you won't be inheriting now."

I finally laugh. I wasn't positive their banter was friendly before the lid toss.

Miller picks up the lid and fists it in his palm. He motions toward me. "This is Clara Grant. She's a friend of mine from school."

A friend? *Okay.* I give Gramps a small wave. "Nice to meet you."

Gramps tilts his head down a little, looking at me very seriously. "Clara Grant?"

I nod.

"When Miller was six years old, he shit his pants at the grocery store because the automatic flusher on public toilets terrified him."

Miller groans and opens the front door, looking at me. "I should have known better than to bring you inside." He motions for me to head outside, but I don't.

"I don't know if I'm ready to leave," I say, laughing. "I kind of want to hear more stories from Gramps."

"I've got plenty," Gramps says. "In fact, you'll probably love this one. I have a video from when he was fifteen and we were at the school—"

"*Gramps!*" Miller snaps, quickly cutting him off. "Take a nap. It's been five minutes since your last one." Miller grabs my wrist and pulls me out of the house, closing the door behind him.

"Wait. What happened when you were fifteen?" I'm hoping he finishes that story, because I need to know.

Miller shakes his head and actually seems a little embarrassed. "Nothing. He makes up shit."

I grin. "No, I think *you're* the one making up shit. I need that story."

Miller puts a hand on my shoulder and urges me toward the porch steps. "You're never getting it. Ever."

"You aren't aware of my persistence. And I like your grandpa. I might start visiting him," I tease. "Once the city limit is moved, I'll order a pepperoni-and-pineapple pizza and listen to your gramps tell embarrassing stories about you."

"*Pineapple? On pizza?*" Miller shakes his head in mock disappointment. "You aren't welcome here anymore."

I walk down the steps, skipping the rotted one again. When I'm safe on the grass, I turn around. "You can't dictate who I get to be friends with. And pineapple on pizza is delicious. It's the perfect combination of sweet and salty." I pull out my phone. "Does your gramps have Instagram?"

Miller rolls his eyes, but he's smiling. "See you at school, Clara. Don't ever come back to my house again."

I'm laughing as I walk back to my car. When I open the car door and turn around, Miller is looking down at his phone. He never once looks back at me. When he disappears inside his house, an Instagram notification pings through on my phone.

Miller Adams started following you.

I smile.

Maybe it's all been in my head.

Before I'm even out of the driveway, I'm dialing Aunt Jenny's number.

CHAPTER THREE

MORGAN

"Morgan, stop." Jenny pulls the knife from my hand and pushes me away from the cutting board. "It's your birthday. You aren't supposed to do any of the work."

I lean my hip into the counter and watch her begin chopping the tomato. I have to bite my tongue because she's slicing the tomato way too thick. The big sister in me still wants to take over and correct her, even in our thirties.

But seriously, though. I could get three slices of tomato out of one of hers.

"Stop judging me," she says.

"I'm not."

"Yes, you are. You know I don't cook."

"That's why I was offering to slice the tomato."

Jenny holds the knife up like she's going to cut me. I raise defensive hands and then push myself up onto the counter next to her.

"So," Jenny says, side-eyeing me. I can tell by the tone of her voice she's about to say something she knows I'm going to disagree with. "Jonah and I decided to get married."

Surprisingly, I have no outward reaction to that comment. But inside, those words feel like claws, hollowing out my stomach. "He proposed?"

She lowers her voice to a whisper because Jonah is in the living room. "Not really. It was more of a discussion. It makes sense for it to be our next move."

"That is the least romantic thing I've ever heard."

Jenny narrows her eyes at me. "Like your proposal was any different?"

"Touché." I hate it when she makes good points. But she's right. There wasn't a fancy proposal—or even a *plain* proposal. The day after I told Chris I was pregnant, he said, *"Well, I guess we should get married."*

I said, *"Yeah, I guess."*

And that was that.

We've been happily married seventeen years now, so I don't know why I'm judging Jenny for the situation she got herself in. It just feels different. Jonah and Chris are two completely different people, and at least Chris and I were in a relationship when I got pregnant. I'm not even sure what's going on with Jonah and Jenny. They haven't spoken since the summer after he graduated, and now he's suddenly back in our lives and potentially our family?

Jonah's father died last year, and even though none of us had seen or spoken to him in years, Jenny decided to go to the funeral. They ended up having a one-night stand, but then he flew back home to Minnesota the next day. A month later, she found out she was pregnant.

I'll hand it to Jonah: he did step up to the plate. He got his life tied up in Minnesota and moved back here a month before Jenny was due. Granted, that was only three months ago, so I guess my hesitation comes more from not really knowing who Jonah is at this point in his life. They dated for two months when Jenny was in high school, and now he moved across the country to raise a child with her.

"How many times have the two of you even had sex?"

Jenny looks at me in shock, like my question is too intrusive.

I roll my eyes. "Oh, stop acting modest. I'm serious. You had a one-night stand and then didn't see him until you were nine months pregnant. Have you even been cleared by your doctor yet?"

Jenny nods. "Last week."

"And?" I ask, waiting for her to answer my question.

"Three times."

"Including the one-night stand?"

She shakes her head. "Four, I guess. Or . . . well . . . *five*. That night counts as two times."

Wow. They're practically strangers. "Five times? And now you're *marrying* him?"

Jenny is finished cutting the tomatoes. She plates them and starts slicing up an onion. "It's not like we just met. You liked Jonah just fine when I dated him in high school. I don't understand why you have an issue with it now."

I pull back. "Uh . . . let's see. He dumped you, moved to Minnesota the next day, disappeared for seventeen years, and now he suddenly wants to commit to you for the rest of his life? I think it's odd that you think my reaction is odd."

"We have a child together, Morgan. Is that not the same reason you've been married to Chris for seventeen years?"

There she goes, bringing up another good point.

Her phone rings, so she wipes her hands and pulls it out of her pocket. "Speaking of your child." She answers her cell. "Hey, Clara."

She has it on speakerphone, so it stings when I hear Clara say, "You aren't with my mother, are you?"

Jenny's eyes widen in my direction. She begins backing toward the kitchen door. "Nope." Jenny takes the phone off speaker and disappears into the living room.

It doesn't bother me that Clara always calls my sister for advice, rather than asking me. The problem is Jenny has no idea how to give

Clara advice. She spent her twenties partying, struggling through nursing school, and coming to me when she needed a place to stay.

Usually when Clara calls Jenny with something important that Jenny doesn't know how to answer, she'll make an excuse to hang up, and then she'll call me and relay everything. I'll tell her what to tell Clara; then she'll call Clara back and relay the advice like it came from her.

I like the setup, although I'd much rather Clara just ask me. But I get it. I'm her mom. Jenny is the cool aunt. Clara doesn't want me to know about certain things, and I get that. She'd die if she knew that I was aware of some of her secrets. Like when she asked Jenny to make her an appointment to get on birth control a few months ago, *just in case*.

I hop off the counter and continue slicing the onion. The kitchen door swings open, and Jonah walks in. He nudges his head toward the cutting board. "Jenny told me I have to take over because you aren't allowed to do anything."

I roll my eyes and drop the knife, moving out of his way.

I stare at his left hand, wondering what a wedding ring is going to look like on his ring finger. It's hard for me to imagine Jonah Sullivan committing to someone. I still can't believe he's back in our lives, and now he's here, in my kitchen, chopping onions on a cutting board that was given to me and Chris at the wedding Jonah didn't even attend.

"You okay?"

I look up at Jonah. His head is tilted, his cobalt eyes full of curiosity as he waits for me to answer him. Everything inside of me feels like it thickens—my blood, my saliva, my resentment.

"Yeah." I flash a quick smile. "I'm fine."

I need to give my focus to something else—*anything* else. I walk to the refrigerator and open it, pretending to look for something. I've successfully avoided one-on-one conversation with him since he moved back. I don't feel like making it a thing right now. Especially on my birthday.

The kitchen door swings open, and Chris walks in with a pan of burgers fresh off the grill. I close the refrigerator and stare at the kitchen door, which continues to swing back and forth behind him.

I hate that door more than I hate any other part of this house.

I'm grateful for the house, don't get me wrong. Chris's parents gave it to us as a wedding present when they moved to Florida. But it's the same house Chris grew up in, and his father, and his grandfather. The house is a historical landmark, complete with the little white sign out front. It was built in 1918 and reminds me daily that it's over a century old. The creaky floorboards, the plumbing that's constantly in need of repair. Even after we remodeled six years ago, the age still screams out any chance it gets.

Chris wanted to keep the original floor plan after the remodel, so even though a lot of the fixtures are new, it doesn't help that every room in this house is secluded and closed off from every other room. I wanted an open floor plan. Sometimes I feel like I can't breathe in this house with all these walls.

I certainly can't eavesdrop on Jenny and Clara's conversation like I'd like to.

Chris sets the pan of burgers on the stove. "Gotta grab the rest, and then it'll be ready. Is Clara almost home?"

"I don't know," I say. "Ask Jenny."

Chris raises his eyebrows, sensing my jealousy. He exits the kitchen, and the door continues to swing. Jonah stops it with his foot and then goes back to cutting up the vegetables.

Even though the four of us used to be best friends, sometimes Jonah seems like a stranger to me. He looks mostly the same, but there are subtle differences. When we were teens, his hair was longer. So long he'd sometimes pull it back in a ponytail. It's short now and a richer brown. He lost some of the honey-colored streaks that would show up by the end of every summer, but the darker color just brings out the blue in his eyes even more. His eyes have always been kind, even when he was angry. The only time you could tell he was upset was when his angular jawline would tense.

Chris is his opposite. He has blond hair and emerald eyes and a jawline he doesn't keep hidden behind stubble. Chris's job requires him to be clean cut, so his smooth skin makes him appear years younger than he actually is. And he has this adorable dimple that appears in the center of his chin when he smiles. I love it when he smiles, even after all these years of marriage.

When I compare the two of them, it's hard to believe Jonah and Chris are both thirty-five. Chris still has a baby face and could pass for being in his twenties. Jonah looks all of thirty-five and seems to have grown several inches, even since high school.

It makes me wonder how much different I look now than I did as a teenager. I'd like to think I still appear as youthful as Chris, but I certainly feel a lot older than thirty-three.

Well. Thirty-*four*, now.

Jonah brushes past me to grab a plate from the cabinet. He glances at me when he does and holds his stare. I can tell by the look on his face he has something to say, but he probably won't say it because he's always inside his head. He thinks more than he speaks.

"What?" I stare back at him—waiting for a response.

He shakes his head and turns around. "Nothing. Never mind."

"You can't look at me like that and not tell me what you were about to say."

He sighs, his back still to me as he grabs the head of lettuce and sticks the knife into it. "It's your birthday. I don't want to bring it up on your birthday."

"Too late for that."

He faces me again with a hesitant look in his eye, but he concedes and tells me his thoughts. "You've barely spoken to me since I moved back."

Wow. He cuts right to the chase. I can feel my chest and neck heat from the embarrassment of being called out. I clear my throat. "I'm speaking to you now."

Jonah folds his lips together, like he's trying to remain patient with me. "It's different. Things feel different." His words tumble around in the kitchen, and I want to dodge them, but the kitchen is too damn small.

"Different from what?"

He wipes his hands on a dish towel. "From how it used to be. Before I left. We used to talk all the time."

I almost scoff at that ridiculous comment. Of course things are different. We're adults now, with lives, and children, and responsibilities. We can't just go back to the carefree friendships we all had back then. "It's been over seventeen years. Did you think you could show back up and the four of us would fall right back into place?"

He shrugs. "Things fell back into place with me and Chris. And me and Jenny. Just not with me and you."

I waver between wanting to duck out of the kitchen and yelling all the things I've been wanting to yell at him since he left in such a selfish way.

I take a sip of my wine to stall my response. He's staring at me with eyes full of disappointment as I formulate a reply. Or maybe he's staring at me with contempt. Whatever he's feeling, it's the same look he gave me seconds before he walked away all those years ago.

And just like back then, I don't know if his disappointment is directed inward or outward.

He sighs. I can feel the weight of all his unpackaged thoughts.

"I'm sorry I left the way I did. But you can't stay mad at me forever, Morgan." His words come out quietly, like he doesn't want anyone else to hear our conversation. Then he walks out of the kitchen and ends it.

It isn't until this moment that I'm reminded of the heaviness I used to feel when he was around. Sharing the same air with him sometimes felt stifling back then, like he was selfishly taking more of it than he needed and I was hardly left with any air at all.

That same stifling feeling is back again, surrounding me in my own kitchen.

Even though he's no longer in the kitchen and the door is swinging back and forth, I can still feel the heaviness bearing down on my chest.

As soon as I stop the swinging kitchen door with my foot, Jenny pushes it back open. The conversation I refused to partake in with Jonah gets shoved to the back of my mind for me to stew over later, because now I need to know everything Clara said to my sister.

"It was nothing," Jenny says flippantly. "She gave some guy from her school a ride, and he started following her on Instagram. She wasn't sure if he was flirting with her."

"What guy?"

Jenny shrugs. "Morris? Miller? I can't remember. His last name is Adams."

Chris is in the kitchen now, setting another pan on the stove. "Miller Adams? Why are we talking about Miller Adams?"

"You know him?" I ask.

Chris shoots me a look that lets me know I should know *exactly* who Miller Adams is, but the name rings no bells. "He's Hank's boy."

"Hank? There are still people named *Hank* in this world?"

Chris rolls his eyes. "Morgan, come on. Hank Adams? We went to school with him."

"I vaguely remember that name."

Chris shakes his head. "He's the kid who used to sell me weed. Ended up dropping out junior year. Got arrested for stealing the science teacher's car. And a load of other shit. Pretty sure he's been in jail a few years now." Chris gives his attention to Jenny. "Too many DUIs or something. Why are we talking about his son? Clara isn't dating him, is she?"

Jenny grabs the pitcher of iced tea from the refrigerator and closes the door with her hip. "No. We're talking about a celebrity named Miller Adams. You're talking about someone local. Different people."

Chris blows out a rush of air. "Thank God. That's the last family she needs to be involved with."

Anything involving his daughter and a boy is not an easy subject with Chris. He takes the tea from Jenny and leaves the kitchen to go place it on the dining room table.

I laugh once I know Chris is out of earshot. "A celebrity?"

Jenny shrugs. "I don't want to get her in trouble."

Jenny has always been quick on her feet. She's so good at improvising it's scary.

I glance at the door to make sure it's closed, then look back at her. "Jonah thinks I hate him."

Jenny shrugs. "Feels that way sometimes."

"I've never hated him. You know that. It's just . . . you barely know him."

"We have a child together."

"It takes thirty seconds to make a baby."

Jenny laughs. "It was more like three hours, if you really want to know."

I roll my eyes. "I *don't* want to know."

Chris yells from the dining room to let us know the food is ready. Jenny walks out of the kitchen with the burgers, and I plate the rest of the vegetables and take them to the table.

Chris sits across from Jenny, and I sit next to Chris. Which means Jonah is directly across from me. We successfully avoid eye contact while making our plates. Hopefully the rest of dinner will go much the same way. It's all I really want for my birthday—little to no eye contact with Jonah Sullivan.

"Are you excited for tomorrow?" Chris asks Jenny.

Jenny nods vigorously. "You have no idea."

She's a nurse at the same hospital where Chris is head of quality control. She's been on maternity leave since Elijah was born six weeks ago, and tomorrow is her first day back.

The front door bursts open, and Clara's best friend, Lexie, walks in. "You started eating without me?"

"You're perpetually late. We always start without you. Where's Clara?"

"On her way, I guess," Lexie says. "I was going to catch a ride with her, but Mom let me use the car." Lexie looks around the table, taking in who all is here. She nods at Jonah. "Hey, Uncle Teacher."

"Hi, Lexie," he says, seemingly annoyed at the nickname she's given him.

Jonah got a job at Clara's school as a history teacher when he moved back. I still can't believe he's a teacher. I don't ever remember him talking about wanting to *become* a teacher. But I guess there weren't a lot of options in our small East Texas town when he decided to move back and help Jenny with Elijah. He came from the business world, but all you need to become a teacher around here is a bachelor's degree and an application. They're in short supply thanks to the shitty pay scale.

"You sure you don't mind keeping Elijah this week?" Jenny asks me.

"Not at all. I'm excited."

I really am excited. He'll be in day care starting next week, so I've agreed to keep him for the four days Jenny works this week.

Sometimes I'm surprised that Chris and I never had another child after Clara. We talked about it, but we never seemed to be on the same page at the same time. There was a stretch where I wanted another, but he was working so much that he wasn't ready. Then when Clara was about thirteen, Chris brought up the idea of having another one, but the thought of having an infant and a teenager at the same time seemed a little terrifying. We haven't brought it up since, and now that I'm thirty-four, I'm not sure I want to start over.

Elijah is the perfect solution. A part-time baby I get to play with and send back home.

"Too bad I'm still in high school," Lexie says. "I'd be a great babysitter."

Jenny rolls her eyes. "Weren't you the one who put a random dog in my backyard because you thought it was mine?"

"It looked like your dog."

"I don't even *have* a dog," Jenny says.

Lexie shrugs. "Well, I thought you did. Excuse me for being proactive." Lexie finally takes her seat after having made her plate. "I can't stay long. I have a Tinder date."

"I still can't believe you're on Tinder," Jenny mutters. "You're sixteen. Don't you have to be eighteen to even open an account?"

Lexie grins. "I *am* eighteen on Tinder. And speaking of things that surprise us, I'm still shocked you've had the same boyfriend for more than one night. It's so unlike you." She looks at Jonah. "No offense."

"None taken," Jonah says with a mouthful.

Jenny and Lexie have always had this kind of banter. I find it entertaining, mostly because they're so much alike. Jenny had a string of boyfriends throughout her twenties, and had there been Tinder back then, Jenny would have been Tinder Queen.

Me, not so much. Chris is the only guy I've ever dated. The only guy I've ever kissed. That happens when you meet the man you're going to marry at such a young age. Hell, I met Chris before I even knew what I wanted to study in college.

I guess it didn't matter, though, because I didn't last that long in college. Having Clara so young put a hold on any dreams I had for myself.

I've been thinking a lot about that lately. Now that Clara is getting older, I've been feeling this gaping hole inside me, like it's sucking the air out of each day that passes by, where all I do is live for Chris and Clara.

Clara finally walks into the house in the middle of my self-deprecating thought. She stops about five feet from the table, ignoring everyone and everything around her as her finger moves over her phone screen.

"Where have you been?" Chris asks her. She's only about thirty minutes later than usual, but he notices.

"Sorry," she says, placing her phone down on the table next to Lexie's. She reaches over Jonah's shoulder to grab her plate. "Theater meeting after school and then one of my classmates needed a ride." She smiles at me. "Happy birthday, Mom."

"Thank you."

"Who needed a ride?" Chris asks her.

Jenny and I look at each other right when Clara says, "Miller Adams."

Shit.

Chris drops his fork to his plate.

Lexie says, "*Excuse* me? Where was my phone call about this?"

Chris looks at Jenny and then at me like he's about to scold us for lying to him. I grip his leg under the table. A sign I don't want him to mention we were talking about it. He knows as well as I do that Jenny is a good source of information for what's going on in our daughter's life, and if he reveals Jenny was telling me about their conversation, we'll all suffer.

"Why are you giving Miller Adams a ride?" he asks her.

"Yes," Lexie says. "Why did you give Miller Adams a ride? Don't leave out a single detail."

Clara ignores Lexie, responding only to her father. "It was barely a mile. Why do you seem so bothered by it?"

"Don't do it again," Chris says.

"I vote *do* it again," Lexie says.

Clara looks at Chris in disbelief. "It was hot out—I wasn't going to make him walk."

Chris raises his eyebrow, something he doesn't do very often, which makes it all the more intimidating when he does. "I don't want you involved with him, Clara. And you shouldn't be giving guys rides. It isn't safe."

"Your father is right," Lexie says. "Only give hot guys rides when *I'm* with you."

Clara falls down into her seat and rolls her eyes. "Oh my God, Dad. He's not a stranger, and I'm not dating him. He's had the same girlfriend for a year."

"Yeah, but his girlfriend is in college, so it's not like she'll be in your way," Lexie says.

"Lexie?" Chris says her name as more of a warning.

Lexie nods and runs her fingers across her mouth, like she's zipping her lips shut.

I'm a little in shock that Clara is sitting here acting like she didn't just call Jenny and slightly freak out that this kid was flirting with her. She's acting like she doesn't care, to both Chris *and* Lexie. But I know she does, thanks to Jenny. I stare at Clara in awe of her ability to pretend otherwise, but that awe is accompanied by a slight disturbance. I'm equally as impressed by her ability to lie as I am *Jenny's* ability to lie.

It's scary. I couldn't lie if my life depended on it. I get flustered, and my cheeks flush. I do whatever I can to avoid confrontation.

"I don't care if he's single or married or a billionaire. I would appreciate it if you wouldn't give him another ride."

Lexie makes a move like she's unzipping the imaginary zipper on her lips. "You're her dad—you shouldn't say it like that. If you make a guy off limits to a teenage girl, that only makes us want him more."

Chris points his fork at Lexie and looks around the table. "Who keeps inviting her to these things?"

I laugh, but I also know Lexie is right. This isn't going to end well if Chris keeps this up. I can feel it. Clara already has a crush on the guy, and now her father has made him off limits. I'll have to warn Chris later not to bring it up again unless he wants Hank Adams to be Clara's future father-in-law.

"I feel out of the loop," Jonah says. "What's so bad about Miller Adams?"

"There's no loop, and there's nothing wrong with him," Clara assures him. "It's just my parents, being overprotective as usual."

She's right. My mother didn't shelter me as a child in any sense, which is part of the reason I ended up pregnant with Clara at seventeen. Because of that, Chris and I take it overboard with Clara sometimes. We admit that. But Clara is our only child, and we don't want her to end up in a situation like we did.

"Miller is a good kid," Jonah says. "I have him in class. Nothing like Hank was at that age."

"You have him in class for forty minutes a day," Chris says. "You can't know him that well. Apples don't fall far from their trees."

Jonah stares at Chris after that response. He chooses not to continue the conversation, though. Sometimes when Chris wants to make a point, he doesn't let up until the person he's arguing with gives in. When we were younger, I remember him and Jonah always going toe to toe. Jonah was the only one who wouldn't give in and let Chris win.

Something has changed since he's been back, though. He's quieter around Chris. Always lets him get the final word. I don't think it's a show of weakness, though. In fact, it impresses me. Sometimes Chris still comes off as the hotheaded teenager he was when I met him. Jonah, however, seems above it. Like it's a waste of time to try to prove Chris wrong.

Maybe that's another reason I don't like that Jonah's back. I don't like seeing Chris through Jonah's eyes.

"What makes you say that about him? Apples don't fall far from their trees," Clara asks. "What's up with Miller's parents?"

Chris shakes his head. "Don't worry about it."

Clara shrugs and takes a bite of her burger. I'm glad she's letting it go. She's a lot like Chris in that she can sometimes be combative. You never know which way it's going to go with her.

I, on the other hand, am not combative at all. It bothers Chris sometimes. He likes to prove a point, so when I give in and don't give him that opportunity, he feels like I win.

It's the first thing I learned after marrying him. Sometimes you have to walk away from the fight in order to win it.

Jonah seems just as ready to move on from the conversation as the rest of us. "You didn't turn in your application for the UIL film project."

"I know," Clara says.

"Tomorrow is the deadline."

"I can't find anyone to sign up with. It's too hard to take on by myself."

It bothers me that Jonah entertains this idea of hers. Clara wants to go to college and study acting. I have no doubt she'd be good at it because she's phenomenal onstage. But I also know what the odds are of actually succeeding in such a competitive industry. Not to mention if you are one of the few who do succeed, you're dealing with the price of fame. It's not something I want for my daughter. Chris and I would love acting to be a backup major to something that can actually sustain her financially.

"You don't want to help her with it?" Jonah asks, his attention on Lexie.

Lexie makes a face. "Heck no. I work too much."

Jonah returns his attention to Clara. "Meet me before first period starts tomorrow. There's another student looking for a partner, and I'll see if they're interested."

Clara nods, just as Lexie starts to wrap up the rest of her burger. "Where are you going?" Clara asks.

"Tinder date," Jenny answers for her.

Clara laughs. "Is he at least our age?"

"Of course. You know I hate college boys. They all smell like beer." Lexie leans down and whispers something in Clara's ear. Clara laughs, and then Lexie leaves.

Clara begins asking Jonah questions about the film project requirements. Jenny and Chris are in a conversation of their own, discussing everything she missed at the hospital while on maternity leave.

I talk to no one and pick at my food.

It's my birthday, and I'm surrounded by everyone important to me, but for some reason, I feel more alone than I've ever felt. I should be happy right now, but something is off. I can't put my finger on it. Maybe I'm getting bored.

Or worse. Maybe I'm *boring*.

Birthdays can do that to you. I've been analyzing my life all day, thinking about how I need something of my own. After having Clara so young, Chris and I married, and he's always taken care of us financially since graduating college. I've always taken care of the house, but Clara will be seventeen in a couple months.

Jenny has a career and a new child and is about to have a new husband.

Chris got a promotion three months ago, which means he's at the office even more now.

When Clara is away at college, where will that leave me?

My thoughts are still stuck on the state of my life an hour after we've finished dinner. I'm loading the dishwasher when Jonah walks into the kitchen. He stops the door from swaying before it even starts. I appreciate that about him. He's a good dad, and he hates my kitchen door. *That's two things.*

Maybe there's hope for our friendship yet.

He's holding Elijah against his chest. "Wet rag, please."

That's when I see the spit-up all over Jonah's shirt. I grab a rag and wet it, then hand it to him. I take Elijah from him while he cleans himself up.

I look down at Elijah and smile. He looks a little like Clara did at this age. Fine blond hair, dark-blue eyes, a perfect little round head. I start to sway back and forth. He's such a good baby. Better than Clara. She was colicky and cried all the time. Elijah sleeps and eats and cries so little that sometimes Jenny will call me when he does cry just so we can gush over how cute he sounds when he's upset.

I glance up, and Jonah is watching us. He looks away and reaches toward the diaper bag. "I got you a birthday present."

I'm confused. Before dinner he seemed so tense with me. Now he's giving me a birthday present? He hands me an unwrapped gift. A gallon-size ziplock bag full of . . . candy.

What are we, twelve?

It takes me a moment, but as soon as I see that it's an entire bag of watermelon Jolly Ranchers, I want to smile. But I frown, instead.

He remembered.

Jonah clears his throat and tosses the rag into the sink. He takes Elijah from me. "We're about to head home. Happy birthday, Morgan."

I smile, and it's probably the only genuine smile I've given him since he's been back.

There's a moment between us—a five-second stare, where he smiles and I nod—before he leaves the kitchen.

I don't know exactly what that five seconds meant, but maybe we've come to some kind of truce. He really is trying. He's great to Jenny, great to Elijah, one of Clara's favorite teachers.

Why—when he's so great to everyone I love—have I been wishing he wasn't in any of our lives?

Once Jenny, Jonah, and Elijah leave, Clara goes to her room. It's where she spends the majority of her evenings. She used to want to spend her evenings with me, but that stopped when she was around fourteen.

Chris spends his evenings with his iPad, watching Netflix or sports.

I waste mine away watching cable. The same shows every night. My weeks are so routine.

I go to bed at the same time every night.

I wake up at the same time every morning.

I go to the same gym and do the same workout routine and run the same errands and cook the same scheduled meals.

Maybe it's because it's my thirty-fourth birthday, but I've felt like this cloud has been hanging over me since I woke up this morning. Everyone around me seems to have a purpose, yet I feel like I've reached the age of thirty-four and have absolutely no life outside of Clara and Chris. I shouldn't be this boring. Some of my friends from high school haven't even started families yet, and my daughter will be out of the house in twenty-one months.

Chris walks into the kitchen and grabs a bottle of water out of the fridge. He picks up the bag of Jolly Ranchers and inspects it. "Why would you buy an entire bag of the worst flavor?"

"It was a gift from Jonah."

He laughs and drops the bag on the counter. "What a terrible gift."

I try not to read too much into the fact that he doesn't remember watermelon is my favorite flavor. I don't necessarily remember all the things he liked when we first met.

"I'll be late tomorrow. Don't bother with dinner."

I nod, but I already bothered with dinner. It's in the slow cooker, but I don't tell him that. He starts to walk out of the kitchen. "Chris?"

He stops short and faces me.

"I've been thinking about going back to college."

"For what?"

I shrug. "I don't know yet."

He tilts his head. "But why now? You're thirty-four."

Wow.

Chris immediately regrets saying that when he sees how much his choice of words hurts me. He pulls me in for a hug. "That came out wrong. I'm sorry." He kisses the side of my head. "I just didn't know it's something you were still interested in since I make plenty of money to support us. But if you want a degree"—he kisses me on the forehead—"go to college. I'm gonna take a shower."

He leaves the kitchen, and I stare at the kitchen door as it swings back and forth. *I really hate that door.*

I kind of want to sell the house and start over, but Chris would never go for it. It would give me something to put my energy into, though. Because right now, my energy is pent up. I feel swollen with it as I think about how much I want a new kitchen door.

I might remove the whole door tomorrow. I'd rather have no door at all than a door that doesn't even work like a door should work. Doors should slam shut when you're angry.

I open a Jolly Rancher and pop it in my mouth. The taste gives me a feeling of nostalgia, and I think back to when we were all teenagers, craving the nights the four of us would spend driving around in Jonah's car, me and Chris in the back seat, Jenny in the front. Jonah had a thing for Jolly Ranchers, so he always kept a bag in the console.

He never ate the watermelon ones. It was his least favorite flavor, and my favorite, so he always left the watermelon for me.

I can't believe it's been that long since I've had one. I swear, sometimes I forget who I was or what I loved before I got pregnant with Clara. It's like the day I found out I was pregnant, I became someone else. I guess that happens when you become a mother, though. Your focus is no longer on yourself. Your life becomes all about this beautiful tiny little human you created.

Clara walks into the kitchen, no longer a beautiful tiny little human. She's beautiful and grown, and I ache at the loss of her childhood sometimes. When she'd sit in my lap or I'd snuggle up to her in bed until she fell asleep.

Clara reaches to my bag. "Yay. Jolly Ranchers." She grabs one and walks to the refrigerator, opening it. "Can I have a soda?"

"It's late. You don't need the caffeine."

Clara turns around and eyes me. "But it's your birthday. We still haven't done your birthday board."

I forgot about the birthday board. I actually perk up for the first time today. "You're right. Grab me one too."

Clara grins, and I go to my craft closet and pull out my birthday board. Clara may be too old to sit with me while I rock her to sleep, but at least she still gets just as excited about our traditions as I do. We started this one when she was eight years old. Chris doesn't involve himself in this tradition, so it's just something Clara and I do twice a year. It's like a vision board, but rather than making a new one every year, we just add to the same one. We each have our own, and we add to them only on our respective birthdays. Clara's birthday is still a couple months away, so I grab my board and leave hers in the closet.

Clara takes a seat next to me at the kitchen table and then selects a purple Sharpie. Before she starts writing, she looks over stuff we've put on it over the years. She runs her fingers over something she wrote on my board when she was eleven. *I hope my mom gets pregnant this year.* She even cut out a tiny picture of a rattle and pasted it next to her wish.

"Still not too late to make me a big sister," she says. "You're only thirty-four."

"Not happening."

She laughs. I look over the board, searching for one of the goals I wrote for myself last year. I find the picture I pasted of a flower garden in the top left of the board because it was my goal to uproot the bushes in the backyard and replant them with flowers. I met that goal in the spring.

I find the other goal I had, and I frown when I read it. *Find something to fill all the empty corners.*

I'm sure Clara thought I was being literal when I wrote it last year. I didn't actually want to fill every corner in my house with something. My goal was more of an internal one. Even last year, I'd been feeling unfulfilled. I'm proud of my husband and proud of my daughter, but when I look at myself and my life separate from theirs, there's very little I can find to be proud of. I just feel like I'm full of all this untapped potential. Sometimes my chest feels hollow, as if I've lived a life with nothing significant enough to fill it. My heart is full, but that's the only part of me that feels any weight.

Clara begins to write her goal for me, so I lean toward her and read it. *Accept that your daughter wants to be an actress.* She snaps the cap back on the Sharpie and puts it in the package.

Her goal makes me feel guilty. It's not like I don't want her to follow her dreams. I just want her to be realistic. "What are you going to do with an unusable degree if the acting thing doesn't work out for you?"

Clara shrugs. "We'll cross that bridge when we come to it." She pulls her leg up onto the chair and rests her chin on her knee. "What about you? What did you want to be when you were my age?"

I stare at my board, wondering if I can even answer that question. I can't. "I had no idea. I didn't have any special talents. I wasn't extremely smart in any one particular subject."

"Were you passionate about anything like I am about acting?"

I think about her question for a moment, but nothing comes to mind. "I liked hanging out with my friends and not thinking about the future. I assumed I'd figure it out in college."

Clara nods at the board. "I think that should be this year's goal. You need to figure out what you're passionate about. Because it *can't* be being a housewife."

"It could," I say. "Some people are perfectly fulfilled in that role." I *used* to be. I'm just not anymore.

Clara takes another sip of her soda. I write down her suggestion. *Find my passion.*

Clara may not want to know this, but she reminds me of myself at her age. Confident. Thought I knew everything. If I had to describe her in one word, it would be *assured*. I used to be assured, but now I'm just . . . I don't even know. If I had to describe myself with one word based on my behavior today, it would be *whiny.*

"When you think of me, what one word comes to mind?"

"Mother," she instantly says. "Housewife. *Overprotective.*" She laughs at that last one.

"I'm serious. What one word would you use to describe my personality?"

Clara tilts her head and stares at me for several long seconds. Then, in a very honest and serious tone, she says, "Predictable."

My mouth falls open in offense. *"Predictable?"*

"I mean . . . not in a bad way."

Can *predictable* sum a person up in a *good* way? I can't think of a single person in the world who'd want to be summed up as predictable.

"Maybe I meant *dependable,*" Clara says. She leans forward and hugs me. "Night, Mom. Happy birthday."

"Good night."

Clara goes to her bedroom, unknowingly leaving me in a pile of hurt feelings.

I don't think she was trying to be mean, but *predictable* is not something I wanted to hear. Because it's everything I know I am and everything I feared I would grow up to be.

CHAPTER FOUR

CLARA

I probably shouldn't have called my mother predictable last night, because this is the first time in a long time that I've woken up for school and didn't find her in the kitchen cooking breakfast.

Maybe I should apologize, because I'm starving.

I find her in the living room, still in her pajamas, watching an episode of *Real Housewives*. "What's for breakfast?"

"I didn't feel like cooking. Eat a Pop-Tart."

Definitely shouldn't have called her predictable.

My father walks through the living room, straightening out his tie. He pauses when he sees my mother lying on the couch. "You feeling okay?"

My mother rolls her head so that she's looking up at us from her comfy position on the couch. "I'm fine. I just didn't feel like making breakfast."

When she gives her attention back to the television, Dad and I look at each other. He raises a brow before walking over to her and pressing a quick kiss on her forehead. "See you tonight. Love you."

"Love you too," she says.

I follow my dad into the kitchen. I grab the Pop-Tarts and hand him one. "I think it's my fault."

"That she didn't cook breakfast?"

I nod. "I told her she was predictable last night."

Dad's nose scrunches up. "Oh. Yeah, that wasn't nice."

"I didn't mean it in a bad way. She asked me to describe her using one word, and it's the first thing that came to mind."

He pours himself a cup of coffee and leans against the counter in thought. "I mean . . . you aren't wrong. She does like routine."

"Wakes up at six every morning. Breakfast is ready by seven."

"Dinner at seven thirty every night," he says.

"Rotating menu."

"Gym at ten every morning."

"Grocery shopping on Mondays," I add.

"Sheets get washed every Wednesday."

"See?" I say in defense. "She's predictable. It's more of a fact than an insult."

"Well," he says, "there was that one time we came home, and she'd left a note saying she went to the casino with Jenny."

"I remember that. We thought she'd been kidnapped."

We really did think that. It was so unlike her to take a spontaneous overnight trip without planning months in advance, so we called both of them just to make sure she was the one who wrote the note.

My father laughs as he pulls me in for a hug. I love his hugs. He wears the softest white button-up shirts to work, and sometimes when his arms are around me, it's like being wrapped in a cozy blanket. Only that blanket smells of the outdoors, and it sometimes disciplines you. "I need to get going." He releases me and pulls at my hair. "Have fun at school."

"Have fun at work."

I follow him out of the kitchen to find Mom no longer on the couch but standing in front of the television. She's pointing the remote at the TV screen. "The cable just froze."

"It's probably the remote," Dad says.

"Or the operator," I say, taking the remote from my mother. She always hits the wrong button and can't remember which one to press to get her back to her show. I hit all the buttons and nothing works, so I power everything off.

Aunt Jenny walks into the house as I'm attempting to power the television back on for my mother. "Knock, knock," she says, swinging open the door. Dad helps her with Elijah's car seat and an armful of stuff. I power the television back on, but it doesn't do anything.

"I think it's broken."

"Oh, *God*," my mother says, as if the idea of being home all day with an infant and no television is a nightmare of an existence.

Aunt Jenny hands my mother Elijah's diaper bag. "You guys still have cable? No one has cable anymore."

There's only a year of age difference between Aunt Jenny and my mom, but sometimes it feels as though my mother is the parent of both of us.

"We try to tell her, but she insists on keeping it," I say.

"I don't want to watch my shows on an iPad," my mother says in defense.

"We get Netflix on our television," my father says. "You can still watch it on the television."

"Bravo isn't on Netflix," my mother responds. "We're keeping the cable."

This conversation is making my head hurt, so I take Elijah out of his car seat to get a minute in with him before I have to leave for school.

I was so excited when I found out Aunt Jenny was pregnant. I always wanted a sibling, but Mom and Dad never wanted more kids after they had me. He's as close as I'll ever get to a brother, so I want to be familiar to him. I want him to like me more than anyone else.

"Let me hold him," my father says, taking Elijah from me. I like how much my dad likes his nephew. Kind of makes me wish he and

Mom *would* have another one. It's not too late. She's only thirty-four. I should have written it down again on her birthday board last night.

Aunt Jenny hands my mother a list of written instructions. "Here's his feeding times. And how to heat the breast milk. And I know you have my cell phone number, but I wrote it down again in case your phone dies. I wrote Jonah's number down too."

"I've raised a human before," my mother says.

"Yeah, but it was a long time ago," Aunt Jenny says. "They might have changed since then." She walks over to my father and gives Elijah a kiss on the head. "Bye, sweetie. Mommy loves you."

Aunt Jenny starts to leave, so I grab my backpack in a hurry because there's something I need to discuss with her. I follow her out the front door, but she doesn't realize I'm behind her until she's almost to her car.

"Miller unfollowed me on Instagram last night."

She turns around, startled by my sudden presence. "Already?" She opens her car door and hangs on to it. "Did you say something that made him angry?"

"No, we haven't spoken since I left his house. I didn't post anything. I didn't even comment on any of his pictures. I just don't get it. Why follow me and then unfollow me hours later?"

"Social media is so confusing."

"So are guys."

"Not as confusing as we are," she says. She tilts her head, eyeing me. "Do you like him?"

I can't lie to her. "I don't know. I try not to, but he's so different from all the other guys at my school. He goes out of his way to ignore me, and he's always eating suckers. And his relationship with his grandpa is adorably weird."

"So . . . you like him because he ignores you, eats suckers, and has a weird grandpa?" Aunt Jenny makes a concerned face. "That's . . . those are weird reasons, Clara."

I shrug. "I mean, he's cute too. And apparently, he wants to go to college as a film major. We have that in common."

"That helps. But I mean, it sounds like you barely know him. I wouldn't take the unfollow too personal."

"I know." I groan and fold my arms over my chest. "Attraction is so stupid. And knowing he unfollowed me already put me in a shit mood, and it's only seven in the morning."

"Maybe his girlfriend saw the follow and didn't like it," Aunt Jenny suggests.

I thought about that possibility for a brief moment this morning. But I didn't like thinking about Miller and his girlfriend discussing me.

My father walks out the front door, so Aunt Jenny gives me a hug goodbye and goes to leave because she's parked behind both of us. I get in my car and text Lexie while I wait for Jenny to pull out of the driveway behind me.

I hope you got my text last night about me picking you up half an hour early. You never responded.

She still hasn't responded when I pull into her driveway.

Just when I'm about to call her, she comes tumbling out of her house, her backpack hanging from the crease of her elbow while she attempts to slide on a shoe. She has to stop and press her hand to the hood of the car to finish getting the shoe on. She stumbles to the door, her hair in disarray, mascara still under her eyes. She's like a drunk hurricane.

She gets in the car and shuts the door, dropping her backpack to the floorboard. She pulls out her makeup bag.

"You just woke up?"

"Yeah, four minutes ago when you texted. Sorry."

"How'd the *Tinder* date go?" I say sarcastically.

Lexie laughs. "I can't believe your family still believes I have a Tinder account."

"You lie to them about having it every time you're around. Why would they believe otherwise?"

"I work too much. All I have time for is school and work and maybe a shower if I'm lucky." She opens her makeup bag. "By the way. Did you hear about Miller and Shelby?"

I whip my head in her direction. "No. What about them?"

She opens her mascara just as I pull up to a stop sign. "Stop here for a second." She begins putting on her mascara, and I wait for her to finish whatever she was going to say about Miller Adams and his girlfriend. How random that it's the first thing she brought up and it's the only thing I've been able to think about since I gave him a ride yesterday.

"What about Miller and Shelby?"

Lexie moves her mascara wand to her other eye. She still doesn't answer me, so I ask her again. "Lexie, what happened?"

"Jeez," she says, stuffing the mascara wand back into the tube. "Give me a sec." She motions for me to continue driving while she pulls out her lipstick. "They broke up last night."

That's my favorite sentence that's ever come out of Lexie's mouth.

"How do you know?"

"Emily told me. Shelby called her."

"Why'd they break up?" I'm trying not to care. *Really* trying.

"Apparently, it's because of you."

"Me?" I look back at the road. "That's ridiculous. I gave him a ride to his house. He was in my car for three minutes tops."

"Shelby thinks he cheated on her with you."

"Shelby sounds like she has trust issues."

"That's really all it was?" Lexie asks. "A ride?"

"Yes. It was *that* inconsequential."

"Do you like him?" she asks.

"No. Of course not. He's an asshole."

"He is not. He's super nice. Annoyingly nice."

She's right. He is. *He's only an asshole to me.* "Isn't it weird that my father thinks he's such a bad person?"

Lexie shrugs. "Not really. Your father doesn't even like me, and I'm awesome."

"He likes you," I say. "He only teases the people he likes."

"And maybe Miller is the same way," she suggests. "Maybe he only ignores the people he likes."

I ignore that comment. Lexie focuses on putting on her makeup, but my mind is whirling. *Did their fight really have to do with a silly car ride?*

It was probably the car ride coupled with the Instagram follow. Which would explain why he unfollowed me last night. Which proves he's trying to get her back.

"Do you think their breakup will stick?"

Lexie glances at me and grins. "What's it matter to you? It was *inconsequential.*"

⌐

Jonah makes me call him Mr. Sullivan at school. I'm sure he'd like it if I called him Uncle Jonah outside of school, but he's just Jonah to me. I haven't known him long enough to feel like he's my uncle yet, even though he just had a baby with my aunt Jenny. Maybe after they're actually married, I'll add the title. But for now, all I really know of him is what I've heard my parents say—that he broke Aunt Jenny's heart in high school and moved away without warning. I've never asked any of them why he broke up with her. I don't guess I really cared, but for some reason, I'm curious today.

Jonah is at his desk grading papers when I walk in.

"Morning," he says.

"Morning." I have him for first period, so I toss my backpack in my usual seat, but I take the seat right in front of his desk.

"Did Jenny get Elijah dropped off with your mom?" he asks.

"Yep. Cute as ever."

"He really is. Looks just like his daddy."

"Ha. No. He looks just like *me*," I correct.

Jonah stacks his pages together and scoots them aside. Before he gets into the whole film project thing, I let my curiosity get the best of me. "Why'd you break up with Aunt Jenny in high school?"

Jonah lifts his head quickly, his eyebrows raised. He laughs nervously, like he doesn't want to have this conversation with me. Or with anyone. "We were young. I'm not sure I even remember."

"Mom wasn't happy when you got Aunt Jenny pregnant last year."

"I'm sure she wasn't. It wasn't very well thought out."

"Kind of hypocritical of her, considering they had me at seventeen."

Jonah shrugs. "It isn't hypocritical unless the action she's objecting to occurs *after* the objection."

"Whatever that means."

"It means people who make mistakes usually learn from them. That doesn't make them hypocrites. It makes them experienced."

"Didn't they teach you in college not to dole out life lessons before the morning bell rings?"

Jonah leans back in his seat, a hint of amusement in his eyes. "You remind me of your mother when she was your age."

"Oh, God."

"It's a compliment."

"How?"

Jonah laughs. "You'd be surprised."

"Stop insulting me."

Jonah laughs again, but I'm only half kidding. I love my mother, but I do not aspire to *be* my mother.

He grabs one of two folders on his desk and hands it to me. "Please fill this out, even if you don't end up doing it. If you place in the top, it'll be great to put on your film school applications. Not to mention you'll have footage for your acting reel."

I open the folder to look through it. "So who is it that's looking for a partner?"

"Miller Adams." My head snaps up when Jonah says his name. He continues speaking. "When you guys were talking about him last night, I remembered reading in the notes from the teacher who sponsored this program last year that Miller was on a team that placed. Which means he has the experience. I asked him to sign up this year, but he ultimately turned it down. Said he's got a lot going on and it's a big commitment. But if the two of you do it together, he might be interested."

I'm not gonna lie—I was secretly hoping it was Miller Adams, especially because he told me he was into film. *But was Jonah not at the same dinner I sat through last night?*

"Why would you try to pair me up with him on a project after what my dad said?"

"I'm a teacher, not a matchmaker. Miller is the perfect partner on this. And he's a good kid. Your father is misinformed."

"Either way, Dad set hard boundaries." *That I already know I'm not going to follow.*

Jonah stares at me thoughtfully for a second, then crosses his arms over his desk. "I know. Listen, it's just a suggestion. I think the project will be good for you, but if your dad doesn't want you to do it, there's not much I can do. But . . . you also don't need a parent's permission to sign up. You only need it for submission, and that's still several months away."

I kind of like that Jonah is encouraging me to disobey my father. Maybe he and Aunt Jenny really are perfect for each other.

The door opens, and Miller Adams walks in. *Thanks for the heads-up, Jonah.*

The first thing I notice are his crimson, puffy eyes. It looks like he hasn't slept. His shirt is wrinkled; his hair is a mess.

Miller looks from Jonah, to me, to Jonah. He remains by the door and tosses a hand in my direction while looking at Jonah. "*This* is who you want me to sign up with?"

Jonah nods, confused by Miller's reaction. *I'm* not confused by it. I'm used to him not wanting anything to do with me.

"Sorry, but that's not gonna work out," Miller says. He looks at me. "No offense, Clara. I'm sure you understand why."

I guess his girlfriend really *is* the reason. "I gathered when you unfollowed me on Instagram five hours after following me."

Miller walks farther into the room and drops his backpack on a desk and plops down into the chair. "According to Shelby, I shouldn't have followed you in the first place."

I laugh. "Your girlfriend broke up with you because I gave you a ride in one hundred and two–degree weather. There's something off about that."

"She broke up with me because I lied to her about it."

"Yeah. And you lied to her about it because you knew she'd break up with you if she found out. Therein lies the issue."

Jonah inserts himself into our conversation by leaning forward and looking back and forth between us. He pushes back his chair and stands. "I need coffee." He tosses the other folder on Miller's desk and heads for his classroom door. "You two figure this out and let me know what you decide by the end of the day."

Jonah leaves, and it's just Miller and me left in the room, staring at each other. He looks away and browses through the contents of the folder.

He really could have used those extra minutes of sleep. I feel bad Jonah called him in early for this. He looks like a truck ran over him between me dropping him off at his house yesterday and him waking up this morning. I can tell whatever fight he and Shelby had, it's taken a toll on him.

"You look really heartbroken," I say.

"I am," he says with a dull tone.

"Well . . . not all is lost. Heartbreak builds character."

That makes Miller laugh, although it's a dry laugh. He closes the folder and looks at me. "If Shelby finds out I'm working with you on this film submission, she'll never forgive me."

"So that's a yes?"

Miller doesn't laugh at that. In fact, he seems a little bummed that I'm making jokes at his expense. He's obviously not in the mood. And honestly, I kind of don't blame Shelby for dumping him. If my boyfriend lied to me about being in the car with another girl, then followed that girl on Instagram, he'd be my ex-boyfriend too.

"Sorry, Miller. I'm sure she's great. If I can help in any way—maybe back up your story—let me know."

Miller smiles at me appreciatively and then stands up, heading for the classroom door. He leaves the folder on the desk. "You should do the project anyway."

I nod, but I don't really care to sign up alone. For a few hopeful seconds, I was excited I might get to work with Miller on the project. Now that I had a taste of that thought, every other option tastes bitter.

Seconds later, Miller is gone.

I stare at the folder on his desk, then grab it and fill out the form, anyway. You never know—Shelby and Miller may not get back together, and it would suck if he didn't sign up just because his girlfriend has jealousy issues.

Jonah returns with two coffees, just as I've finished both forms. He hands me one of the coffees and casually leans against his desk.

He's been around for a few months now, and he still has no idea how much I hate coffee. This is why I don't refer to him as *Uncle* Jonah yet.

"What was that all about?" he asks.

"His girlfriend hates me. Well . . . *ex*-girlfriend." I take a sip of the coffee to be nice. It's putrid.

"Shouldn't be a problem then, right?"

I laugh. "You would think." I hand him both the folders. "I filled them out, anyway. Don't mention it to Miller. If he changes his mind, at least we'll have met the deadline for signups."

"I like the way you think," Jonah says. He sets his coffee on his desk and picks up a piece of chalk. He's writing the date on the board when two of my classmates walk in.

I go back to my seat. When the classroom begins to fill up, Jonah turns around and eyes the coffee on my desk. "Clara. Students aren't allowed to have drinks in class. Do it again and I'll give you detention."

I roll my eyes at him, but I want to laugh at his ability to switch into teacher mode so easily, even if he is just toying with me. "Yes, Mr. Sullivan," I say mockingly.

I trash the coffee, then pull out my phone and text Aunt Jenny on the way back to my seat.

Me: You busy?

Aunt Jenny: On my way to work.

Me: It'll only take a sec. Two things. Your baby daddy is a smartass. Also, Miller and Shelby broke up. Not sure how long it'll last.

Aunt Jenny: Why'd they break up? Because you gave him a ride?

Me: Apparently it was the Instagram follow that did it.

Aunt Jenny: That's good news! Now you get to date the guy with the weird grandpa.

Me: I didn't say his grandpa was weird. I said their relationship was adorably weird. Also, he's trying to get his girlfriend back, so I don't know that I have a chance.

Aunt Jenny: Oh, that stinks. Don't pursue him, then. You don't want to be the other girl. Trust me.

Me: You were the other girl once? I need to hear this story. Is that why you and Jonah broke up in high school?

The dots on my phone indicate Aunt Jenny is typing. I wait to hear about her juicy teenage drama, but the dots stop.

Me: I tell you everything. You can't hint that you've had an affair and not elaborate.

Me: Jenny?

Me: Aunt Jenny?

"Clara, put your phone away."

I drop my phone into my backpack with frightening speed. I don't know who Aunt Jenny cheated with, but if Jonah doesn't know about it, I don't think him confiscating my phone and reading my texts would be good for their relationship.

I'll call her at lunch and force her to tell me. Even if it involves Jonah, I want to know.

CHAPTER FIVE

MORGAN

I once heard someone say we're all just one phone call away from our knees.

It's the absolute truth. My voice comes out in a shaky whisper when I ask, "Is he okay?"

I wait for the nurse on the other end of the line to tell me that Chris will be fine. But all I get is a long stretch of silence. It feels like someone is wringing my spine like a wet towel. I want to double over from the pain, but the pain isn't physical. It's an intangible anguish that feels terminal.

"I don't know details," the nurse says. "All I know is that he was brought in a few moments ago, so try to get here as soon as possible."

I choke out an okay before ending the call, but I'm almost positive she would have given me more information if the news were better.

If the news were better, Chris would have called me himself.

I'm holding Elijah. I was holding him when the phone rang, and now I'm clutching him even tighter, still on my knees. For at least a minute, I'm frozen on my living room floor. But then Elijah yawns, and it snaps me back into a grim reality.

I call Jenny first, but her phone goes to voice mail. It's her first day back to work. She won't have her phone on her until her lunch break. But word will spread fast at the hospital, and she'll find out soon enough.

I start to call Jonah next so that he can come get Elijah, but I don't even have his phone number saved in my phone. I rush to the sheet of paper Jenny left me this morning and enter the number she wrote down to reach him. It goes straight to voice mail. *He's in class.*

I'll call the school to get in touch with him soon, but every second I spend trying to contact someone is a second longer it's going to take me to get to the hospital. I strap Elijah into his car seat, grab his diaper bag and my keys, and leave.

The trip to the hospital is a blur. I spend it whispering prayers and gripping the steering wheel and stealing glances at my phone resting in the passenger seat, waiting for Jenny to call me back.

I don't call Clara at school yet. I need to know that Chris is okay before I worry her.

If they haven't already notified Jenny that Chris was in a wreck, I'll have them page her when I get inside. She can take Elijah then.

For now, he's with me, so I take his diaper bag and his car seat and run toward the entrance. I'm faster than the automatic sliding doors of the emergency room. I'm forced to pause my sprint for a couple of seconds so they can open wide enough for me to enter. As soon as I'm inside, I go straight to the nurse's desk. It's a nurse I don't recognize. I used to know almost everyone in this hospital because I thought it made Chris look good for me to know everyone at his office parties, but they come and go so often, I don't even try to keep up anymore.

"Where's my husband?" The words tumble out in a panic. Her eyes are sympathetic.

"Who is your husband?"

"Chris." I gasp for air. "Chris Grant. He works here, and he was just brought in."

Her expression changes when I say his name. "Let me get someone who can help you. I just got on shift."

"Can you page my sister? She works here too. Jenny Davidson."

The nurse nods but rushes away from the window without paging Jenny.

I set Elijah's car seat on the closest chair. I try Jenny again and then Jonah's cell phone again, but they both go straight to voice mail.

I don't have time to wait on the nurse to figure out her shit. I call the hospital and ask for Labor and Delivery. They connect me after the most excruciating thirty seconds of hold time in my life.

"Labor and Delivery, how may I direct your call?"

"I need to speak to Jenny Davidson. One of your nurses. It's an emergency."

"Hold, please."

Elijah starts to cry, so I put my phone on speaker and set it in the chair so that I can pull him out of his car seat. I pace back and forth, waiting for Jenny to answer, waiting for a nurse, waiting for a doctor, *waiting, waiting, waiting.*

"Ma'am?"

I grab my phone. "Yes?"

"Jenny isn't on schedule until tomorrow. She's been out on maternity leave."

I shake my head, frustrated. Elijah is growing more agitated. He's hungry. "No, she started back this morning."

There's a moment of hesitation from the woman on the other line before she repeats herself. "She isn't on schedule until tomorrow. I've been here all day, and she's not here."

Before I start to argue with her, the doors to outside open, and Jonah rushes in. He pauses for a second, almost as if he wasn't expecting to see me here already. I hang up the phone and toss it in the chair. "Thank God," I say, handing Elijah to him. I reach into the bag and pull out a pacifier. I put it in Elijah's mouth and then head back to the window and ring the bell three times.

Jonah is standing next to me now. "What do you know?"

"Nothing," I say, exasperated. "All I was told on the phone is that it was a car wreck."

I finally look up at Jonah, and I've never seen him like this. Pale. Expressionless. For a moment, I worry about him more than myself, so I take Elijah from him. He backs up to a chair and sits down. In the midst of my internal hysteria, irritation begins to claw its way out. Chris is my husband. Jonah should be worried about me more than himself right now.

The waiting room is alarmingly empty. Elijah only becomes fussier, so I sit three seats down from Jonah and pull a bottle out of Elijah's diaper bag. It's cold, but it'll have to do. The second I put it in his mouth, he stops fussing and begins to devour it.

He smells like baby powder. I close my eyes and press my cheek against the top of his warm head, hoping the distraction will keep me from breaking down. I can feel in my gut that it might not be good. If they aren't allowing us to go see Chris, that means he's probably in surgery. Hopefully for something minor.

I want my sister. Jonah isn't really someone who can bring me comfort at a time like this. In fact, I'd rather he not be here, but if I can get in touch with Jenny, she'll make the situation better. And she can probably find out more information about Chris. Maybe Jonah has already spoken with her.

"Is Jenny on her way over?" I lift my head just as Jonah swings his gaze in my direction. He doesn't answer my question. He just stares at me, his brow furrowed, so I continue. "I tried calling her, but whoever answered the phone in Labor and Delivery kept telling me she isn't on the schedule today."

Jonah's eyes squint with a shake of his head. "I'm confused," he says.

"I know. I told her she started back today, but the woman tried arguing with me."

"Why are you trying to call Jenny?" He's standing now. The confusion dripping from him is making me more nervous than I already am.

"She's my sister. Of course I'm going to call her and tell her about Chris."

Jonah shakes his head. "What *about* Chris?"

What about Chris?

I'm so confused. "What do you mean? They called me and said Chris was in a wreck. Why else would I be here?"

Jonah swallows, dragging his hands down his face. Somehow, his eyes fill with even more concern. "Morgan." He steps closer to me. "I'm here because *Jenny* was in a wreck."

If I wasn't already sitting, I would have fallen.

I don't make a noise. I just stare at him and try to process everything. I shake my head and try to speak, but my words are weak. "You must have misunderstood them. They can't both have been . . ."

"Wait here," Jonah says. He strides to the window and rings the bell. I pull my cell phone out of my purse and dial Jenny's number. Voice mail again. I dial Chris's number. Maybe there was a mistake in the computer. His phone goes to voice mail too.

This has to be some mistake.

A few seconds pass with no sign of anyone, so Jonah moves to the doors that lead to the emergency room. He beats on them until someone finally appears at the window. A nurse I instantly recognize. Her name is Sierra. She has a daughter in Clara's class. She looks at me, and then her eyes fix on Jonah.

"I think there's been a mistake," Jonah says.

I'm next to him at the window now, holding Elijah. I can't feel my legs. I don't even know how I walked from the chair to here. "Who had a wreck? Who was brought in?" I can't stop the questions from spilling out of me. "Was it my husband or my sister?"

Sierra's eyes dart from me to Jonah and then down to the desk in front of her. "Let me get someone who can help you, Morgan."

Jonah grabs at his hair when she walks away. *"Dammit."*

It's not lost on me that no one seems to want to be in our presence. We're being avoided, and that terrifies me. No one wants to be the bearer of bad news.

"They can't both be hurt," I whisper. "They can't."

"They're not," Jonah says. His voice is so full of confidence I almost believe him. But then he rubs his forehead and leans against the wall for support. "Who called you? What did they say?"

"The hospital. About twenty minutes ago. They specifically said Chris. There was no mention of Jenny."

"Same, but they told me Jenny."

Just then, Sierra reappears, this time through the doors. "You guys can come with me."

She doesn't take us to a hospital room. She takes us to another waiting room, farther inside the ER.

Jonah is holding Elijah now. I didn't even notice he took him from me. Sierra tells us to have a seat, but neither of us does.

"I don't have news on their conditions yet."

"So, it *is* both of them?" Jonah asks. "Jenny *and* Chris?"

She nods.

"Oh my God," I whisper. I drop my head in my hands. Two huge tears slide down my cheeks.

"I'm so sorry, Morgan," she says. "You guys can wait in here, and as soon as I know something, I'll be back." Sierra leaves the room and closes the door.

Jonah sits next to me.

We've been in the emergency room less than ten minutes, but the fact that we still don't know anything makes it seem like hours have gone by.

"Maybe one of their cars broke down," Jonah mutters. "That's probably why they were together."

I nod, but my mind can't even process that sentence right now. I don't know why they were together, in the same car. I don't know why Jenny lied to us and said she was working today. I don't even care. I just need to know that they're okay.

Jonah straps a sleeping Elijah into his car seat, then stands and begins pacing the room. I look at the time on my cell phone. I should call someone to pick up Clara. A friend of mine. Or Lexie. I want someone to get to Clara before she finds out about the wreck from someone else.

I should call Chris's parents.

No, I'll wait. Make sure he's okay first. They live in Florida. Not much they can do from there but worry unnecessarily.

Jonah calls his mother and asks if she can come pick up Elijah. Before he hangs up, I get his attention. "Would she mind going to get Clara?"

Jonah nods in understanding, then asks his mother to pick up Clara from school. He then calls the school and hands me his phone. I let them know his mom will be picking her up.

Clara has met Jonah's mother a couple of times, but she's going to be confused, and Jonah's mother isn't anyone on the pickup list for Clara. I just don't want Clara driving up here alone. She'll be full of worry and panic, and she hasn't had her license all that long.

A few more minutes pass. Jonah spends it calling the police station, trying to get information about the wreck. They won't tell him much. He asks what the model of the vehicle is that was involved. It was Jenny's car. A Toyota Highlander. A male was driving. But that's all they'll tell him.

"Why was Chris driving her car?" Jonah asks. I treat it as a rhetorical question, but he mutters another. "Why did she lie about working today?"

I keep watching my phone as if Jenny or Chris is going to call me and tell me they're fine.

"Morgan," Jonah says.

I don't look at him.

"Do you think . . . are they having an—"

"Don't say it," I spit out.

I don't want to hear it. Or think it. It's absurd. It's incomprehensible.

I stand up and start to pace the portion of the room Jonah hasn't paced yet. I've never been so irritated by sounds before. The beeping coming from the hallway, the tapping of Jonah's fingers against his phone screen as he shoots off texts to Jenny's and Chris's phones, the paging system overhead calling doctors and nurses from one place to another, the squeaking of my shoes against the hardwood floor of this room. I'm so incredibly annoyed by every single thing, but the cacophony of sounds is the only thing I want in my head right now. I don't want to think about why Chris and Jenny were together.

"Clara will be here soon. And my mother," Jonah says. "We need to come up with a reason why Chris and Jenny were together."

"Why lie to them? I'm sure it was a work-related thing."

Jonah is staring at the floor, but I can see that his expression is full of doubt. Concern. *Fear.*

I swipe tears away, and I nod, because he could be right. I choose to believe he's wrong, but his mother and Clara might begin to ask us questions. They'll want specifics, or they'll start having the same thoughts Jonah and I are having. We can't tell them we don't know why they were together. It could cause unnecessary suspicion in Clara.

"We can tell them Chris had a flat and Jenny gave him a ride to work," I suggest. "At least until Jenny and Chris can explain it themselves."

We make eye contact . . . something we've barely done since he walked into the emergency room. Jonah nods while pressing his lips together, and something about the look in his eyes breaks me.

As if Jonah can sense I'm beginning to crack . . . to fade . . . he walks over to me and pulls me in for a comforting hug. I'm clinging to him in fear, my eyes squeezed shut, when the door finally opens.

We separate. Jonah steps forward, but when I see the look on the doctor's face, I step back.

He begins to speak, but I don't know exactly what he says because his words mean nothing to me. I can see our answer in his apologetic eyes. In the way his lips turn down at the corners. In his remorseful stance.

When the doctor tells us there was nothing they could do, Jonah falls into a chair.

I just . . . *fall.*

CHAPTER SIX

CLARA

I used to collect snow globes when I was younger. They lined a shelf in my bedroom, and sometimes I would shake them up, one after the other, then sit on my bed and watch as the flurries and the glitter swirled around inside the glass.

Eventually, the contents inside the globe would begin to settle. All would grow still, and then the globes on my shelf would return to their quiet, peaceful states.

I liked them because they reminded me of life. How sometimes, it feels like someone is shaking the world around you, and things are flying at you from every direction, but if you wait long enough, everything will start to calm. I liked that feeling of knowing that the storm inside always eventually settles.

This week proved to me that sometimes the storm doesn't settle. Sometimes the damage is too catastrophic to be repaired.

For the past five days since Jonah's mother showed up at my school to take me to the hospital, it feels like I've been inside a snow globe that someone shook up, then dropped. I feel like the contents of my life have shattered, and fragments of me have spilled out all over someone's dusty hardwood floor.

I feel irreparably broken.

And I can't even blame what happened to them on anyone but myself.

It's unfair how one event . . . one second . . . can shake the world around you. Toss everything on its head. Ruin every happy moment that led up to that earth-shattering second.

We're all walking around like lava coats our throats. Painfully silent.

My mother keeps asking if I'm okay, but all I can do is nod. Other than those words, she's been just as quiet as I have. It's like we're living in a nightmare—one where we don't want to eat or drink or speak. A nightmare where all we want to do is scream, but nothing comes out of our hollow throats.

I'm not a crier. I guess I get that from my mother. We cried together at the hospital. So did Jonah and his mother. But as soon as we left the hospital and went to the funeral home, my mother became as poised and put together as people expect her to be. She's good at putting on a brave face in public, but she saves the tears for her bedroom. I know because I do the same thing.

My father's parents flew in from Florida three days ago. They've been staying with us. My grandmother has been helping out around the house, and I'm sure it's been good for my mother. She's had to deal with funeral planning for not only her husband but also her sister.

Aunt Jenny's funeral was yesterday. My father's is right now.

My mother insisted they be separate, which made me angry. No one wants to sit through this two days in a row. Not even the dead.

I'm not sure what's more exhausting. The days or the nights. During the days since the accident, our house has had a revolving front door. People bringing food, offering their condolences, stopping by to check in. Mostly people who worked at the hospital with my father and aunt Jenny.

The nights are spent with my face buried into my soaking wet pillow.

I know my mother wants it to be over. She's ready for her in-laws to go home.

I'm ready to go home.

I've been holding Elijah through most of the service. I don't know why I've been wanting to hold him so much since it happened. Maybe I find his newness kind of comforting amid all this death.

He begins to grow restless in my arms. He's not hungry—Jonah's mom just fed him. I changed him right before the service started. Maybe he doesn't like the noise. The preacher my mother selected to conduct the service doesn't seem to know how to hold a microphone. His lips keep brushing across it. Every time he takes a step toward the speakers, they screech.

When Elijah begins to full-on cry, I first look at the end of the aisle for Jonah, but his previously occupied seat is now empty. Luckily, I'm sitting on the edge of the pew, closest to the wall. I quietly leave the room without having to walk down the middle of the aisle. The service is beginning to wind down, anyway. They'll have the prayer, and then everyone will walk past the casket and hug us, and then it'll be over.

I hugged most of these same people at Aunt Jenny's funeral yesterday. I don't really feel like doing it all over again. It's part of the reason I've been insistent on holding Elijah. I can't really hug people when my arms are occupied with my baby cousin.

When I'm outside the chapel and back in the foyer, I put Elijah in his stroller and take him outside. Ironically, it's a beautiful day. The sun warms my skin, but it doesn't feel good. It feels unfair. My father loved days like this. One time, he called in sick and took me fishing, simply because the weather was so nice.

"He okay?"

I glance to my left, and Jonah is leaning against the building in the shade. He pushes off the brick and walks toward us. I find it odd that he isn't inside right now. My father and Jonah were supposedly best friends, and he's skipping his service?

I guess I don't have room to talk. I'm out here too.

"He was getting restless, so I brought him outside."

Jonah places his palm on the top of Elijah's head, brushing his thumb over his forehead. "You can go back in. I'll probably just take him home now."

I'm jealous he gets to leave. *I* want to leave.

I don't go back inside. I take a seat on a bench right outside the front door to the chapel and watch Jonah push the stroller across the parking lot. After strapping Elijah into his car seat and loading the stroller into his trunk, Jonah gives me a small wave as he climbs into the car.

I wave back, unable to mask the empathy in my expression. Elijah isn't even two months old yet, and Jonah will be raising him alone now.

Elijah will never know what Aunt Jenny was like.

Maybe I should write down some of my favorite memories of her before I start to forget.

That thought breathes new life into my grief. I'm going to start forgetting them. I'm sure it won't happen at first, but it will, after time. I'm going to forget how my father sounded off key when he sang John Denver songs at the top of his lungs every time he mowed the yard. I'm going to forget how Aunt Jenny used to wink at me whenever my mother would say something that exposed her overbearing side. I'll start to forget how my father always used to smell like coffee or fresh grass and how Aunt Jenny used to smell like honey, and before I know it, I'll forget how their voices sounded and what their faces looked like in person.

A tear falls down my cheek, and then another. I lie down on the bench and curl up my legs. I close my eyes and try not to get swallowed up in more guilt. But the guilt wraps its arms around me, squeezing the breath out of my lungs. Since the moment I found out they had the wreck, I knew in my gut what caused it.

I was texting Aunt Jenny.

She was responding to my texts at first . . . and then she wasn't. I never heard back from her, and then two hours later, I found out about the wreck.

I'd like to believe it wasn't my fault, but Aunt Jenny said she was on her way to work when I texted her. I should have been more concerned about her reading my texts while driving, but I was only concerned about myself and my issues.

I wonder if Mom knows my conversation with Jenny is what caused them to crash. Had I not been texting her in that moment—had I just waited until she was at work—my mother wouldn't have lost both her sister and her husband. She wouldn't be struggling right now with being forced to bury two of the most important people in her life.

Jonah wouldn't have lost Jenny. Elijah wouldn't have lost his mother.

I wouldn't have lost my father—the only man I've ever loved.

Did they look at Aunt Jenny's phone? Could they determine she was texting and driving?

If my mother does find out it was because I wanted Aunt Jenny to read my texts and respond to me when I knew she was driving, that will only add to her heartache.

That knowledge makes me not want to be here at a funeral where every single tear being shed inside is all because of me.

"Hey."

My eyes pop open at the sound of his voice. Miller is standing over me, his hands in the pockets of his pants. I sit up on the bench, straightening out my dress so that it covers my thighs. I'm surprised to see him. He's wearing a suit. Black on black. I feel terrible that my body can somehow feel this much grief, yet be sparked with a twinge of attraction as soon as Miller is in my presence. I use my palms to wipe tears from my face. "Hi."

He presses his lips together and looks around, like this is as uncomfortable as I fear it is. "I wanted to stop by. See how you were doing."

I'm not doing well. Not at all. I want to tell him that, but the only thing that comes out of my mouth is, "I don't want to be here." I'm not asking him to take me anywhere. I'm just being honest about what I'm feeling this very moment. But he nudges his head toward the parking lot.

"Then let's go."

—

Miller is driving the old blue truck that was sitting in front of their house the day I dropped him off. I don't even know what kind of truck it is, but it's the same color of blue as the sky is right now. The windows are down, so I'm guessing his air conditioner no longer works. Or maybe he just likes to drive with the windows down. I pull my hair up and tie it in a knot so it'll stop blowing in my face. I tuck flyaways behind my ears and then rest my chin on my arm as I stare out the window.

I don't ask him where we're going. I don't even care. I just know that with every mile he puts between me and that funeral home, I feel more and more pressure release from my chest.

A song plays, and I ask Miller to turn it up. I've never heard it before, but it's beautiful and has nothing to do with any of the thoughts I'm having, and the singer's voice is so soothing it feels like a bandage. As soon as it ends, I ask him to play it again.

"I can't," Miller says. "It's the radio. Truck is too old for Bluetooth."

"What was the song?"

"'Dark Four Door,' by Billy Raffoul."

"I liked it." I look back out the window, just as another song begins to play. I like his taste in music. I wish I could just do this all day, every day. Ride around listening to sad songs while Miller drives. For some reason, sadness in music eases the sadness in my soul. It's like the worse the heartache in a song is, the better I feel. Dramatic songs are like a drug, I imagine. Really bad for you, but they make you feel good.

I wouldn't know. I've never done drugs before, so I've never tested that particular comparison. I've never even been high. It's hard to do normal rebellious teenage things when you have two parents who over-compensate for the mistakes they made when *they* were teenagers.

"You hungry?" Miller asks. "Thirsty?"

I pull away from the window and turn to look at him. "No. I kind of want to get high, though."

His eyes move swiftly from the road to me. He smiles a little. "I'm sure you do."

"I'm serious," I say, sitting up straighter. "I've never tried it before, and I really want to get out of my head today. Do you have any weed?"

"No," he says.

I sink back into my seat, disappointed.

"But I know where you can get some."

Ten minutes later, he's pulling up to the local movie theater. He tells me to wait in the truck. I almost tell him never mind, that it was just a random thought. But part of me is curious if it'll help with the grief. I'll try anything at this point.

He walks into the theater, and less than a minute later, he's walking out with a guy who looks a little older than us. Maybe in his twenties. I don't recognize him. They walk to the guy's car, and within fifteen seconds, cash and weed are exchanged. *Just like that.* It seems so easy yet fills me with a nervous energy. It's not legal in Texas, and even if it were, Miller is only seventeen.

Not to mention, he has a brand-new dashcam in this old truck. I'm positive the dashcam didn't catch the transaction, but if he were to be arrested right now, the police would search his truck and probably watch the video and hear that the drugs are for me.

My knee is bouncing nervously when Miller climbs back into his truck.

He drives to the side of the movie theater and faces the road so that we can see the entire parking lot. He pulls a baggie out of his pocket. There's an already-rolled joint in it.

The truck is so old it still has one of those built-in cigarette lighters. He pushes it in to heat up and then hands me the joint. I stare at it, unsure of what to do with it. I look at Miller expectantly. "You aren't going to light it for me?"

He shakes his head. "I don't smoke."

"But . . . you have a dealer."

Miller laughs. "His name is Steven. He's my coworker, not a dealer. But he always has weed on him."

"Well, shit. I didn't think I'd have to do it myself. I've never even lit a cigarette before." I pull out my phone and open YouTube. I search for how to light a joint and start playing a video.

"YouTube has weed-smoking tutorials?" he asks.

"Shocking, I know."

Miller is finding this amusing. I can tell by the expression on his face. He scoots closer to me and watches the video with me. "You sure you want to get high? Your hands are shaking." He takes the phone from me.

"It would be rude to change my mind now. You already paid for it."

Miller continues holding the phone for us. When the video is over, I pull the lighter out of its socket and stare at it hesitantly.

"Here. I can try."

I hand it to him, and he lights the joint as if he's a pro. Kind of makes me question his initial claim. He inhales once, then blows the smoke away from me, out his open window. He hands it to me next, but when I attempt to inhale, I just end up coughing and sputtering through the whole thing. I'm not nearly as graceful as he was.

"If you don't smoke weed, how come you did it so easily?"

He laughs. "I didn't say I've never tried it. I've just never lit a joint before."

I try it again, but I still can't get it to go down smooth. "It's so disgusting," I choke.

"Edibles are better."

"Then why didn't you get me an edible?"

"Steven didn't have any, and drugs aren't really my thing."

I hold the joint between my fingers, looking down at it, wondering how I ended up here when I should be at my father's funeral. Drugs aren't my thing, either, I guess. It feels so unnatural. "What *is* your thing?" I ask, looking back at Miller.

He leans his head back against his seat and thinks on this for a moment. "Iced tea. And cornbread. I love cornbread."

I laugh. Not what I expected. I wait a moment before taking another hit. Lexie would be horrified if she saw me right now.

Shit. Lexie.

I didn't even tell her I was leaving the funeral. I look at my phone, but she hasn't texted. I only have one text from my mother, sent fifteen minutes ago.

Mom: Where are you?

I flip my phone facedown. If I can't see the text, it doesn't exist.

"What about you?" Miller asks. "What's your thing?"

"Acting. But you already know that."

He makes a face. "When you asked what my thing was, for some reason, I thought we were talking about things we like to consume."

That makes me smile. "No, it includes anything. What are you the most into? What is the one thing you would never be willing to give up in life?" *He's probably going to say Shelby.*

"Photography," he says quickly. "Filming, editing. Anything that puts me behind the camera." He tilts his head and smiles at me. "But you already know that."

"That why you have a dashcam?" I say, pointing at it. "You have a need to be behind a camera, even when you're driving?"

He nods. "I also have this." He opens the glove box and pulls out a GoPro. "I always have some kind of camera on me. Never know when that perfect photographic moment will arise."

I think Miller might be just as into filming as I am when it comes to acting. "Too bad your ex won't let us work on the film project together. We might actually make a good team." I lift the joint back to my mouth, even though I hate everything about it. "How much do I have to smoke before it makes me feel numb?"

"It might *not* make you feel numb. It might make you feel nervous and paranoid."

I look at the joint, disappointed. "Well, crap." I look for somewhere to snuff it out, but there's not an ashtray in his truck. "What do I do with it? I don't like it."

Miller takes it from me and pinches the end of it with his fingers. He gets out and throws it in a trash can, then comes back to his truck.

Such a gentleman. Buying me weed and then disposing of it for me.

What a weird day. And I don't feel anything at all yet. Still just full of grief.

"I'm back together with Shelby."

I take it back. I felt that.

"That sucks," I say.

"Not really."

I roll my head and look at him pointedly. "No . . . it does. It sucks. You shouldn't have even brought it up."

"I didn't," he says. "You did. You called her my ex a minute ago, and I felt I needed to clarify that we got back together."

I don't even know why he's telling me this. I tilt my head, narrowing my eyes. "Do you think I'm into you? Is that why you keep informing me of your relationship status when we're together?"

Miller smiles. "You're abrasive."

I laugh, turning away from him because I'm scared my laugh will result in tears. It's funny, though. Sad and funny, because my mother used to refer to my father as abrasive. I guess the apple didn't fall far from my father's tree either.

Miller must think he insulted me, because he leans forward a little, trying to get my attention. "I didn't mean that in a negative way."

I wave him off, letting him know I'm not offended. "It's fine. You're right. I am abrasive. I like to argue, even when I know I'm wrong." I face him. "I'm getting better, though. I'm learning that sometimes you have to walk away from the fight in order to win it." *My aunt Jenny told me that once. I try to remember it every time I feel like I'm on the defensive.*

Miller smiles gently at me, and I don't know if the weed is finally kicking in or if his smile is making me light headed. Either way, it beats the headache I've had for five days from all the crying.

"If you're back together with Shelby, why are you checking on me right now? Pretty sure she wouldn't approve of this."

A flash of guilt crosses his face. He grips his steering wheel, then slides his hands down it. "I'd feel even guiltier if I *didn't* check on you."

I'd really like to ruminate on that comment, but our conversation is ruined by the intrusion of a car that pulls up next to us. I glance out my open window, then sit up straight. "Crap."

"Get in the car, Clara." My mother's words are firm and loud, but it could be because the windows are down and she pulled up so close to Miller's truck that I'm not sure I'll be able to open the door.

"Is that your mother?" Miller whispers.

"Yep." But oddly it doesn't faze me as much as it probably should. Maybe the weed really did help, because I kind of want to laugh that she's here. "I forgot we have that app. She can track me anywhere."

"Clara," my mother says again.

Miller raises an eyebrow. "Good luck."

I shoot him a tight-lipped smile and then open my door. I was right—I can't get out. "You parked too close, Mom."

My mother inhales a slow breath and then puts the gearshift in reverse. When I'm clear to open my door, I don't even look back at Miller. I walk to my mother's car and get inside. She says nothing as she begins to drive away from the theater.

Nothing until the words "Who was that?"

"Miller Adams."

I can feel her disapproval, despite her silence. A few seconds later, she swings her head in my direction. "Oh my God. Are you high?"

"Huh?"

"Were you just getting high with that guy?"

"No. We were just talking." *I don't sound convincing.*

She makes a *hmph* sound and then says, "You smell like weed."

"Do I?" I sniff my dress, which is stupid, because anyone who knows they don't smell like weed wouldn't sniff themselves to see if they do smell like weed.

Her jaw clenches even tighter when we make eye contact. Something has completely given me away. I flip down the visor and look at my bloodshot eyes. *Wow, that happened fast.* I flip up the visor.

"I can't believe you skipped your father's funeral to get high."

"I stayed for most of it."

"It was your father's *funeral*, Clara!"

She is so pissed right now. I sigh and stare out my window. "How long am I grounded for?"

She releases a frustrated breath. "I'll let you know after I talk to your fath—" Her mouth clamps shut when she realizes what she was about to say.

I'm not certain because I'm staring out my window, but I think she cries the entire way home.

CHAPTER SEVEN

MORGAN

Two years, six months, and thirteen days. That's exactly how long Clara and I can live off Chris's life insurance policy if we continue to live like we're living. His Social Security check won't come close to what his actual paycheck was, which means decisions need to be made. Finances need to be reconfigured. Clara's college fund may need to be decreased. I need to find a job. A *career*.

Yet . . . I can't seem to get out of bed or off the couch to face any of it. I feel like with the more hours I can put between the accident and the current moment, the pain will get better. When the pain is better, maybe my lack of desire to tackle everything that needs to be done will lessen.

I figure the quickest way to get from point A (grief) to point B (less grief) is to sleep my way through it. I think Clara feels the same way, because both of us spent most of the weekend sleeping.

She's barely spoken to me since the funeral. I took her phone as soon as I found out she'd gotten high. But I haven't been in the mood for conversation lately, either, so I don't push her.

I don't push her, but I do hug her. I don't know if the hugs are more because I need them or because I'm worried about how she's taking everything. Tuesday will make a week since the wreck, and I have no idea if she's going back to school tomorrow or if she still needs more time. I'd give her more time if she needs it, but we haven't discussed it yet.

I peek into her room just to make sure she's okay. I don't know how to confront this kind of grief with her. We've never had to navigate something this awful. I feel lost without Chris. Without Jenny, even. They were always my go-tos when I needed to vent or needed reassurance about how I'm parenting Clara.

My mother died a few years ago, but she's the last person I'd want to get parenting advice from, anyway. I have friends, but none of them have experienced this level of unexpected loss. I feel like I'm navigating waters that are uncharted by anyone I know. I plan on putting Clara in therapy, but maybe not for another month or so. I want to give her time to work out the most painful part of the grief before I force her into something I know she isn't going to want to do.

The house has never been so quiet. Not even the sound of the TV fills the background, because the damn cable is still broken. Chris took care of all the bills, so I'm not even sure what the name of our cable company is. I'll figure it out eventually.

I lower myself to the living room floor. It's dark, and I attempt to meditate, but really all I'm doing is thinking of everything I can possibly think of that doesn't involve a thought of Chris or Jenny, but it's hard. Almost every memory I have includes one of them.

They were both a part of every single milestone or event in my life. My entire pregnancy with Clara. Her birth. Our wedding, our anniversaries, graduations, family holidays, birthday cookouts, movie dates, fishing and camping trips, Elijah's birth.

Every important moment of my life included the two of them. They were my whole world, and I was theirs. Which is why I refuse to give another thought as to why they might have been together. There's no way they would have betrayed me like that. Betrayed *Clara* like that. I would have known.

I *absolutely* would have known.

My thoughts are interrupted when the doorbell rings.

I get a glimpse of Jonah's car out the window as I'm heading toward the front door. I don't feel relieved to see him, because I'd rather not have any visitors at all, but I also don't feel the irritation I usually feel at the sight of him when I open the door. My sympathy for his situation overshadows my irritation. Of course, I'm devastated about Jenny and Chris, but I'm reasonable enough to know that this affects Jonah more than it affects me. He's got an infant to raise.

I at least had Chris, Jenny, and Chris's parents to help with Clara. Jonah only has his mother.

I guess he has me too. But I'm not much help right now.

I open the door, shocked by what I see. Jonah hasn't shaved in a few days. He doesn't even look like he's showered. Or slept. He probably hasn't, because *I* haven't, and I don't even have an infant to care for.

"Hey," he says, his voice flat.

I open the door to let him in. "Where's Elijah?"

"My mother wanted him for a few hours."

That makes me feel good. Jonah needs the break.

I don't know why he's here, but I'm scared it's because he wants to talk about what happened. He's probably here to dissect why they were together. If I could have my way, I'd never speak of it. I want to pretend it didn't happen. The grief of losing them is enough. I don't want to pile anger and feelings of betrayal on top of that.

I just want to miss them. I don't think I have enough strength left to hate them.

We're standing quietly in the living room for only five seconds, but it feels like longer. I don't know what to do. Take him to the back patio to sit? Take a seat at the dining room table with him? The couch? This is awkward because I don't have that kind of ease with Jonah anymore.

My routine with him since he showed back up has been avoidance, and since I can't really avoid him right now, I feel like this is all-new territory.

"Is Clara home?"

I nod. "Yeah. In her room."

He glances down the hallway. "I'd like to talk to you in private if you have a minute."

The living room is the farthest room from Clara's bedroom. I have a straight view down the hallway and will see her if she comes out of her room, so I point him toward the love seat, and I take the couch facing the hallway.

He leans forward, elbows on his knees, fingers coming to a point against his chin. He sighs heavily. "I don't know if it's too soon to discuss it," he says, "but I have so many questions."

"I don't *ever* want to discuss it."

He sighs, leaning back against the couch. "Morgan."

I hate how he says my name. Full of disappointment. "What good would it do, Jonah? We don't know why they were together. If we start dissecting it, we might find answers we don't want."

He squeezes his jaw. We sit in a stark, uncomfortable silence for an entire minute. Then, as if it's a brand-new thought, Jonah's eyes flicker to mine. "Where is Chris's car?" Jonah can tell by the way I avert my eyes that this is something else I was trying to avoid. "He left here in his car that morning, didn't he?"

"Yes," I whisper.

I've been wondering where his car is, but I haven't done anything about trying to locate it. I'm afraid of what the location might prove. I'd rather just not know where it is forever, rather than find out it's parked at some hotel.

"Did he have OnStar?"

I nod. Jonah pulls out his cell phone and goes outside to make the phone call. I rush to the kitchen because I need a drink. I feel nauseated.

I find the bottle of wine Jonah and Jenny brought over last week for my birthday. We never got around to opening it because we had a bottle leftover. I unscrew the cork and pour myself a glass.

The glass is almost empty when Jonah walks into the kitchen.

His face has completely drained of color, and I know with that one look that this isn't good. My biggest fear is probably about to come true, and even though I don't want to know, I still can't help but ask.

I cover my mouth with a hesitant hand. "Where is it?" I whisper.

His face conveys his words before they even come out of his mouth. "It's parked at the Langford."

My hand drops from my mouth, and I clench my stomach. I must look like I'm about to faint because Jonah takes the glass of wine from my hand and sets it carefully on the counter.

"I called the hotel," he continues. "They've been leaving voice mails on Chris's phone. They said we can come get the keys and the stuff that was left in their room."

Their room.

My sister and my husband's hotel room.

"I can't, Jonah." My voice is a pained whisper.

His expression is sympathetic now. He puts his hands on my shoulders and dips his head. "You have to. His car will be towed tomorrow if we don't pick it up tonight. You need his car, Morgan."

My eyes are filled with tears. I press my lips together and nod. "Okay, but I don't want to know what's in the room."

"That's fine. You can drive Chris's car home, and I'll take care of the rest."

⌒⌐

Chris and I stayed at the Langford once. It was our two-year anniversary, and it was before I had finally dropped out of college. He couldn't take the time off his weekend job, so he booked us a Wednesday night.

My mother kept Clara, and we spent the entire night in bed together. *Sleeping.*

It was heaven.

We were both exhausted from having a toddler and trying to finish school, so as soon as we got a moment of peace, we took advantage of it. We were only nineteen and twenty years old. Not even old enough to drink alcohol, but already tired enough to have been twice our age.

It eventually got to a point where day care was costing more than I was making at my part-time job, we were barely making ends meet, and the only logical solution at that time was for me to stay home with Clara. Chris said I could finish my degree after he finished his, but I never reenrolled. Once Chris found a job, the financial struggles subsided, and we fell into a comfortable routine.

I was content with my life. We both were, I thought. But maybe Chris was less content with his life than I assumed.

I'm sitting in Jonah's car. We're parked next to Chris's SUV. Jonah got a key from the front desk and went inside the hotel room to find Chris's car key. He's been in there for five minutes. I lean my head back and close my eyes, saying a silent prayer. Hoping he'll come tell me that whatever he found proved we're way off base. But I already know. In my heart, I know that I've been betrayed in the worst way possible by the one person I never thought would hurt me.

My sister. My best friend.

Chris doing something like this was a knife to my heart.

But Jenny? That's an obliteration of my soul.

When Jonah is back in the driver's seat, he tosses Jenny's duffel bag into the back. The one Chris and I bought her for Christmas last year. He hands me the keys to Chris's car.

I'm staring at the bag, wondering why she would have needed it. She left her house that morning for a twelve-hour shift—not for an overnight trip. Why would she need an overnight bag?

"Why was her bag in there?"

Jonah doesn't respond. His jaw is like concrete as he stares forward.

"Why did she need a bag, Jonah? She told you she was going to work, right? She wasn't staying the night anywhere."

"Her scrubs were in there," he says. But the way he says it makes me think he's lying.

She had an overnight bag so she could change *out* of her scrubs after leaving my house. But what was she changing into?

I reach to the back seat, and he grabs my wrist and stops me. I pull away from him and turn around in my seat, attempting to reach for the duffel bag again. He blocks me with his arm, so we spend the next several seconds scuffling in the car until he has both arms around me, trying to pull me back into my seat, but I've already unzipped it.

As soon as I see the black lace trim edging a piece of dainty lingerie, I fall back into the front seat. I stare ahead. Motionless. I try not to let the images flash through my mind, but knowing my sister was planning to wear lingerie for my husband is quite possibly one of the worst things imaginable.

Jonah is also immobile.

We each silently grapple with the reality of what this means. My doubt is devoured by our new grim reality. I curl into myself, pulling my knees to my chest.

"Why?" My voice strains against the walls of my throat. Jonah reaches a comforting arm out, but I push him away. "Take me home."

He doesn't move for a moment. "But . . . Chris's car."

"I don't want that *fucking* car!"

Jonah eyes me for a beat, then nods once. He cranks his car and reverses out of our parking spot, leaving Chris's car where it's sat untouched for the past week.

I hope the car gets towed. It's in Chris's name—not mine. I don't want to see the car at my house. The bank can repossess it as far as I'm concerned.

As soon as Jonah pulls back up in my driveway, I swing open the passenger door. It feels like I've been holding my breath since we left the Langford, but stepping out of the car and into the fresh night air does nothing to refill my lungs.

I don't expect Jonah to get out, but he does. He begins to follow me across my yard, but before I open my front door, I turn around to face him. "Did you know about their affair?"

He shakes his head. "Of course not."

My chest is heaving. I'm angry, but not at Jonah. I don't think. I'm angry at everything. Chris, Jenny, every single memory I have of them together. I'm angry because I know this is now my new obsession. I'll be constantly wondering when it started, what every look meant, what every conversation between them meant. Did they have inside jokes? Did they say them in front of me? Did they laugh at my inability to sense what was happening between them?

Jonah takes a hesitant step forward. I'm crying now, but these tears weren't born from the grief I've been grappling with this entire past week. These tears are born from a more innate anguish, if that's even possible.

I attempt to inhale a breath, but my lungs feel clogged. Jonah's concern grows as he watches me, so he moves even closer, invading my personal space, making it even harder for me to catch a breath.

"I'm sorry," he says, attempting to soothe the panic within me. I push him away, but I don't go inside yet. I don't want Clara to see me like this. I'm audibly gasping now, and it's not helping that I'm trying to stop the tears. Jonah leads me to a chair on the front patio and forces me to sit.

"I can't . . ." I'm winded. "I can't breathe."

"I'll go get you some water." He heads inside the house, and as soon as the door closes, I burst into sobs. I cover my mouth with both hands, wanting it to stop. I don't want to be sad. Or angry. I just want to be numb.

I see something out of the corner of my eye, so I look at the house next door. Mrs. Nettle is peeking out at me from behind her living room curtains, watching me as I cry.

She's the nosiest neighbor we've ever had. It makes me angry that she's watching me right now, probably getting pleasure from seeing me in the middle of a panic attack.

When she moved in three years ago, she didn't like the color of grass in our yard because it didn't match the grass in her yard. She tried to petition the homeowner's association to force us to replant our yard with alfalfa rather than Saint Augustine.

And that was just the first month she lived here. She's gotten so much worse since then.

God, my random anger at my eighty-year-old neighbor is making it even harder to breathe.

My heart rate is so fast right now I can feel it pounding in my neck. I put a hand on my chest just as Jonah returns with the water. He takes a seat next to me, ensuring I take a sip. Then another. He places the glass on the table between us.

"Lean forward and put your head between your knees," he says.

I do it without question.

Jonah inhales a slow breath, intending for me to mimic it. I do. He repeats it about ten times, until my heart rate has slowed down significantly. When I feel less on the verge of a heart attack, I lift my head and lean back in the patio chair, attempting to refill my lungs with air. I let out a long sigh, then glance next door. Mrs. Nettle is still staring at us from behind her curtain.

She doesn't even try to hide her nosiness. I flip her off, which works. She snatches the curtains shut and turns off her living room light.

Jonah makes a small sound in his throat, like he wants to laugh. Maybe it is funny, seeing me flip off an eighty-year-old. But there's no way I could possibly find it in me to muster up even a modicum of laughter right now.

"How are you so calm?" I ask him.

Jonah leans back in his chair with a sidelong look in my direction. "I'm not calm," he says. "I'm hurt. I'm angry. But I'm also not as invested as you, so I think it's natural for us to have different reactions."

"Not as invested as me?"

"Chris wasn't my brother," he says, matter-of-factly. "Jenny wasn't someone I've been married to for half my life. They've cut you deeper than they've cut me."

I look away from Jonah because his words make me want to wince. I don't like that description. *They've cut you . . ."*

It's the perfect explanation for how I feel, but I never imagined Jenny and Chris would be the ones to make me feel it.

Jonah and I don't speak for a while after that. I'm no longer crying, so I should probably go inside now that I'm in the clear. I've been trying to hide my emotions from Clara. Not the grief. The grief is natural. I don't mind being sad in front of her. But I don't want her to sense my anger. What Jenny and Chris did is something I never want Clara to find out. She's gone through enough.

No telling how she'd lash out if she uncovered the truth about them. She's already lashed out enough with behavior that is so unlike her.

"Clara left Chris's funeral early. I found her at the movie theater getting high with that guy. Miller Adams. The one you claimed was a good kid?" *I don't know why I threw in that last part, like it's somehow Jonah's fault.*

Jonah releases a sigh. "Wow."

"I know. And the worst part is I don't even know how to deal with it. Or how long I should ground her for."

Jonah pushes himself out of the chair, coming to a stand. "She's suffering. We all are. I doubt it's something she'd have done if it were under different circumstances. Maybe give her a pass on her behavior this week."

I nod, but I disagree with him. A free pass would be appropriate for something milder than doing drugs. It's more appropriate for something like breaking curfew. I can't just let it slide that she left Chris's funeral to get high. Not to mention she was with the one guy her father told her not to spend time with. If I let either of those things slide, what will that leniency lead to?

I stand up, ready to go inside. I open the front door and turn to face Jonah. He's in the doorway now, staring at his feet, when he says, "I need to pick up Elijah." He lifts his eyes, and I can't tell if he's holding back tears or if I just forgot that when you're this close to Jonah Sullivan, the blue in his eyes looks liquefied. "Will you be okay?"

I let out a half-hearted laugh. I still have tears on my cheeks that haven't even dried, and he's asking me if I'll be okay?

I haven't been okay for a week. I'm not okay now. But I shrug and say, "I'll survive."

He hesitates like he wants to say more. But he doesn't. He walks back to his car, and I close my front door.

"What was that about?"

I spin around to find Clara standing at the entrance to the hallway. "Nothing," I say, almost too quickly.

"Is he okay?"

"Yeah, he just . . . he's struggling. Raising Elijah on his own. He had questions."

I'm not the good liar in this family, but that technically wasn't a lie. I'm sure Jonah *is* struggling. It's his first child. He just lost Jenny. I remember when Clara was a baby and Chris was a full-time student and worked all the days he didn't have class. I know how hard it is to do everything on your own. I've been there.

Granted, Elijah is an easier baby than Clara. They look like they could be twins, but their personalities are nothing alike.

"Who has Elijah?" Clara asks.

I hear that question come from Clara, but I can't answer it because my thoughts aren't moving forward. They're stuck on the last thing that went through my head.

They look like they could be twins.

I grip the wall after being hit by what feels like a ten-thousand-pound realization.

"Why did you leave the house with Jonah?" Clara asks. "Where did y'all go?"

Elijah doesn't look anything like Jonah. He looks just like Clara.

"Mom," Clara says with more emphasis, trying to get a response from me.

And Clara looks just like Chris.

The walls in front of me begin to pulsate. I wave Clara off because I know what a terrible liar I am, and I feel like she can see right through me. "You're still grounded. Go back to your room."

"I'm grounded from the *living* room?" she asks, puzzled.

"Clara, *go*," I say firmly, needing her to leave the room before I completely break down right in front of her.

Clara storms off.

I rush to my own bedroom and slam the door.

As if their deaths weren't enough, the blows just keep coming, and they're getting more and more severe.

CHAPTER EIGHT

CLARA

I left the house as soon as my mother went to her bedroom and slammed her door. I'm not supposed to leave, so I'm sure this will extend however long I'm grounded for, but at this point, I don't care. I can't be cooped up inside that house for another minute. Everything reminds me of my father. And every time I look at my mother, she's sitting quietly in random spots, staring at nothing.

Or snapping at me.

I know she's hurting, but she's not the only one. All I did was ask her where Elijah was and why she left the house with Jonah, but she completely overreacted.

Will this be how it is from now on? My father is gone, so now she feels she has to compensate for his absence and be even stricter on me? *Who gets grounded from their own living room?*

I'm grounded from my phone, so my mother won't be able to see where I am. I was afraid she'd call the police, so before I left, I wrote her a note that said, *"I'm really hurting. I'm going to Lexie's for a couple of hours, but I'll be home by ten."* I knew if I threw in the "hurting" part that maybe she wouldn't be so angry. Grief is a beast, but it's also a great excuse.

I drove to Lexie's house after leaving my own, hoping she'd be home, but she wasn't.

Now I'm sitting in the parking lot of the movie theater, staring at Miller's truck.

I pulled in because I was thinking how nice it would be to sit in the dark theater for an hour and a half and forget the outside world even exists. But now that I know Miller is working tonight, I'm not sure I want to go in. It'll seem like I came here on purpose, seeking him out.

Maybe I did? I don't even know.

Either way, I'm not going to stop going to the movies anytime he's working, simply because he's got a girlfriend. I'm also not going to stop going just because I'm worried it'll be awkward.

I mean, the guy bought me drugs. Can't get much more awkward than that.

The outdoor ticket counter window is closed, but Miller is inside. I watch him through the glass doors for a moment. He's wiping down the concession stand counters while Steven, the guy who sold him the weed, sweeps up random spills of popcorn.

The lobby of the theater is quiet when I walk inside, so both of them look up when they hear the door open.

Miller shoots me a small smile and stops cleaning when he sees me. I'm suddenly more nervous than I anticipated I'd be.

He presses his palms onto the counter and leans forward as I approach him. "I figured you'd be grounded."

I shrug. "I am. She took my phone and banished me to my bedroom." I look at the menu over his head. "I escaped."

He laughs. "Final showings started between thirty and forty-five minutes ago, but you can take your pick. Theater four is the emptiest."

"What's playing in four?"

"*Interstate.* It's an action flick."

"Gross. I'll take it." I pull money out of my purse, but he waves it away.

"Don't worry about it. Family gets in free. If anyone asks, tell them you're my sister."

"I'd almost rather pay than pretend we're siblings."

Miller laughs and grabs a large cup. "What do you want to drink?"

"Sprite."

He hands me the Sprite, then wets a handful of napkins in the sink behind him. I look at him with confusion as he hands me the wet napkins.

"You have stuff," he says, dragging a finger down his cheek. "Makeup. From crying."

"Oh." I wipe at my cheeks. I don't even remember putting on mascara today. I seem to be going through the motions of life without actually being aware of any of the motions. I wasn't even aware that I was crying the entire way here. Hell, I'm probably still crying. I can't even tell anymore. My guilt over knowing I was texting Aunt Jenny the moment she had the wreck, coupled with the gaping loss I feel for both of them, doesn't feel like it'll ever go away. The tears that seemed to only come at night are starting to follow me into the daytime. I thought time would make it better, but so far, time has just allowed my feelings to build and build. My heart feels swollen, like it might explode if even one more small tragedy finds its way in.

Miller makes me a large bag of popcorn as I wipe away my mascara. "You want butter?"

"Lots of it." I toss the napkin in a nearby trash can, not even concerned if I got it all. He douses the popcorn in butter.

"Don't forget. If an employee asks for a ticket, you're my sister," he says as he hands the popcorn to me.

I put a few pieces of popcorn in my mouth as I back away. "Thanks, bubba."

He makes a pained face after I call him that, almost as if it's a gross thought. I like that the thought of us being relatives repulses him. That means there's a chance he's imagined us together in an entirely different capacity.

⟋

The popcorn is stale.

I'm sure it's because the concession stand was shutting down when he made me a bag. Can't expect fresh popcorn at the end of the night. But it's so bad that I'm pretty sure this popcorn is the reject pile that's been resting untouched at the bottom of the popcorn machine since it was first popped this morning.

I'm eating it anyway.

I chose to sit in the back row in the corner because there are only two other people in here, and they're in the middle. I didn't want to sit in front of them because I planned on crying through the whole thing, but it's actually an interesting enough movie to keep my mind off things.

I didn't say it was a *good* movie. Just interesting.

At least, the main character is interesting. She's a no-holds-barred badass with shoulder-length hair that whips and sways with her every movement. I've focused more on her hair than on the story line. My hair is long, down to the middle of my back. My dad loved my hair long and talked me out of cutting it off every time I got the urge.

I pull at a strand of my hair and slide my fingers down the length of it. I'm tired of it. I think I'll cut it off soon. I'm due for a change.

"Hey," Miller whispers. I look up just as he's taking a seat next to me. "How's the movie?"

"I don't know. I'm thinking about cutting off my hair."

He reaches into my popcorn and grabs a handful, then leans back in his seat and props his feet up on the chair in front of him. "I have scissors behind the concession stand."

"I didn't mean right now."

"Oh. Well, whenever you're ready. The scissors stay here, so just show up, and I'll cut it."

I laugh. "I didn't mean I wanted *you* to cut it."

"Okay, but fair warning. Steven is better at sweeping up popcorn and selling weed than he is at cutting hair."

I roll my eyes, resting my feet on the back of the seat in front of me.

"New flip-flops?" he asks, staring at my feet.

"Yep. Did some real shady shit for these."

Miller grabs another handful of popcorn, and we don't speak for the next few minutes. The movie comes to an end, and the only other people in the theater get up to leave when the credits begin rolling. He digs his hand into the popcorn again.

We're not doing anything wrong, but it feels like we are. Before he sat down next to me, I felt numb, but now my body is charged with adrenaline. Our arms aren't even touching. I'm hogging both armrests, and he's leaned away from me, probably to avoid any form of contact.

But still, it feels wrong. He's sitting next to the one girl we both know he shouldn't be sitting next to. And even though it makes me feel guilty, it also makes me feel good.

The credits are still rolling when Miller says, "This popcorn is really stale."

"It's the worst popcorn I've ever had."

"It's almost gone," he says, indicating the bag. "Doesn't seem like you minded."

I shrug. "I'm not picky."

More silence passes between us. He smiles at me, and a surge of heat rushes through me. I look into the bag of popcorn and shake it around like I'm trying to find a good piece because I don't want to look at him and feel this for someone who has a girlfriend. I don't want to feel this for anyone. Feeling anything remotely good makes me feel like a shit human considering the circumstances of the past week. But he's still staring at me and hasn't made a move to leave yet, and since he's blocking me from the aisle, I feel forced to make conversation.

"How long have you worked here?"

"A year." He settles into his seat a little more. "I like it okay. I think the idea of working at a theater is more exciting than the reality of it. It's mostly just a lot of cleaning."

"But you get to watch all the movies you want, right?"

"That's why I still work here. I've seen every movie released since I started. I look at it as preparation for my career. Research."

"What's your favorite movie?"

"Of all time?" he asks.

"Pick one from the past ten years."

"I can't," he says. "There are so many great ones, and I love them all for different reasons. I love the technical aspect of *Birdman*. I love the performances in *Call Me by Your Name*. *Fantastic Mr. Fox* is my favorite cartoon because Wes Anderson is a goddamn genius." He glances at me. "What about you?"

"I don't think *Fantastic Mr. Fox* counts. It seems older than ten years." I lean my head back and stare up at the ceiling. It's a tough question. "I'm like you. I don't know that I have a favorite movie. I tend to judge more on the talent than the story line. I think Emma Stone is probably my favorite actress. And Adam Driver is the best actor of our time, but I don't think he's landed the role of his lifetime yet. He was great in *BlacKkKlansman*, but I'm not crazy about some of the other movies he's been in."

"But did you see the Kylo Ren skit?"

"Yes!" I say, sitting up. "On *SNL*? Oh my God, it was so funny." I'm smiling, but I hate that I'm smiling. It feels weird to smile when I'm so full of sadness, but this is how Miller makes me feel every time I'm around him. He's the only thing that seems to be able to take my mind off everything, yet he's the one person I can't really hang out with. *Thanks for that, Shelby.*

It sucks. I don't like thinking about it, even though we're together right now. But when I eventually return to school, things will go back to how they've been. Miller will keep his distance. He'll respect his relationship with Shelby, which will only serve to make me respect him even more.

And I'll just continue to be in a depressing funk.

"I should go," I say.

Miller hesitates before moving. "Yeah, I think my break was over ten minutes ago." We both stand up, but I can't get out of the aisle because he's blocking my way, facing me, not making an effort to walk away. He's just staring down at me as if he wants to say something else. Or *do* something else.

"I'm really sorry about what happened," he says.

At first, I'm not sure what he's talking about, but then it hits me. I press my lips together and nod, but I don't say anything because it's the last thing I want to talk or think about.

"I should have said that the other day. At the funeral."

"It's fine," I say. "I'm fine. Or at least I'll *be* fine. Eventually." I sigh. "Hopefully."

He's staring at me like he wants to pull me in for a hug, and I really wish he would. But instead, he turns and walks out of the aisle, toward the exit.

I stop at the restroom on our way out. He grabs a trash can and starts to pull it toward the theater we just came out of.

"See ya, Clara."

I don't tell him goodbye. I walk into the restroom and don't even bother pretending things will be the same between us the next time I see him. He'll avoid me while being all faithful and shit, and *whatever*. That's okay. I need to stop interacting with him anyway, because as good as it feels when I'm around him, it's starting to hurt when I'm not. And I don't need another painful thing added to my already existing pile of excruciating feelings.

When I get home, I expect my mother to be waiting up for me, pissed and ready to argue. Instead, the house is quiet. Her bedroom light is off.

When I get to my own bedroom, I'm surprised to find my cell phone on my pillow.

A peace offering. That's unexpected.

I lie back on my bed and catch up on my messages. Lexie wants to know if I'll be at school tomorrow. I wasn't planning on going back so soon, but the thought of being in this house sounds way worse than school, so I tell her I'll be there.

I open Instagram and browse through Miller's profile. I know I said I needed to stop interacting with him, and I will. But first, I need to send him a message. Just one. Then we can go back to how things have been between us for the past year. Nonexistent.

> Just wanted to say thank you for the free movie and the shitty popcorn. You're the best sibling I've ever had.

He doesn't follow me, so I expect it to go to his filtered messages and take him a month to read, but he actually responds within a few minutes.

> Miller: You got your phone back?

I grin and roll onto my stomach when his message comes in.

> Me: Yeah. It was on my pillow when I got home. I think it's a peace offering.

> Miller: She sounds like a cool mom.

I roll my eyes. *Cool* is being very generous.

Me: She's great.

I even put one of those smiling face emojis to make my response more believable.

Miller: You coming back to school tomorrow?

Me: I think so.

Miller: Good deal. I should probably stop talking to you here. I think Shelby knows my password.

Me: Wow. That's like next level. You proposing soon?

Miller: You love to make fun of my relationship.

Me: It's my favorite pastime.

Miller: I guess I make it easy.

Me: Has she always been a jealous person? Or did you do something to make her that way?

Miller: She's not a jealous person. She's only jealous when it comes to you.

Me: What?! Why?

Miller: It's a long story. A boring one. Good night, Clara.

It's a boring story? *Whatever.* The fact that Miller has a story that includes me in the narrative is going to be the only thing I can think about for the rest of the night.

Me: Good night. Make sure you delete these messages.

Miller: Already have.

I stare at my phone, knowing I should stop, but I send him one more message.

Me: Here's my number in case you get your heart broken again.

I send him my phone number, but he doesn't respond. Probably for the best.

I go back to his page and scroll through his pictures. I've looked through his page before, but not since I've actually had a conversation with him. Miller is good with a camera. There are a few pictures of Miller with Shelby, but most of his pictures are of random things. None of him by himself, which I like for some reason.

The picture that catches my eye is a black-and-white photo he took of the city limit sign. It makes me laugh, so I double tap the picture to like it.

I'm still scrolling through my feed when a text comes through from a number I don't recognize.

Troublemaker.

His text makes me laugh. I honestly didn't like his picture with any ill intent. I genuinely thought it was funny, and for a minute, I forgot that me even liking it could send him back to the interrogation room with Shelby.

I immediately save his number in my contacts. It makes me wonder if he's going to save my number under my real name or a fake name. Shelby would flip if she knew he had my number in his phone. And I'm sure if she has his Instagram password, she probably goes through his phone.

Me: You saving my number under a fake name so you don't get in trouble?

Miller: I was thinking about it. What about Jason?

Me: Jason is a good name. Everyone knows a Jason. She wouldn't be suspicious.

I smile, but my smile only lasts a fleeting second. I remember the last thing Aunt Jenny texted me. *"You don't want to be the other girl. Trust me."*
She's right. Aunt Jenny was always right. *What am I doing?*

Me: Never mind. Don't save me under a fake name. I don't want to be Jason in your phone and I don't want to be your fake sibling at the movie theater. Call me someday when I can just be Clara.

The dots appear on my phone. They disappear.
He doesn't text me back.
After a few minutes, I screenshot our messages and then delete his number.

CHAPTER NINE

MORGAN

I've just slipped into a light sleep when I hear a banging on the door that startles me. I sit up in bed and reach over to shake Chris awake.

His side of the bed is empty.

I stare at it, wondering when things like that are going to stop. It's been less than two weeks since they died, but I've picked up my phone at least five times to call him or Jenny. It's so natural that I just forget. Then I'm forced to relive the grief.

Another pounding on the door. My head swings in the direction of the noise. My heart rate picks up because I'm going to have to deal with this whether I'm prepared to or not. In the past when something happened unexpectedly in the middle of the night, Chris would always take care of it.

I pull on a robe and rush to the door before whoever it is wakes up Clara. The pounding is so incessant it's starting to make me angry. It better not be Mrs. Nettle from next door here to blame me for something. She once woke us up at two in the morning to complain about a squirrel in our backyard tree.

I flip on the porch light and look through the peephole, relieved to see it isn't Mrs. Nettle. It's just Jonah, disheveled and holding Elijah tightly against his chest. But my relief only lasts for a second when I realize that it's midnight, and Jonah doesn't just randomly stop by at midnight. Something must be wrong with Elijah.

I swing open the door. "Is everything okay?"

Jonah shakes his head, his eyes frantic as he pushes past me. "No."

I close the door and walk over to them. "Does he have a fever?"

"No, he's fine."

I'm confused. "You just said he's not okay."

"*He's* fine. *I'm* not fine." He hands Elijah to me, and I check his forehead for a temperature anyway. He doesn't have a fever, so I start to check him for a rash. I can't think of any other reason he'd be here this late at night. "He's *fine*," Jonah repeats. "He's perfect, he's happy, he's fed, and I . . ." He shakes his head and walks back toward the front door without Elijah. "I'm done. I can't do this."

A sinking feeling consumes me. I rush after Jonah and intercept him, pressing my back against my front door. "What do you mean you can't *do* this?"

Jonah takes a step back and then faces the other direction. He clasps his hands behind his head. I realize what I initially thought was fear is nothing less than devastation. Jonah doesn't even have to tell me why he's so upset. I already know.

He spins around, facing me again, his eyes full of heartache and lined with tears. He waves a hand toward Elijah. "He smiled for the first time tonight." He pauses, as if what he's about to say next is too painful to put into words. "Elijah—my *son*—has Chris's fucking *smile*."

No, no, no. I shake my head, feeling the heartache pouring out of him. "Jonah—" I hear Clara's bedroom door open before I can process what this all means. My sympathetic expression immediately changes to a pleading one. "Please don't do this right now," I beg him in a whisper. "I don't want her to find out what they did. It'll break her."

Jonah's eyes move past me. I'm assuming to Clara.

"What's going on?" she asks.

I spin around, and Clara is standing at the entrance of the hallway, rubbing sleep from her eyes. Jonah mutters, "I can't do this. I'm sorry," under his breath and opens the door. He leaves.

I walk over to Clara and shove Elijah into her arms. "I'll be right back."

Jonah is almost to his car when I shut the front door and rush after him. He hears me following him, so he spins around. "Why would Jenny lie to me about something this *huge*?" He's full of anguish, gripping his hair and then slapping his palms against the car, like he has no idea what to do with his hands. His head hangs between his shoulders in defeat. "Having an affair is one thing, but to lead me to believe I fathered her *child*? Who *does* that, Morgan?"

He pushes off the car and strides toward me. I've never seen him this angry, so I find myself taking small steps backward.

"Did you know he wasn't mine?" He's looking at me like I was in on this somehow. "Is that why she showed up out of the blue at my father's funeral last year? She needed to cover up who really got her pregnant? Was this some kind of sick plan?"

His words kind of hurt, because of course I didn't know any of that. I only just recently suspected Chris could be Elijah's father, but this is the first time I've seen Jonah since having that suspicion. "Do you actually think I would have let them get away with that?"

He grips the sides of his head in frustration, then throws his arms out. "I don't know! You've been with Chris half your life. How could you *not* suspect that he was Elijah's father?" He walks back toward his car but then thinks of something else to say that will likely make me even angrier with him. "You knew they were sleeping together, Morgan. Deep down, you had to know, but we both know how good you are at ignoring what's right in front of you!"

Yep. I'm definitely a lot angrier than I was ten seconds ago.

Jonah steps back, as if his own words boomeranged back into his gut. His anger is immediately swallowed by the apologetic look in his eyes.

"Are you done?" I ask.

He nods, but barely.

"Where's Elijah's diaper bag?"

Jonah walks to the car and opens the back door. He hands me the diaper bag. He stares down at the concrete beneath his feet, waiting for me to walk away.

"You're *all he has*, Jonah."

He lifts his head and stares at me a moment and then slowly shakes his head. "Actually, *you're* all he has. He's your sister's child. He has absolutely nothing of me in him." His words don't come out with the vengeance that was coursing through him earlier. Now he's just quiet and broken.

I look at him pleadingly. I can't imagine what this must be like for him, so I'm doing my best not to judge his reaction, but he loves Elijah. There's no way he can walk away from an infant he's raised for two months, no matter how hurt he is right now. He'll end up regretting this. I soften my own voice when I speak. "You're the only parent he knows. Go home. Sleep it off. Come back and get him in the morning."

I walk back to my house. I don't mean to slam the door, but I do, and it startles Elijah. He begins to cry. Clara is seated on the couch with him, so I take him out of her arms so she can get back to bed.

"What's wrong with Jonah?" she asks. "He seemed angry."

I play it down as much as I can, even though I know I'm a terrible liar. "He's just exhausted. I offered to keep Elijah for the night to give him a break."

Clara stares at me for a moment. She knows I'm lying, but she doesn't press me. She does roll her eyes when she passes me, though.

When she's back in her room, I take Elijah to my bedroom and sit down on the bed, holding him. He's wide awake now, but he's no longer crying.

He's smiling.

And Jonah is right. When he smiles, there's a deep dimple that forms in the center of his chin.

He looks *exactly* like Chris.

CHAPTER TEN

CLARA

Everyone thought Jonah would be back teaching his classes on Monday, but he wasn't. Mom said Jonah would pick up Elijah on Monday, but it's Wednesday now, and he didn't.

I don't know what's going on because my mother won't tell me anything, so when Lexie comes to my locker after last period and says, "What's going on with Uncle Teacher?" I have no idea what to say.

I close my locker and shrug. "I don't know. I think he's having a breakdown. He dropped Elijah off with us Sunday night, and all I heard him say before he stormed out of the house was, *'I can't do this. I'm sorry.'*"

"Shit. So your mom still has Elijah?" The way Lexie is chewing her gum makes it seem like we're chatting about going to the mall rather than Jonah possibly abandoning his infant son.

"Yep."

Lexie leans against the locker next to me. "That's not good."

"It's fine. He'll probably pick him up today. I think he just needed to catch up on sleep."

Lexie can tell I'm making excuses. She shrugs and pops a bubble with her gum. "Yeah, maybe. But fair warning. My dad has been 'catching up on sleep' for thirteen years."

I humor her with a laugh, but Jonah is nothing like Lexie's dad. Not that I've ever met her biological father. But Jonah would never do something like that to Elijah.

"My mother said it was the day after Christmas when he stormed out of the house and yelled, *'I'm done!'* He never came back." She pops another bubble. "If there's one thing my dad is good at, it's being done. He's been 'being done' for thirteen years." She suddenly clamps her mouth shut and looks over my shoulder. She's focused on something else now. Or *someone* else.

I turn around and see Miller heading this direction. His eyes land on mine, and for a substantial three seconds, he holds my stare. His entire focus is on me so hard he has to crane his neck a little as he passes us before he looks away almost forcefully.

We haven't spoken since that night over text. I like that he's not pursuing me, but I also hate it. I want him to be a good human, but I'd also very much like it if he didn't care so much about his current relationship.

Lexie whistles out a breath. "I felt that."

I roll my eyes. "No, you didn't."

"I did. That look he gave you . . . it was like . . ."

"Back to Jonah," I say, pushing off my locker. "He's a good dad. He just needed a break."

"Fifty bucks says he doesn't come back." Lexie follows me toward the exit to the parking lot.

"Back to where?" I ask. "To school? Or to Elijah?"

"Both. Didn't he only move here because Jenny was pregnant? He probably had a life outside of this town that he'd love to get back to. Start over. Pretend the past year never happened."

"You're terrible."

"No. *Men* are terrible. Dads are the *most* terrible," she says.

My shoulders shrink a little at her comment. I sigh, thinking about my father. "Mine wasn't. He was the greatest."

Lexie pauses her steps. "Clara, I'm so sorry. I'm a dumbass."

I step back and grab her hand, pulling her forward with me. "It's fine. But you're wrong about Jonah. He's like my dad. He's one of the good ones. He loves Elijah too much to just up and abandon him like this."

We make it another five feet before Lexie stops again, pulling me to a stop with her. I turn around, my back to the parking lot, my eyes on her. "What's wrong?"

"Don't look right now, but Miller just pulled up next to your car."

My eyes widen. "He did?"

"Yes. And I need you to take me home, but I don't want to make it awkward if he's wanting to talk to you, so I'm going back inside the school. Text me when it's safe to come out."

"Okay." I'm nodding, my stomach full of nerves.

"Also, you're full of it. You are so into him. If you use the word *inconsequential* one more time in reference to him, I'll slap you."

"Okay."

Lexie walks back toward the school, and I take a breath. I spin around and head for my car, pretending not to notice Miller's truck until I'm at my driver's-side door. His windows are up and his truck is running, but he's just sitting in it, staring ahead with a sucker hanging from his mouth. He's not even paying attention to me.

He probably doesn't even know he parked next to me, and here I am assuming it was deliberate. I feel stupid.

I start to turn around and open my car door but stop short when he unlocks his passenger door.

That's when he lazily turns his head and looks at me expectantly, like I'm supposed to get in his truck.

I contemplate it. I like the way I feel around him, so even though I know I shouldn't give him the satisfaction of being able to summon me into his truck with one simple look, I get in his truck anyway. I am that pathetic.

When I close the door, it feels as if I've trapped a live wire inside the truck with us. The silence between us only makes the feeling more noticeable. I can actually feel my heart beating from my stomach all the way up to my throat, as if my heart has swollen to fill my entire torso.

Miller's head is resting against his seat, his body is facing forward, but his eyes are on me. I'm looking at him much the same way, but I'm not as relaxed. My back is straight against the leather of his seat.

He does have air-conditioning, despite what I assumed last time I was in his truck. It's on high, and it's blowing my hair into my mouth. I flick the vent closed and then pull a strand of hair away from my lips with my fingers. Miller's eyes follow my movements, lingering on my mouth for a moment.

The way he's looking at me is making it really difficult to inhale a proper breath. As if he can tell I'm having a physical reaction to just being in his presence, his eyes fall even more to my heaving chest, albeit very briefly.

He pulls his sucker out of his mouth and grips his steering wheel, looking away from me. "I changed my mind. I need you to get out of my truck."

I'm dumbfounded by his words. And also very confused. "Changed your mind about what?"

He looks at me again, and for some reason, he looks torn. He drags in a slow breath. "I don't know. I feel really confused around you."

He feels confused around *me*? That makes me smile.

My smile makes him frown.

I don't even know what's happening right now. I don't know if I like it or hate it, but I do know that whatever it is that makes me feel the way I do when I'm around him is a feeling that can only be fought for so long. He's looking back at me like he's almost at the end of his fight.

"You really need to figure out your shit, Miller."

He nods. "Believe me. I know I do. That's why I need you to get out of my truck."

This entire interaction is so bizarre I can only laugh about it. My laugh finally makes him smile. But then he groans and grips his steering wheel with both hands, pressing his forehead against it.

"*Please* get out of my truck, Clara," he whispers.

I should hate that he's battling some sort of moral struggle right now. I like this feeling—thinking he might be attracted to me—a lot more than thinking he hates me.

I try to keep Shelby at the forefront of my mind. Knowing he has a girlfriend that he loves and cares for keeps me from climbing across this seat and kissing him like I want to. But I know I'm not doing anything to help prevent him from having the same urge, because I'm still sitting in his truck, despite him asking me to get out no less than three times.

I might even make it worse when I reach over and pull his sucker out of his grip. "Miller?" He tilts his head, still pressed against the steering wheel, and stares at me. "You're confusing me too." I put his sucker in my mouth and grab the door handle.

Miller keeps his head tilted just enough so that he can watch me exit his truck. As soon as I shut the door, he locks it, then puts the truck in reverse like he can't get away from me fast enough.

I get into my car, fully convinced that Aunt Jenny was wrong about one thing. She said girls were more confusing than guys. I don't believe that for a second.

I back out of my parking spot after Miller is gone. When I pull onto the road, my phone rings. It's Lexie.

Shit. Lexie.

I answer it. "I'm sorry. I'm turning around."

"You forgot me."

"I know. I'm the worst. Coming back now."

CHAPTER ELEVEN

MORGAN

Two years, six months, and thirteen days. That's how long Chris's life insurance was *supposed* to last in a worst-case scenario when I did the math. But adding an infant into the mix is going to throw us into poverty level. I can't get a job if I have an infant. I can't afford day care if I get a job. I can't sue Jonah for child support because he's not even the father.

When Elijah begins to cry, I pile the paperwork together and go tend to him. *Again.* I thought Elijah was nothing like Clara was at this age, but I'm beginning to think I was wrong. Because all he's done for the last few days is cry. He naps occasionally, but he's mostly been crying. I'm sure it's because I'm not familiar to him. He's used to Jenny, and he hasn't heard her voice in a while. He hasn't heard Jonah's since Sunday night. I'm doing the best I can at pretending this will turn out okay, but I'm starting to worry it won't, because Jonah hasn't responded to a single one of my texts.

Jonah very well may not come back. And do I blame him? He's right—I'm the one related to this baby by blood. Not him. It's as if Elijah *is* more my responsibility now. Despite being on the birth certificate, Jonah really doesn't have an obligation to raise a child who was created by my sister and my husband.

I was hoping the two months Jonah has spent with Elijah would be enough to form that unbreakable bond between parent and child and that he'd come to his senses and show up, apologetic and heartbroken. But that didn't happen. It's going on day four and here I am, possibly about to raise a newborn in the midst of this chaos.

Last night, I couldn't stop thinking about it while I sat in the living room, holding Elijah as he screamed his head off for an hour straight. I actually started laughing hysterically in the middle of all the screaming. It made me wonder if I was going crazy. That's how they always depict crazy people on television. Laughing in dire situations, when they should be reacting more appropriately. But all I could do was laugh, because my life is complete and utter shit. It's shit. It. Is. Shit. My husband is dead. My sister is dead. Their illegitimate child has been handed over to me to raise, when my own daughter barely speaks to me anymore. I'm not qualified for this.

And I can't even escape this shit life to watch television because the damn TV is still broken.

"I should call them."

"Call who?"

I spin around, shocked to find Clara home. I didn't even hear her walk through the door.

"Call who?" she repeats.

I didn't realize I said that out loud. "The cable company. I miss television."

Clara shakes her head as if she wants to say, *Cable is so outdated, Mom.* But she doesn't. She walks over and takes Elijah from me.

There are two cable companies in this town, but I get lucky and call the one we actually have an account with first. I'm on hold forever before I finally get an appointment confirmed. When I hang up, Clara is looking up at me from her position on the couch.

"Have you even slept yet?"

I'm assuming she asks this because I'm in yesterday's clothes and I haven't brushed my hair. I can't even remember if I brushed my teeth. I usually do it before I go to sleep and as soon as I wake up, but I haven't done either of those things, because Clara is right. I *haven't* slept. I wonder how long someone can go on no sleep.

Apparently for Elijah, it's seven hours, because that's how many have passed between his last nap and this one.

"Call Jonah and tell him to come get his son. You look like you're about to break."

I avoid responding to her comment, lifting Elijah out of her arms. "Can you run to the store and grab some diapers? I only have one left, and he needs changing."

"Jonah can't bring you more?" Clara asks. "Isn't that his responsibility?"

I look away from Clara, since she's staring at me like I'm water and she can see right through me. "Cut Jonah some slack," I say to her. "His world has been turned upside down."

"Our worlds were turned upside down too. Doesn't mean we'd abandon an infant."

"You wouldn't understand. He needs time. My wallet is in the kitchen," I say, continuing to avoid throwing Jonah under the bus, no matter how much I want to.

Clara takes my money and leaves for the store.

When it's just me and Elijah, I lay him on the pallet I made for him. He's finally asleep, and I have no idea how long it'll last, so I take advantage of it and use the time to go to the kitchen and rinse out his bottles.

He hasn't had breast milk since Jenny died, but he seems to be taking to formula pretty well. It just makes for a hell of a lot of dishes.

I'm scrubbing one of the bottles when it happens.

I start crying.

Lately, when I start crying, I can't turn it off. I cry with Elijah at night. I cry with him during the day. I cry in the shower. I cry in my car.

I have a perpetual headache and a perpetual heartache, and sometimes I just wish it would end. All of it. The whole world.

You know your life is shit when you're handwashing baby bottles, praying for Armageddon.

CHAPTER TWELVE

CLARA

There are several routes I can take to get from my house to the grocery store, or my house to the school, or my house to basically anywhere in town. One of them is the main road through the center of downtown, which is the shortest way. The other is the loop, which is out of my way, but even still, it's the only road I've taken to get anywhere for almost two weeks now.

Because it's the only road that takes me right by Miller Adams's house.

The city limit sign has moved a little more, and I can see now why he's moving it in small increments. Unless you're looking to see if it's been moved, it would be hard to notice a twenty-foot shift every week. I've noticed, though. And it makes me smile every time I see it in a different spot.

I drive this way in hopes he'll be on the side of the road again, and I'll have an excuse to stop. He's never out here, though.

I continue my drive to the grocery store to get diapers, even though I have no idea what kind of diapers or what size to get. Texts to my mother when I arrive at the store go unanswered. She must be busy with Elijah.

I open my contact for Jonah. I stare at it, wondering why my mother wouldn't call him for diapers. I'm also curious as to why she's had Elijah for as long as she has.

I could tell she was lying to me when she said he just needed a break. I could see it in her eyes. She was worried. She's hoping a break is *all* he needs.

But what if Lexie is right? What if Jonah decides not to come back for him?

If that's the case, it's one more thing to add to the long list of tragedies I'm responsible for. Jonah is stressed because he lost the mother of his child and has no idea how to raise him alone, and none of this would be happening if it weren't for me.

I need to fix whatever is going on, but I can't do that when I don't know what, exactly, is going on.

I decide not to call Jonah. I put my phone in my pocket and leave the store without buying diapers, and then I drive straight to Jonah's house because Aunt Jenny isn't here to give me answers and my mother certainly isn't being honest with me. No better way to get answers than to go straight to the source.

I can hear the television when I approach Jonah's front door. I breathe out a little bit of relief, knowing if the television is on, he probably hasn't skipped town. *Yet.* I ring the doorbell and hear rustling inside of the house. Then footsteps.

The footsteps fade, as if he's walking away, attempting to avoid his visitor. I start beating on the door, wanting him to know I'm not going away until he opens this door. I'll go through a window if I have to.

"Jonah!" I yell.

Nothing. I try the doorknob, but it's locked, so I knock again with my right hand and ring the doorbell with my left. I do this for a full thirty seconds before I hear footsteps again.

The door swings open. Jonah is pulling on a T-shirt. "Give a guy a second to get dressed," he says.

I push open the door and move past him, entering his house without permission. I haven't been here since a week before Jenny died. It's incredible how fast a man can let something go to complete shit.

Not that it's reached the point of disgusting, but it has definitely reached the point of pathetic. Clothes on the floor. Empty pizza boxes on the counter. Two open chip bags on the couch. As if he's embarrassed by the state of his house, *which he should be*, he starts to gather trash and carry it toward the kitchen.

"What are you doing?" I ask.

He steps on the trash can lever, and the lid pops open. I think his plan was to drop the trash into the trash can, but it's too full for that, so he releases the lever and sets the trash on the kitchen counter with a pile of other trash. "Cleaning," he says. He takes the lid off the trash can and begins to tie the bag shut.

"You know what I mean. Why has my mother had Elijah since Sunday?"

Jonah pulls the bag of trash out of the can and sets it next to the kitchen door that leads to the garage. He pauses for a moment and looks at me, as if he might actually be honest with his answer. But then he shakes his head. "You wouldn't understand."

I am so sick of hearing those words. It's as if adults assume that being sixteen prevents a person from understanding the English language. I understand enough to know that there's nothing in the world that should keep a parent from their child. Not even grief.

"Are you even concerned about him?"

Jonah looks offended by my question. "Of course I am."

"You have a funny way of showing it."

"I'm not in a good place."

I laugh. "Yeah. Neither is my mother. She lost her husband and her sister."

Jonah's response is flat. "I lost my best friend, my fiancée, and my son's mother."

"And now your son lost you. That seems fair."

Jonah sighs, leaning against the counter. He looks down at the floor, and I can tell my being here is making him feel guilty. *Good.* He deserves to feel guilty. And I'm not even done yet.

"Do you think you're hurting more than my mother?"

"No," he says instantly. Convincingly.

"Then why are you putting your responsibilities on her? It's not like you're grieving more than she is, and now you've dropped your kid off with her, like your grief is more important than what she's going through."

Jonah takes in what I'm saying. I can see it sinking in because he looks guilt ridden. He pushes off the counter and turns away from me, like my presence alone is making him feel remorse.

"Elijah rolled over last night," I say.

Jonah spins around, his eyes darting back to mine. "Did he really?"

I shake my head. "No. But he will soon, and you're going to miss it."

Jonah's jaw hardens. I can see the shift in him seconds before it happens. "What the hell am I doing?" he whispers. He rushes to the dining room table, swiping up a set of car keys. He begins to head for the garage door.

"Where are you going?"

Jonah pauses, then faces me. "To get my son."

He opens the garage door, but before he leaves, I call after him. "I'll stay and clean your house for fifty bucks!"

Jonah then walks back through the living room as he pulls his wallet out of his pocket. He takes out two twenties and a ten and hands the three bills to me. Then he does something unexpected. He leans in and gives me a quick kiss on the forehead. When he pulls back, he's staring at me with an intense expression. "Thank you, Clara."

I smile and shake the three bills in my hand, but I know he isn't thanking me for staying to clean his house. He's thanking me for knocking some sense back into him.

CHAPTER THIRTEEN

MORGAN

I'm in the laundry room, rewashing the few outfits I have of Elijah's when I hear the front door open and close. Clara must be back from the store with diapers. I'm still crying. Big surprise. I wipe at my eyes before turning on the dryer and heading back into the living room.

When I round the corner, I pause.

Jonah is standing in my living room.

He's holding Elijah. Cradling him against his chest, kissing him over and over on top of his head.

"I'm sorry," I hear him whispering. "Daddy is so, so sorry."

I don't want to interrupt the moment. It's heartwarming, which is odd, since I was so full of anger just minutes before. But I can see in Jonah's expression that he realizes he can't just walk away from Elijah. No matter who fathered him, Jonah has raised him. Jonah is the one Elijah knows and loves. I'm happy that Jonah didn't make my worst fears come true.

I walk to my bedroom and give them a moment while I repack Elijah's diaper bag. When I return to the living room, Jonah hasn't moved. He's still cradling him as if he can't apologize enough to Elijah. As if Elijah even understands what happened.

Jonah glances up, and we make eye contact. As much relief as I feel right now from knowing his love for Elijah overpowers any DNA they do or don't share, I'm still a little pissed that it took him almost four days to come to his senses.

"If you abandon him again, I'm filing for custody."

Without wasting a second, Jonah crosses the room and wraps an arm around me, tucking my head under his chin. "I'm sorry, Morgan. I don't know what I was thinking." His voice is desperate, as if I might not forgive him. "I'm so sorry."

The thing is . . . I don't even *blame* him.

If Chris and Jenny weren't already dead, I'd kill them for doing this to Jonah. It's all I've been able to think about for the past few days. Jenny had to know there was a chance Chris could be Elijah's father. And if Jenny knew, *Chris* knew. I've asked myself why they would allow Jonah to think for one second that he fathered a child that wasn't his. The only reason I can come up with isn't good enough.

I believe they kept it a secret because they were afraid of the fallout the truth would bring. Clara would have never forgiven them. I think Jenny and Chris would have done anything in their power to keep the truth from Clara. Even if that meant pulling Jonah into the lie.

For Clara's sake, I'm relieved they did such a good job of hiding it.

But on Jonah's behalf—and Elijah's—I'm livid.

Which is why I don't say anything else to Jonah to make him feel guilty. He needed time to adjust to such traumatic news. He doesn't need to feel guilty. He's back and he's remorseful, and that's all that matters right now.

Jonah is still clinging to me, still apologizing, as if I need more of an apology than Elijah. I don't. I understand completely. I'm just relieved to know that Elijah won't have to grow up without a father. That was my biggest concern.

I pull away from Jonah and hand him Elijah's diaper bag. "There's a load of his onesies in the dryer. You can come get them later this week."

"Thank you," he says. He kisses Elijah on the forehead again and stares at him for a moment before going to leave. I follow them across the living room. When Jonah reaches the front door, he turns around and says it again, somehow with even more conviction. "*Thank* you."

I shake my head. "It's okay, Jonah. Really."

When the door closes, I fall onto the couch with relief. I don't think I've ever been this exhausted. From life. From death. From *everything*.

I wake up an hour later in the same position when Clara finally returns home.

Without diapers.

I rub sleep from my eyes, wondering where she's been if she wasn't out getting diapers like I asked her to. As if having an infant all week wasn't exhausting enough, having a teenager who decided to start her rebellious period on the day of her father's funeral takes the cake.

I follow her into the kitchen. She opens the refrigerator, and I'm behind her, trying to see if she smells like weed again. She doesn't, but nowadays they all eat those gummies. It's easier to hide.

Clara looks at me over her shoulder with a raised brow. "Did you just sniff me?"

"Where have you been? You were supposed to be out getting diapers."

"Is Elijah still here?"

"No. Jonah came and got him."

She sidesteps around me. "Then we don't need diapers." She pulls the diaper money out of her pocket and sets it on the counter. She heads for the kitchen door, but I've been way too lenient on her. She's sixteen. I have a right to know where she's been.

I block her from leaving the kitchen. "Were you with that guy?"

"What guy?"

"The guy who got you high at your father's funeral."

"I thought we were past this. And no."

She tries to step around me again, but I stay in front of her, still blocking the door. "You can't see him anymore."

"Uh. I'm *not*. And even if I were, he's not a bad guy. Can I please go to my room now?"

"After you tell me where you've been."

She throws her hands up in defeat. "I was cleaning Jonah's house! Why do you automatically assume the worst?"

I feel like she's lying to me. Why would she be cleaning Jonah's house?

"Check the app if you don't believe me. Call Jonah." She squeezes past me and pushes open the kitchen door.

I guess I could have checked the app. I just feel like, even with the app, I don't know what she's up to. Her app said she was at the movie theater the day of Chris's funeral, but it certainly didn't tell me she was doing drugs while she was there. I feel like the app is useless at this point.

I should probably just cancel it because it costs money. But Chris is the one who subscribed us to the app, and Chris's phone probably got smashed in the wreck. It wasn't in the box of belongings they gave us from Jenny's car.

I wouldn't know the password to his phone even if I *did* find it. That should have been my first clue that he was hiding so many things from me. But who needs clues when you don't even realize you're supposed to be playing detective? I never even suspected anything was amiss.

Here I go again.

I kind of wish Elijah were still here. He kept my mind preoccupied. I didn't have to think about what Jenny and Chris did when every minute was consumed by Elijah. Jonah is lucky in that regard. Elijah will probably keep him so busy and exhausted that his brain will have time for little else.

I'll pour myself some wine. Maybe take a bubble bath. That might help.

Clara stormed out of here a good thirty seconds ago, but the kitchen door is still swinging back and forth. I hold it with my hand, then stare at the back of my hand, my palm pressed flat against the door. I fixate on my wedding ring. Chris gave me this one for our tenth wedding anniversary. It replaced the gold band he bought me when we were teenagers.

Jenny helped Chris pick this one out.

Was their affair happening way back then?

For the first time since the day I put on this ring, I feel the urge to get it off me. I slip it off my finger and throw it at the door. I don't know where it lands, and I don't care.

I push the kitchen door open and go to the garage in search of something that can take care of at least *one* problem in my life.

I really want a machete, or an ax, but all I find is a hammer. I take it back to the kitchen with me to take care of this damn door once and for all.

I swing the hammer at the door. It makes a nice dent.

I swing at it again, wondering why I didn't just try to take the door off the hinges. Maybe I just really needed something to take out my aggression on.

I hit the door in the same spot, over and over, until the wood begins to chip. Eventually, a hole begins to form, and I can see from the kitchen into the living room. It feels good. That kind of worries me.

I keep hacking away, though. Every time I swing at the door, the door swings away from me. I swing again when it comes back. My hammer and I fall into a rhythm with the door until there's at least a twelve-inch hole.

I put all my strength behind the next swing, but the hammer gets stuck in the wood and slips out of my hands. When the door swings back toward me, I stop it with my foot. I can see Clara through the hole in the door. She's standing in the living room, staring at me.

She looks bewildered.

My hands are on my hips now. I'm breathing heavily from the physical exertion this hole took to make. I wipe sweat from my forehead.

"You have officially lost your mind," Clara says. "I'd be better off as a homeless runaway."

I push at the door, holding it open with my hand. If she really thinks it's so bad, being here with me . . . "Run away, then, Clara," I say flatly.

She shakes her head, as if *I'm* the disappointing one, then walks back to her bedroom.

"That's not the way to the front door!" I yell.

She slams her bedroom door, and it only takes three seconds for me to regret yelling at her. If she's anything like I was at that age—*which she is*—she's probably packing a bag and is about to climb out her window.

I wasn't serious. I'm just frustrated. I need to stop taking it out on her, but her attitude with me is making her an easy target.

I go to her bedroom and open her door. She's not packing a bag. She's just lying on her bed, staring up at the ceiling. *Crying.*

My heart clenches with guilt. I feel terrible for snapping at her. I sit down on her bed and run an apologetic hand over her head. "I'm sorry. I don't really want you to run away."

Clara rolls over dramatically and faces the other direction. She pulls a pillow to her chest. "Get some *sleep*, Mom. Please."

CHAPTER FOURTEEN

CLARA

I finished my first ever full cup of coffee about two weeks ago, the morning after my mother knocked a random hole in our kitchen door. Since then, I've discovered the one thing that just might save me from my monthlong depression.

Starbucks.

Not that I've never been to a Starbucks before. I've just always been that teenager who orders tea at coffee shops. But now that I know what it's like to be sleep deprived, I've been through almost every drink on the menu and know exactly which one is my favorite. The classic Venti Caramel Macchiato, no substitutions.

I take my drink to an empty corner table, one that I've sat at almost daily for the last two weeks. When I'm not at Lexie's house after school, I'm here. Things have gotten so tense at home I don't even want to be there. My curfew on school nights is ten, as long as I don't have homework. My curfew on weekends is midnight. Suffice it to say, I haven't been home before ten p.m. since the last argument my mother and I got into.

If she's not demanding to know where I am and who I'm with or sniffing me for signs of drug use, she's moping around the house, knocking random holes in the doors.

And then there's everything we haven't talked about. The fact that I was texting Jenny when they died. And I know where she and Jonah went when they left the house together—the Langford. I saw it on the app. I asked her that night where they'd gone, but she wouldn't tell me. If I brought it up to her now, I have a feeling she'd lie to me.

Things just feel uneven with her. We aren't on the same page. We don't know how to talk to each other now that Dad and Jenny are gone.

Or maybe it's me. I don't know. I just know I can't take being in our house right now. I hate the feeling I get when I'm there. It feels weird without my father there, and I'm scared it'll never go back to the way it used to be. It used to feel like home. Now it feels like an institution, and my mom and I are the only patients.

It's sad that I feel more comfortable at Starbucks than in my own home. Lexie works at Taco Bell five days a week, and tonight she's back at it, so I get comfortable in my quiet little corner of Caffeine Land and open a book.

I'm only a few pages in when my phone vibrates on the table. I flip it over to look at the new Instagram notification.

Miller Adams started following you.

I stare at the notification, allowing the meaning of it to soak in for a moment. Did Shelby break up with him again? Is this his way of getting back at her?

I feel a smile attempting to form on my lips, but I bite it back because I'm kind of getting whiplash. *Get in my truck. Get out of my truck. Let's be friends on Instagram. No, let's not be friends. Okay, yeah, let's be friends.*

I won't allow myself to feel happy about this until I know what the hell he's up to. I open our Instagram messages, since I deleted his number, and I send him one.

Me: Get your heart broken again?

Miller: I think I did the breaking this time.

There's no biting back my smile this time. It's too big to fight.

Miller: What are you doing right now?

Me: Nothing.

Miller: Can I come over?

My house is the *last* place I want him.

Me: Meet me at Starbucks.

Miller: On my way.

I set my phone down and pick up my book again, but I know I won't be able to concentrate on the words while I wait for him. It doesn't matter, though, because five seconds later, Miller is pulling an empty chair over to my table. He sits, straddling the chair backward. I pull my book to my chest and stare at him.

"You were already here?"

He grins. "I was standing in line to get coffee when I messaged you."

Which means he probably saw me grinning like an idiot. "That feels like an invasion of privacy."

"It's not my fault you're severely unaware of your surroundings."

He's right. When I'm here, I don't have a clue what's going on around me. Sometimes I sit here for two hours reading, and when I close the book, I'm surprised to look up and see that I'm not at home.

I slide the book into my bag and take a sip of my coffee. Then I lean back in my chair, my gaze rolling over Miller. He looks better. Not so heartbroken this time. He actually looks content, but I have no idea how long that'll last before he realizes how much he misses Shelby and unfollows me on Instagram again.

"I don't know how I feel about being your backup plan every time things go south with your girlfriend."

He smiles gently. "You aren't a backup plan. I like talking to you. I don't have a girlfriend anymore, so I no longer feel guilty talking to you."

"That's essentially what a backup plan is. Priority doesn't work out . . . move on to second tier."

A barista calls Miller's name, but he stares at me for five long seconds before he scoots his chair away from the table and goes to retrieve his coffee. When he comes back, he doesn't revisit the conversation. He changes the subject entirely.

"Feel like going for a ride?" He takes a sip of his coffee, and I have no idea how something as simple as a cute guy sipping coffee could be appealing, but it is, so I grab my bag and stand up.

"Sure."

⌐

Aside from a few dates I went on with a guy named Aaron last year without my parents' permission, I've never been on a date with anyone else. Not that I consider whatever this is we're doing an actual date, but I can't help but compare it to what little experience I've had in the past. My parents have been extremely overprotective, so I never even bothered asking if I could go out with a guy. The rule has always been that I could date at sixteen, but I've been sixteen for almost a whole year and have avoided it. The idea of bringing a guy into my house to meet my parents always sounded dreadful, so if I wanted to hang out with a guy, I usually just did it behind their backs with Lexie's help.

I do know enough to know that silence is your enemy on dates. You try to fill that silence by asking trivial questions that no one really wants to answer, and then, if you can get past the terrible answers, you might get to make out at the end of the night.

But whatever this is between me and Miller is *not* a date. Not even close. We haven't said one word to each other since we got into his truck, even though that was over half an hour ago. He isn't forcing me to answer questions I don't want to be asked, and I'm not forcing every ounce of information out of him about his breakup with Shelby. It's just two people, listening to music, *enjoying* the silence.

I love it. It might even beat my cozy corner in Starbucks.

"This was Gramps's truck," Miller says, breaking our comfortable silence. But I'm not annoyed by the break. I've actually been wondering why he drives such an old truck and if there's a story behind it. "He bought it brand new when he was twenty-five. Drove it his whole life."

"How many miles are on it?"

"There were just over two hundred thousand before it was gutted and everything was replaced. Now there are . . ." He lifts his hand to look at the dash behind his steering wheel. "Nineteen thousand, two hundred and twelve."

"Does he still drive it?"

Miller shakes his head. "No. He's not in any shape to drive."

"He seemed like he was in pretty good shape to me."

Miller scratches his jaw. "He has cancer. The doctors are giving him six months, tops."

That feels like a brutal punch to my gut, and I've only met the man once.

"He likes to pretend it isn't happening and that he's fine. But I can tell he's scared."

It makes me wonder more about Miller's family. Like what his mother is like, and why my father seemed to hate his father so much.

"Are the two of you very close?"

Miller just nods. I can tell by his refusal to verbally answer that question that he's going to take it hard when it does happen. That makes me sad for him.

"You should write everything down."

He gives me a sidelong glance. "What do you mean?"

"Write it all down. Everything you want to remember about him. You'll be surprised how soon you start to forget everything."

Miller smiles at me appreciatively. "I will," he says. "I promise. But I also have a camera in his face most of the time for that very reason."

I smile back and then stare out the window. That's all that's said between us until he pulls back into the Starbucks parking lot fifteen minutes later.

I stretch my back and then my arms before unbuckling my seat belt. "Thank you. I needed that."

"Me too," Miller says. He's leaning against his driver's-side door, his head resting on his hand as he watches me gather my bag and open my door.

"You have good taste in music."

"I know," he says, a soft smile playing on his lips.

"See you at school tomorrow?"

"See ya."

The way he's looking at me makes me think he doesn't want me to go, but he's not saying anything to indicate otherwise, so I exit his truck. I shut the door and turn to my car, but I can hear him scrambling out of his truck while I search for my keys.

He's next to me now, leaning against my car. Miller's stare is intense. I feel it everywhere. "We should hang out again. You busy tomorrow night?"

I halt the search for my keys and make eye contact with him. Tomorrow night sounds good, but tonight sounds even better. It's still another hour before I have to be home. "Let's just hang out right now."

"Where do you want to go?"

I glance at the doors to Starbucks, already craving more caffeine. "Another coffee sounds really good."

All the smaller tables were taken, which meant we were left choosing between a table with six chairs or the love seat.

Miller went for the love seat, and I wasn't sad about that. We're both relaxed into the couch, our heads pressed into the back of the cushions, facing each other. I've pulled my legs onto the love seat, and Miller has one leg propped up.

Our knees are touching.

Most of Starbucks has cleared out by now, and my drink is almost empty, but we haven't stopped talking and laughing, not even for a few seconds. This version of us is so different than when we were in his truck earlier but just as comfortable.

It just feels natural with him. The silence, the conversation, the laughter. All of it feels so comfortable, and that's something I didn't even know I'd been missing. But I have missed it. Since the moment of the wreck, everything in my life has felt like it's edged in sharp corners, and I've been tiptoeing around this world in the dark for the past month, trying not to injure myself.

We haven't talked about his breakup, despite my curiosity about what happened. I was hoping we would avoid talking about the wreck and all that has transpired since then, but he just asked me how my mother is doing.

"Okay, I guess." I down the last sip of my coffee. "I walked in on her trying to tear down the kitchen door with a hammer for no reason at all. Now there's a huge random hole in the center of our door that's been there for two weeks."

Miller smiles, but it's an empathetic smile. "What about you?" he asks. "Any destruction on your part?"

I shrug. "Nah. I'm okay. I mean . . . it's only been a little over a month. I still cry every night. But I don't feel like I can't get out of bed anymore." I shake my empty coffee cup. "Acquiring a taste for coffee helped."

"Want another one?"

I shake my head and set my cup on the table next to me. Then I reposition myself on the couch to get more comfortable. Miller does the same, so we're even closer now.

"Will you do me a favor?" I ask him.

"Depends on what it is."

"When you become a famous director someday, will you make sure the coffee cups actually have liquid in them when actors hold them in scenes?"

Miller laughs at this. Loudly. "That is my biggest pet peeve," he says. "They're always empty. And when they set them down, you can hear the hollowness of the cup when it hits the table."

"I was watching this one movie where an actor was angry, holding a cup of coffee, and he was slinging it around, but not a single drop spilled. It pulled me out of the moment and ruined the entire movie for me."

Miller smiles and squeezes my knee. "It's a promise. Every coffee cup on my set will be full." His hand remains on my knee. It's too obvious to pretend I don't notice, but I try. I keep glancing down, though. I like seeing his hand there. I like feeling his thumb brush back and forth.

I like how I feel when I'm with him. And I'm not positive, but I think he likes how I make him feel. Neither of us has stopped smiling. I know I've blushed at least three times during our conversation.

We both know we're interested, so we aren't even trying to play coy. It's just a matter of me not knowing where his head is. What he's thinking . . . if he's thought about Shelby at all.

"So," he says. "You decided on a college yet? Still planning on majoring in acting?"

This question elicits a big sigh from me. "I really want to, but my mother is so against it. So was my father."

"Why?"

"The odds aren't in my favor, so they want me to do something more practical."

"I've seen you act. It's what you were born to do."

I sit up a little straighter. "Really? What have you seen me in?" I always do theater every year at school, but I've never really noticed Miller there before.

"I can't remember what it was. I only remember you onstage."

I can feel myself blushing again. I lean back against the couch and smile shyly. "What about you? Did you at least apply to UT yet? Or anywhere?"

He shakes his head. "No. We can't afford a school like that, and honestly, I need to stay around here. For Gramps."

I want to ask him more about that, but he seems sad when he talks about it. I don't know if it's because there isn't anyone else to care for his grandfather if he were to move away or if it's because he'd never leave him regardless. Probably a combination of both.

I don't like that this conversation is sending his mind in that direction, so I try to redirect his thoughts. "I have a confession."

He looks at me expectantly, waiting for me to spill it.

"I filled out the form for the film submission."

Miller smiles. "Good. I was worried you wouldn't do it."

"I might have filled it out for you too."

He stares at me, his eyes narrowed. "In case I broke up with Shelby?"

I nod.

He laughs a little and then says, "Thank you." There's a pause. "So does this mean we're partners?"

I shrug. "If you want to be. But I mean, if you end up getting back together with Shelby, I'll understand if you can't do—"

Miller leans forward, dipping his head as he stares at me. "I'm not getting back together with her. Get that out of your head."

Such a short sentence, but such a big statement. One that sends a surge of heat up my chest.

He has such a serious look in his eye that it makes me nervous when he begins to speak again. "Earlier, when you called yourself my backup plan, I wanted to laugh. Because if anything, Shelby was my backup plan to *you*." A reserved smile spreads across his face. "I've had a thing for you for almost three years."

His words stun me into a momentary silence. Then I shake my head, confused. "Three years? Why'd you never do anything about it?"

"Timing," he says quickly. "I almost did once, but then you started dating that one guy . . ."

"Aaron."

"Yeah. *Aaron.* Then I started dating Shelby. Then you and Aaron broke up two months later."

"And then you began to go out of your way to avoid me."

Miller looks apologetic when I say that. "You noticed?"

I nod. "You paid a guy twenty bucks to switch lockers with him on the first day of school this year. I took that very personally." I say it with a laugh, but I'm being completely transparent.

"I was trying to keep my distance. Shelby and I were friends before we started dating, so she knew I used to have a thing for you."

That explains so much. "That's why you said she's only jealous of me and not other girls?"

"Yeah." Miller leans casually against the couch again, his head resting against the back of it. He's watching me process everything he just said. He's staring back at me with so much vulnerability—like it just took a hell of a lot of courage for him to admit what he did, and he's nervous about how I might respond.

I don't even know how to react. I kind of want to change the subject because I feel awkward now. I don't have anything to say that'll impress him or make him feel as good as his words just made me feel. For those reasons, the most random thing comes out of my mouth. "Does your truck have a name?"

Miller squints, as if he's wondering what the hell I'm talking about. Then he just laughs, and it's the greatest, deepest laugh. "Yeah. Nora."

"Why Nora?"

He hesitates. I love the smile that's playing on his lips. "It's a Beatles song."

I recall the Beatles poster hanging in his bedroom. "So you're a Beatles fan?"

He nods. "I have a lot of favorite bands. I love music. It feeds my soul."

"What are your favorite lyrics?"

He doesn't even hesitate. "They're not from the Beatles."

"Who are they from?"

"A band called Sounds of Cedar."

"Never heard of them, but I like the name."

"If I tell you my favorite lyrics by them, you'll want to listen to every song they've ever written."

I smile hopefully. "Good. Give me a couple of lines."

He leans in just a little and smiles as he repeats the lyrics. "I've believed in you since the moment I met you. I believe in myself now that I've finally left you."

I let the lyrics simmer as we stare at each other. It makes me wonder if those are his favorite lyrics because of his recent breakup with Shelby or if they were his favorite lyrics even before that. I'm not about to ask him, though. Instead, I release a sigh.

"Wow," I whisper. "Those words are somehow both tragic *and* inspiring."

He smiles gently. "I know."

I can't hide how he makes me feel in this moment. I'm appreciative that being with him gives me a respite from my grief. I'm appreciative that he's not pretending to be someone he's not. I'm appreciative that he broke up with his girlfriend before making a move on me. And even though I don't know him really well, I know him enough to be able to tell that there's a lot of good in him.

I'm severely drawn to that part of him—the part of him that showed up to my father's funeral, simply because he wanted to check on me. I'm drawn to that part even more than his looks or his humor or his terrible singing voice.

There are so many feelings swirling around in my chest right now, and I'm afraid the room will start spinning if I don't find my center of gravity. I lean forward and press my lips against his, if only just to balance myself.

It's a quick kiss. Unexpected for both of us, I think. When I pull away, I'm biting my lip nervously, wondering if I should have done that. I rest my head against the couch and wait for his reaction. He doesn't take his eyes off me.

"I didn't think our first kiss would be like that," he says quietly.

"Like what?"

"Sweet."

"How did you think it would be?"

His eyes wander to the few remaining customers still lingering. "I can't show you in here."

When his gaze meets mine again, the satisfaction in his lazy smile fills me with confidence. "Then let's go to your truck."

The anticipation for our second kiss makes me even more nervous than our first. We're holding hands when we exit Starbucks. He heads to his truck and opens the passenger door for me. I get in and he shuts it, then walks around to the driver's side.

I don't know why I'm so nervous now. Probably because this is actually happening. Me and Miller. Miller and me. What would our ship name be? Cliller? Millerra?

Ugh. They both sound terrible.

Miller closes his door. "What's that look for?"

"What look?"

He points at my face. "That one."

I laugh, shaking my head. "Nothing. I'm getting ahead of myself."

He reaches for my hand and pulls me closer to him. We meet in the middle of his seat. That's the thing about older trucks. The seats are long, without a console to separate the passengers. We're even closer now than we were on the couch. Our faces are closer, our bodies are closer. Everything is so much closer. His hand is on my outer thigh, and I'm wondering what flavor of sucker he's going to taste like.

"What do you mean you're getting ahead of yourself? Do you regret kissing me?"

I laugh because that's the last thing I regret. "No. I was thinking how terrible our ship names would be."

I see relief take over his expression. But then his eyes crinkle at the corners. "Oh. Yeah. They're terrible."

"What's your middle name?"

"Jeremiah. What's yours?"

"The quintessential *Nicole*."

"That's a really long middle name."

I laugh. "Smartass."

I can see the wheels turning behind his eyes. "Jerecole?"

"That's so bad." I'm thinking about it when it hits me how odd this is. We've had one small peck. We've only spent part of an evening together without him being attached to someone else, yet here we are, discussing ship names. I want to believe how he makes me feel, but the truth of the matter is he hasn't even been single long enough to decide if he even wants this to go anywhere.

"You're making that face again," he says.

I sigh, breaking eye contact with him. I look down and grab his hand. "Sorry. I just . . ." I pause for a moment, then look back up at him. "Are you sure about this? I mean, you just broke up with Shelby today. Or yesterday. I don't even know when, but either way. I don't want to start something if you're going to back out of it in a week."

The silence after I finish speaking lingers in the truck for a lot longer than I feel comfortable with. We're still holding hands, and Miller is lightly stroking the outside of my thigh with his other hand. He sighs, more heavily than I want him to. That kind of sigh is usually followed up with words that aren't good.

"You know the day in my truck when you told me to figure out my shit?"

I nod.

"That was the day I broke up with Shelby. It wasn't today or yesterday. It was weeks ago. And to be honest, my shit was already figured out long before that day. I just didn't want to hurt her."

Nothing else is said with words. It's all said with a look. His eyes pierce mine with such a concentrated honesty that I suck in a breath. He moves his hand from my leg to my elbow and then slowly drags his fingers up my arm and neck, coming to a stop at my cheek.

I'm pulling in shallow breaths, watching his eyes as they scroll over my face and pause on my lips.

"Nicomiah sounds okay," I whisper.

The moment is interrupted by his laughter. Then his hand slides to the back of my head, and he pulls me to his mouth, still grinning. It's a sweet kiss at first, much like the one I gave him inside. But then his tongue slips past my lips and touches mine, and the sweetness is gone.

This just got serious.

I respond with an almost embarrassing hunger, pulling him closer, wanting him and his kiss to take away the last few droplets of grief that are still swimming around inside of me. My hands are in Miller's hair now, and one of his hands is sliding down my back.

I've never felt anything so good and perfect before. I can actually feel the dread building inside of me, knowing this kiss will eventually come to an end.

He grips my waist and guides me closer so that I'm straddling him. Our new position makes him groan, and his groan makes me kiss him even deeper. I can't get enough. He tastes like coffee rather than suckers, but I don't mind because I actually love the taste of coffee now.

His fingers graze the skin of my lower back, and I'm amazed at how such a small touch can cause such a consequential reaction. I tear my mouth from his, afraid of that feeling. That intensity. It's new to me, and I feel somewhat jarred by it.

Miller pulls me to him, burying his face against my neck. My arms are wrapped around him, and my cheek is pressed against the top of his head. I can feel his breaths falling in heavy, heated waves against my neck.

He sighs, circling his arms more tightly around me. "That's more along the lines of the kind of first kiss I was expecting."

I laugh. "Oh yeah? You like that one better than the sweet one I gave you?"

He shakes his head and puts a little separation between us so that he can look at me. "No, I loved the sweet kiss too."

I smile and press my lips gently against his so that I can give him another sweet kiss.

He sighs against my mouth and kisses me back, no tongue, just soft lips and a gentle release of air. He peeks over my shoulder, glancing at his radio, and then leans back against the seat.

"You're late for curfew." He says it sort of with dread, like he wishes we could stay in his truck all night.

"How late?"

"It's fifteen after."

"Well, crap."

Miller slides me off of him and then exits the truck. I open my door to get out, and then Miller laces his fingers through mine as he walks me to my car. He opens the door for me, resting an arm on the top of my doorframe. We kiss one more time before I take a seat in my car.

I cannot believe how much I'm feeling right now. Before I showed up here today, I lived without Miller in my life perfectly fine. Now I feel like every minute I spend without him is going to be torture.

"Night, Clara."

"Good night."

He stares at me for a moment without shutting my door. Then he just groans. "Tomorrow seems so far away now."

I love the way he put exactly how I'm feeling into the perfect string of words. He closes my door and backs away a few steps. But he doesn't stop watching me, and he doesn't return to his truck until I'm out of the parking lot and on my way home . . . late.

This should be fun.

CHAPTER FIFTEEN

MORGAN

I've been sitting on the back patio, contemplating. I'm not sure what I'm contemplating. My mind is like a Ping-Pong ball, bouncing from thoughts about Chris, to thoughts about how I need to start applying for jobs, to thoughts about going back to college, to thoughts about Clara and how she's way past curfew. It's almost ten thirty now, so I text her. *Again.*

You're late. Please come home.

She's been staying out a lot, and I have no idea who she's with because she barely talks to me anymore. When she *is* here, she's in her bedroom. The app shows she's always either at Lexie's or Starbucks, but who in the world spends that much time at a coffee shop?

There's a soft knock on my back patio door, and I glance up, almost having forgotten that Jonah has been here for the past twenty minutes, fixing the kitchen door. I stand up and tuck my hair behind my ears when he walks outside.

"Do you have pliers?"

"I'm pretty sure Chris does, but his toolbox has a lock on it. But I might have a pair." I walk into the house and go to the laundry room. I keep my own toolbox for when I needed to fix stuff when Chris wasn't around. It's black and pink. Chris got it for me for Christmas one year.

He also got one for Jenny. The thought pierces me.

Sometimes I think it's getting better, but then the simplest memories remind me how much it still sucks. I pull my toolbox down and hand it to Jonah.

Jonah opens it and sorts through it. He doesn't find what he needs. "They're old hinges," he says. "I can't get the last one off because it's stripped so bad. I have something that'll work at the house, but it's late, so I'll just come back tomorrow if that's fine?"

He says it like it's a question, so I nod. "Yeah. Sure."

I texted him yesterday, telling him I couldn't get the kitchen door off the hinges and asking if he could help. He said he'd be over tonight but that it would be late because he was picking his sister up at the airport. He didn't even ask why I needed the door off the hinges. When he got here earlier, he never even asked why there was a huge hole in it. He just walked straight to the door and got to work.

I'm waiting for him to ask what happened as we walk toward the front door, but he doesn't. I don't like the quiet, so I throw a question in the mix that I don't even really care to know the answer to.

"How long is your sister in town for?"

"Until Sunday. She'd love to see you. She just . . . you know. She didn't know if you'd want company."

I don't, but for some reason, I smile and say, "I'd love to see her."

Jonah laughs. "No, you wouldn't."

I shrug because he's right. I barely know her. I met her once when we were teens, and I saw her for a few minutes the day after Elijah was born. And she was at both funerals. But that's the extent of my relationship with her. "You're right. It was the polite thing to say."

"You don't have to be polite," Jonah says. "Neither do I. It's the only positive thing to come out of this. We get at least a six-month pass to be assholes." I smile, and he nudges his head toward his car. "Walk me out?"

I follow him to his car, but before he gets in, he rests his back against the driver's-side door and folds his arms over his chest. "I know you probably don't want to talk about it any more than I do. But it affects our kids, so . . ."

I slide my hands into the back pockets of my jeans. I sigh and look up at the night sky. "I know. We have to discuss it. Because if it's true . . ."

"It makes Clara and Elijah half siblings," Jonah says.

It's weird hearing it out loud. I blow out a slow breath, nervous about what it means. "Are you planning on telling him someday?"

Jonah nods, slowly. "Someday. If he asks. If it comes up in conversation." He sighs. "I honestly don't know. What do you think? Do you want Clara to know?"

I'm hugging myself now. It's not cold out, but I have chills for some reason. "No. I never want Clara to find out. It would devastate her."

Jonah doesn't look angry that I'm essentially asking him not to tell Elijah the truth. He only looks sympathetic to our situation. "I hate that they left this mess for us to clean up."

I agree with him on that. It's a disaster of a mess. One I still haven't even wrapped my head around fully. It's too much to think about so soon and too much for me to want to discuss it right now. I change the subject, because either way, decisions aren't being made tonight.

"Clara's birthday is in two weeks. I'm thinking about keeping the tradition going with a cookout, but I'm not sure if she would want me to. It won't be the same without them here."

"You should ask her," Jonah suggests.

I laugh half-heartedly. "We aren't on the best terms right now. I feel like I'm walking on eggshells around her. She'd disagree with anything I suggested."

"She's almost seventeen. It would be more out of the ordinary if things were perfect between the two of you."

I appreciate him saying that, but I also know it's not entirely true. I know a lot of mothers who get along just fine with their teenagers. I'm just not one of the lucky ones. Or maybe it isn't about luck. Maybe I went wrong somewhere along the way.

"I can't believe she's about to be seventeen," he says. "I remember the day you found out you were pregnant with her."

I remember it too. *It was the day before he left.*

I divert my gaze to the concrete beneath my feet. Looking at him brings back too many emotions, and I'm really sick of emotions at this point. I clear my throat and take a step back, just as headlights brighten the yard around us. I look up and watch as Clara finally pulls into the driveway.

Jonah takes that as his cue to leave, so he opens his car door. "Good night, Morgan." He waves at Clara before getting into his car. I give him a silent wave and watch him drive away. He's already at the end of our street before Clara gets out of her car.

I fold my arms over my chest again and stare at her expectantly.

She shuts her door and acknowledges me with a nod but walks toward the front door. I follow her inside the house, where she kicks her shoes off by the couch. "What was that?" she asks.

"What was what?"

She tosses a hand toward the front yard. "You and Jonah. In the dark. It was weird."

I narrow my eyes at her, wondering if she's just trying to deflect right now. "Why are you late for curfew?"

She looks down at her phone. "I am?"

"Yes. I texted you. Twice."

She swipes her finger across the screen. "Oh. I didn't hear them come through." She slips her phone in her back pocket. "Sorry. I was studying at Starbucks . . . lost track of time. I didn't realize it was so late." She points over her shoulder as she backs toward the hallway. "I need to shower."

I don't even bother pushing for a more honest answer. She wouldn't give me one anyway.

I walk to the kitchen and grab a Jolly Rancher. I lean against the counter and stare absentmindedly at the hole in my kitchen door, wondering why Jonah so casually brought up the day I found out I was pregnant, like it wasn't one of the worst days of my life.

Maybe he brought it up because his leaving the next day didn't mean as much to him as it did to the rest of us.

I've forced myself not to think about that week since it happened, but now that Jonah brought it up, every moment of that day begins running through my mind.

We were at the lake. The three of them had been swimming, and I was sitting on a blanket in the grass, reading a book. They all came out of the water at the same time, but Jonah was the only one who walked in my direction. Chris and Jenny ran up the embankment toward the playground.

"Morgan!" Jenny yelled. "Come swing with us!" She was running backward up the hill, trying to entice me over.

I shook my head and waved her on. I wasn't in the mind-set to be playful that day. I hadn't even wanted to go to the lake in the first place, but Chris insisted on it. I wanted a night alone with him, without Jonah and Jenny tagging along. I needed to talk to him in private, but we hadn't had a single second of privacy that day. Sometimes he was oblivious to my moods, even though I had certainly been in a mood since realizing I was late for my period last night.

"What's eating you today?" Jonah said as he dropped onto the grass next to me. "You've been acting strange."

I almost laughed at his timing. "Did Chris send you over to fish it out of me?"

Jonah stared at me like I had somehow insulted him. "Chris lives in blissful oblivion."

Jonah's response surprised me. I noticed he had been making jabs at Chris. Little ones. Harmless ones. But I noticed. "I thought you guys were supposed to be best friends."

"We are," Jonah said. "I'd do anything for him."

"Sometimes you act like you don't even like him."

Jonah didn't deny it. Instead, he gave his attention to the lake in front of us, like my comment forced him into contemplation.

I picked up a pebble and threw it toward the lake. It didn't even hit the water.

"We're out of drinks," Chris said, jogging up to us. He dropped onto the grass dramatically and pulled me to him. He kissed me. "I'm gonna run to the store. Wanna come?"

I was relieved to finally get some alone time with him. We had a lot to talk about. "Sure."

"I have to pee," Jenny said. "I'm coming too."

I had to stop myself from rolling my eyes, but every time I thought I might get one minute alone to talk to Chris about what was going on with me, something or someone inserted themselves into our scene. "Take Jenny," I said with a sigh. "I'll wait here."

"You sure?" Chris asked as he hopped to his feet.

I nodded. "Better hurry—she's already racing you up the hill."

Chris looked behind him and then took off in a sprint. "Cheater!"

I turned back around and looked at Jonah, who was sharing the blanket with me, his knees pulled up, his arms resting on them. He was staring out at the lake. I could sense something was brewing in him.

"What's eating *you* today?" I said, repeating his own question.

His eyes cut to mine. "Nothing."

"It's something," I said.

The look he gave me in that moment was heart stopping. It was the same feeling I was starting to get every time he looked at me—like it had somehow reached past my eyes and slid down my spine.

The reflection of the lake in front of us made his eyes look liquefied. The realization started to grow on me that I was staring back at him much the same way, so I ripped my gaze from his.

Jonah sighed heavily and then whispered, "I'm worried we got it wrong."

His statement made my breath hitch. I didn't ask him what we might have gotten wrong because I was too scared of his answer.

I was scared he was going to say we weren't with the person we were meant to be with. Of course, he could have been about to say anything, but that's where my mind went, because why else did he look at me the way he looked at me sometimes? I tried to ignore it because Jonah and I had never been romantic in any sense. But we had a connection—one Chris and I didn't even have.

I hated it. I hated that Jonah always knew when something was bothering me, but Chris was clueless. I hated that Jonah and I could give each other a look and know exactly what the other was thinking. I hated how he always saved the watermelon Jolly Ranchers for me because it was a sweet gesture, and I didn't like that my boyfriend's best friend did sweet things for me. Besides, he and Jenny had just started dating. Unlike Jenny, I never would have betrayed my own sister.

Which is why that day on the shore of the lake when Jonah whispered, *"I'm worried we got it wrong,"* I said the one thing I knew would put us both in our place.

"I'm pregnant."

Jonah stared at me in stunned silence. I saw the color drain from his face. My confession shook him.

He stood up and walked a few feet away from me. It was as if all the what-ifs sank into him at once. He looked like he'd shrunk two inches by the time he walked back over to me. "Does Chris know?"

I shook my head, watching how his eyes had gone from liquefied to frozen in a matter of seconds. "No. I haven't told him yet."

Jonah chewed on his bottom lip for a moment, nodding in thought. He looked angry. Or destroyed.

When he turned and walked back through the sand and waded out into the water, I stared at him with tears in my eyes. The sun was setting, and the lake was murky. I couldn't see how far out he swam. But he was out there long enough that when he finally began making his way back to the shore, Chris and Jenny were pulling back into the parking lot.

Jonah sat back down on my blanket, soaking wet and holding his breath. I remember watching beads of water drip from his mouth. "I'm breaking up with Jenny."

His admission left me aghast. Then he looked at me pointedly, as if what he was about to say next were the most important words he would ever speak. "You'll be a great mother, Morgan. Chris is very lucky." His words were sweet, but the look in his eyes was painful. And for some reason, those words felt like a goodbye, before I even knew it *was* a goodbye.

With that, he pushed off the grass and walked toward the parking lot.

My head was spinning. I wanted to run after him, but the weight of the whole day anchored me in place. All I could do was watch as he told Jenny he was ready to go. I watched as they got in his car and pulled away.

When Chris started making his way down the hill, I should have been relieved to finally have that alone time with him, but I was devastated. Chris sat down next to me on the blanket and handed me a bottle of water.

I loved Chris. I was going to have his baby, even though I hadn't told him that yet. But I felt guilty because in all the time Chris and I had been dating, he'd never once given me a look that trickled down my spine. I was scared I'd never feel that again. I was scared I was wrong and that maybe I loved Chris, but maybe I wasn't *in* love with him.

He put his arm around me. "Babe? What's wrong?"

I wiped at my eyes, blew out a breath, and said, "I'm pregnant."

I didn't wait for Chris's reaction. I immediately stood up and cried the entire walk back to his car. Even then, I was blaming the tears on hormones. On finding out I was pregnant. I blamed the tears on everything besides what actually caused them.

The next day, Jonah told Jenny he wanted to move in with his sister and go to college in Minnesota. He packed up his things, bought a plane ticket, and didn't even come tell me or Chris goodbye.

Chris and Jenny were so upset that Jonah had selfishly up and left, but as I was more stunned by the news that I was pregnant, I didn't really have time to care about Jonah leaving. For the next several weeks, I mended Jenny's heartache and forced Chris to focus on us and my pregnancy, rather than the best friend who had abandoned him. I tried not to give Jonah another thought.

Little did I know, that routine would go on for a long time. Me being Chris's devoted wife, taking care of his house and his daughter and his needs. Me being loyal to my little sister, helping her study her way through nursing school, cleaning up the messes she made of her twenties, giving her a place to stay every few years when she'd need help getting back on her feet.

The day I found out I was pregnant, I stopped living life for myself.

I think it's time I figure out who I was meant to become before I started living my life for everyone else.

CHAPTER SIXTEEN

CLARA

Despite knowing I just pissed my mother off by being half an hour late for curfew, I still can't stop smiling. That kiss with Miller was worth it. I bring my fingers to my lips.

I've never been kissed like that. The guys I kissed in the past all seemed like they were in a hurry, wanting to shove their tongue in my mouth before I changed my mind.

Miller was the opposite. He was so patient, yet in a chaotic way. It was like he'd thought about kissing me so often that he wanted to savor every second of it.

I don't know that I'll ever not smile when I think about that kiss. It kind of makes me nervous for school tomorrow. I'm not sure where that kiss leaves us, but it felt like it was a statement. I just don't know what exactly that statement was.

My phone buzzes in my back pocket. I roll over and pull it out, then fall onto my back again. It's a text from Miller.

Miller: I don't know about you, but sometimes when something significant happens, I get home and think of all the things I wish had gone differently. All the things I wish I would have said.

Me: Is that happening now?

Miller: Yes. I don't feel like I was entirely forthcoming with you.

I roll onto my stomach, hoping to ease the nausea that just passed through me. It was going so well . . .

Me: What weren't you honest about?

Miller: I was honest. Just not entirely forthcoming, if there's a difference. I left a lot out of our conversation that I want you to know.

Me: Like what?

Miller: Like why I've liked you for as long as I have.

I wait for him to elaborate, but he doesn't. I'm staring at my phone with so much intensity that I almost throw it when it rings unexpectedly. It's Miller's phone number. I hesitate before answering it, because I rarely ever talk on the phone. I much prefer texting. But he knows I have my phone in my hand, so I can't very well send it to voice mail. I swipe my finger across the screen and then roll off the bed and head to my bathroom for more privacy. I sit on the edge of the tub.

"Hello?"

"Hey," he says. "Sorry. It's too much to text."

"You're kind of freaking me out with all the innuendos."

"Oh. No, it's all good. Don't be nervous. I just should have said this to you in person." Miller inhales a deep breath, and then on the exhale, he starts talking. "When I was fifteen, I watched you in a school play. You had the lead role, and at one point, you performed a monologue that went on for like two whole minutes. You were so convincing and you looked so heartbroken I was ready to walk onto the stage and hug you. When the play was finally over and the actors came back out onto the stage, you were smiling and laughing, and there wasn't a trace of that character left in you. I was in awe, Clara. You have this charisma about you that I don't think you're aware of, but it's captivating. I was a scrawny kid as a sophomore, and even though I'm a year older than you, I hadn't quite filled out yet, and I had acne and felt inferior to you, so I never worked up the courage to approach you. Another year went by, and I continued to admire you from afar. Like that time you ran for school treasurer and tripped walking off the stage, but you jumped up and did this weird little kick and threw your arms up in the air and made the entire audience laugh. Or that time Mark Avery popped your bra strap in the hallway, and you were so sick of him doing it that you followed him to his classroom, reached inside your hoodie, and took off your bra and then threw it at him. I remember you yelling something like, *'If you want to touch a bra so damn bad, just keep it, you perv!'* Then you stormed out. It was epic. Everything you do is epic, Clara. Which is why I never had the courage to approach you, because an epic girl needs an equally epic guy, and I guess I've just never felt epic enough for you. I've said *epic* so many times in the last fifteen seconds—I'm so sorry."

He's out of breath when he finally stops talking.

I'm smiling so hard my cheeks ache. I had no idea he felt this way. *No* idea.

I wait a few seconds to make sure he's done; then I finally respond. I'm pretty sure he can hear from my voice alone that I'm smiling. "First of all, it's hard to believe you were *ever* insecure. And second, I think you're pretty epic, too, Miller. Always have. Even when you were scrawny and had acne."

He laughs a little. "Yeah?"

"Yeah."

I can hear him sigh. "Glad I got that off my chest, then. See you at school tomorrow?"

"Good night."

We end the call, and I don't know how long I sit and stare at my phone. I can't even process the gravity of this. He actually has real feelings for me. He's *had* feelings for me. I can't believe I've been so oblivious to it.

I eventually unlock my screen because I need to call Aunt Jenny and tell her every bit of that conversation. I'm scrolling through my contacts when it hits me.

I *can't* call her. I can never call her again.

When is that finally going to sink in?

—

Lexie doesn't even have a chance to fasten her seat belt before I assault her with the news. "I kissed Miller Adams, and I think maybe we're a thing now."

"Wow. Okay," she says, nodding. "But . . . what about Shelby?"

"He broke up with her two weeks ago."

She takes a moment to let this sink in. I back out of her driveway, and she's staring forward, thinking hard about it. Then she looks at me and says, "I don't know, Clara. Seems a little quick, like maybe it's a rebound."

"I know. I kind of thought the same thing, but it doesn't feel that way at all. I can't explain it, but . . . I don't know. I get the feeling he didn't have this kind of connection with Shelby."

I can feel her giving me a look. "I'm your friend, so I feel the need to say this, but you sound kind of crazy right now. He dated Shelby for an entire year. You made out with him once, and you think he has more feelings for you than he does for her?"

It does sound insane, but she wasn't there. "You know me better than anyone, Lex. You know I don't fall for guys like this. I think you should take me a little more seriously."

"Sorry," she says. "Maybe you're right. Maybe Miller Adams is madly in love with you, and his twelve-month relationship with Shelby was some kind of move to make you jealous."

"Now you're just making fun of me."

"It was just a kiss, Clara! You're acting like the two of you are official already. Of course I'm making fun of you."

I do see the ridiculousness of it from her point of view. But I still think she's wrong. I drop it, though, because she won't understand it. "It was an amazing kiss, though," I say with a smile.

She rolls her eyes. "Good for you. Just don't make it official yet. It's *not* official, is it?"

"No. I don't guess so. All we did was kiss. He didn't even ask me out on a date."

"Good. When he does ask you, pretend you're busy."

"Why?"

"So it doesn't seem like you like him this much."

Her advice is confusing. "Why wouldn't I want him to know I like him?"

"Because he might lose interest. You'll scare him away."

"That makes no sense."

"It's just how guys work."

"Let me get this straight. If I like a guy, and he likes me, we have to pretend *not* to like each other, or we'll stop liking each other?"

"Hey, I didn't make the rules," she says. She falls back into her seat in kind of a slump. "I can't believe this. We've always been single together. This is going to change our friendship."

"No, it won't."

"It will," she says. "You'll sit by him at lunch. He'll start meeting you before and after school. You'll be too busy to hang out with me on weekends."

"You work all the time, anyway."

"Yeah, but I could have a day off someday, and you won't want to spend it with me now."

"Next time you have a day off, I'm going to spend it with you."

"Promise?"

I hold up my pinkie, and she grips it just as we're pulling into the school parking lot.

Lexie nudges her head. "Gross. He's waiting for you."

Miller is standing next to his truck in the parking spot next to where I always park. Just the sight of him waiting for me makes me smile. Lexie groans when she sees Miller smiling back at me. "I hate it already," she says.

She gets out of the car as soon as I put it in park and looks at Miller over the hood. "How serious is this thing between you two?"

Oh my God. I scramble out of the car and look at Miller, wide eyed. "Don't answer that." I turn to Lexie. "*Stop* it."

She's looking past me, at Miller. "Got any single friends, since you stole mine?"

Miller laughs. "I'm sure I can scrounge up a couple."

Lexie shuts her door. "Only a couple?" She winks at me, then starts walking toward the school by herself. I feel kind of bad, because she's right. Things will change between us a little bit.

"How was your night?" Miller asks, pulling my attention back to him.

"I couldn't sleep."

"Me neither," he says, hoisting his backpack up higher onto his shoulder. He leans in and kisses me, just a quick peck on the mouth. "Were you up all night thinking about me?"

I lift a shoulder. "Maybe."

He walks with me toward the school. "Is Lexie serious? Does she really want a boyfriend?"

"I don't know. She's my best friend, but I still can't tell when she's kidding or when she's serious."

"So it's not just me?"

I shake my head just as Miller opens the door for me. Once we're in the hallway, he reaches down between us and grabs my hand like it's second nature. I might be biased, but I like how we fit. He's taller than me by at least five inches, but our hands clasp together comfortably.

It feels so right . . . *until it doesn't.*

Forty-five days. That's how long they've been dead, and I have no idea how I can possibly walk through these hallways, smiling like I didn't just lose two of the most important people in my life. It fills me with guilt because my mother never smiles anymore. Neither does Jonah. Not only have I stolen lives because of my disregard for Aunt Jenny's safety while she was driving, but now I've stolen the smiles of all the people my father and Aunt Jenny left behind.

I head toward Jonah's classroom, and Miller walks with me, holding the door for me when we reach it. Jonah is the only one inside when we walk into the room, still hand in hand.

Jonah is staring at our hands, and again, I feel the guilt coursing through me. How long will it take until I don't feel guilty for feeling happy? Shouldn't I be in a depression every second of the day? Not just at intervals? I pull my hand from Miller's as I set my stuff onto my desk.

Jonah tilts his head in curiosity. "You two dating now?"

"Don't answer that either," I say to Miller.

"*Okay*, then," Jonah says, giving his attention back to the work laid out in front of him. "Gotten very far on the film project?"

"No. I just told Miller I signed him up for it last night."

Jonah looks up at Miller. "You still waiting on permission from the girlfriend?"

"I don't have a girlfriend anymore." Miller looks at me. "Or maybe I have a new one?" He looks confused when he gives his attention back to Jonah. "It doesn't seem like she wants me telling people we're a thing now."

"Are we?" I ask. "A thing?"

"I don't know," Miller says. "You're the one who keeps telling me not to answer anyone."

"I just didn't want you to feel pressured to label us."

"Now I feel pressured *not* to label us."

"Well, Lexie said if I acted like I liked you, it would scare you away."

Miller raises a brow. "If that phone call didn't scare you away last night, I think we're fine. If you like me, I want you to act like you like me, or I'll get a complex."

"I like you. A lot. Don't get a complex."

"Good," Miller says. "I like you too."

"Good," I say in return.

"*Good*," Jonah says, reminding us of his presence. "Project is due before the end of the semester. Get started."

"Okay," Miller and I say in unison.

Jonah rolls his eyes and walks back around his desk. Miller backs away from me. "I'll meet you after class."

I smile.

He smiles back, but when he leaves the room, my smile turns to a frown. Once again, I feel guilty for even smiling.

"Whoa."

I look up at Jonah. "What?"

"The look on your face. Your smile disappeared as soon as he did. You okay?"

I nod, but I don't elaborate.

Jonah doesn't let it go, though. "Clara. What's wrong?"

I shake my head, because it's stupid. "I don't know. I just . . . I feel guilty."

"Why?"

"It's only been forty-five days, and I woke up happy today. I feel like a terrible person for even feeling good for one second." *Especially since their wreck was my fault.* I leave that part out of my confession, though.

"Welcome to the theme park," Jonah says.

I look at him quizzically, so he begins to offer up an explanation.

"Right after something tragic happens, you feel like you've fallen off a cliff. But after the tragedy starts to sink in, you realize you didn't fall off a cliff. You're on an eternal roller coaster that just reached the bottom. Now it's gonna be up and down and upside down for a long, long time. Maybe even forever."

"Is that supposed to make me feel better?"

Jonah shrugs. "I'm not here to make you feel better. I'm on the same roller coaster you are."

The door opens, and students begin to file in. I can't stop staring at Jonah. His eyes have crinkled at the corners, and his lips have a slight downward turn to them.

It tugs at my heartstrings a little, seeing him stressed out, or sad, or whatever that look is. I don't like it. He's always been quiet and a little serious, but his eyes have always seemed happy. I guess I haven't really looked at him long enough since the wreck to really see how much it changed him.

It makes me wonder how much it's changed my mother. I hardly look at her anymore either. I wonder if that's because of my guilt.

—

Miller isn't waiting for me after class like he said he would be. I'm not even sure where he has first period, so I linger in the hallway for a minute and wait for him.

"Clara?"

I spin around at the sound of my mother's voice. She's holding a folder in one hand, her Louis Vuitton bag in the other. She only breaks out the Louis on special occasions, so I'm not sure what she's doing here and why the Louis is out, but it instantly makes me nervous.

"What are you doing?"

She holds up the folder. "Applying for a job."

"Here?"

"They're hiring substitute teachers. I thought I could do that for a few months. See if I like it. I've decided to go back to college."

The hall is starting to clear out. I look around to make sure no one is near us. "Are you *serious*?"

She looks at me like I just offended her. "What's wrong with me going to college?"

I didn't mean to offend her. If she wants to go to college, I'm happy for her. But the last thing I want is for her to test the waters at the school I attend daily. We already can't get along at home. I can't imagine potentially having her in class.

I shake my head. "I didn't mean—" My words are cut off when lips meet my cheek and an arm snakes around my waist.

"I was trying to find you. Where do you go for study period?"

I look at Miller, wide eyed. I look back at my mother. My expression prompts Miller to look from me to my mother. I feel him stiffen, and then he drops his arm to his side. It's the first time I've seen Miller look flustered. He holds out his hand to my mother to formally introduce himself. She just stares at his hand and then looks at me.

Miller starts to mumble an apology. "I'm so sorry, Mrs. Grant. I thought you were just one of Clara's friends. You . . . you look really young."

My mother is staring daggers at me, ignoring him.

"She *is* young," I say to Miller. "She had me when she was seventeen."

My mother doesn't miss a beat as she finally addresses Miller. "We're very fertile women. Be careful."

Oh my God.

I cover my eyes for a brief moment. I can't even look at him when I say, "I'll see you at lunch."

I can see him nod out of the corner of my eye, and he quickly walks in the opposite direction.

"I can't believe you just said that to him."

"You're dating him now?" she says, motioning over my shoulder. "I thought you said he had a girlfriend."

"He broke up with her."

"Why didn't you tell me?"

"Because I knew you wouldn't like it."

"You're right—I don't." She's raising her voice now. I'm relieved the hallway is empty. "Since the day you started hanging out with him, you've skipped out on your father's funeral, you've done drugs, you're never home, you're late for curfew. He's not good for you, Clara."

I don't want to argue with her right now. But she couldn't be more wrong about him. It makes me angry that she's placing my behavior on a guy, rather than on the fact that maybe the few bad decisions I've made have been a result of what happened forty-five days ago. That's had way more of an effect on me than a boyfriend—knowing my texts to Aunt Jenny are what caused this entire terrible situation to begin with.

"I know nothing about what's going on in your life. You tell me nothing."

I roll my eyes. "Now that Aunt Jenny isn't here to tell you every little secret?"

Her anger gives way to an expression of shock, like she honestly didn't think I was aware Aunt Jenny used to tell her everything. Then she just looks angry. Hurt.

"Why do you think she told me everything, Clara? It's because all the advice she ever gave you *came* from me. She's spent the last five years cutting and pasting texts I wrote, and then she'd send them to you and pretend they were hers."

"That's not true," I snap.

"It *is* true. So stop treating me like I don't know what's best for you or that I have no clue what I'm talking about."

What she's saying about Aunt Jenny isn't true.

And even if it were . . . even if my mother was the one to relay most of the advice Jenny gave me, why would she ruin that for me? Jenny is never coming back thanks to me, and my mother just took the one thing I cherished most about my aunt and threw it in a blender and fed it to me.

I hate that I feel like I'm about to cry. I'm so angry with her. At myself. I turn around to walk away before I say something that will get me grounded, but my mother grips my arm.

"Clara."

I yank my arm from her hand. I spin and take a lunging step toward her. "Thank you, Mom. Thank you for taking one of the things I loved the most about my aunt and *ruining* it for me!"

I really want to call her a bitch, but I don't want to make her angry. I want to make her feel guilty. I want her to feel as guilty as I've felt since the accident.

It works, because she immediately looks ashamed for taking credit for the close relationship I had with Aunt Jenny.

"I'm sorry," she whispers.

I walk away, leaving her standing alone in the hallway.

CHAPTER SEVENTEEN

MORGAN

Why did I say all that? Why did I feel the need to take the credit now that Jenny is gone?

I know why. I'm upset and hurt by what Jenny did to me, and it hurts even more to know that Clara still considers her a saint. I wanted Clara to know that Jenny had no clue how to offer mature advice and everything she learned from Jenny, Jenny learned from me. For some reason, I wanted credit for that. Credit I don't need. I'm taking all the anger I have toward Jenny and Chris, and I'm wanting Clara to feel anger toward them too.

I feel terrible. She's right. I hurt her and ruined a memory she had of Jenny, and it was all for selfish reasons. Because I'm mad at Jenny. Because Jenny hurt *me*.

This is all the more proof that I can't let Clara find out about what Jenny and Chris did. Just finding out this one small thing absolutely gutted her. She almost started crying right when I said it.

God, this hurts. It all hurts so much that I just want out of here. Out of this building. I want to go home. I should have never even considered applying for a job here. What teenager wants to spend all day, every day with their mother?

I turn and rush down the hallway, attempting to hold back tears until I make it outside. I'm ten feet from the door.

"Morgan?"

I freeze at the sound of my name. I spin around on my heels, and Jonah is standing in his doorway. He can tell immediately that I'm not okay. "Come here," he says, motioning me into his empty classroom. A huge part of me wants to keep walking, but a small part of me wants to take refuge somewhere, and his empty classroom seems like a good place to do that.

He presses a hand to the small of my back and ushers me to a seat. He hands me a Kleenex. I take it and wipe at my eyes, pressing back the tears. I don't know where it comes from, but it's as if the last few weeks of feeling like I'm losing control of Clara hit me, and I'm forcing Jonah into being my temporary therapist. I just begin to ramble.

"I always thought I was a good mom. It's been my only job since I was seventeen. Chris worked at the hospital, and my job was to raise Clara. So every time she did something good or surprised us in some way, I felt a sense of pride. I cultivated her into this wonderful little human, and I was so proud of her. Proud of myself. But since the day Chris died, I'm starting to think maybe I had nothing to do with all the good parts of her. She never acted out before he died. She didn't do drugs or lie about having a boyfriend or where she is. What if all this time, I thought she was so great because I was a great mom, but this whole time, Chris is the one who brought out the best side of her? Because now that he's gone, she and I just bring out the worst in each other."

Jonah was leaning against his desk when I started saying all that, but now he's seated in the desk across from me. He leans forward, clasping his hands between his knees. "Morgan, listen to me."

I suck in a breath and give him my attention.

"You and I are in our thirties . . . we expect a fair amount of tragedy in our lives. But Clara is only sixteen. No one her age should have to deal with something this damaging. She's lost in grief right now. You just have to let her find her way, like you did with me."

Jonah's voice is so gentle right now I actually find a semblance of comfort in his words. I nod, appreciative he pulled me into his classroom. He reaches out and squeezes one of my hands reassuringly in both of his. "Clara isn't struggling because Chris is no longer here. She's struggling because he's never coming back. There's a difference."

A lone tear slides its way down my cheek. I wasn't expecting Jonah to actually make me feel better, but he's right. He's right about Clara, and it also makes me think what he's saying applies to me. Chris's presence wasn't nearly as affecting as his absence has been.

Jonah still has both of his hands wrapped around one of mine when the door to his classroom opens. It's Miller. He walks into the classroom and stops a few feet from me. He's looking at me like Clara might have gotten hold of him and told him how much I upset her in the hallway.

I raise an eyebrow in warning. "I hope you aren't about to tell me how to raise my daughter."

Miller takes a sudden small step back. His eyes dart from me to Jonah. He looks uncomfortable when he says, "Um. No, ma'am? I'm just . . ." He points at the desk I'm sitting in. "You're in my seat."

Oh. He's here for class.

I look to Jonah for confirmation. Jonah nods and says, "He's right. That's his seat."

Can I mortify myself any more today?

"It's fine, I can sit somewhere else," Miller says.

I stand up, motioning toward the chair. Miller hesitantly walks to it and sits down. "I'm not crazy," I say to Miller, excusing my behavior just now. And maybe even my behavior in the hallway earlier. "I'm just having a really bad day."

Miller looks to Jonah for confirmation. Jonah nods and says, "She's right. She's not crazy."

Miller raises an eyebrow and sinks into his chair, pulling his cell phone out of his pocket, wanting out of our conversation completely.

More students begin to file into the room, so Jonah walks me toward the door. "I'll be over later to finish taking the door off the hinges."

"Thank you." I start to walk out but realize how much I dread going home alone to think about the embarrassment of the day. The only thing that could get my mind off everything is Elijah. "Do you mind if I get Elijah from day care? I miss him."

"He'd love that. I already have your name on the pickup list. I'll be over as soon as school lets out."

I smile, tight lipped, before turning away. I walk to my car, regretting that I didn't hug Jonah or give him more of a thank-you. He deserves it.

CHAPTER EIGHTEEN

CLARA

Miller slides his tray onto the table next to me. "Your mother hates me."
He casually opens a can of soda and takes a drink.

I'm not going to sugarcoat it and tell him he's wrong. "That makes
two of us."

He swings his head in my direction. "You *both* hate me?"

I laugh, shaking my head. "No. My mother hates both of *us*." I
mindlessly spin my water bottle on the table. "We got into an argument
after you walked away. Not about you. Just about . . . stuff. She kind
of hurt my feelings."

Miller isn't so casual now. He can see I'm bothered by it, so he turns
toward me, ignoring the food in front of him. "You okay?"

I nod. "Yeah. We're just in a rut."

He leans forward and presses his forehead to the side of my head.
"I'm sorry this year sucks for you." He plants a quick kiss on the side of
my head and then pulls back, grabbing the pickle spear from his plate
and putting it on mine. "You can have my pickle. Maybe that'll help?"

"How do you know I like pickles?"

Miller smiles a little. "I've spent three years trying not to stare at
you while you eat lunch. Creepy, I know."

"But also sweet."

He grins. "That's me in a nutshell. A sweet creep."

"*Such* a sweet creep."

Lexie drops her tray onto the table across from us. "I want a sweet creep. Found me a boyfriend yet?"

"Not yet," Miller says. "It's only been four hours since you put in a request."

Lexie rolls her eyes. "Listen to you, talking about time like it matters. You're the one kissing my best friend within minutes of dumping a girl you dated for a year."

I groan. "Be nice, Lexie. Miller doesn't know you well enough yet to be the butt of your sarcasm."

"It's not sarcasm. He literally dumped his girlfriend and jumped right into a relationship with you." She looks at Miller. "Is that inaccurate?"

Miller doesn't look like she's pushing any of his buttons. He pops a chip into his mouth. "It is quite accurate," he says. He looks at me and winks. "Clara knows what's up, though."

"Well, I don't," Lexie says. "I don't know anything about you. I don't even know your middle name. Is it also a brand of beer?"

I turn to Miller when her question sinks in. "Oh, wow. I didn't realize your first *and* last name are brands of beer."

"It wasn't intentional. Miller was my mother's maiden name." He faces Lexie. "It's Jeremiah."

"So *normal*," Lexie says, seemingly disappointed. She eats a spoonful of pudding and sucks on the spoon for a second. She pops it out of her mouth and points at Miller. "Who's your best friend, Miller Jeremiah Adams? Is he hot? Single?"

"They're all hot and single," Miller says. "What exactly are you looking for?"

Lexie shrugs. "I'm not picky. I prefer blond men with blue eyes. Someone with a dry sense of humor. A little rude. Hates spending time with people. Doesn't mind a girlfriend who has a shopping addiction and likes to be right about everything. Athletic. Taller than six foot. And Catholic."

I laugh. "You aren't even Catholic."

"Yeah, but Catholics are strict and have to confess a lot, so he might sin less than, say, a Baptist."

"Your reasoning is so, so flawed," I say.

"I know just the guy," Miller says, standing up. "Want me to go get him?"

"Right now?" Lexie asks, perking up.

"I'll be right back." Miller walks away, and Lexie looks at me, wiggling her eyebrows.

"Maybe I do like your boyfriend. He cares about your best friend."

"I thought you said I wasn't allowed to refer to him as my boyfriend yet."

"There was a pause when I said that word," she states. "I like your boy . . . *friend*."

We watch Miller as he takes a seat at his usual lunch table. He's talking to a guy named Efren. I know him from theater, but he doesn't match any of Lexie's requests. Or *demands*, rather.

Efren has black hair, he's shorter than Lexie, and he's certainly not athletic. He moved here from the Philippines before starting high school a few years ago. Efren smiles at Lexie from across the lunchroom, but she groans and lifts a hand to her face, hiding her view of him.

"Is he serious right now? Efren Beltran?"

"I was in theater with him. He's really nice. And cute."

Lexie's eyes widen, like I'm betraying her. "He's like five seven!" She peeks through her fingers and sees Miller walking Efren over to the table. She groans and drops her hand but doesn't hide her disappointment with Miller's selection.

"This is Efren," Miller says. "Efren, this is Lexie."

Lexie's eyes narrow in Miller's direction before she drags them to Efren. "Are you even Catholic?"

Efren takes a seat next to her. He seems more amused by her reaction than insulted. "No, but I live half a mile from a Catholic church. I'm not opposed to converting."

I already like him, but I have a feeling it's not going to happen so easily on Lexie's part. "You look kind of inexperienced," she says, almost accusingly. "Have you even had a girlfriend before?"

"Does online count?" Efren asks.

"No. It most certainly does not."

"Then . . . no."

Lexie shakes her head.

Miller pipes up and looks at Efren. "I thought you and Ashton dated for a while. That counts, right?"

Efren indicates it doesn't count with a shake of his head. "Fizzled out before it even started."

"Bummer," Miller says.

"How tall is your dad?" Lexie asks him. "Do you think you're finished growing?"

"I don't know," Efren says, shrugging. "My dad left when I was three. I have no idea what he looks like."

I can see Lexie's eyebrow rise, albeit very subtly. "Mine too. Christmas Day."

"That explains the attitude," Efren says.

Lexie shrugs. "I don't know. I think I had this attitude before I was three. It's probably why he left."

Efren agrees with a nod. "Probably. If we start dating, don't get used to me being around, because I'll probably get tired of your attitude and leave too."

Lexie tries not to smile at that, but I'm pretty sure Efren's sarcasm is sexier to her than his height would be, if he were tall.

177

I honestly didn't expect this to go anywhere, but they're on equal ground when it comes to the jabs. Maybe she'll actually let him take her out on a date.

I turn away from them and face Miller. He smiles mischievously before crunching on another chip. "He's a really good guy," he whispers. "She might be surprised if she'd just give him a chance." He takes a chip and holds it up to my mouth. I eat it, and then he leans in and kisses me.

It's just a peck—lasts maybe two seconds—but it's two seconds too long because a moment later, someone is tapping us on the shoulder. We both look up to see the lunchroom monitor glaring at us.

"No PDA in the cafeteria. Put up your trays and come with me. Lunch detention."

I look at Miller and shake my head. "I've been dating you fourteen hours, and you're already getting me in trouble."

Miller laughs. "You were doing illegal things with me long before fourteen hours ago. You forget about the sign?"

"Let's *go*," the lunch monitor says.

She follows us as we put our trays away. Miller swipes the bag of chips off my tray when she's not looking and shoves them into the front of his jeans, covering them with his T-shirt.

The monitor leads us to the library, where she signs us in for lunch detention. I have literally never had lunch detention in my life. This is a first, but I'm actually a little excited about it.

We take a seat at an empty table. The teacher who's monitoring detention is playing a game on his phone while his feet are propped up on the desk. He doesn't pay us any attention.

Miller begins to move his chair a little bit at a time so that it goes unnoticed. It reminds me of how he's been moving the city limit sign.

He's eventually sitting so close to me that our thighs and arms are touching. His proximity is nice. I like the way it feels being close to him. I also like the way he smells. Normally, he smells like bodywash.

Axe, maybe. Sometimes he smells like suckers. But right now, he smells like Doritos.

My stomach growls, so Miller leans carefully back in his seat and sticks his hand in the band of his jeans. He removes the bag of chips and coughs a little when he opens them to cover the noise of the crinkling bag.

The detention monitor looks in our direction. Miller stares down at the table and tries to look innocent. When the guy goes back to playing his game, Miller holds the bag of chips toward me. They're all crushed, so I take the most solid one I can find and slip it into my mouth before the teacher notices.

We eat the entire bag this way, taking turns sneaking chip fragments, sucking them until they're soggy so we don't crunch too loud. When the bag is gone, I wipe my hands on my jeans and raise an arm. "Excuse me?"

The detention monitor looks up.

"Can we get a book off the shelf to read?"

"Go ahead. You have sixty seconds."

A few seconds later, we end up on the same aisle, and Miller's mouth is on mine, my back against a wall of books. We're laughing while we kiss, making every attempt at being quiet. "We're gonna get detention again," I whisper.

"I hope so." His mouth meets mine again, and we both taste like Doritos now. His hands slide from my cheeks down to my waist. His tongue is soft, but his kisses are quick. "We better hurry. We only have thirty seconds left."

I nod but wrap my arms around his neck and pull him even closer. We kiss for about ten more seconds before I push him away. His hands remain on my hips.

"Come to the theater tonight," he whispers.

"You working?"

He nods. "Yeah, but I can get you in free. I'll make fresh popcorn this time."

"Sold."

He pecks me on the cheek and grabs a random book off the shelf behind me. I grab one, too, and we both return to our seats.

It's hard to sit still now. He got me all worked up, and I want to hold his hand or kiss him again, but we have to settle for playing footsie instead. After a while, he leans over and whispers, "Mind if we trade books?"

I look at his book, and he closes it so I can read the cover. *An Illustrated Guide to the Female Reproductive Cycle.*

I cover my laughter with my hand and slide him my book.

When we're back at my locker after detention, Lexie appears. She wedges herself between Miller and me. "He's funny." I think she's talking about Efren. "Short, but funny."

"You two should come to the movies with me tonight," I offer.

Lexie makes a gagging sound. "In all the years you've known me, have I ever gone to the theater with you?"

I think about that, and she hasn't. I've just never questioned it.

"Do you have something against movie theaters?" Miller asks.

"Uhhh, *yeah.* They're disgusting. Do you know how much semen is on a theater seat?"

"Gross," I say. "How much?"

"I don't know, but they should probably research it." She pushes off the locker and walks away. Miller and I both stare at her.

"She's interesting," he says.

"She is. But now I'm not so sure I want to come to the theater tonight."

Miller leans in toward me. "I clean that theater, and it's spotless. You better show up. Seven?"

"Fine. I'll be there. But if you could Lysol the entire back row of every room, that would be great." Miller leans forward to kiss me goodbye, but I push his face away with my hand. "I don't want detention again."

He laughs while he backs away. "See you in six hours."

"See ya."

I don't tell him there's a chance I might not be there. I haven't talked to my mother about it yet. After what happened in the hallway today, it's clear she doesn't want me dating Miller. I'll probably hang out at Lexie's after school for a while and then lie to her and tell her we're going to the movies.

I'm getting pretty good at lying to her. It's easier than telling her the truth.

CHAPTER NINETEEN

MORGAN

Jonah knocks softly on the front door before opening it.

I'm on the couch with a sleeping Elijah when he lets himself in.

"I picked him up right before they were about to lay him down for a nap," I whisper.

Jonah looks down at Elijah and smiles. "They sleep so much at this age. I kind of hate it."

I laugh quietly. "You'll miss it when he starts refusing to take naps."

Jonah nods toward the garage. "I didn't have time to run home after work. Mind if I try to unlock Chris's toolbox?" I shake my head. Jonah heads in that direction, and I put Elijah in his bassinet. I move it to the far side of the living room so that the noise from the kitchen hopefully doesn't wake him.

Jonah walks back into the house with Chris's toolbox and carries it into the kitchen. I follow him to help him with the door.

I hand him a knife, and it only takes him a few seconds to pick the lock. After he opens the lid, he lifts the top tray out so that he can search through the larger section in the bottom.

There's a perplexed look that suddenly appears on his face. That look prompts me to walk over to the toolbox and look inside.

We both stare at the contents that were hidden beneath the top tray. Envelopes. Letters. Cards. Several of them, all addressed to Chris. "Are these from you?" Jonah asks.

I shake my head and take a step back, as if the distance will make them disappear. Every time I feel like one of my many wounds might be starting to heal, something happens to rip it open again.

Chris's name is written in Jenny's handwriting on the outside of all the open envelopes. Jonah is sifting through them.

My heart begins to race, knowing there could be answers to all of our questions inside those envelopes. When did it start? Why? Was Chris in love with her? Did he love her more than he loved me?

"Are you going to read them?" I ask.

Jonah shakes his head with assurance. His decision is so final. I'm envious of his lack of curiosity. He hands them all to me. "You do what you need to do, but I don't care to know what they say."

I stare at the letters in my hands.

Jonah grabs what he needs from the toolbox and pushes it aside, then gets to work on the last stubborn door hinge.

I walk the letters to my bedroom and drop them onto the bed. Even just holding them feels too painful. I don't want to look at them while Jonah is here, so I leave my bedroom and close the door. I'll confront them later.

I push myself up onto the counter in the kitchen, and I stare at my feet, thinking of nothing but the letters, no matter how hard I try to think of something else.

If I read them, will it give me a sense of closure? Or will it only deepen the wound?

Part of me is afraid it'll make it worse. The small memories I have make it bad enough, like the one I had this morning that almost brought me to tears.

Jenny and I were downtown last year, a week before Chris's birthday. She was adamant about getting him a particular abstract painting she saw hanging in a store. In all the years I'd been married to Chris, I'd never known him to be interested in art. But the painting reminded Jenny of Chris somehow. I never thought much about it. After all, she was his sister-in-law. I loved how well they got along.

The painting hangs above the portable kitchen island I keep shoved against the wall.

I'm staring at it now.

"Jenny was adamant about getting Chris that painting for his birthday last year."

Jonah pauses what he's doing and looks over his shoulder at the painting. Then his eyes sweep quickly over me, and his focus is given back to the door.

"I told her he would hate it, and do you know what she said to me?"

"What'd she say?" Jonah asks.

"She said, *You don't know him like I do.*"

Jonah's shoulders tense, but he doesn't respond to that.

"I remember laughing at her because I thought she was joking. But now, knowing what we know, I think she actually meant it. She was serious about knowing my husband better than I did, and I don't think she meant to say that out loud. Now, every time I look at that painting, I can't help but wonder what story it holds. Were they together the first time he saw it? Did he tell her he loved it? Every memory I have of them I thought was set in stone. But the more I think about it—about them—those memories are all changing shape. And I hate it."

Jonah finally gets the door off the hinges. He props it up against the wall and then leans against the counter and grabs a Jolly Rancher. I'm surprised when he pops it in his mouth.

"You hate watermelon."

"Huh?"

"You just ate a watermelon Jolly Rancher. You used to hate them."

He doesn't respond to my observation. He's staring at the painting when he begins talking. "The night before they died, when we were all eating dinner at the table? Chris asked her if she was excited about the next day. And I thought nothing of it when she said, *'You have no idea,'* because she was supposedly starting back to work the next day, and I assumed that's what they were talking about. But they were talking about staying together at the Langford. They were talking about it right in front of us."

I hadn't thought about that moment. But he's right. Jenny looked Chris in the eye and more or less told him she was excited about getting to sleep with him. Chills creep up my arms, so I rub them away. "I hate them. I hate them for lying to you about Elijah. I hate them for rubbing it in our faces."

We're both staring at the painting now. "It's such an ugly painting," Jonah says.

"It really is. Elijah could probably paint something better."

He opens the refrigerator and pulls out a carton of eggs. When the refrigerator door falls shut, he opens the eggs and pulls one out, cupping it in his hand. Then he throws it at the painting. I watch the yolk trickle down the right side and fall onto the floor.

I hope he knows he's cleaning that up.

Jonah is in front of me now, holding out an egg. "Feels good. Try it."

I take the egg and hop off the counter. I draw my arm back like I'm throwing a softball, and then I hurl the egg at the painting. He's right. It feels good watching it splatter over a memory Jenny and Chris made together. I take another egg from the carton and throw it. Then another.

Sadly, there were only four eggs in the carton to begin with, so now I'm out, but I feel like I'm just getting started. "Find something else," I say, urging Jonah to open the refrigerator. Something about destroying one of their memories fills me with an adrenaline rush I didn't even know I'd been missing. I'm bouncing on my toes, ready to toss something else, when Jonah hands me a plastic cup of chocolate pudding. I look at it, shrug, and then throw it at the painting. Part of the plastic punches through the canvas.

"I meant for you to *open* the pudding, but that works too."

I laugh and grab another pudding from him, then tear open the film. When I try to throw the pudding at the painting, the contents are too thick and too hard to get out. It's not as satisfying as the egg until I dip my fingers into the cup and walk to the painting. I smear the pudding across the canvas.

Jonah hands me something else. "Here. Use this."

I look down at the jar of mayo and smile. "Chris hated mayonnaise."

"I know," Jonah says with a grin.

I dip my whole hand inside of it, scooping out a cold glob of mayonnaise before smearing it on as much of the painting as I can. Jonah is next to me now, squirting mustard on the canvas. Normally, I'd be freaking out about the mess we're making, but the satisfaction far outweighs the dread of the eventual cleanup.

Besides, I'm actually laughing. The sound is so foreign I'd smear mayonnaise all over the house just to keep up this feeling.

I've smeared almost an entire jar of mayonnaise over the painting when Jonah starts at it with a bottle of ketchup.

God, this feels good.

I'm already thinking about what else in this house might hold secret memories between the two of them that we could destroy. I bet there's stuff in Jenny and Jonah's house too. And Jonah might even have more eggs than I did.

The jar of mayonnaise is finally empty. I try to turn around so I can find something else to throw, but the combination of bare feet, egg yolk, and tile flooring doesn't make for a reliable surface. I slip and grab at Jonah's arm on my way down. In a matter of seconds, we're both on our backs on the kitchen floor. Jonah tries to push himself off the floor, but the mess we've made is everywhere. His palm slips on the tile, and he's on his back again.

I'm laughing so hard I roll onto my side in the fetal position because I'm using muscles I feel like I haven't used in forever. It's the first time I've laughed since Chris and Jenny died.

It's also the first time I've heard Jonah laugh since they died.

Actually . . . I haven't heard him laugh since we were teenagers.

Our laughter begins to subside. I sigh, just as Jonah turns his head toward me.

He's not laughing at all anymore. He's not even smiling. In fact, everything funny about this moment seems to be forgotten as soon as we make eye contact, because it's so quiet now.

The adrenaline coursing through me begins to change shape and morphs from a need to destroy a painting into an entirely different need. It's jarring, going from such a fun moment to such a serious one. And I don't even know why it became so serious, but it did.

Jonah swallows, and then in a rough whisper he says, "I've never hated watermelon Jolly Ranchers. I only saved them because I knew they were your favorite."

Those words roll through me, slowly warming up the coldest parts of me. I stare at him silently, not because I'm speechless but because that's probably the sweetest thing a man has ever said to me, and it didn't even come from my husband.

Jonah reaches a hand out, wiping away a sticky strand of hair stuck to my cheek. As soon as he touches me, I feel like we're back to that night, sitting together on the blanket in the grass by the lake. He's looking at me the same way he was looking at me back then, right before he whispered, *"I'm worried we got it wrong."*

I feel like he's about to kiss me, and I have no idea what to do, because I'm not ready for this. I don't even *want* it. A kiss between us comes with complications.

So why am I leaning in toward him?

Why is his hand now in my hair?

Why am I completely caught up in the thought of what he might taste like?

Other than the quickening of our breaths, the kitchen is quiet. So quiet I can hear the hum of an engine as Clara's car pulls into the driveway.

Jonah releases me and quickly rolls onto his back.

I sit up in a snap, gasping for a breath. We both pull ourselves off the floor and immediately begin cleaning.

CHAPTER TWENTY

CLARA

Jonah's car is in the driveway. Hopefully he hasn't lost his mind again and is here dropping off Elijah for another week. That's the last thing my mother and I need right now.

I'm not sure what we need, but we need something. An intervention? Separate vacations?

Hopefully she's as ready as I am to forget about what happened at school today. If there's one thing I like about my mother, it's her ability to avoid confrontation when she needs time to think about something. I don't want to have to stay home and talk it out tonight, because all I want is to go inside, change clothes, and head to the theater to see Miller. *But I doubt it's going to be that easy.*

When I walk into the house, I see Elijah asleep in the bassinet next to the wall. I start to walk toward him to give him a quick kiss, but my attention is pulled to the kitchen.

The door isn't there anymore, but that's not the weird part.

The weird part is my mother and Jonah. *And the mess.*

My mom is on her hands and knees, wiping up the floor with paper towels. Jonah is pulling down the painting that Aunt Jenny bought my dad for his birthday. There's stuff all over it. I tilt my head, trying to get a closer look, but can't tell exactly what it is.

Food?

I take a few steps toward the kitchen before I'm able to put it all together. There's an empty mayonnaise jar on the counter. Empty pudding cups on the floor. An empty carton of eggs on the counter. There's food on Jonah's shirt and in my mother's hair.

What the hell?

"Did you guys just have a *food* fight?"

My mother's head whips in my direction. She had no idea I was even here. Jonah spins around and almost slips. He drops the painting but catches himself by gripping the counter. He and my mother look at each other; then they both look back at me.

"Uh," Jonah says, stuttering. "We, um . . . don't really have an acceptable explanation for this."

I raise an eyebrow but keep my thoughts to myself. If I don't judge them for behaving strangely, maybe they won't judge me for not wanting to be here.

"Okay. Well . . . I'm going to the movies with Lexie."

I expect my mother to protest, but she does the opposite. "My purse is on the couch if you need money."

My eyes narrow in suspicion. *Is this some kind of test?* Maybe she feels guilty for what she said to me today.

Something isn't right, but if I stand here much longer, she might realize it too. I spin on my heels and head toward my bedroom to change. I don't bother taking money out of her purse. Miller never charges me for anything, anyway.

~

As soon as I walk into the building, Miller's whole face lights up, and he stops what he's doing to come around the counter. There's no one around, so he pulls me in for a hug and then kisses me. "Meet me in theater one. I'll be there in five minutes."

"But . . ." I point at the concession stand. "Popcorn."

He laughs. "I'll bring you some."

I head toward theater one, surprised to see it's completely empty and the lights are on. There's nothing even showing on the screen. I take the top row like I always do and wait for Miller. In the meantime, I pull up the theater guide on my phone to see what's playing in theater one.

Nothing.

The last showing was a cartoon, and it ended an hour ago.

I text Miller.

Me: Did you say theater one? There's nothing playing in here tonight.

Miller: Stay there. I'm on my way.

Miller rounds the corner a couple of minutes later, holding a tray of food. Nachos, hot dogs, popcorn, and two drinks. He walks to the top row and takes a seat next to me. "I feel like we were mistreated at school today," he says. "I'm pretty sure it's a law that students should get to eat. Even if that means taking our food to detention with us." He hands me a drink and balances the tray of food on the back of the seats in front of us. "Steven owes me about five favors, so he's manning the concession stand for the next hour."

I grab a hot dog and a packet of mustard. "Nice. Does that mean this is a date?"

"Don't get used to it. I don't normally go to such extravagant lengths."

We spend the next several minutes eating and talking. I let him do most of the talking because it's nice. He's animated and he smiles a lot, and every time he touches me, I get a stomach full of cliché butterflies.

When he's finished eating, he pulls a sucker out of his pocket. "Want one?" I hold out a hand, so he pulls another one out and gives it to me.

"Do you keep a stash of suckers on you at all times? You're always eating them."

"I have an issue with grinding my teeth. The suckers help."

"If you keep eating them at the rate you do, you won't have any teeth left to grind."

"I've never even had a single cavity. And don't act like you don't enjoy how I taste."

I grin. "You do taste pretty good."

"Shelby hated my sucker habit," he says. "She said they made my lips sticky."

"Who?" I'm only teasing when I ask that, but he takes it like I've been insulted that he brought her up.

"Sorry. I didn't mean to go there. I don't want to be that boyfriend who talks about his ex."

"I actually have a lot of questions, but I don't want to be that girlfriend who makes you talk about your ex."

He pulls the sucker out of his mouth. "What do you want to know?"

I think about his question for a moment. There's a lot I want to know, but I ask him the most pressing question. "When she broke up with you after I gave you a ride that day, why did you seem so heartbroken?" I've been wondering how he could seem so affected by it *that* day but be perfectly okay with it now. It makes me worry he's hiding something.

His finger gently brushes over the top of my hand. "I wasn't necessarily upset about her breaking up with me. I was upset because she thought I cheated on her. I didn't want her thinking that, so I was hell bent on making her believe me."

"Does she know you broke up with her for me?"

"I didn't break up with her for you."

"Oh," I say, a little taken aback. "You sort of made it sound like you did."

Miller readjusts himself in the seat, sliding his fingers through mine. "I broke up with her because when I went to sleep at night, I wasn't thinking about her. And when I woke up in the morning, I wasn't thinking about her. But I didn't break up with her just so I could date you. I would have broken up with her whether you and I ended up together or not."

It doesn't seem like there's much of a difference in breaking up with someone *for* someone else or *because* of someone else, but it feels like it makes all the difference in the world when he explains it.

"Has it been a weird adjustment? You guys were together for a long time."

He shrugs. "It's been different. Her mom never cared if I spent the night at her house on weekends, so Saturday nights at home with Gramps are taking some getting used to."

"Her mom let you sleep at her house? Like . . . in her bed?"

"It's unconventional, I know. But her parents are pretty lenient in a lot of areas. And technically, she's an adult in college. I guess that had a lot to do with it."

"My mom will never let you spend the night. Just putting that out there."

Miller laughs. "Believe me, I got that vibe from her. I'll be surprised if I'm even allowed to visit you in broad daylight."

I hate that he feels this way. I hate that my mother *made* him feel this way. And if I'm being honest, it worries me that it'll be a turnoff for him later down the line, if she never accepts that he's my boyfriend.

I can't even believe I'm saying that. Miller Adams is my *boyfriend*.

We're both facing each other now, our bodies turned toward each other in the theater seats. It's so quiet in here that we can hear the rumbling of the movie playing on the other side of the wall.

I try not to think about everything he just said, because now I'm worried about all the times he stayed at Shelby's house. All the times he slept in her bed. Will he eventually miss that? I've never had sex, and with the way my mother has been acting, I'm not sure she'll ever allow Miller to come over. She might even put a stop to me going out altogether, just to try and break us up. I hope not, but with her behavior this past month, I wouldn't put it past her.

I feel like Miller has been completely honest with me, so I want to do the same. I pull the sucker out of my mouth and stare at it. "So. Just so you're aware. I'm a virgin."

"I know a cure for that," Miller says.

My eyes flash up to his, but then he laughs. "I'm kidding, Clara." He leans toward me and kisses me on the shoulder. "I'm glad you told me. But I'm not in any hurry. At all."

"Whatever. You're used to getting it every weekend. You'll eventually grow bored with not having sex, and you'll go back to her." I immediately cover my mouth with my hand. "Oh my God, why do I sound so insecure? Please pretend I didn't just say all that."

He laughs a little, but then he looks at me intently. "You don't have to worry. I already get more out of *not* having sex with you than I did during my entire relationship with her."

I like him so much. More than I thought possible. Every minute we spend together makes me like him more than I liked him the previous minute. "When I decide I'm ready . . . I hope it's with you."

Miller smiles at that. "Trust me—I'm not going to talk you out of it."

I think about what our first time might be like. *When* it'll be. I look over at him and grin. "Our first kiss was a cliché coffee shop kiss. Maybe losing my virginity should be cliché too."

Miller raises an eyebrow. "I don't know. They might ban us from Starbucks."

I laugh. "I'm talking about prom. It's five months from now. If we're still together, I'd like it to be a cliché after-prom deflowering."

My choice of words makes Miller laugh. He takes his sucker out of his mouth and grabs mine from my hand and sets them on the food tray. Then he leans in and kisses me, briefly. When he pulls back, he says, "You're getting ahead of yourself. I haven't even asked you to prom yet."

"You should ask me, then."

"You don't want one of those elaborate promposals?"

I shake my head. "Promposals are stupid. I don't want an elaborate anything."

He hesitates, like maybe he doesn't believe me. Then he nods once and says, "Okay, then. Clara Grant, will you go to prom with me and have cliché after-prom sex with me?"

"I would love to."

Miller grins and kisses me. I kiss him back with a smile, but I can feel part of myself sinking.

Aunt Jenny would have loved this story.

CHAPTER TWENTY-ONE

MORGAN

My kitchen might be cleaner than it's ever been. I'm not sure if it was because Jonah is an excellent cleaner (he cleaned the majority of it) or if it's because he's trying to erase any proof of that near kiss in the kitchen so that we don't have a single reminder of it.

My guilt has been palpable since Clara left to go to the movies. Jonah must feel the same, because neither of us spoke as we cleaned. And as soon as Elijah began to wake up, I offered to feed him because Elijah is the only thing I feel like I'm doing right in my life. It seems he's starting to recognize me because he smiles when he sees me.

I've been keeping him occupied in the living room for an hour now. Jonah cleaned the entire kitchen. I didn't expect him to, and even told him not to worry about it at one point, but he kept cleaning. I would have done it, but I was honestly relieved when Elijah woke up. I'd rather not be in the same room as Jonah right now.

Elijah is getting stronger. I'm sitting back on the couch and holding him up while he pushes his legs against my stomach. I'm making baby sounds at him when Jonah carries my kitchen door to the garage.

Elijah yawns, so I pull him to my chest and pat him gently on the back. It's past his bedtime, and despite the thirty-minute nap he took while Jonah and I destroyed the kitchen, Elijah still seems like he's ready to pass out. He grows limp against my chest as he begins to fall into slumber. I press my cheek to the top of his head, wishing more than anything that I didn't grow sad when I think about the hand he's been dealt.

He's lucky to have Jonah. A man who stepped up, knowing there's a huge possibility he didn't father him. I hope, for Jonah's sake, that Elijah doesn't resent him if he ever finds out. I hope it makes Elijah appreciate Jonah even more.

Jonah walks into the living room and smiles when he sees Elijah asleep on my chest. He sits down next to us on the couch and rubs a hand over Elijah's back. Jonah releases a quiet sigh, and when I look at him, he's staring back at me. He's sitting so close our legs are touching.

The feelings that came about unexpectedly in the kitchen earlier are being shaken awake. I was hoping that was a fluke and that this reaction Jonah elicits from me would remain dormant from here on out.

"Scoot over," I whisper.

Jonah's eyes squint, as if he doesn't understand my direction.

"You're too close. I need space."

Jonah understands that. He almost seems a little surprised by my reaction. He moves to the other end of the couch in a dramatic display. Now I feel like I just insulted him.

"I'm sorry," I say. "I'm just . . . confused."

"It's fine," Jonah says.

I crane my neck and look down at Elijah. He's limp enough that I can probably move him back to the bassinet. I do that because I need fresh air. After placing him gently onto the mattress, I wait to make sure he doesn't wake up; then I cover him up.

I don't even make eye contact with Jonah as I make my way to the back patio. I'm sure he'll follow me, whether I ask him to or not. And honestly, we need to discuss what almost happened in the kitchen because the last thing I need is for Jonah to think there's any kind of possibility there.

Jonah slides the glass door shut after he follows me out. I'm pacing the back patio, staring at the stones beneath my feet. Chris installed them a few years ago. Jenny and I helped him, and I remember how much fun we had. We kept making fun of Chris because for some reason, he listened to John Denver while doing yard work and would sing at the top of his lungs. He never listened to John Denver any other time. Only when he did yard work. Jenny and I ridiculed him the entire time we were helping, so he locked us out of the backyard and finished the patio without us.

I wonder if their affair started before then.

I wonder, more often than I should, when it did start. I don't know why I keep hoping it's more recent. The idea that it's been going on for years makes it feel even more personal. I guess if I work up the courage to read the letters we found earlier, I might find out some of the answers to all the questions I have.

Jonah takes a seat in what used to be Chris's favorite chair. Jenny bought it for him.

My God, how can I be so stupid? What brother- and sister-in-law get along as well as they did? Why did I never see it?

"Sit down," Jonah says. "It makes me nervous when you pace."

I flop down into the chair next to Jonah. I close my eyes for a moment, trying to push all the memories back. I don't want to think about all the things in this house that tie Jenny and Chris together. I've already destroyed the painting. I don't want to have to destroy the patio furniture and anything else I actually use.

When I open my eyes, I look over at Jonah. His head is resting comfortably against the back of the chair. It's tilted in my direction, but he doesn't say anything. He thinks a lot, but he doesn't verbalize a lot.

I don't know why the silence is irritating me right now. "Say something. It's too quiet."

As if he already had words on the tip of his tongue, he says, "If you never would have gotten pregnant with Clara, would you have left Chris?"

"What kind of question is that?"

He shrugs. "I've just always wondered. I wasn't sure if you decided to stay with him because of Clara or if it was because you were in love with him."

I look away from him, because honestly, it's none of his business. If he wanted to know how my life was going to play out, he shouldn't have left without warning.

His voice is quieter when he continues. "You didn't answer the question."

"Jonah, stop."

"You told me to say something."

"I didn't mean . . ." I sigh. "I don't know what I meant."

It suddenly seems too stuffy outside. I go back inside, wanting to put space between Jonah and me. But he follows me all the way to my bedroom. Again, he closes the door behind him so our conversation doesn't wake Elijah. He seems a little annoyed that I keep moving from room to room to get away from him.

The letters strewn out over my mattress feel like they're staring back at me, taunting me.

"Are we going to address what happened in the kitchen?" he asks.

I'm pacing again, whether he likes it or not. "Nothing happened in the kitchen."

He looks at me like he's disappointed in my inability to face this in a mature way. I grip my forehead with my hand, trying to massage away an oncoming headache. I don't look at him when I speak.

"You want to talk about it? Fine. Okay. My husband has only been dead for a matter of weeks, and I almost kissed someone else. And if that isn't bad enough, it was *you* I almost kissed. It makes me feel like shit."

"Ouch."

"What if Clara had caught us? Would it really have been worth it?"

"This isn't about Clara."

"It *is* about Clara. *And* it's about Elijah. It's about everyone *but* us."

"I feel differently."

I laugh. "Of course you would."

"What's that supposed to mean?"

I shake my head, frustrated. "You cut ties with your best friends for seventeen years, Jonah. All you do is think about yourself and what *you* want. You never think about how your actions affect other people."

I feel the look he's giving me deep in my core. He's staring at me in a way I've never seen him look at anyone. It's a mixture of confusion and injury. He whispers, "*Wow*," then turns and walks out of my bedroom, slamming the door behind him.

Jonah Sullivan, running away again. Why am I not surprised?

I'm angry now. I storm out of my bedroom, prepared to yell at him, but he's walking out the door with Elijah. He sees me following after him, and he can tell how angry I am because our expressions match. He just shakes his head and says, "Don't. I'm leaving."

I follow him outside anyway because I don't feel empty yet. I still feel like an endless well, full of things I need him to hear. I wait until he buckles in Elijah's car seat and closes the door before I start in on him.

As soon as he faces me, waiting for me to speak, I can't think of a single thing to say.

I just stand in my yard with absolutely nothing left to say.

I honestly don't even know why we're arguing. We didn't even kiss. And I'll never put myself in a position like that with him again, so I don't even know why I'm so angry to begin with.

Jonah leans against his car and folds his arms over his chest. He waits a moment, allowing calm to settle between us. Then he lifts his head and looks at me with so much emotion in his expression.

"Jenny was your *sister*. No matter how I felt about you, I would have never come between the two of you. I left because unlike Jenny and Chris, I had *respect* for them. For *you*. Please don't ever call me self-ish again, because that was the hardest decision I've ever had to make in my entire life."

He gets in his car, slams the door, and leaves.

I'm left standing alone in my front yard, in the dark, full of infor-mation I'm not sure I wanted and feelings I've never allowed myself to confront.

My knees feel weak. I don't even have the energy to walk back to the house to think about everything that happened tonight, so I just lower myself to the grass, right where I've been standing since Jonah pulled away.

I drop my head into my hands, feeling the weight the day brought with it. Everything that happened with Clara at the school. Everything that happened with Jonah in the kitchen. Everything he just said. And even though there's a part of me that needed to hear all that from him, it doesn't change anything. Because it could never work between Jonah and me, no matter how long Jenny and Chris are out of the picture. It would make *us* look like the bad guys.

Clara wouldn't understand it. And what would we tell Elijah when he's older? That we all just switched partners? What kind of example is that?

Nothing between Jonah and me is a good idea. It'll be a lifetime of reminders that I so desperately want to forget. And now that he threw everything out there that he's probably been needing to say for seventeen years, I want him to take it back. I want to go back to yesterday, when it was easier. When he could bring Elijah over without all the awkwardness that will be between us from now on.

I feel like he said all that hoping it would solve something, but for me, it only created an even larger wedge. And I don't know that it'll ever get better.

We were teenagers. We weren't in love. What we experienced was attraction, and attraction is confusing, but it's also not worth uprooting Clara's life over.

I glance up when I see headlights turning in my direction.

Clara.

She parks the car, and when she gets out, she doesn't immediately say anything to me. I'm not even sure she notices me until she pivots at the sidewalk and comes to sit next to me on the grass. She pulls her knees up to her chin and hugs them as she stares out into the dark street. "I'm worried about you, Mom."

"Why?"

"It's late. And you're sitting alone in the dark in the front yard. Crying."

I reach a hand up to my cheek and wipe away tears I hadn't even acknowledged yet. I blow out a breath and look at her. "I'm sorry about today. I shouldn't have said that."

Clara just nods. I'm not sure if she's accepting my apology or agreeing that I shouldn't have said what I said.

"Were you with Miller tonight?"

"Yes."

I sigh. At least she was honest with me.

"He's not a bad person, Mom. I promise. If you'd just get to know him."

She's defending him, but I get it. When you're sixteen, you ignore all the warning signs. I blow out a breath. "Just be careful, Clara. I don't want you making the same mistake I did."

Clara stands up and wipes the back of her jeans. "I'm not you, Mom. Miller isn't Dad. And I really wish you'd stop referring to me as a mistake."

"You know that's not what I meant."

I have no idea if she heard that, because she's already walking into the house. She slams the door behind her.

I'm too exhausted to run after her. I lower my back to the grass and stare up at the stars. What little I can see of them, anyway.

I wonder if Chris and Jenny are up there somewhere. I wonder if they can see me down here. I wonder if they feel bad for what they turned my life into.

"You suck," I whisper to Chris. "I hope you can see us right now, because you've ruined a lot of lives, you fucking *prick*."

I hear footsteps in the grass and sit straight up, startled. I clasp my hand around my throat and release a breath at the sight of Mrs. Nettle standing a few feet away.

"I thought you were dead," she says. "But then I heard you call the Lord a prick." She turns around to head back toward her house. When she reaches her front door, she waves her cane toward me. "That's blasphemy, you know! You should probably start going to church!"

Once she's inside her house, I can't help but laugh. She really hates me.

I push off the grass and go inside. When I get to my bedroom, I look at the letters and cards spread out over my bed. My hands shake as I count them. There are nine total letters and three cards.

I want to know what they say, but I don't. I'm confident they'll only upset me more, and I've had enough for one day.

I stick them in the bottom of my dresser and decide to save them for a better day.

If that ever comes.

CHAPTER TWENTY-TWO

CLARA

It was a long weekend. Lexie and Miller both worked late shifts. Other than sitting with Miller during his break Saturday night and spending two hours on the phone with him last night, I haven't seen him. I haven't seen much of my mother either. After Friday night's weirdness, she spent all day Saturday on the computer applying for jobs. I spent most of Sunday in my room catching up on homework.

I'm later than usual when I get to Jonah's class. I'm the last one to arrive before the bell rings, so I'm surprised when Jonah approaches my desk and kneels in front of it. He usually doesn't pay me individual attention in front of other students.

"How's your mother?"

I shrug. "Good, I guess. Why?"

"She didn't return my texts this weekend. I just wanted to make sure she was okay."

I lean forward, not wanting anyone else to hear what I'm about to say. "I came home Friday night, and she was sitting in the front yard, crying. It was weird. Sometimes I think she's on the verge of a breakdown."

He looks concerned. "Did she say why she was crying?"

I look around, and everyone is talking, not paying attention to us. "I didn't ask. She cries more than she doesn't, so I just stopped asking her about it."

The bell rings, so Jonah returns to his desk. But he seems distracted as he starts to explain the lesson for the day. He looks tired. He looks like he's over it.

It disappoints me a little. Sometimes I feel like being an adult is so much easier than being a teenager, because you should have it all figured out as an adult. You're more emotionally mature, so you can handle crises better. But seeing Jonah right now as he tries to pretend he's not distracted, and watching my mother try to navigate her life as if her will still exists, is all the proof I need that grown-ups might not have their shit figured out any more than we do. They just wear more-convincing masks.

That disappoints me.

My phone vibrates in my pocket. I wait until Jonah's back is to the classroom before pulling my phone out and setting it on my desk. I swipe the screen and read Miller's text.

Miller: I'm off work today. Want to work on the video submission?

Me: Yes, but I really don't want to be around my mother right now. Can we do it at your house?

Miller: Sure. Come over around 5. I need to take Gramps to the doctor at 3 so I won't see you after school.

Miller is on the porch waiting for me when I pull into his driveway at ten after five. He jogs toward my car and hops into the passenger seat before I even have time to get out.

"Gramps is asleep," he says. "Let's go to Munchies first and let him rest for a while."

"What's Munchies?"

Miller looks at me like I've just blown his mind. "You've never been to Munchies? The food truck?"

I shake my head. "Nope."

He's completely taken aback. "You mean you've never had the Mac?"

"Is that a food?"

He laughs and pulls on his seat belt. "Is that a *food*," he mimics. "I hope you're hungry, because you're about to have the best experience of your life."

~

Fifteen minutes later, I'm sitting at a picnic table, staring at the camera Miller propped up with a tripod right before he went to order our food. It's pointed right at me. He said he's going to start filming random things when we're together because it'll be good for the film project to have extra footage. Or *B-roll*, as Miller referred to it. He already talks like a director sometimes.

He told me never to stare directly at the camera because we need to pretend it's not there, so of course I stare at it and make faces the entire time he's in line at the food truck.

I've honestly never seen Miller this enthusiastic over something. I'm actually more jealous of the sandwich than I've ever been of Shelby. He's *that* excited about it. Apparently, *the Mac* is a grilled cheese sandwich stuffed with macaroni and cheese that was boiled in holy water.

Okay, so holy water isn't really an ingredient, but with the way he talks about it, I wouldn't be surprised if it were.

When he approaches the table, he sets the tray in front of me, kneeling down on one knee like he's presenting a queen with a gift. I laugh and pull the tray from him, grabbing one of the sandwiches.

He sits next to me, rather than across from me, and straddles the bench. I like it. I like how much he wants to be near me.

When our sandwiches are unwrapped, he waits to take a bite of his because he wants to watch my reaction to my first bite. I bring the sandwich to my mouth. "I feel pressured to like it now."

"You're gonna love it."

I take a bite and then rest my arms on the table while I chew. It's delicious. Not only is it the crispiest, most buttery toast I've ever tasted, but the mac and cheese is so warm and gooey I feel like rolling my eyes.

But I shrug because I like teasing him. "It's okay."

He leans forward in disbelief. "It's . . . *okay?*"

I nod. "Tastes like a sandwich."

"We're breaking up."

"Bread's a little stale."

"I hate you."

"Cheese tastes processed."

He sets his sandwich down, grabs his phone, and opens Instagram. "I'm unfollowing you again."

I laugh after swallowing my first bite and then peck him on his cheek. "It's the best thing I've ever tasted."

He grins. "Promise?"

I nod. Then I shake my head. "It's second to how you taste after eating suckers."

"Good enough for me." He picks up his sandwich and takes a bite. He groans, and the sound he makes causes me to redden a little. I don't think he notices, because he tears off a miniscule piece of bread and reaches across the table, placing it next to an ant. The ant eventually carries it away.

Miller kisses my cheek, then takes another bite of his sandwich. "You thought about what kind of film we're going to make?"

I shake my head and wipe my lips with a napkin. He reaches up and brushes something away from my mouth with his thumb.

"We don't have a lot of time," he says.

"We have three months."

"That's not a lot of time. It's a lot of work."

"Dang," I say with a sarcastic undertone. "Guess that means we're gonna have to spend a lot of time together."

He's holding his sandwich with one hand and rubbing my leg with his other while we eat. He's super affectionate. And he's not afraid to kiss me in public. Or in front of a camera.

I suspect we'll be getting detention more than once this year.

"Stop looking at it," he says, referring to the camera.

"I can't help it," I say, looking away. "It's just right there in our faces."

"And you want to be an actress?"

I nudge him with my elbow. "That's different. This"—I wave to the camera—"is awkward."

"Get used to it because I want a lot of footage to work with. I want to win this year. Last time I submitted, we got fourth place."

"In the whole region?"

"The state."

"What? Miller, that's fantastic!"

He shrugs. "Not really. Fourth place cut deep. They only post the top three finalists to YouTube. No one cares about fourth place. I decided me and you are going for gold." He leans in and kisses me, then pulls back and takes another bite of his sandwich. "Does it bother you that I kiss you so much?" He's talking with his mouth full, but it's kind of adorable.

"What a strange thing for a person to be bothered by. Of course not."

"Good."

"I like that you're an affectionate person."

He shakes his head, wiping his mouth with a napkin. "That's just it, though. I'm not. I wasn't like this with Shelby."

"Why is it different with me?"

He shrugs. "I don't know. I've been trying to figure that out. I just crave you more than I've ever craved anything in my life."

That comment makes me smile, but I raise a teasing eyebrow. "I don't know, Miller. You were pretty damn stoked for your sandwich."

He has half a sandwich still left to eat, but as soon as I say that, he stands up and walks over to a nearby trash can and tosses it inside. He sits back down. "That sandwich meant nothing to me. I'd take your tongue in my mouth over that sandwich any day."

I crinkle up my nose and pull back. "Was that supposed to be sexy? Because it wasn't."

He laughs and pulls me closer to him, pressing his mouth to mine. It's not a sweet kiss, though. This one is full of tongue. And . . . *bread.*

I push him away. "You still have *food* in your mouth!" I fake gag and take a sip of my drink.

His drink is already empty, so he takes mine from me and drinks some of it.

A moment later, he looks longingly over at the trash can and sighs. "I threw it away to make a point, but I really wanted to eat the rest of it." He looks back at me. "Would it be gross if I dug it back out of the trash?"

I laugh. "Yes. And I'd never kiss you again." I slide him the rest of my sandwich. "Here. You can eat the rest of mine. I'm not even hungry."

He takes my sandwich and eats it, then finishes off my drink. He gathers all the trash and throws it away, then returns to the picnic table and straddles the bench again, sliding me closer to him. He presses his forehead to mine and smiles, then pulls back, tucking a lock of my hair behind my ear. "I think I'm psychic. I knew we would be good together, Clara."

"You aren't psychic. We've been together for less than a week. It could go downhill before tomorrow."

"It won't, though. I have a good feeling about us."

"That's just attraction. It's not a sixth sense."

"You think that's all this is? Attraction?"

"What else would it be? We barely know each other."

"I gave up half a sandwich for you. That's *way* more than attraction."

I laugh at his persistence. "You're right. That was a pretty grand gesture." I lean in and kiss him, but when I start to pull back, he moves forward, unwilling to break the kiss. I turn my body toward him and lean into his mouth.

I normally wouldn't be this affectionate with him in public, but we're the only ones out here. For a food truck that makes such amazing sandwiches, I'm surprised it's not busier than it is.

Miller finally pulls away from me and glances at the camera. "We should stop. You're underage, and I could get arrested if this turns into a porno."

I love how much he makes me laugh when I don't feel like laughing.

⌒

Before we left the food truck, Miller ordered his gramps a sandwich. He hands it to him when we walk into the living room.

"Is this what I think it is?" Gramps asks.

"One and only."

The grin on Gramps's face makes me smile. "I ever tell you you're my favorite grandson?"

"I'm your *only* grandson," Miller says. He takes his grandpa's glass and walks it to the kitchen to refill it.

"That's why you're inheriting everything I own," Gramps says.

Miller laughs. "A lot of air, apparently."

Gramps turns to me. "Clara, right?" He's unwrapping his sandwich. I take a seat in one of the green chairs and nod.

"I ever tell you about the time Miller was fifteen and we were at the school—" A hand comes around Gramps's chair and rips his sandwich away. Gramps looks down at his empty hand. "What the hell?" Gramps says to Miller.

Miller takes a seat in the other green chair, holding his grandpa's food hostage. "Promise me you won't repeat that story, and I'll give you back your sandwich."

"Come on, Miller." I groan. "This is twice you've stopped me from hearing it."

Gramps looks at me apologetically. "Sorry, Clara. I would tell you, but have you ever had a Mac?"

I nod in understanding. "It's okay. One of these days I'll come over when Miller isn't here so you can finish telling me."

Miller hands Gramps back his sandwich. "Clara and I have a project to work on. We'll be in my room."

"You don't have to lie to me," Gramps says. "I was seventeen once."

"I'm not lying," Miller says. "We really do have to work on a project."

"Whatever you say."

Miller rolls his eyes as he pushes out of the chair. He grabs my hand and pulls me up. "I apologize on behalf of my grandpa."

"Why? You're lying to him. We don't have a project to work on."

Miller rolls his head. "Yes, we *do*." He looks at his grandpa disapprovingly. "You two aren't allowed to hang out anymore. You're too much alike."

Gramps smiles at me as we leave the living room. When we walk down the hallway, I glance into their bathroom. Miller sees my pause. There are multiple pill bottles lined up on the counter, and the reminder that his grandpa is sick makes my stomach twist into a knot.

Once we're in Miller's bedroom, he can tell my mood has shifted. "Thinking about Gramps?"

I nod.

"Yeah. Sucks. Bad." He kicks off his shoes and lies down in the middle of the bed, patting the mattress next to him. I kick off my shoes and crawl in, tucking myself to his side, draping my arm over him.

"How'd the doctor visit go today?"

He pushes back my hair, running his fingers all the way to the ends. "We talked about what to expect over the next few months. It's not really safe for him to be here alone while I'm in school, so they're putting him on hospice soon. Once he's on hospice, an aide will be here with him most of the time, so that's a relief. I won't have to drop out of school."

I sit up on my elbow. "Was that really your only option?"

"Yeah. My mother died when I was ten, and he's her father. I have an uncle who lives in California, but he's not much help from there. Other relatives stop by a lot. Make sure we have what we need. But I've lived with him since I was ten, so most of the responsibility falls on my shoulders."

I had no idea his mother passed away. "I'm so sorry." I shake my head. "That's a lot of pressure for someone your age."

Miller rests a hand on my cheek. "You're only sixteen and look what you've been through. Life doesn't play favorites." He pulls my head to his chest. "I don't want to talk about it anymore. Let's talk about something else."

He smells good. Like lemon this time. "When's your birthday?" I ask.

"December fifteenth." He pauses. "Yours is next week, right?"

I nod, but I'd like to forget. With my birthday comes the traditional birthday dinner, but this will be the first one without my dad and Aunt Jenny. I don't want to think about it, so I change the subject. "What's your favorite color?"

"I don't have one. I like all of them except orange."

"Really? I like orange."

"You shouldn't. It's a terrible color," he says. "What's your least favorite color?"

"Orange."

"You just said you *like* orange."

"You made me doubt it, like maybe there's something wrong with it that I'm not aware of."

"There's a *lot* wrong with orange," he says. "It doesn't even rhyme with anything."

"Is it the color or the word you don't like?"

"Both. I hate them both."

"Did something in particular spark this immense hatred?"

"No. It came about naturally, I guess. Maybe I was born this way."

"Is it a particular shade of orange you loathe?"

"I hate them all," he says. "Every shade of orange, from mango to coral."

I laugh. "This is the stupidest conversation I've ever had."

"Yeah, we're kind of bad at this. Maybe we should just kiss."

I pull my head from his chest and look up at him. "Hurry, because I'm starting to forget why I'm even attracted to you."

He grins and then rolls on top of me, brushing back my hair while he smiles lazily. "Need a reminder?"

I nod. This is the most connection our bodies have ever had. We've kissed standing up. We've kissed in his truck. We've kissed sitting down. But we've never kissed on a bed with his body between my legs. He rests his mouth against mine, but doesn't kiss me. He adjusts the pillow beneath my head; then he kicks the covers away, all while barely teasing my lips with his.

"This sure is taking a long time," I say.

"I want you to be comfortable." He keeps his mouth near mine and lifts my neck a little, pulling my hair out from beneath me. He piles it over my shoulder and whispers, "Ready?" against my lips.

I start to laugh, but the laugh never happens because Miller's tongue parts my lips, and my near laugh turns into a gasp. It feels different like this—with him on top of me. *Better.* The kiss is nice. Slow flicks of his tongue. His fingers trailing down my arm. Mine trailing up his back.

But then I feel him begin to harden between my legs, and it both surprises me and gives me confidence. I wrap my legs around his waist, wanting to ease the ache I'm beginning to feel there, but it only makes it worse. His kiss deepens, and he pushes against me, forcing a moan up my throat. He pauses the kiss for a second, as if that sound does something to him, but then he brings his mouth back to mine with an even more profound urge.

I lift the back of his shirt, wanting to feel his skin beneath my palms. I run my hands up his back until I reach the tight curves of his shoulder muscles. Before I know it, I'm tugging at his shirt, wanting it off him. He obliges and separates us for the three seconds it takes for him to take off his shirt and throw it on the floor.

The next few minutes don't escalate beyond the shirt removal, but it doesn't deescalate either. The make-out session just leaves us both aching and panting and not at all in the mood to work on our project.

Miller eventually rolls off of me, onto his side, with his mouth still on mine. We kiss like that for a minute—it's not as exciting, but I think that's the point. He's trying to slow down something I don't think he intended to start.

His eyes are closed when he finally stops kissing me, and then he presses his forehead to mine. He brings his hand to my chest and rests it there, feeling my heart thumping wildly against his palm. When he pulls away and opens his eyes, he's smiling down at me. "You know what else sucks about the color orange?"

I laugh. "What?"

"All the celebrities used that orange square to announce Fyre Festival. And look how that turned out."

"You're right. Orange is the worst."

He falls onto his back and stares up at the ceiling. It's quiet for a moment, and my heart is still racing.

"Did you want me to stop?" he asks.

"Stop what?"

"Making out with you."

I shrug. "Not really. I was enjoying it."

"I wasn't sure. I didn't want to move too fast, but I really wanted to take off your shirt. Not your bra. Just your shirt."

"I'm cool with that."

He raises an eyebrow. "Yeah?"

"Sure."

"Is your bra orange?"

"No, it's white."

"Good." He rolls back on top of me and starts kissing me again.

Suffice it to say, we don't get anything done on the project, but he also stays true to his word and doesn't even attempt to remove my bra.

CHAPTER TWENTY-THREE

MORGAN

I wake up to the sound of my phone vibrating on my nightstand. I look over at the window, but the sun hasn't even fully risen yet.

No one calls me this early.

I reach over and pick up my phone and see Jonah's name at the top of the screen. I drop the phone on the nightstand and fall back onto my pillow.

We haven't spoken in over a week. Not since the night we almost kissed. He's texted twice, asking how I'm doing. I didn't respond to either text.

It's hard, because I want to separate myself from him, but at the same time, I want to spend time with Elijah. It sucks that Jonah and Elijah are a package deal.

I'm hoping we can work out some kind of visitation schedule. It would be even better if we didn't have to go to each other's houses to exchange Elijah. We could Uber Elijah back and forth.

That thought makes me laugh. Ubering babies from house to house. I wonder if there's a minimum age limit for Uber passengers.

My phone pings. A text. I swing my arm back to my nightstand and pull my phone to my face. I sit up in bed when I see how many missed calls and texts I have from Jonah.

I throw the covers off and stand up, urgently pressing the screen to call him back. He answers on the first ring. "Morgan?"

"Is Elijah okay?"

Jonah sighs with relief at the sound of my voice. "I'm sorry to even ask you, but he's been up all night with a fever, so I can't take him to day care. But I can't call in to work today. It's state testing day for the freshmen, and after school lets out, I have two conferences sch—"

"Of course." My hand is on my chest. My heart is pounding. I thought it was something worse. "Of course. Bring him over."

Jonah's voice is softer. Less panicked. "I won't be able to pick him up until after six."

"It's fine. I miss him."

I spend the next twenty minutes in the kitchen cooking. Jonah sounded so stressed on the phone, and if Elijah was up all night with a fever, that means Jonah is going to need some energy today. I used to do this for Chris. I'd make breakfast burritos packed with protein and send a bag with him on his busiest days.

I might also be making Jonah breakfast as somewhat of an apology. I feel like I was too harsh on him last week. Maybe I've been too harsh on him since he came back into our lives. Either way, burritos will make it better.

I'm also hoping this is a step forward. Maybe we can work out some sort of deal to where Elijah can be a huge part of my life, and Jonah and I can build an actual friendship. I stay up most nights thinking about what he said to me in the driveway, and while it did have a profound impact on the resentment I've been holding toward him, I also realize that the feelings he was talking about were in the past.

We were teenagers back then. We were different people. He wasn't saying that he *still* felt that way. He was simply saying he *used* to feel that way.

He's been back in our lives for several months now, and nothing outside of that near kiss has indicated he still has those same feelings, so whatever he thought he felt for me when we were teenagers is something he obviously worked through during the years he was away. Otherwise, he wouldn't have slept with Jenny when they ran into each other last year. And he wouldn't have moved in with her or agreed to marry her if he still had feelings for me.

That gives me hope that a friendship between us might actually work.

~

I'm stuffing the burritos into a bag when there's a knock at the door. I let Jonah in, but I pause for a second when I take him in. He's dressed up today. He's wearing a black long-sleeved dress shirt with a black-and-silver tie. He shaved his stubble and finally got a haircut. He looks younger. I start to comment on how nice he looks but think better of it.

Elijah is fussing in the car seat, so I unbuckle him and take him out of it. He's warm when I pull him to my chest. "Poor thing." He sounds congested. "Are you giving him anything?"

Jonah nods and pulls a couple of prescription bottles out of the diaper bag. "I took him to the ER around midnight. They gave me these, said to rotate them every four hours." He holds one of them up. "Give him this one in two hours." He sets the diaper bag down. "I packed extra clothes and rags. You might need them today."

"You took him to the emergency room? Have you even slept?"

As if the thought of it is a trigger, Jonah yawns, covering his mouth with a fist. He shakes his head. "I'll be okay. I might have time to make a Starbucks run." He opens the living room door to leave.

"Wait." I go to the kitchen and grab the sack of breakfast burritos, running them back to him before he escapes. "I made these for you. Breakfast burritos. Sounds like you're about to have a long day."

Jonah looks at me with a soft appreciation as he takes it from me. "Thank you." There's a little bit of surprise in his voice, and I try not to let that please me, but it does. It feels good to do something nice for him. I've been so hard on him for so long.

"I'll text you with updates on Elijah. Don't worry. He's in good hands."

Jonah smiles. "I don't doubt that for a second. See you tonight."

As soon as he leaves, Clara walks around the corner, dressed for school. She sees Elijah in my arms and lights up, holding her arms out in front of her. "Gimme."

I hand him to her. "He's sick. Don't kiss him—you might catch it."

She cradles him against her chest and kisses his forehead anyway. "Sick babies need all the kisses they can get."

She's right. When Clara was a baby, the sicker she was, the more I coddled her and kissed her and just wanted to take all her aches and pains away. *God, I miss those days.*

I'm sure sometime in the near future, I'll miss *these* days. I feel like Clara and I are an impossible pair this year, but I know I'll miss it after she moves out and starts a life of her own. I'll miss it all—the arguments, the silent treatments, the groundings, the rebellious behavior.

"Why are you looking at me like that?" Clara asks.

I smile and pull her in for a hug. She's holding Elijah, so she can't reciprocate the hug, but it's enough that she isn't pulling away. I kiss the side of her head. "I love you."

When I pull back, she's looking at me with a cautious expression. But then she smiles and says, "Love you, too, Mom."

She goes to the couch to sit with Elijah.

"I made breakfast burritos. Left you some on the counter."

Clara perks up. "Bacon or sausage?"

"Both."

"*Yes*," she whispers. She gives her attention back to Elijah. "I love you, buddy, but I have breakfast to eat."

I shoot Jonah a text around ten to let him know Elijah's fever has gone down a little. He responds at noon.

Jonah: Is he sleeping at all?

Me: Not really. I bet he'll crash once his fever finally breaks, though.

Jonah: Hopefully he waits until I'm ready to crash. This has been the longest day and it's only noon. The breakfast was a godsend. Thanks for that.

Me: I have a roast in the crockpot. Clara and I won't eat it all, so I can send some home with you when you pick up Elijah.

Jonah: Perfect. Thanks again.

Two hours later, I get another text from Jonah.

Jonah: Is he asleep yet?

Me: He took a fifteen minute nap. Still has fever, but he's not as fussy as he was.

Then, a text from Clara.

Clara: Miller and I need to work on our project after school. We'll be at Starbucks.

Me: What project? This is the first I'm hearing about a project with Miller.

Clara: Jonah partnered us up for the UIL film submission. We have less than 4 months to finish.

I text Jonah.

Me: You partnered Clara up with Miller Adams on the film project?

Jonah: Yes. Is that an issue?

Me: I'm assuming in more ways than one, considering he introduced her to drugs. And Chris already told her to stay away from him.

Jonah: Miller isn't as bad as you seem to think he is. Chris didn't even know the kid, so his opinion doesn't count.

Me: I've formed my own opinion of the kid. He talked Clara into leaving her father's funeral. He got her high. And according to a voice mail I received from the school, they both had detention last week due to PDA. She never did any of this before he was in the picture. And even if he's not the cause of her actions, I'd still rather her be with someone who would talk her OUT of doing those things, rather than be the type of teenage boy to encourage her behavior.

Jonah: I don't think that kind of teenage boy exists in real life.

Morgan: You're not making me feel better about this.

I wait for his response, but I don't get one.

⌐⁀

I spend the rest of the afternoon trying to keep Elijah awake so that he'll sleep for Jonah tonight, but once six o'clock hits, there's no hope left. He's out cold. His tiny body is limp in my arms, deep in sleep as I place him in his bassinet. His fever finally broke a couple of hours ago, so I think the worst is over, but I have a feeling after Elijah sleeps for a few hours, he'll be up all night with Jonah. Maybe I should offer to keep him for the night so Jonah can rest.

I pull out my phone to text Jonah those exact words when he knocks on the front door. I look down at Elijah, and the sound doesn't even make him flinch. When I open the front door, I whisper, "He just fell asleep."

Jonah is no longer wearing a tie. The top two buttons of his shirt are undone, and his hair is messier than it was this morning. He looks even better than he did this morning, despite the exhaustion consuming him. *Why am I even having these thoughts?*

I motion for him to come to the kitchen so I can make him a plate of food to take with him. I pull Tupperware from the cabinet.

"Have you already eaten?" Jonah asks.

"Not yet."

"I'll just eat here, then." He opens the cabinet next to me, where I keep the plates, and he removes two of them. I replace the Tupperware in the cabinet and take a plate from him.

This is good. This is casual. Friends eat food together.

We both make our plates and take a seat at the table. As normal as it is for two people to eat a meal together, Jonah and I have never done so without Chris and Jenny. That part seems off. Like there are two huge gaping holes sucking the comfort out of the meal.

"This is really good," Jonah says, taking another bite. "So were your burritos."

"Thanks."

"Is everything you cook this good?"

I nod confidently. "I'm a great cook. Chris hated going out to eat because he said restaurants never compared to what he got at home."

"How was he not fat?" Jonah shakes his head. "I'd get so fat eating this every day."

"He worked out twice a day. You know that."

It feels weird talking about Chris like we don't hate him, but I like it. Eventually, I'd like to remember all the good memories without the shadow of the bad ones. We had a lot of good memories together.

"Where's Clara?"

I point my fork at him. "With that boy. All your fault."

Jonah laughs. "He's still one of my favorite students. I don't care what you think of him."

"What kind of student is Clara?"

"Great," he says.

"No, for real. Don't tell me what I want to hear. I want to know what she's like when she's not around me."

Jonah regards me quietly for a moment. "She's good, Morgan. Really good. Always turns her homework in on time. Makes good grades. Doesn't act up in class. And she's funny. I like her sarcasm." He smiles. "She gets that from you."

"She is a lot like I was at that age."

"She's a lot like you are now. You haven't changed."

I release a half-hearted laugh. "Okay."

He looks at me with a little too much seriousness. "You haven't. At all."

I look down at my plate and mindlessly scoot food around. "I don't know if that's a compliment. It's kind of pathetic that I'm still the same person I was at seventeen. No education. No work experience. Not a single thing to put on my résumé."

Jonah stares at me a moment, then looks down at his plate, poking his fork into a carrot. "I wasn't talking about your résumé. I'm talking about everything else. Your humor, your compassion, your levelheadedness, your confidence, your discipline." He pauses for a quick breath, then says, "Your smile." He shoves the bite of food into his mouth.

I look down, completely losing the smile he's referring to, because I felt that. Everything he just said. Every compliment felt like darts stabbing at my heart. It makes me sigh. I lose my appetite. I stand up and toss the remaining food from my plate into the trash can.

I rinse the plate off in the sink. My chest is constricted. My hands are shaking. I don't like that I'm having a physical reaction to his presence, but friends don't say those things to friends while having the look in their eyes that Jonah just had.

He still has feelings for me.

I don't know how to process that because it fills me with so many more questions. Jonah brings his empty plate to the sink and rinses it under the water. I pull my hands back and grip the counter, staring into the sink.

He's standing next to me, staring at me.

I can't look at him. I'm embarrassed that I even feel anything right now, but I do, and it's confusing, because all I feel is jealousy. It's a feeling that's always been there, but it's something I've never allowed myself to acknowledge. But the jealousy is there, and it's loud, and it's forcing me to confront it.

"Why did you sleep with her last year?"

As soon as the question passes my lips, I regret it. But since the day Jenny came home from Jonah's father's funeral and told me she'd had a one-night stand with him, I've been full of anger. It somehow felt as if Jonah had betrayed me, even though he didn't belong to me.

Jonah takes a step closer. Not close enough that we're touching, but close enough that it feels like we are. "I don't know. Maybe because she was there," he says quietly. "Or maybe because you *weren't*."

I cut my eyes to his. "I wouldn't have slept with you, if that's what you're saying."

"That's *not* what I'm saying. What I mean is that I was hurt that my father died and you weren't there. Even though we didn't keep in touch, you knew about the funeral because Jenny was there." He sighs regretfully. "Maybe I did it hoping it would hurt you."

"That's a terrible reason to sleep with someone."

He laughs unconvincingly. "Yeah, well, I don't expect you to understand. You were never in my shoes. You didn't have to stand on the sidelines and watch the girl you were in love with build a life with your best friend."

Those words leave me breathless.

He breaks eye contact with me. "Jealousy can make a person do some shitty things, Morgan." He stands up straight, sensing he's worn out his welcome. "I should go."

"Yes." My voice comes out raspy and coarse. I clear my throat. "You should."

He nods, disappointed that I'm agreeing with him. He taps the fridge twice with an open palm, then walks out of the kitchen.

As soon as he's no longer in the same room with me, I refill my lungs with air. His presence still lingers all around me as he gathers Elijah's things. Before he lifts him out of the bassinet, he pauses and walks back to the kitchen. He stands in the doorway, the diaper bag draped over his shoulder.

"Was it mutual?"

I shake my head a little, revealing my confusion. "I don't know what you mean."

"How I felt about you. I could never tell. Sometimes I thought you felt the same way, but I knew you'd never admit it back then because of Jenny. But . . . I need to know. Did you feel what I felt?"

The hammering in my chest is back. He's never confronted me like this. I wasn't expecting it. It's hard to admit something out loud to someone else that you've only just admitted to yourself.

Jonah drops the diaper bag to the floor and strides across the kitchen. He doesn't stop until his body and his mouth are both pressed firmly against mine.

It's a shock to my system. I grip the counter behind me just as his hold tightens on my cheeks. I feel so much I'm afraid I might sink to the floor.

I press my palms against his chest, fully prepared to push him away, but instead, I find myself pulling him closer with two fistfuls of his shirt.

When he parts my lips with his and I feel his tongue slide against mine, I experience a full-body shiver. It's so much all at once. It's an awakening, but it's also a death. It's the realization that I've gone my whole life being kissed by the wrong man.

Jonah gets the answer to his question by the way I respond to him. His feelings are definitely mutual. They always have been, no matter how much denial I've shoveled on top of that mutual attraction.

My body conforms to his like I'm afraid something will wedge itself between us if I let go.

And then, sadly, it does.

CHAPTER TWENTY-FOUR

CLARA

"Mom?"

It's the only word I can manage to say, but it's powerful enough to put a five-foot divide between them. My mother turns away from me. Jonah looks down at his feet.

I just stare at them in disbelief.

I'm shaking my head, trying to convince myself that I didn't just see that. My mother . . . kissing her dead sister's fiancé. My mother . . . kissing her dead husband's best friend.

I take a step out of the doorway, as if the room is contaminated with betrayal and I'm afraid I might catch it. My mother takes a breath and then faces me, tears rimming her eyes. "Clara . . ."

I don't give her the chance to explain. I don't really want to know why that was happening. I run to my room because I need solitude before they're able to reach me. I slam my door and lock it; then for extra reassurance, I scoot my nightstand in front of it.

"Clara, open the door," my mother says, her tearful voice muffled by the door, her knuckles rapping against it.

"Clara." Jonah is speaking now. "Please open the door."

"Leave me alone!"

My mother is crying. I can hear Jonah apologizing, but it's so quiet I know he's not apologizing to me. He's apologizing to my mother.

"Just go," I hear her say. Jonah's footsteps fade down the hallway.

She knocks on the door again. "Clara, *please* open the door. You don't understand. It's . . . just open the door."

I flip off my light. "I'm going to bed! I don't want to speak to you tonight! Go! Away!" I fall onto my bed. The knocking against my bedroom door finally stops. Not even two minutes later, I hear the front door slam shut.

My mother tries one more time to get me to open the door, but I roll onto my side and ignore her, covering my ears with a pillow. After a few minutes of attempting to regulate my breathing, I release the pillow. The knocking has ceased, hopefully for good this time. I hear her bedroom door close across the hall, which means I have until morning to talk myself out of murdering her.

I push myself off the bed. I begin to pace my room, my skin buzzing with anger. *How could she do this? They just died two months ago.*

A thought rips through me and causes me to fall back onto the bed. How *long* has she been doing this?

I start to think back on the last several weeks. Jonah has been over here so many times since my father and Aunt Jenny died. My memory is awakened with an entirely new perspective of every moment—the night they were outside in the dark when I got home, the night he came to fix the door, the excuse he made that he needed to come back the next day to finish the door. That time they left the house together, and when I looked on the app, it showed my mom's phone had been at the Langford Hotel.

That was only a week after their deaths.

I feel like I might be sick.

How long have they been having an affair?

I feel so stupid. Jonah is always asking about her in class—pretending it's concern.

Did Elijah really even have a fever this morning? Hell, Jonah probably stayed the night last night and I had no idea because I was in my bedroom. It would explain why he was here so early. Why my mother finally cooked breakfast for the first time since before my father died.

I pray my father had no idea. This whole time I've been feeling so guilty for possibly having a hand in ruining everyone's lives, but Jonah and my mother have been ruining everyone's lives since before the accident!

How could my mother do this to Jenny? I don't have a sister, but what kind of human would do that to their own flesh and blood?

I hate her so much right now. I hate her so much I'd be fine if I never even spoke to her again. I hate her so much I sit on the edge of my bed and think of all the ways I can get revenge for what they've been doing to our family.

I'm running out of ways to rebel. I've done drugs, I've gotten detention, I've lied, I've missed curfew. The only thing left I could do that I know would upset her is if I were to have sex with Miller. She's always begged me to wait until I was at least eighteen, which I probably wasn't going to do anyway, but if she knew I lost my virginity at sixteen, *and to Miller Adams*, it would destroy her.

I look at my alarm clock. It's not even eight o'clock yet. I still have four hours to make it happen before my birthday tomorrow. And I really need Miller right now, anyway. His presence is very calming, and I could use some calming vibes.

I grab my phone and call Miller.

"Hey," he says, answering right away. "What's up?"

"What time do you get off work?"

"Not for another half hour. You can still come kiss me good night before your curfew, though."

"Will you come to my house when you leave?"

"Your house?" he pauses. "Are you sure?"

"Yeah, but use the bedroom window."

"Oh, are we being sneaky?" I can hear the grin in his voice. "Okay, but I've never been inside your house. I don't know which window yours is."

"First window, right side of the house."

"Facing the house?"

"Yes. And . . . bring a condom."

He pauses for several long seconds. "Are you sure?"

"Positive."

"It's . . . Clara, we don't have to."

"You promised you weren't going to talk me out of it."

"I don't know that it was a promise. And I assumed it would be a while before we . . ."

"I changed my mind. I don't want to wait until prom."

He's silent again. Then he says, "Okay. Yeah. Be there in less than an hour."

I turn on my radio to help drown out any noise Miller or I might make. I light two candles and put one by my bed and one by the window so that he can make his way around my dark bedroom. I take a shower while I wait for him. I try to get all my tears out before he shows up. Surprisingly, there aren't that many. I'm too angry to cry, I think. I didn't know I was capable of reaching this level of anger, but I've reached it, and there might even be room for *more* anger. Who knows? Guess I'll see what I'm really capable of when my mother and I come face to face tomorrow.

I get out of the shower and wrap a towel around myself. I blow-dry my hair a little so that it's not dripping wet. I apply some mascara and pinch my cheeks because I look pale right now. Realizing your own mother is not the person you thought she was can really drain the color from your face.

I'm looking for lip gloss when I hear a light tap on my window. I rush to my closet to find something to put on, but then I remember why Miller is here in the first place. He's here to get me naked. The towel will do just fine.

I open my bedroom window while Miller takes off the screen. When he climbs inside, he glances around the room before he takes me in. When his eyes finally land on me, I can see his realization sink in. I'm pretty sure up until this point, he didn't think I was serious about losing my virginity to him tonight. But now that I'm standing in front of him, wearing nothing but a towel, his reaction becomes physical.

He bites his fist and winces as he looks at me from head to toe. "Holy *shit*, Clara."

I would laugh, but I'm still too angry. I don't want him to feel my mood, though. I need to shake it off long enough to get this over with.

Miller cups my face in his hands. "Are you absolutely positive this is what you want?" He's whispering, thank God. The last thing I need is for my mother to ruin this part of my life too.

I nod. "Yes."

"What about your mom? Where is she?"

"She's in her room. My door is locked. We'll be quiet. Plus, my music is on, so she won't hear us."

Miller nods, but he seems nervous. I didn't expect him to be nervous. "I'm sorry I keep asking if you're sure. I just wasn't expecting this to happen for a while, so . . ."

"Seventy percent of couples have sex on the first date. I think we've been really patient."

Miller laughs quietly. "Did you just make up a fake statistic to try and get in my pants?"

"Did it work?"

He pulls his shirt over his head, and it falls to the floor. "It would have worked *without* the fake statistic." He kisses me then. A full-body kiss—the kind where our legs and bodies and arms are pressed together so close not even air could pass between us. He backs me up to my bed but stops before my legs meet my mattress.

His kiss made this real. Before, when it was my anger fueling my actions, I felt like this probably wouldn't happen. But now that he's here and his shirt is on my floor and I'm only wearing a towel and we're about to be on my bed, it is very real. I'm about to have sex with Miller Adams.

And I'm ready. *I think.*

If my mother knew what was happening just ten feet down the hall from her bedroom, it would destroy her.

Yep. I'm definitely ready.

My anger prompts me to drop my towel. When I do, Miller gasps and looks up at the ceiling. I'm confused that he's looking at the ceiling and not at me.

"I'm down here."

His hands move to my hips, and he just rests them there, still staring up. "I know. I just . . . I guess I'm used to sex being like baseball. You know, lots of bases I have to make it to before I reach home plate. I feel like I'm cheating at the game."

That makes me laugh. "You hit a home run, Miller. It's your lucky night."

He finally lowers his head, but he only looks at my face. "Get under the covers."

I grin and climb under the covers as he attempts to avert his eyes the whole time. He starts to climb under the covers with me, but I stop him.

"Take off your pants first."

He tilts his head. "Why are we in such a hurry?"

"Because. I don't want to change my mind."

"Maybe that's a sign you aren't ready yet."

God, why can't he just be like other guys and be a complete asshole about this?

"I'm ready. I'm very ready."

He focuses on my face for a moment, as if he's searching for a piece of me that's lying to him. He forgets what a great actress I am. He finally stands up and unbuttons his pants, then kicks them off. He's wearing boxer shorts with pineapples all over them.

"Sexy."

He grins. "Thought you might like these."

I lift the covers, and he slides into my bed with me but then holds up a finger. "One sec." He rolls over and reaches to the floor to grab his jeans. When he rolls back over, he's holding four condoms up like the choice is all mine. "Got them at the Valero on the corner. They're fruit flavored."

"Why are they flavored? Are condoms edible?"

My question makes Miller laugh. "No. It's for . . ." He suddenly blushes. "You know. If you put your mouth on it."

His answer makes me redden. My question shows just how inexperienced I am. The furthest I've ever gone with a guy is when Miller took my shirt off and we made out on his bed for an hour.

I take the orange-flavored condom out of Miller's hand and set it on the nightstand. "Not the orange one. It'll ruin the moment. Can't even believe you brought that into my house."

He laughs. "Sorry. It was a vending machine in the men's bathroom. I didn't get to choose what came out of it." Miller picks one of the remaining condoms and tosses the other two on the nightstand with the orange one. When he turns back to me, he slips his arm under the covers and pulls me against him.

It scares me. The feeling of his skin against mine. Knowing his boxer shorts are the only thing separating us right now. He wraps a leg over me, and part of me is sad that I'm rushing it, because making out with him at his house was nice. But this is different. This isn't as intimate because so many steps are being skipped, and I know this, but I feel like I'm too far into it to change my mind. I bury my face in the crevice of his neck because I don't want him to look at me. I'm afraid of what he'll see when he looks in my eyes.

"I don't have to put it on yet," he whispers. "We can do other stuff first. I mean . . . technically I haven't even touched your boob yet."

I grab his hand and slide it over my stomach, up to my breast. He groans, and then he's the one burying his face in *my* neck.

"Let's just get the hard part over with first. Then we can do other stuff," I whisper.

Miller nods, then pulls back and kisses me gently. I can feel him taking off his boxer shorts as he kisses me. He pulls away from my lips while he puts on the condom, but he keeps his mouth close to mine. His breath crashes against me in short spurts.

When he rolls on top of me, he's looking down at me with eyes full of so many things. Longing, appreciation, wonder. I want to feel all the things he's feeling as we experience each other for the first time, but all I feel is betrayed. Lied to. *Stupid.*

"Relax a little more," he says. "It'll hurt less if you aren't so tense."

I try to relax, but it's difficult when all I can think of is how sorry I feel for Jenny. And Dad. And how this is the first time I've ever hoped that an afterlife doesn't exist. At least not one where Jenny and Dad can see how little Jonah and my mother are grieving for them.

Miller's lips meet mine, and I'm grateful for the distraction. Then something else distracts me. There's a pain and pressure between my legs when he begins to push into me, and then an even deeper pain, coupled with a rush of air passing Miller's lips.

I wince. He stops moving and kisses me gently on the corner of my mouth. "You okay?"

I nod.

He's kissing me again, and this time when he pushes against me, I feel it happen. It's a significant feeling, like there was a barrier deep inside me keeping us apart, but that barrier is gone and Miller is moving against me now and *I just lost my virginity.*

It's both special and not.

It's both painful and not.

I regret it and I don't.

I lie still, my hands on his back, my legs around his. I like the feel of him against me, although I'm not sure I like the feel of what's happening as a whole. My heart isn't in it, which means my body is struggling to be in it. He's being gentle and sweet, and the sounds he's making are extremely sexy, but I don't feel it in my soul. My soul is too full of resentment to allow room for any of what's happening right now to enter.

Part of me wishes I'd have waited. But it would have been with Miller regardless. In the grand scheme of things, would dragging it out a few more months have even made a difference?

Probably.

Okay, *all* of me wishes I'd have waited. I feel bad that I rushed it. I feel bad that my anger fueled this rash decision. But Miller seems to be enjoying himself, so there's that, at least.

Maybe I don't really feel the way I expected to feel in this moment because I realized tonight that love is full of so much ugliness and betrayal and maybe I don't want anything to do with it. What I think I feel for Miller is what Jenny probably felt for Jonah and what my father probably felt for my mother, and look where that got them.

Miller's mouth is on my neck now. One of his hands is gripping my thigh, and I kind of like the position we're in. Maybe the next time we're in this position, it'll hurt less, both physically and emotionally. Maybe I'll actually appreciate how much he enjoys it next time it happens. Maybe *I'll* actually enjoy it.

But right now, I'm not enjoying anything. My mind won't stop going there. Their actions make me not believe in whatever Miller and I feel for each other, and that makes me sad. It hurts because I so want to believe in Miller and me. I want to believe in the way he looks at me, but I've seen my mother look at my father like that, so does it even mean anything? I want to believe Miller when he says he's never craved anyone like he craves me, but how long will that be true? Until he grows bored with me and finds a girl he craves more than me? *Thank God I don't have a sister for him to fall in love with.*

I pull Miller closer, wanting my face hidden against his skin. I hate having these thoughts, *especially* right now, but Miller is the only thing in my life that's made me happy since they died, and now I'm scared my mother and Jonah have ruined that. Not only am I questioning them, and now Miller, but I'm questioning the whole stupid idea of monogamy and the validity of love and thinking how losing my virginity really *isn't* all that special. Because if love isn't real, then sex is just sex, no matter if it's your first time or your fiftieth time or your last time.

It's just one body part inside another body part. Big freaking deal.

Maybe that's why people find it so easy to cheat: because sex is actually inconsequential. No different than two people shaking hands. Maybe having sex with your boyfriend for the first time means as little as having sex with your dead sister's fiancé.

"Clara?" Miller says my name between heavy breaths. Between movements. Then he stops.

I open my eyes and pull away from his neck, allowing my head to fall back onto my pillow.

"Am I hurting you?"

I shake my head. "No."

He brushes hair from my face and runs a thumb down my wet cheek. "Why are you crying?"

I don't want to talk about it. Especially not right now. I shake my head. "It's nothing." I try to pull him against me again, but he separates himself from me and then rolls off me. I feel strangely empty now.

"Did I do something wrong?" he asks.

I hate the worry in his eyes. I hate that he's thinking any part of my reaction has anything to do with him, so I adamantly shake my head. "No. It's not you, I swear."

He looks relieved, but only for a fraction of a second. "Then what is it? You're scaring me," he whispers.

"It's not you. It's my mother. We got in a really bad argument tonight, and I'm just . . ." I wipe the tears away with my hands. "I'm so angry at her. I'm *so* angry, and I don't know how to process it." I roll over onto my side so I can face him. "She and Jonah are having an affair."

Miller pulls back a little, shocked. *"What?"*

I nod, and I see the sympathy in his expression. He places a soothing hand on the side of my head.

"Earlier, when I got home, I walked in on them in the kitchen. I got so angry. It's the angriest I've ever been in my life, and I think I might actually hate her. Like . . . I'm having all these thoughts about how much she's betrayed my dad and my aunt. I can't stop thinking about everything I can do to get back at her and punish her because all I can think about is how she deserves to suffer too." I lift up on my elbow. "They haven't been gone long enough for her to even be thinking about anyone other than my father. Which is why I'm pretty sure it was happening *before* the wreck."

Miller is quiet for a moment, staring at me with a perplexed look, probably unsure how to comfort me when I'm this upset. He falls onto his back and stares up at the ceiling. "That's why you called me over here?" His voice has a sharp edge to it, even though it's still a whisper. "Because you're mad at your *mother?*"

His reaction is staggering. I reach out and put my hand on his chest, but he grabs my wrist and flicks it off him. He rolls over and sits on the edge of the bed, his back to me.

"No. Miller, *no*." I'm saying no, but that word is a lie, and we both know it. I place a hand on his shoulder, but he flinches when I touch him. He stands up, and I hear the snap of the condom as he pulls it off and tosses it angrily into the trash can next to my bed. He slides his boxers on and then steps into his jeans. He won't even look at me.

"Miller, I swear. That's not why I called you over here."

He's walking across my bedroom. "Why'd you call me, then? You weren't ready for this to happen tonight." He snatches up his shirt and finally looks at me. I expect to see anger in his eyes, but all I see is hurt.

I'm sitting up on the bed, the blanket pulled up to my chest. "I *was*, though. I promise. I wanted to be with you—that's why I called you." I'm desperately trying to recover, but I think I've ruined this. It's terrifying me.

He takes a step forward, waving a hand in my direction. "You're upset with your *mother*, Clara. You didn't want me—you wanted revenge. I knew you weren't ready. It was weird . . . it was . . ." He releases a frustrated rush of air.

I use the sheet to wipe some of my tears away. "I called you because I was upset, yes. But being so upset is what made me want to be with you."

He's already got his shirt over his head, but he pauses as he's pulling it down over his chest. "I would have come over, Clara. Without the sex. You know that."

Why can't I stop offending him? I don't want to hurt him, but that's all I'm doing right now.

He reopens the window, and the last thing I want him to do is leave. I didn't mean to hurt him. I didn't mean to drag him into this. But I don't want him to leave me alone right now.

"Miller, wait." He's about to climb out the window, so I plead with him again, moving to the edge of my bed, still wrapped up in my blanket. "*Please*. It wasn't personal. I swear."

Those words pull him away from the window and back toward the bed. He lowers himself in front of me and cups my face with both hands. "You're right. That's why I'm so upset with you. The one thing that should be the *most* personal to us wasn't personal at all."

His words rip through me, and a loud sob breaks from my chest. I can't believe I did this. It feels like I've stooped to my mother's level. Miller releases me and starts to climb out the window, and I cover my mouth with both hands, unable to stop the feelings from tearing through me. It's not just what I've done to Miller. It's everything. I feel *everything*. I feel the loss of Jenny and the absence of my father and the guilt over how they died and the betrayal of my mother and the pain I caused Miller, and it's so much all at once that I don't think I can do this anymore. I crawl back up my bed and bury my face into my pillow, but I really just want to pull the covers over my head and close my eyes and never feel any of it again. It's too much. It's not fair. It's not fair, it's not fair, it's not fair.

I feel the mattress dip beside me, and when I roll toward him, he wraps his arms around me and pulls me against him. It makes me cry even harder.

I try to tell him I'm sorry, but I'm crying so much I can't even get words out. Miller presses soft lips against the side of my head, and I struggle to say it, but the only word I'm sure he can make out is *sorry* between sobs.

He doesn't tell me it's okay or that he forgives me. He doesn't say anything. He spends the next several minutes silently comforting me while I cry.

My face is pressed against his chest—buried deep into his shirt. When I can finally find my words again, I use them. Over and over.

"I'm sorry. I'm so sorry. You're right, and I feel terrible." My words are muffled against him. "I'm so sorry."

He's gently cupping the back of my head. "I know you feel bad," he whispers. "I forgive you. But I'm still mad at you."

Despite his words, he presses a kiss into my hair, and that's all the forgiveness I need from him right now. He *should* be mad at me. I don't blame him. *I'm* mad at me.

He lies with me for a while, but when I'm no longer crying, he pulls away and looks down at me, running his hand over my cheek. "I should probably go. It's getting late."

I shake my head and look pleadingly into his eyes. "Please don't. I don't want to be alone right now."

I can see the three seconds of contemplation swirling around in his eyes before he nods. Then he sits up on the bed and takes off his T-shirt. He bunches it up and then reaches over and slides it over my head. "Wear this."

I slip my arms into the T-shirt, and with the covers still on top of me, I pull the T-shirt over my hips.

It's not lost on me that even after everything that's happened tonight, he still hasn't seen me naked. He never even looked when I dropped my towel.

He slips under the covers with me and pulls me to him so that my back is pressed against his chest. We share a pillow. We hold hands. And eventually, we both fall asleep, angry at different people, but both hurting the same.

CHAPTER TWENTY-FIVE

MORGAN

I thought washing baby bottles while praying for Armageddon was rock bottom, but maybe I was wrong. I think this might be rock bottom.

What do people do when they hit rock bottom? Wait until someone throws them a rope? Wither away to skin and bones until the vultures come and find them?

I'm on my bed, where I've been since last night, except I gave up trying to sleep. Now that the sun's about to come up, I don't see the point.

I walked to Clara's room a couple more times but didn't even bother trying to knock. She turned her music up to drown me out, so I decided to give her the night to hate me before attempting to ask for her forgiveness.

Maybe waiting to start therapy was a bad idea. I thought it would be better to wait a few months—let the hardest parts of the grief settle. But obviously, that was a mistake. I need to talk to someone. Clara and

I *both* need to talk to someone. I'm not sure this is something we can fix on our own.

I don't want to talk to Jonah about it because he'll just apologize and tell me it'll be okay and assure me it'll get better. And maybe it will. Maybe a rain will come that'll flood the pit I'm in, and I can float to the top and climb out. Or at least *drown*. Either one seems appealing.

Even if we start therapy right away, nothing will change what happened last night. Nothing will change the fact that my daughter saw her mother kissing her dead father's best friend so soon after his death. It's unfathomable. Unforgiveable.

All the school counselors and therapists and conversations and self-help books in the world will never get that image out of her head.

I'm completely mortified. Ashamed.

And no matter how many texts he sends me—*seven since he left here last night*—I am not speaking to Jonah again. Not for a long time. I don't want him in my house. I don't like what his presence does to me. I don't like the person it turns me into. Kissing him last night was one of the biggest mistakes I've ever made, and I knew that before I even let his lips touch mine. Yet still, I did it. I allowed it. And the worst part is I *wanted* it. I've wanted it for a long time. Probably since the day I met him.

Maybe that's why I feel like such a piece of shit right now, because I know if Jonah hadn't left all those years ago, we might have eventually ended up in the same position as Jenny and Chris. Sneaking around, betraying our spouses, lying to our families.

My anger with them hasn't subsided since last night. I've just developed a new anger that is just as intense, but this time it's directed toward myself. There isn't a life lesson I could teach Clara at this point that wouldn't make me out to be a hypocrite. I feel like anything I say to her from this point forward will mean nothing to her. And maybe it shouldn't. Who am I to raise a human? Who am I to teach someone morals? Who am I to help guide someone else through life when I'm wearing a blindfold and running in the wrong direction?

I jolt upright in bed when I hear a rapping on my door. So help me God, if it's Jonah Sullivan, I am going to be pissed.

I throw my covers off and pull on my robe. I haven't even had a chance to speak to Clara yet, so until I speak to her, I don't want to even bother talking it out with Jonah. I rush through the house to get to the door before he wakes her.

I swing it open but take a step back when I see Mrs. Nettle standing on my patio with the screen door open.

"Just making sure you're alive," she says. "Guess you are." She releases my screen door, and it slams shut against the frame. I speak through it.

"Why were you assuming I'd be dead?"

She keeps walking, limping away with her cane. "There's a window screen on the ground over on the side of your house. Thought someone might have broken in and murdered you last night."

I watch her until she makes it to her patio, ensuring she doesn't fall. Then I close the door and lock it. *Great.* A broken window screen. Something else Chris would have taken care of if he were still alive.

I'm walking into my bedroom when I pause.

I was Clara's age once. Window screens don't just fall off on their own. *Did she sneak out last night?*

I spin and walk straight to her bedroom. I don't even knock because she's probably not even inside to answer me. I push at the door, but it's locked. It's just one of those hook locks that can easily be lifted and bypassed. I hate that I'm resorting to breaking into her room, but I need to see if she's actually gone before I get dressed and go find her.

I grab a hanger from my closet, then slip the hanger up the crack in her door until it catches on the lock. When it releases, I push at the door, but it doesn't open right away. Did she barricade herself in her room?

God, she might be angrier than I thought.

I shove my hip against the door, moving whatever it is she pushed against it. I get the door open a few inches, and I peek inside.

I release a huge sigh of relief. She's still asleep. She didn't sneak out. Or if she did, she's home now, and that's the most important thing.

I start to pull the door shut, but I pause when I see movement. An arm wraps over Clara's stomach. *An arm that isn't hers.*

I throw my whole body against the door to open it. Clara sits straight up in bed, startled. So does Miller.

"What the *hell*, Clara?"

Miller is standing now, scrambling to put on his shoes. He reaches to the nightstand and grabs condoms, shoving them in the pocket of his jeans like he's trying to hide them before I see them, but I *definitely* saw them, and I'm angry, and I want him out of my damn house right now.

"You need to leave."

Miller is nodding. He looks at Clara with eyes full of apology.

Clara covers her face. "Oh my God, this is so embarrassing."

Miller starts to walk around the bed but then pauses and looks at Clara, then me, then Clara, then down at his bare chest. That's when I realize Clara is wearing his shirt.

Does he expect her to give it back to him? Is he an idiot? *He is. She's dating an idiot.* "Get out!"

"Wait, Miller," Clara says. She snatches the shirt she was wearing yesterday off the floor and walks to her closet. She closes herself inside so she can change shirts. Miller looks like he doesn't know if he should listen to her and wait for his shirt or run before I murder him. Lucky for him, it only takes Clara a few seconds to change.

She opens the door and hands him his shirt.

Miller pulls on the shirt, so I yell at him again, this time with more force. "Get *out*!" I look at Clara, wearing just a T-shirt that barely covers her ass. "Get dressed!"

Miller rushes to the window and starts to open it. *He really is an idiot.* "Just use the front door, Miller! *Jesus!*"

Clara is wrapped in her bedsheet now, sitting on her bed, full of rage and embarrassment. *That makes two of us.*

Miller slips past me nervously, looking back at Clara. "See you at school?" He whispers it, as if I'm unable to hear him. Clara nods.

Honestly. She could sneak any guy into her bedroom, and *this* is the guy she chooses? "Clara won't be at school today."

Clara looks at Miller as he reaches the hallway. "Yes, I will."

I look at Miller. "She won't be there. Goodbye."

He spins and leaves. *Finally.*

Clara tosses the sheet away and reaches to the floor to grab the jeans she wore yesterday. "You can't ground me from school."

My worry about whether I have the right to parent her is nonexistent right now thanks to my anger. She isn't going anywhere today. "You are sixteen years old. I have every right to ground you from whatever the hell I want to ground you from." I glance around her room, looking for her phone so I can confiscate it.

"Actually, *Mother.* I'm seventeen." She slips a leg into her jeans. "But I guess you were too busy with Jonah to remember that today's my birthday."

Shit.

I was wrong.

This is rock bottom. I try to recover by muttering, "*I didn't forget,*" but it's obvious I did.

Clara rolls her eyes as she buttons her jeans. She walks to her bathroom and comes back out with her purse.

"You aren't going to school like that. You wore those clothes yesterday."

"Watch me," she says, shoving past me.

I'm pressed against the frame of her bedroom door as I watch her walk down the hall. I should be running after her. This isn't okay.

Sneaking a boy into her bedroom is *not* okay. Having sex with a guy she just started dating is *certainly* not okay. There is so much wrong here, but I'm scared it's beyond my parenting abilities. I don't even know what to say to her or how to punish her or if I even have the *right* to at this point.

I hear the front door slam, and I flinch.

I grip my head and slide down to the floor. A tear rolls down my cheek and then another. I hate it because that means a raging headache is going to follow. I've had headaches every single day since the accident, thanks to the tears.

This time, I deserve the headache. It's like my own actions have given permission to her rebellion. *They have.* She'll never respect me again. A person can't learn from someone they don't respect. It just doesn't work that way.

I can hear the faint sound of my phone ringing down the hall. I'm sure it's Jonah, but part of me wonders if it could be Clara, even though she hasn't even had time to back out of the driveway. I rush to my bedroom, but I don't recognize the number.

"Hello?"

"Mrs. Grant?"

I grab a Kleenex and wipe my nose. "This is she."

"I'm the technician who'll be repairing your cable today. I just wanted to let you know that someone will need to be home from nine until five so that I can have access to do the repairs."

I sink onto the bed. "Seriously? You expect me to sit in this house for the entire day?"

There's a pause. He clears his throat and says, "It's just policy, ma'am. We can't enter an empty residence."

"I get that it's policy for someone to be here, but you can't give me a smaller window of time? Maybe two hours? Three?"

"It's difficult for us to pinpoint a particular time because every repair varies in need."

"Yeah, but come on. An entire day? Why do I have to stay in this house for eight *fucking* hours?" *Oh my God. I'm cussing at the cable technician.* I shake my head, pressing my palm against my forehead. "You know what? Just cancel it. I don't even want cable. No one has cable anymore. In fact, you should probably start looking into other careers, because apparently being a cable technician is no longer sustainable."

I end the call, and then I toss my phone on the bed and stare at it. Okay. Okay. *This* is rock bottom. This is *definitely* rock bottom.

CHAPTER
TWENTY-SIX

CLARA

I get to school half an hour early. There are only a handful of vehicles in the student parking lot, and Miller's truck isn't even one of them. There's no way I'm walking into Jonah's classroom early, so I pull the lever on my seat and lean back.

I'm not going to cry.

In fact, I'm not even angry right now. If anything, I'm numb. So much has happened in the last twelve hours that I feel like my brain must have an emergency shutoff valve. I'm not sad about it. I prefer this feeling of numbness to the anger I had last night and the embarrassment I had this morning when my mother was so rude to Miller.

I get it. I snuck a boy into my room. I had sex. That's really shitty, but she lost her privilege last night to tell me what is and isn't shitty behavior.

I flinch at the knock on my passenger window. Miller is standing next to my car, and I no longer feel numb because seeing him springs a little bit of life back into me. He opens the door and takes a seat, handing me a coffee.

He's never looked so good. Sure, he's tired, and neither of us have brushed our teeth or our hair, and we're wearing the same clothes we wore yesterday, but he's holding coffee and looking at me like he doesn't hate me, and that's a beautiful thing.

"Figured you could use the caffeine," he says.

I take a sip and savor the heat against my tongue and the sweet caramel sliding down my throat. *I don't know why it took me so long to appreciate coffee.*

"For what it's worth . . . happy birthday?"

He says it like a question. I guess it is. "Thank you. Even though this is the second-worst day of my life."

"I think yesterday was the second-worst day of your life. Today still has a chance of looking up."

I take another sip and grab his hand, squeezing it, sliding my fingers through his.

"What happened after I left? Did she ground you?"

I laugh at that. "No. And she won't."

"You snuck me into your room last night. Not sure how you can get out of that one, even if it *is* your birthday."

"My mother is a liar, a cheat, and a very bad example for me. I decided this morning I'm no longer following her rules. I'll be better off just raising myself."

Miller squeezes my hand. I can tell he doesn't like what I'm saying, but he doesn't talk me out of feeling this way. Maybe he thinks I just need time to calm down, but time won't help. I'm done with her.

"What'd Lexie say when you told her what happened?"

I glance at him, raising an eyebrow. "Lexie?"

He nods, sipping his coffee.

"Shit! Lexie!" I crank my car. "I forgot to pick her up."

Miller laughs. "Well, in your defense, you've had an eventful morning." He leans in and kisses me. "I'll see you at lunch."

I kiss him back. "Okay."

He grabs the door handle and goes to get out of the car. I squeeze his arm, needing to say one more thing. When he falls back into his seat and looks at me, I lift my hand to the side of his head, not knowing what words to use to convey how sorry I am for last night. I stare at him, my heart full of remorse, but I seem to have forgotten how to verbalize anything at this point.

Miller leans forward and presses his forehead to mine. I close my eyes, and he remains there for a moment. He brings his hand up to the back of my neck and caresses it. "It's okay, Clara," he whispers. "I promise." His lips briefly meet my forehead before he gets out of my car and closes the door.

I am fully aware of what an asshole move that was last night. I'm still mortified by it. So much so I already know I'm not telling Lexie what happened between Miller and me. I'll never tell anyone. And I hope someday we'll have a redo of that moment, because I certainly did a great job of ruining it.

I was so early to school that when I finally made it to Lexie's house, she didn't even know I had forgotten her. She walked out of her house with a wrapped gift and a Mylar balloon that said "Get Well Soon" on it.

She does that a lot. Waits until the last minute until it's too late to find the appropriate card, or balloon, or wrapping paper. Half the stuff she gives me is normally wrapped in Christmas paper, no matter what time of year it is.

I still can't believe my mother forgot my birthday. At least Miller and Lexie remembered.

Even though I've only been seventeen for a few hours, I'm proud of my newfound maturity. When I walked into Jonah's classroom half an hour ago, I made it all the way to my seat without punching him. Even when he told me good morning. Even when his voice cracked as he said it. I didn't even make eye contact with him.

He's been lecturing for about twenty minutes now, and I haven't done a single thing I've fantasized about doing during the twenty minutes I've been in his class. I've wanted to scream at him, call him an adulterer, tell the entire class about his affair with my mother, hack the intercom system to tell the whole school.

But I haven't done any of those things, and I'm proud of myself for it. I've remained extremely calm and composed, and as long as I keep my eyes off him, I think I might be able to make it through the entire class and escape without a confrontation.

Seventeen looks good on me. I'm practically an adult now, thank God, because I can't rely on my mother to raise me anymore.

Lexie: Efren is growing on me. I'll have my first Friday off since we've been talking and he just asked if I wanted to go on a date.

I smile when I get her text.

Me: What'd you say to him?

Lexie: I told him no.

Me: Why?

Lexie: Kidding. I actually said yes. I'm shocked. He's so short. But he's kind of mean to me, so it makes up for all the many things he lacks.

She's the pickiest person I know when it comes to guys. I'm honestly very surprised she agreed to go out with him. Relieved, but surprised.

I start to type out a text to her when Jonah says, "Clara, please put your phone away."

My chest heaves at the sound of his voice. It makes my skin crawl. "I'll put it away when I'm finished with my text."

I hear a couple of people gasp in the room, like I just cussed at him or something. I continue typing my response to Lexie.

I need to ask administration if I can switch classes. There's no way I can look at Jonah for the rest of the year. I don't want to be in the same room as him, the same house as him, the same town as him, the same *world* as him.

"Clara." He says my name with a gentleness, almost as if it's a plea not to make a scene. He can't allow me to text when no one else is allowed to have their phones out. I understand his awkward predicament, not wanting to call me out but being forced to. I should feel bad, but I don't. I kind of like that he's uncomfortable right now. He deserves a dose of how I've felt since I saw his hands pawing at my mother while his tongue was in her throat.

God, I can't get it out of my head no matter how hard I try.

I lift my eyes and look at him for the first time since walking into his classroom. Jonah is standing at the front of his desk, leaning against it, his feet crossed at the ankles. He's in teacher mode. Normally I would respect that, but right now, all I see when I look at him is the man who cheated on my aunt Jenny. With my *mother*.

When he nods his head toward my phone with a pleading expression, silently asking me to put it away again, all I see is red. I grip my phone in my right hand, and I hurl it toward the trash can near the classroom door. My phone crashes against the wall and falls to the floor in pieces.

I can't believe I just did that.

Apparently, no one else in the class can believe it either. There's a collective gasp. I think one of those gasps is mine.

Jonah stands up straighter and walks to the classroom door. He opens it and points out into the hallway. I snatch up my backpack and push myself out of the desk. I march to the door, more than ready to leave this room. I glare at him as I pass through the doorway. I'm sure he's about to walk me to the office, so it doesn't surprise me when he closes the door to his classroom and follows me.

"Clara, stop."

I don't. I'm not listening to him. Or my mother. I'm done listening to the remaining adults in my life. I feel it might be counterproductive to my mental health.

I feel Jonah's hand grip my upper arm, and the fact that he's trying to stop me and have a conversation with me infuriates me. I yank myself from his grip and spin around. I don't know what's about to come out of my mouth, but I can feel the anger raging its way up my throat like a rapid.

Right before I can lash out at him, he closes the gap between us and wraps his arms around me, pressing my face against his chest.

What the hell?

I try to push against him, but he doesn't let go. He just squeezes me tighter.

His hug enrages me, but it also causes me to lose focus for a moment. I wasn't expecting this. I was expecting to be sent to the office or suspended or expelled, but I certainly wasn't expecting a hug.

"I'm sorry," he whispers.

I try one more time to push him away, but I don't try very hard because he's wearing the same kind of shirt my dad was wearing the last time he hugged me goodbye. A soft white button-up shirt that feels nice against my skin. My cheek is pressed against one of the plastic buttons, and I squeeze my eyes shut, not knowing what to do, because even though I hate Jonah right now, his hug reminds me of my dad.

He even smells like my dad a little. Like fresh-cut grass in a thunderstorm. When his hug doesn't ease up at all, I start to cry. Even Jonah's hand against the back of my head feels just like my dad's. I hate myself for this, but I lean into him and let him hug me while I cry. I miss my dad so much. I feel more sadness than anger right now, so I let Jonah hug me because it feels better than fighting.

I miss him so much.

I don't know how this happened. I don't know how I went from throwing my phone across the room to sobbing against his chest, but I'm just glad he's not dragging me to the office. He waits until I've calmed down a little, and then he presses his cheek to the top of my head.

"I'm sorry, Clara. We both are."

I don't know how truthful he's being, but even if he is sorry, I don't think it's going to change anything. He *should* be sorry. Being sorry is the least he could do to right his wrong.

I just can't understand this level of betrayal. I can't understand how my mother can walk around one minute, supposedly full of grief because she lost her soul mate, but then the next minute, her tongue is down his best friend's throat.

"It's like neither of you even cared about them."

Maybe I wouldn't be this mad if I had walked in on my mother kissing a random stranger. But Jonah isn't a stranger. He's Jonah. He's *Jenny's* Jonah.

He pulls back, dropping his hands to my shoulders. "Of course we care about them. What you saw . . . that had nothing to do with them."

I pull away from his hands. "It had *everything* to do with them."

Jonah sighs, folding his arms over his chest. He really does look remorseful. A small part of me wants to stop being so angry, just so he won't have that look on his face anymore.

"Your mom and I . . . we just . . . I don't know. I can't explain what happened last night. And honestly, I don't want to. That's for you and your mother to discuss." He takes a step forward. "But that's the thing,

Clara. You *need* to discuss it with her. You can't lock yourself in your bedroom forever. I know you're angry, and you have every right to be, but promise me you'll talk to her about this."

I nod, but only because he seems so sincere about it. *Not* because I'm actually going to talk to my mother about it.

I don't feel quite as angry with Jonah as I am with my mother, because this really isn't even his fault. I feel like 90 percent of my anger is placed on my mother. Jonah and Jenny weren't even married. They hadn't even been dating that long. And my dad isn't Jonah's brother, so his betrayal and my mother's betrayal are on two different levels. Two different *continents*.

Jonah should feel guilty, but my mother should feel like scum.

I look up at the ceiling and run my hands down my face. I drop them to my hips. "I can't believe I threw my phone."

"It's your birthday. You get a free outburst. Just don't tell the other students."

I'm surprised, but I actually find it in me to laugh at that. Then I sigh heavily. "It sure doesn't feel like my birthday."

It's hard for today to feel like my birthday when my own mother forgot about it. Guess that means our traditional birthday dinners are over for good.

Jonah points to the classroom door. "I have to get back in there. Go wait out the rest of this period in your car. I at least need the class to think I punished you."

I nod and take a step away from him. He walks back toward his classroom, and part of me wants to tell him thank you, but I have a feeling I'd immediately regret that. I don't really have anything to thank him for. If we're keeping score, he still owes me about a million free passes.

The next three class periods sail by without a single assault. *Progress.*

I haven't seen Miller since first thing this morning, and it's kind of killing me. We usually text each other throughout the day, but my phone is probably at the bottom of Jonah's wastebasket. When I finally make it to the cafeteria for lunch, I can see the relief spread across Miller's face when I approach the table. He scoots over and puts space between him and Efren.

"You okay?" he asks as I take a seat. "Rumor has it you threw your phone at Mr. Sullivan."

"I might have hurled it in his general direction, but I was aiming for the trash can."

"Did you get detention?"

"No. He took me out to the hallway and gave me a hug."

"Hold up," Lexie says. "You threw your phone, and he *hugged* you?"

"Don't tell anyone. I had to pretend I got punished."

"I wish *I* had an Uncle Teacher," Lexie says. "Unfair."

Miller presses his lips to my shoulder and then rests his chin there. "You okay, though?" he whispers.

I nod because I want to be okay, but the truth is today sucks. Last night sucked. These past few months have sucked, and I can't seem to catch a break. I can feel heat behind my eyes, and then Miller brings a hand up and squeezes the back of my neck. "It's nice out. Wanna go for a drive in Nora?"

That's the only thing that could probably make me feel any sense of relief right now. "I would love that."

I've skipped a funeral with him, done drugs with him, gotten detention with him, snuck him into my bedroom, lost my virginity to him. In comparison, skipping half a day of school seems like an improvement in my behavior.

Miller drove us to the city park. It edges a large pond—one my dad used to take me fishing at on days like this. Miller sits under a shade tree and spreads his legs, patting the ground between them. I sit down with my back against his chest, and he wraps his arms around me as I adjust myself until I'm comfortable.

My head is leaning against his shoulder, and his cheek rests against the top of my head when he says, "What was your father like?"

It hasn't been that long, but I still feel like I have to jog my memory to answer his question. "He had such a great laugh. It was loud and filled up the entire room. Sometimes it would embarrass my mother in public because people would turn and look at us when he laughed. And he laughed at *everything*. He worked a lot, but I never held it against him. Probably because when we were together, he was actually present. Wanted to know about my day, would always tell me about his." I sigh. "I miss that. I miss telling him about my day, even when there was nothing to tell."

"He sounds great."

I nod. "What about yours?"

I feel a movement in Miller's chest, like a silent, unconvincing laugh. "He's not like your dad was. At all."

"Did he raise you?"

I can feel Miller shake his head. "No. I spent time with him here and there growing up, but he was in and out of jail. Finally caught up to him when I was fifteen, and he got a longer sentence. He'll be out in a couple of years, but I doubt I'll have anything to do with him when he gets out. It had been a while since I'd seen him when he got arrested, anyway."

So *that's* why my father made that comment about Miller's dad, about the apple not falling far from the tree. *My father was wrong, obviously.*

"Do you keep in touch at all?"

"No," Miller says. "I mean . . . I don't hate him. I just realize some people are good at being parents and some people aren't. I don't take it personally. I'd just rather not have a relationship with him."

"And your mom?" I ask. "What was she like?"

I feel him deflate a little before he says, "I don't remember her very well, but I don't have any negative memories of her." He wraps one of his legs around my ankle. "You know, I think that's where my love for photography came from. After she died . . . I had nothing to remember her by. She hated the camera, so there are very few pictures of her. Not much video. It wasn't long after that when I asked Gramps for my first camera. I've had it in his face ever since."

"You could probably make an entire movie just of him."

Miller laughs. "I could. I might. Even if it's just something I do for myself."

"So . . . what happens when he—"

"I'll be okay," he says with finality, like he doesn't want to talk about it anymore. I understand why. A father in prison, a dead mom, a grandpa with terminal cancer. I get it. I wouldn't want to talk about it either.

We sit in silence for a while before Miller says, "Crap. I keep forgetting." He pushes me forward a little and then jogs back to his truck. He comes back with his camera and a tripod, then sets it up several feet away from us.

He slips between me and the tree and resumes our position. "Don't stare at it this time."

I'm staring at it when he says that, so I look out at the water. "Maybe we should just cancel the project."

"Why?"

"My mind is all over the place. I've been in a perpetual bad mood."

"How bad do you want to be an actress, Clara?"

"It's the only thing I want to be."

"You're in for a rude awakening if you think you're gonna show up on set in a good mood every day."

I exhale. "I hate it when you're right."

He laughs and kisses the side of my head. "You must really hate me, then."

I shake my head gently. "Not even a little bit."

It's quiet again. Across the lake, there's a man with two little boys. He's teaching them how to fish. I watch him, wondering if he's cheating on their mom.

Then I feel the anger return because now I feel like I'm going to be looking for the worst in people for the rest of my life.

I don't want to talk about Aunt Jenny or my dad, or Mom and Jonah, but the words pour out of me anyway.

"The way Jonah talked today . . . he really did sound remorseful. Like maybe their kiss was an accident or a onetime thing. I want to ask her about it, but I'm scared she'll be honest and tell me it's way more than that. I kind of think it is because I know they went to a hotel not even a week after the accident."

"How do you know that?"

"The app. Why else would they have been there if they weren't already involved?"

"Either way, you need to talk to her about it. There's really no way around it."

"I know." I blow out a rush of air. "You know, it doesn't surprise me that Jonah would do something like that. He only moved back here and started dating Jenny because he got her pregnant. Not because they were madly in love. But my mother . . . her and Dad have been together since high school. It's like she had absolutely no respect for my father."

"You don't know that. Maybe she and Jonah are just grieving."

"That didn't look like grief to me."

"Maybe finding solace in each other helps with the grief."

I don't even want to think about that. It's a weird way to grieve. "Well. Me skipping school helps with *my* grief. So thank you."

"Anytime. Well, anytime except last period. I have a test, so I need to get back soon."

"Whenever you're ready."

"You doing anything for your birthday tonight?"

I shrug. "It's always been tradition to do family birthday dinners. But I guess that's out. We barely have a family left."

Miller's arms tighten around me. It makes me miss my father's hugs. Even Jonah's hug today made me miss him. "Well, if your mom will let you, I'll take you out."

"I highly doubt she's going to let me leave, and I might be too tired to fight her on it."

"It makes me sad to think you might spend your birthday alone in your room."

"Yeah, well. It's just another day."

I wonder what my father would think about seeing me so sad on my birthday. He'd probably be disappointed we aren't continuing the family birthday dinner. I bet Aunt Jenny would be disappointed about it too. We've never missed one for as far back as I can remember.

It makes me wonder why I automatically assumed the tradition would stop with their deaths. They wouldn't want it to stop.

Even though my mother seems to have lost her respect for the tradition, that doesn't necessarily mean the tradition shouldn't continue. At least this way, I could see Miller tonight.

I sit up and look at him. "You know what? I do want a birthday dinner tonight. And I want you to come."

He raises a cautious eyebrow. "I don't know. Your mom didn't seem like she'd ever welcome me back into your house."

"I'll talk to her when I get home. If she has an issue with it, I'll call you."

"You don't have a phone."

"I'll call you from our home phone."

"People still have those?"

I laugh. "She's only thirty-four, but she's an ancient thirty-four-year-old."

I lean back against him, thinking about my birthday. It really isn't fair if she tries to ground me. If she does, I might throw the Langford in her face. I let a slow roll of air pass through my lungs. The more I think about it, the angrier I get. The idea that the two of them were having a hotel tryst just a week after the accident makes me want revenge.

I try not to think about it. I turn around and straddle Miller, and then I kiss him for several minutes. It's a good distraction, but he eventually has to drive us back to the school.

I wait out the final class period in my car before going home, which is probably a bad idea, because the entire time I sit in my car, I think about all the ways I can fight for the vengeance my dad and Jenny deserve.

I head home, even angrier than when I left for school this morning.

CHAPTER
TWENTY-SEVEN

MORGAN

I'm in Clara's bedroom closet hanging up clothes when she gets home from school. I've been keeping myself preoccupied all day with cleaning, laundry, mindless organization. It's not lost on me that I never left the house today, so I really should have never cancelled the cable technician. I could be catching up on *Real Housewives* right about now.

I hear Clara making her way down the hallway, so I brace for impact. I expect her to scream at me or give me the silent treatment. It'll be one or the other. I'm hanging up the last shirt when she walks into her room and drops her backpack on the bed.

"What are we eating for my birthday dinner tonight? I'm hungry."

I stare at her cautiously because I feel like this is some sort of trick. *She still wants to do a dinner?* That surprises me. But I go along with it, just in case it's sincere. *I hope it's sincere.* "I was thinking lasagna," I say. I know lasagna is her favorite.

She nods. "Perfect."

I might need to run to the grocery store now, but I'd do anything at this point to have an opportunity to open up a conversation with her. And this dinner will be the perfect opportunity. Maybe she realizes that too. Without Jenny and Chris here, Jonah won't be here. It'll just be the two of us. We're long past due for a serious heart-to-heart.

—

I'm chopping tomatoes for the salad when the doorbell rings. I wipe my hands on a dish towel and begin making my way to the front door. Surprisingly, I'm intercepted by Clara. She swings open the door, and I'm taken aback by the sight of Jonah and Elijah.

What is he doing here? Did he really think the dinner was still on after last night?

I expect Clara to slam the door in his face, but she doesn't. He hands her a box, and even though I'm on my tiptoes in the doorway to the kitchen, trying to see what it is, I have no idea what he's just given her.

"Seriously?" She sounds excited. I feel like I'm in the twilight zone.

"I had an old phone in a drawer at the house," Jonah says.

"This is the latest model, though."

"I took the old one."

Clara lets him in, and I slip back into the kitchen. Why did he buy her a phone? Is that his way of winning her over? *That's not how you parent, Jonah.*

"I already put your old sim card in it, so it should be ready to go."

"Thanks."

It's nice hearing a hint of joy in her voice, but it's hard to feel relief when Jonah is walking into the kitchen behind me.

"You bought her a new phone?" I ask, without turning around.

"She dropped hers today in class. It broke, so I gave her one of mine."

I suck in air before turning around to face him. I hate how I feel around him after last night. As brief as that kiss was, it feels like it's still lingering. Like I can still taste him on my lips. "What are you doing here?"

"Clara called about an hour ago. She said her birthday dinner was still happening."

I look in the direction of Clara's room with narrowed eyes. "What is she up to?"

Jonah shrugs, adjusting Elijah in his arms. "Maybe she's okay with it."

"With what?"

"With us."

"She's not. And there *is* no *us*." With that, I spin around and finish making the salad.

Jonah takes a seat at the table and begins playing with Elijah by making faces at him. It's adorable and awful. I can't stop stealing glimpses of him because his interaction with his son is breathtaking. Maybe even more so because I know Elijah isn't even his biological child, yet the love Jonah has for him is the same as if he were. I hate that Elijah is a result of Chris and Jenny's betrayal, but I love that it doesn't matter to Jonah.

Seeing him with Elijah is making me think too many good thoughts about him, so I walk over and take Elijah from Jonah, just so I can stop the feelings that are rocketing through me. I sit at the table and turn Elijah toward me. He smiles. He gets excited to see me now, and it melts my heart every time.

"You need help with anything?" Jonah asks.

"You can put icing on the cake," I suggest. Anything to get him out of my line of sight.

Jonah just finishes icing the cake when the doorbell rings again. We both look at each other with confusion. "You expecting anyone else?"

I shake my head, then hand him Elijah before I head to the front door. But once again, Clara is rushing across the living room, beating me to the door. When she opens it, I freeze.

Miller Adams is standing in the doorway. He looks nervous, but I have no time to register his appearance or even yell at him before Clara grabs his hand and pulls him into the house. Jonah is standing next to me now. Clara is dragging Miller toward the hallway when Miller gives us a half wave.

"Hey, Mr. Sullivan." He swallows, and his voice is quieter when he addresses me. "Mrs. Grant."

We don't even have the opportunity to say anything back because Clara has pulled him out of the living room.

"I don't know what to do," I whisper.

"About what?" Jonah asks.

I look at him incredulously, but then I realize he has no idea what Clara did last night. I push on his shoulder, shoving him back to the kitchen. He turns to face me, and I'm trying to keep my voice down despite my anger. "I caught them in bed together this morning," I hiss. "There were condoms on the table. Clara was practically naked. He slept in her room the entire night!"

Jonah's eyes widen. "Oh. Wow."

I fold my arms together and slump down in one of the breakfast nook chairs. "She's testing me." I look up at Jonah for a little bit of advice. "Do I make him leave?"

Jonah shrugs. "It's just dinner. It's not like he's gonna get her pregnant at the table."

"You're way too lenient."

"It's her birthday. She was upset with us last night, so she probably invited him over out of spite. At least he's here and you'll have a chance to get to know him better."

I roll my eyes and push myself out of the chair. "Dinner is ready. Go tell them before he gets her pregnant."

This is so awkward. Not only because I know Miller more than likely took my daughter's virginity last night but because Jonah and I are barely speaking. We haven't discussed what happened between us, and that hangs thickly in the air.

Clara has only given me clipped answers when I try to talk to her, so I finally stopped asking her questions because it was embarrassing. Miller and Clara aren't even really talking because she's scarfing down her lasagna like we're at a food-eating contest.

Jonah is holding Elijah, feeding him a bottle as he eats. It's cute, so I stare down at my plate and avoid looking at them.

"How's the film project coming along?" Jonah asks.

Miller shrugs. "Slowly. We haven't come up with a solid idea yet, but we'll get there."

Yeah, because you're too busy doing other things, I want to say.

Clara points her fork at Miller's plate. "Eat faster."

I can see the confusion in his expression, but he picks up his fork and takes another bite.

I know exactly what she's doing. She's playing nice, hoping all will be forgiven if she spends her birthday dinner with me. She figures if she doesn't put up a fight, then I won't put up a fight when dinner is over, and she wants to leave with Miller.

She's not leaving with him. Not a chance in hell.

Clara finishes her food and stands up. She walks her plate into the kitchen. When she comes back, she looks at Miller. "You finished?" He's midbite when she pulls his plate from him regardless.

"There's still cake to eat," I say, pointing at the three-layer chocolate cake in the center of the table.

Clara stares at me. Hard. She grabs Miller's fork from him without breaking her stare, and she digs it into the center of the cake, then shoves a bite into her mouth.

"Delicious," she says wryly. She drops the fork and takes Miller's hand. "Ready?"

"Where do you think you're going?"

"A ball game," Clara says.

"It's not a game night."

Clara tilts her head. "You sure about that, Mom? I mean, you weren't even sure it was my birthday this morning."

"I knew it was your birthday. I was just momentarily shaken by the fact that your boyfriend slept in your bed last night."

Clara smirks. "Oh, we didn't *sleep*."

Miller mutters, "Yes we did," from behind her.

I look at Miller. "You can go now. Tell Clara good night."

Clara looks at Miller. "Don't leave yet. I'm coming with you."

Miller looks from me to Clara, like he's torn. I'd feel bad for him if I wasn't so angry at him.

"Miller, it's probably best if you just go," Jonah says.

Clara rolls her head, stopping it when her eyes land on Jonah. "If he's leaving, you should go too. You don't live here."

Jonah seems over her attitude just as much as I am. "Clara, *stop*."

"Don't tell me to stop. You aren't my dad."

"I'm not trying to be."

I'm standing now. This is going way too far.

Miller turns and heads for the door, as if he senses the bomb is about to explode, and he doesn't want to be injured by the shrapnel.

Clara backs her way to the front door. "It's my birthday. I'm protesting my punishment on the grounds that it was *your* example that forced me to break the rules last night." She opens the door. "I'll be home by curfew."

I start to walk around the table in a rush to the door, but Jonah grabs my wrist. "Let her go."

I look down at his hand clamped around my wrist. "You can't be serious."

Jonah stands up, forcing my eyes upward because he looms over me. "You need to tell her the truth, Morgan."

"No."

"You're losing control of her. She hates you. She blames you for everything."

"She's sixteen. She'll get over it."

"She's *seven*teen. And what if she doesn't?"

I can't have this conversation with him right now. "She's right. You should go too."

Jonah doesn't protest. He grabs Elijah's things, and they leave. Jonah doesn't even say goodbye.

I stare back at the kitchen table—at all the uneaten food and the near-perfect cake.

I slump into a chair, grab a fork, and take a bite of it.

CHAPTER TWENTY-EIGHT

CLARA

I'm leaning against Miller's truck with him when Jonah comes outside with Elijah. I turn and stare toward the road so I don't have to look at him.

As evidenced in class today, I get a lot angrier when we make eye contact. And even though he was nice enough not to punish me, and then later gave me his phone, I realize he did both of those things out of guilt because he knows what he's done. And now he's here, having family dinner with us like my father never even existed.

I hear him as he's buckling Elijah into place in the back seat of his car. Then I hear the door close. I blow out a quiet breath, relieved he's leaving, but then suck in another rush of air when I realize he didn't open his car door. I glance toward the front of Miller's truck to see Jonah making his way over to us. My posture grows rigid when he stops two feet in front of me.

He places both his hands firmly on my shoulders and then leans forward and kisses me on top of my head. "You're better than this, Clara. We all are." He backs away. "Happy birthday."

When Jonah finally pulls out of the driveway, I roll my eyes and push off Miller's truck. I lean against his chest, just wanting to feel the soothing sound of his heartbeat against my cheek. He presses his chin against the top of my head as he wraps his arms around me. "Is this how it always is?" he asks.

"Lately, yes."

Miller's chest rises and then falls, just once. Heavily. "I don't know if I can do this."

I pull back and look up. "You don't have to come over anymore. I wouldn't even blame you."

Miller is looking at me regretfully. "I don't mean dinner with your family."

I stare at him a moment—long enough to make out irritation in his expression. I take a step back. His arms fall to his sides. "It's my birthday."

"I'm aware of that."

"You're breaking up with me on my *birthday?*"

He drags a hand down his face. "No. I'm just . . ." He can't even finish whatever it is he's about to say. Probably because he knows what a jerk he's being right now.

I take another step back. "You slept with me last night, and now you're dumping me? *Really?*" I spin around and head back to my house. "Guess I was wrong about you too."

I can hear him sprinting after me. He intercepts me before I make it to the front patio. He grips my face with both hands, but it isn't a gentle grip. It's not a rough one, either, but based on the anger in his expression, it's not a touch I really want right now.

"You don't get to throw that in my face, Clara. *I* was the one who was taken advantage of last night. *Not* you." With that, he drops his hands and walks back to his truck. When I hear him open his door, I flinch.

"I'm sorry." I face him. "I'm sorry. That was a really shitty thing to say and an even shittier thing to do." I walk back to his truck. "But why are you doing this? This morning, in my car, you acted like you forgave me for last night." I feel panicky. Miller's expression is torn as he taps his fist against the frame of his door. Then he slams it shut and pulls me in for a frustrated hug.

"I know you and your mother aren't getting along right now." He looks down at me, his hands tilting my face up to his. "But I feel like you're using me as your weapon in all these fights against her. It's not fair to me."

"I didn't know it was going to turn into what it turned into."

"It's your fault it turned into that. You weren't the victim in there tonight, Clara. You were the instigator."

I shrug myself from his grip. "You have a bad memory if you think tonight was my fault. In case you forgot, I found out my *mother* has been having an *affair* with *Jonah*."

Miller opens his door and gets in his truck. I plant myself in the space between him and his door so that he can't shut it. His head falls against the back of his seat. "I want to go home."

"I'll go with you."

He rolls his head until he's looking at me. "I want to go alone."

I'm not going to beg. I did enough of that last night. "That's unfortunate." I back away so that he can shut his door. He cranks his truck but rolls down the window.

"I'll see you at school tomorrow." His voice has lost its edge, but it does nothing to make me feel better. He's leaving me alone on my birthday. I realize dinner was a mess, but my entire *life* is a mess. *What's new?*

I turn around and walk away from his truck.

"Clara."

He's confusing as shit with all this back-and-forth.

I spin around and march back to his window. "You know what? I don't need this. I don't want a boyfriend who makes me feel worse when I'm already down. I don't want to date you anymore. I'm breaking up with *you*." I back away but realize I'm not finished with my point, so I step back toward his truck. "They disrespected the two most important people in my life. They disrespected *me*. Am I just supposed to pretend I'm fine with it? Is that the kind of girlfriend you want? Someone who just gives up and lets other people win every time?"

Miller's arm is hanging casually over his steering wheel. His voice is calm when he says, "Sometimes you have to walk away from the fight in order to win it."

Hearing him repeat those words infuriates me. I stomp my foot. "You don't get to break up with me and then quote my dead aunt!"

"I *didn't* break up with you. And I'm quoting *you*."

"Well, you should stop. Don't quote *any*one! It's . . . it's unattractive!"

If it's possible, Miller somehow looks amused. "I'm going home now."

"Good!"

He looks behind him and begins to back out of the driveway. I'm standing in the same spot, confused by our argument. I don't even know what just happened. "Did we just break up? I can't even tell!"

Miller presses on the brake and leans out his window. "No. We're just having an argument."

"Fine!"

Again, he looks amused as he backs onto the street. I want to wipe the smirk off his face, but he's already leaving. When he rounds the corner, I walk back inside the house. My mother is standing in the living room, staring down at her phone. It's on speaker. She's listening to a voice mail. I walk in on the tail end of it.

"*. . . she didn't sign out at the office, so we're just calling to let you know she'll need to bring a note to excuse her from her afternoon classes today . . .*"

My mother ends the call before the voice mail is over. "You skipped school today?"

I roll my eyes as I brush past her. "It was only three classes. I had to get out of there. I couldn't breathe. I *still* can't breathe." I slam my door, and tears are streaming down my cheeks before I even fall against my mattress. I grab my new phone and call Lexie. She answers on the first ring because she's dependable like that. She's the only dependable thing in my life right now.

"This . . ." I suck in a series of quick breaths, attempting to choke back tears. "This is the worst birthday. The *worst*. Can you . . ." I suck in more breaths. "Come over?"

"On my way."

CHAPTER TWENTY-NINE

MORGAN

I pull a few of Chris's shirts out of the closet and remove the hangers from them. I drop them into a trash bag I'll be donating to a church.

Lexie showed up half an hour ago. I debated on not letting Clara have her over, but I'd almost rather Lexie be here than for Clara to be alone right now. I was relieved to see her when I opened the front door earlier because I could hear Clara crying from my bedroom, and she refuses to speak to me. Or maybe I don't want to speak to her.

I think it's best if we just don't speak until tomorrow.

Now that Lexie is here, Clara is no longer crying, which is good. And even though I can't make out what they're saying, I can hear them talking. At least I know she's home and safe, even if she does hate me right now.

I pull two more of Chris's shirts out of my closet.

Since the week after Chris died, I've slowly been getting rid of his stuff. I've been doing it a little at a time, hoping Clara doesn't notice. I don't want her to think I'm trying to rid this house of the memory of him. He's her father, and erasing him isn't my goal. But I am trying to rid my personal space of him. I threw his pillow away last week. I threw his toothbrush away this morning. And I just finished packing up the last of his dresser.

I expected, in all my digging around, that I would find something he was sloppy about. A hotel receipt, lipstick on a collar. Something that would show he was a little careless in his affair. Aside from the letters he kept locked away in his toolbox, I find nothing else. He hid it well. They both did.

I should probably take the letters out of my dresser and put them away before Clara accidentally runs across them.

I pull a box of his things down from the top closet shelf. After I got pregnant with Clara, Chris and I moved in together. We didn't have much because we were just teenagers, but this box is one of the few things he brought with him. At the time, it held little mementos like photographs and awards he'd won. But over the years, I've been adding other stuff to it. I consider it *our* box now.

I sit on the bed and look through loose pictures of Clara from when she was a baby. Pictures of me and Chris. Pictures of the three of us and Jenny. I inspect every picture, assuming I'll find some kind of hint of when it started. But every picture just paints a portrait of a happy couple.

I guess we really were for a while. I'm not sure where it went wrong for him, but I do wish he'd have chosen any girl in the world other than Jenny. That was the least he could have done.

Or maybe it was Jenny who chose him.

I pull an envelope out of the box. It's full of pictures developed from a roll off one of our old cameras. Jenny isn't in many of the pictures because she was the one who took most of them, but there's a lot of me and Chris. Some include Jonah. I stare hard at the pictures of Jonah, trying to find one where he looks genuinely happy, but there isn't one. He hardly ever smiled. Even now, it's a rare thing. Not that he wasn't happy. He seemed happy back then, but not like the rest of us. Jenny would light up around him, Chris would light up around me, but no one made Jonah light up. It's as if he was stuck in a perpetual shadow, cast by something none of us were aware of.

I flip through the final three pictures, but something about what I see causes me to pause. I pull the three pictures out, taken in sequence, and study them. In the first picture, I'm in the middle, smiling at the camera. Chris is smiling down at me. Jonah is on the other side of me, looking at Chris with a desolate expression.

In the next picture, Chris is smiling at the camera. I'm looking up at Jonah, and Jonah is looking down at me, and I remember that moment. *I remember that look.*

In the third picture, Jonah is out of the frame. He had broken our stare and walked off.

I've tried not to think about that day or the ten minutes before that picture was taken, and I haven't. Not in a long time. But the pictures force me to recall it in vivid detail.

We had been at Jonah's house because he was the only one who had a pool. Jenny was on a towel laid out on the concrete, trying to get a tan near the shallow end of the pool. Chris had just gotten out of the water to go inside the house because he was hungry.

Jonah was holding on to a raft a few feet away from me, his body submerged in the water, his arms stretched out over the raft.

I couldn't touch, and my legs were tired, so I swam over to him and grabbed onto the float. The raft was poorly inflated and probably a few summers old, so it wasn't very reliable. Especially with both of us hanging on to it. I started slipping, so Jonah grabbed my arms, then slid his leg around the back of my knee to anchor me in place.

I don't think either of us expected to be jolted by the contact, but I could tell he felt it too. I could tell because his eyes changed shape and darkened at the same moment I shuddered.

I'd been dating Chris for a while at that point, and in all the times he'd touched me while we dated, I had never felt that kind of current pass through me. The kind that not only left you breathless but left you fearing you'd die from lack of oxygen if you didn't back away. I wanted to slip with Jonah under the water and use his mouth for air.

The thought startled me. I tried to pull away, but Jonah held on to my arms. His eyes were pleading, as if he knew the second I pulled away, he'd never get to touch me like that again. So I stayed. And we stared.

That's all that happened.

Nothing was said. Other than the way he was keeping me afloat with his leg wrapped around mine beneath the water, I wouldn't even say our touch was inappropriate. Had Chris seen it, he wouldn't have thought a thing about it. Had Jenny seen it, she wouldn't have even been mad.

But that's because they didn't feel what was happening between us. They couldn't hear everything that wasn't being said.

A few seconds later, Chris walked back outside and dove into the pool. Jonah unwrapped his leg from around mine, but he didn't let go of my arms. The ripples from the waves Chris's dive had left caused the float to rock, but our eyes never unlocked. Not even when Chris sprang up out of the pool next to me and splashed water on us.

Chris wrapped both arms around my waist, pulling me away from the raft. My arms began to slip out of Jonah's, and I watched Jonah wince when my fingers slid through his and then left him empty.

We were no longer touching. Chris was holding me up, pressing his mouth to mine, and I knew Jonah was watching us kiss.

In that moment, I felt full of guilt. But not because of the moment I had shared with Jonah. Somehow, it felt like Jonah was the one I had *betrayed*. Which made absolutely no sense.

I climbed out of the pool right after that. A moment later, Jenny had her camera out, asking us to pose for a picture. I remember after the first picture, I glanced up at Jonah. He was looking down at me with an expression that felt like it put a crack in my chest. I didn't understand it then. Back then, I thought it was just attraction. A teenage boy, hoping to make out with a teenage girl. But right after Jenny took the second picture, Jonah stormed off, into his house.

His actions confused me, and I wanted to ask him about it, but I never did. A few weeks later, I found out I was pregnant.

Then Jonah Sullivan skipped town.

I stare at the picture. The one of Jonah looking down at me. I finally understand that look in his eyes. It wasn't attraction or contempt.

It's heartache.

I put the pictures back in the box and replace the lid. I stare at the box, wondering what would have happened if he had never left.

If he had stayed, would we have ended up like Jenny and Chris? I don't want to think we would have ended up like that. Sneaking around, betraying the people we love the most.

I've been so angry at Jonah for leaving, but I get it now. He had to. He knew if he stayed, someone besides him would have ended up getting hurt.

I've been avoiding him since his return because my feelings for him were supposed to be dormant. It was supposed to be a teenage crush that fizzled out after I moved on with Chris.

I've been lying to myself, doing everything in my power to convince myself that the feelings Jonah stirs up inside me are nothing more than anger.

I'm a terrible liar, though. I always have been.

⌐⌐

I knock lightly when I reach his front door. If Elijah is asleep, I don't want to wake him.

I take a step back, hugging myself. There's a heavy breeze that swirls around me, but I don't know if the chills on my arms are caused by the wind or seeing Jonah standing in the open doorway. He's in a pair of blue jeans and nothing else. His hair is wet and messy. His eyes are drawing me in like they always have. But this time, I don't force myself to look away.

"Yes," I say.

He looks at me, perplexed. "Did I ask you a question?"

I nod. "You asked me if I would have left Chris had I not gotten pregnant with Clara. My answer is yes."

He stares at me, hard, and then it's as if this invisible wall that's always been shielding him from me suddenly disappears. He becomes a different person entirely. His features soften, his shoulders relax, his lips part, his chest rises and falls with a smooth release of air.

"Is that the only reason you're here?"

I shake my head and take one step closer. My heart is pounding so hard right now that I want to turn around and run, but I know the only thing that can ease this ache I feel is Jonah. I want to know what it feels like to be held by him. To be *with* him. All this time I've never even allowed myself to imagine it. Now I want to experience it.

My hands are at my sides now. Jonah barely lifts his finger, hooking it around one of mine. A jolt of electricity spirals its way through my chest, and then a chill rushes down my arm. Jonah's arms are covered with chills too. They run over his chest and up his neck. I slip my entire hand into his, and he grips it. Squeezes it.

"I might regret this tomorrow," I warn.

He steps forward, wrapping his free hand around the back of my neck, pulling me close to his mouth. Before he touches my lips, his gaze flickers over my face. "You won't."

He pulls me inside and closes the door behind us. He backs me against the living room door, and it feels like I'm swallowing fire when his lips finally touch mine. It's everything I've denied myself from feeling. Our kiss last night felt incredible, but this kiss makes last night's kiss feel like it was a mere teaser.

Jonah presses his entire body against mine, and it feels like a lifetime of ache is being soothed with each brush of his fingertips against my skin. With each flick of his tongue, each sound that escapes our throats. We end up on the couch, him on top of me, my hands dragging over his back, feeling his muscles tense and roll beneath my fingertips.

It's like we're making up for all the years we missed out on this feeling. We kiss like teenagers for ten minutes. Exploring each other, tasting each other, moving against each other.

I eventually have to turn my face away from his, just so I can catch my breath. I feel light headed. He presses his forehead to my cheek and sucks in all the air I've just stolen from him.

"Thank you," he whispers breathlessly. He closes his eyes and brings his mouth to my ear. His breath is warm as it trickles down my neck. "I needed to know I wasn't crazy. That this feeling hasn't all been in my head."

I pull his mouth back to mine. I kiss him gently, and then he drops his head to my neck and sighs. "That day in your pool," I whisper. "Do you remember?"

Quiet laughter meets my skin. "I've been searching for that feeling since the second Chris pulled you away from me."

I want to say, *"Me too,"* but it would be a lie. I haven't searched for that feeling at all. I've spent every year of my marriage trying to *forget* it—attempting to pretend that kind of connection didn't really exist. Every time I caught myself thinking back on that day, I found things to blame. The heat. The sun. The chlorine in the pool. The alcohol we'd been sneaking from Jonah's pantry.

Jonah pulls away from me and grabs my hand, easing me onto my feet. He quietly leads me to the bedroom. We're kissing as he lowers me to the bed, and I love how he takes his time. He doesn't remove a single piece of my clothing. He just kisses me in every position. Him on top, me on top, both of us on our sides. We make out, and it's everything I hoped it would feel like.

He leans over me, dragging his lips down my neck. His breath is warm against the base of my throat when he says, "I'm scared."

Those words send a chill through me. He stops kissing me and presses his cheek to my chest.

I thread my fingers through his hair.

"Scared of what?"

"Your need to protect Clara." He lifts his face. "My need to be honest with Elijah. We aren't on the same page, Morgan. I've waited too long for this to be a onetime thing, but I'm not sure you want what I want."

He scoots up, sliding his hand beneath my shirt, pressing his palm against my stomach. I'm staring up at the ceiling, and I could swear the ceiling is pulsating to the rhythm of my heartbeat. "I don't know what I want." My eyes find his, and I *do* know what I want. I'm lying. I know *exactly* what I want. I just don't know if it's possible. "She'll never understand. And what would we tell Elijah?"

"We would tell him the truth. Do you really think it's better for Clara to think *we're* the bad guys in this scenario?"

"You saw how devastated she was because of a kiss. Imagine if she finds out about Elijah—about what Jenny and Chris did—she'll never be able to forgive that."

I can see a flash of understanding on Jonah's face, but he shakes his head. "So . . ." He falls onto his back. "Chris and Jenny get away with an affair. They get away with lying to me about fathering a child. They get away with being eternal idols in Clara's eyes. And in the meantime, me and you are forced to keep our mouths shut and live separately in misery because of actions we aren't even responsible for?"

"I realize it's not fair." I lift myself up onto my elbow and look at him. I put my hand on his hardened jaw and force him to meet my focused stare. "Chris was a shitty husband. He was a shitty friend to you. But he was a wonderful father." I run my thumb over his lips, pleading with him through my teary eyes. "If she ever finds out Elijah isn't yours, it'll devastate her. *Please* don't tell him. All he knows is you, anyway. It's not the same as if Clara were to find out about Chris. I'll take their secret to my grave if it means protecting her from that kind of pain."

Jonah turns his head, pulling away from my hand. The rejection stings. "I'm not like you. I don't want to lie to my child."

I fall onto my back. More tears come. I shouldn't have come over here. It was a bad idea. I've lived this long suffering through this terrible longing I've kept buried for Jonah. What's fifty more years?

"We have to work this out. Come to an agreement," he says. "I want to be with you."

"That's why I'm here. So you can be with me."

"I want you in more ways than this."

I squeeze my eyes shut for a moment, working out what that would mean. Even in all of Chris's infidelity, I still feel guilty that I'm here, in Jonah's bed. Kissing him felt so good when I wasn't thinking too hard about it. It's the best feeling I've had in a long, long time. But now that he's forcing me to look at where this will lead, I just feel miserable again.

I look him directly in the eye. "You're telling me you're willing to ruin every memory my daughter has with her father. Yet in the same conversation, you're asking me to be with you in more than one way? To fall in love with you?"

"No," he says. "I'm not asking you to fall in love with me, Morgan. You already love me. I'm just asking you to give that a chance."

"I do *not* love you." I roll toward the other side of the bed, away from him. *I need to leave.*

I start to stand, but he grips my arm and pulls me back to the bed, onto my back.

I press my hands against his chest to push him away, but he's on top of me now, staring down at me with a familiar look in his eyes. I'm instantly still. I'm weak beneath that stare. He's looking at me like he was in that picture. Full of heartache.

Or maybe this is what Jonah looks like when he loves something so much it hurts.

I suddenly don't feel an urgent need to leave. I relax beneath him, into him, around him. I suck in air when he lowers his mouth to my jawline, dragging his lips slowly up to my ear.

"You love me."

I shake my head. "I don't. That's not why I'm here."

He kisses me, just below my ear. "You do," he says. "You've just done an excellent job at hiding it, but you've said it in every silent conversation we've ever had."

"There's no such thing as silent conversation."

He's looking into my eyes in a way no man has ever looked at me before. Then, he dips his head and rests his lips against mine. "It's okay, you don't have to say it. I love you too." When his lips close over mine, there's an intensity in his kiss that makes me lose myself.

There's something about being Jonah's first choice—maybe even his *only* choice—that makes every look he gives me and every touch and every word he speaks reach me on a level Chris never could. A level I feel so deep in my soul it makes me ache beneath all the satisfaction his kiss brings.

When he settles himself between my legs, I moan into his mouth and pull him closer to me.

I forget everything. The only thoughts I have are of this moment. How rough his hands are as they pull off my shirt. How soft his lips are when they meet my breasts. How effortless his movements are as he slips out of his jeans. How in sync our gasps are when we're finally skin to skin. How intense his eyes are when he begins to push into me.

It's a completeness I've never experienced before.

It's as if he knows exactly where to touch me, how soft, how firm, where I want his lips. He feels like a professor of my body, and I feel like an inexperienced student, cautiously touching him, unsure if my fingers or my lips can even come close to making him feel how he's making me feel.

I press my mouth against his shoulder and whisper, "I've only ever been with Chris."

Jonah is deep inside me when he stops suddenly and pulls back. Our eyes meet, and he smiles. "I've only ever *wanted* to be with you."

He kisses me tenderly, and that's how it continues—him kissing me, moving gently in and out of me until I can no longer keep silent. I pull him closer so I can bury my face against his neck when it happens.

I finish first, an explosive moment of emotions and pleasure and years of suppression finally coming to the surface. My body is trembling beneath him, and my nails have raked their way down his back when he groans against my cheek, shuddering on top of me.

I expect it to end here, with him catching his breath and then rolling off me with a sigh. That's how the last seventeen years of sex with Chris always ended.

But Jonah isn't Chris, and I need to stop comparing them. *It's unfair to Chris.*

Jonah is gently cradling the side of my head as we continue to kiss. This doesn't feel like it's over yet. This thing between me and Jonah. Now that I've had this side of him, I don't know how I can go on without it.

That scares me, but I'm too satiated to stop his mouth as it moves over mine, across my jaw, finally coming to rest against my chest, where he calmly lays his head. We spend the next few minutes waiting for the current to settle between us.

He slides his hand down my stomach and begins to run his finger lazily over my skin. "I'll do it."

I feel my breath catch.

Jonah lifts up onto his elbow, hovering over me. "I won't tell Elijah. If you promise me you won't put a stop to this—that you'll eventually tell Clara you want to be with me—I won't tell Elijah." He brushes back my hair and looks at me with eyes full of sincerity. "You're right. Clara deserves every great memory she has of Chris. I don't want to take that from her."

I feel a tear slide into my hair as I look up at him. "You're right too," I whisper. "I *do* love you."

Jonah smiles. "I know you do. That's why we're naked."

I laugh. He pulls me on top of him, and I realize as I look down at him that I've never felt like I belonged with another person more than I belong with Jonah Sullivan.

CHAPTER THIRTY

CLARA

"Let me get this straight," Lexie says. She kicks her feet up on the coffee table, nearly knocking over one of the bottles of wine. "Your mom is sleeping with Uncle Teacher?"

I hiccup. Then nod.

"Her dead sister's fiancé?"

I nod again.

"Wow." She leans forward and grabs more wine. "I'm not drunk enough for this." She takes a swig straight from the bottle. I take it from her, not because I think she's gone overboard but because I don't know that I'm drunk enough for it either. I take a sip, then set it between my legs, gripping the top of the bottle.

"How long do you think it's been going on?" she asks.

I shrug. "No telling. She's over there right now. We have that app, and that's where she is. Over there. With him."

"Bastards," she says. After that insult leaves her mouth, she suddenly grows animated, hopping up from the couch. She stumbles but catches herself. "What if your mother and Jonah *caused* the wreck so they could be together?"

"That's ridiculous."

"I'm serious, Clara! Do you not watch *Dateline*?"

I motion toward the television. "We don't have cable anymore."

Lexie begins pacing the living room, a little wobbly but successfully. "What if this is a conspiracy? I mean, think about it. Your dad and Jenny were together when they died. *Why* were they together?"

"My dad had a flat tire. They work in the same building. Jenny was giving him a ride." They're dead because of my texts to Aunt Jenny, but I keep that thought to myself.

Lexie narrows her eyes and snaps her fingers, like she just solved the case. "Flat tires can be staged."

I roll my eyes, grab my fork, and take another bite of the cake sitting on the coffee table. It's the saddest birthday cake I've ever seen. No one has even cut a slice from it. There are just huge chunks of cake missing from the top and sides. I speak with a mouthful. "My mom is a terrible person. But she's not a murderer."

Lexie raises an eyebrow. "What about Uncle Teacher? He hasn't been around that long. Do we even know where he's been? There could be a trail of dead bodies in his wake."

"You watch way too much TV."

She stomps over to me and bends over, coming face to face with me. "*True* TV! I watch crimes that have actually happened! This stuff happens, Clara. More often than you think."

I shove a bite of cake in her mouth to shut her up.

It was unnecessary, though, because as soon as the front door opens, Lexie and I both clamp our mouths shut at the sudden presence of my mother.

Lexie slowly begins to lower herself to the coffee table. "Hello, Morgan," Lexie says, doing everything in her power to appear sober. It might have worked if she wasn't lifting her legs and stretching her back into an awkward position on the coffee table as she tries to hide the bottles of wine from my mother. Her entire body is stiff and contorted now. I appreciate her efforts, but she overestimates my mother's stupidity.

My mother closes the door and stares at us with disappointment. She can see the empty bottles on the table, despite Lexie's attempt to sprawl out in front of them. Lexie forgot I'm also holding a bottle in my lap. Can't very well hide that at this point.

My mother's eyes fall on me. "*Really*, Clara?" Her voice is flat. Unsurprised. It's as if nothing I do could disturb her at this point.

"I was just leaving," Lexie says, pushing off the table. She begins to walk toward the door, but my mother holds out her hand.

"Give me your keys."

Lexie's head rolls back with a groan. She pulls her keys from her pocket and drops them in my mother's hand. "Does that mean I can stay the night?"

"No. Call your mother to come get you." She looks at me. "Clean up this mess." She takes Lexie's keys to the kitchen.

Lexie pulls out her phone.

"Really? You're just going to *leave* me here with her? She could be a murderer," I whisper.

I don't really think that, but I also really don't want to be alone with my mother like this. When she's angry, it doesn't scare me. But right now, she just looks annoyed. That kind of terrifies me. It's out of character, which means I don't know what comes next.

"Uber will be here in two minutes," Lexie says, sliding her phone back into her pocket. She walks over to me and hugs me. "Sorry, but I don't wanna stay for this one. Call me if she murders you, 'kay?"

"Fine," I say, pouting.

Lexie walks outside, and I look at the coffee table, grab the bottle of wine that isn't quite empty yet, and I finish it off. I get the last swig down when it's ripped from my hand.

I look at my mother, and maybe it's the alcohol. It *might* be the alcohol. But I hate her so much I don't even know if I'd be sad if she died. Every time I look at her now, I wonder about their affair. Did it start before her sister got pregnant? Was she still sleeping with Jonah while accompanying Jenny to all her sonogram appointments?

I always thought my mother was a terrible liar, but she's a better liar than anyone. She's better than me, and I'm the actress in the family.

"So," I say, very casually. "How long have you and Jonah been fucking?"

My mother is forced to blow out a calming breath. Her lips thin with anger. I'm not sure I've ever felt worried she might slap me, but I take a step back because she looks pissed enough to slap me right now. "I'm done with this behavior, Clara." She picks up the other wine bottle and the red SOLO Cups Lexie and I started with. When she stands up straight, she looks me in the eye again. "I would have *never* done that to Jenny. *Or* your father. Don't insult me like that."

I want to believe her. I kind of *do* believe her, but I'm drunk, so my judgment is impaired. She walks to the kitchen, so I follow her. "Is that where you've been?"

My mother ignores me as she begins pouring what little is left of the wine down the drain.

"What were you doing at Jonah's . . ." I snap my fingers, trying to think of the word for the things people live in. Words are hard right now. "House!" I finally say. "Why were you at his house just now?"

"We needed to talk."

"You didn't talk. You had sex. I can tell. I'm an expert now."

My mother doesn't deny my accusation. She throws the empty bottles of wine in the trash, then finds the last bottle of wine in the kitchen and uncorks it, then pours it out in the sink.

I point my hands toward her, clapping. "Thinking ahead, I see. Good job. *Good* Mom."

"Well, I can't really trust you with much of anything at this point, so whatever it takes." When that bottle is empty, she tosses it in the trash, then walks back to the living room. She swipes my phone off the table. I follow her down the hallway, even though I keep bumping into the wall with my shoulder. Words are hard, but walking is harder. I eventually just place my hand on the wall and balance myself until I get to my room. My mother is inside, gathering things.

My television.

My iPad.

My books.

"You're grounding me from *books*?"

"Books are a privilege. You can earn them back."

Oh my God. She's taking away everything that brings me any semblance of happiness. I stomp over to the corner where I tossed my favorite throw pillow this morning. It's purple and black sequined, and I like drawing shapes in it with my fingers. Sometimes I draw cuss words. It's fun.

"Here," I say, handing it to her. "This pillow brings me a lot of joy too. Better take it away."

She snatches it out of my hand, and then I look for something else I like. I feel like we're in an upside-down Marie Kondo episode. *Does it spark joy? Get rid of it!*

My earbuds are on my nightstand, so I grab them. "I like these. I can't even use them because you took my phone and my iPad, but I still might be tempted to put them in my ears, so you better take them!" I toss them into the hallway, where she's setting all the other stuff. I grab my blanket off my bed. "My blanket keeps me warm. It's really nice, and it still smells like Miller, so you better make me earn this one back." I throw it past her and pile it on top of my other things.

My mother is standing in my bedroom doorway watching me. I stomp to my closet and find my favorite pair of shoes. They're boots, actually. "You got me these for Christmas, and since Texas winters are nonexistent, I hardly get to wear them. But it's really awesome when I *do* get to wear them, so you better take them before winter comes!" I toss them one at a time into the hallway.

"Stop patronizing me, Clara."

I hear a text sound off on my phone. My mother pulls it out of her pocket, reads it, rolls her eyes, then puts my phone away.

"Who was it?"

"Don't worry about it."

"What did it say?"

"You would know if you hadn't gotten wasted."

Ugh. I walk to my closet and pull one of my favorite shirts off a hanger. Then another. "Better take these shirts. Take *all* my clothes, actually. I don't need them. I can't leave the house anyway. Even if I could, I'd have nowhere to go, because my boyfriend broke up with me on my birthday. Probably because my mother is crazy!" I drop an armload of clothes onto the hallway floor.

"Stop being dramatic. He didn't break up with you. Go to bed, Clara." She closes my bedroom door.

I swing it open. "We *did* break up! How would you know if we broke up or not?"

"Because," she says, turning to face me with a bored expression. "That text was from him. It said, *'I hope you sleep well. See you at school tomorrow.'* People who break up don't text like that—or send heart emojis." She starts to walk farther down the hallway, so I follow her because I need to know more.

"He put a heart emoji?"

She doesn't answer me. She keeps walking.

"What color was it?"

She's still ignoring me.

"*Mom!* Was it red? Was it a red heart?"

291

We're in the kitchen now. I lean against the counter because I feel something speeding through my head. A whoosh. I grip the counter for balance, then burp. I cover my mouth.

My mother shakes her head, her eyes full of disappointment. "It's like you printed off a checklist for ways to rebel and you've been marking them off one at a time."

"I don't have a checklist. But if I did, you'd probably take that from me, too, because I like checklists. Checklists make me happy."

My mother sighs, folding her arms over her chest. "Clara," she says, her voice gentle. "Sweetie. How do you think your father would feel if he could see you right now?"

"If my father were alive, I wouldn't be drunk," I admit. "I respected him too much to do that."

"You don't have to stop respecting him just because he's dead."

"Yeah, well. Neither do *you*, Mom."

CHAPTER
THIRTY-ONE

MORGAN

Clara's comment cut deep.

I realize she drank an entire bottle of wine on her own. Two of them were completely empty. But sometimes drunken stupors make people more honest than they normally would be, which means she truly believes I'm disrespecting her father.

It kills me that she thinks I'm the one in the wrong.

I hope this passes. Her anger, her rebellion, her hatred toward me. I realize she'll never fully get over it, but I hope in the coming days, she can somehow find it in herself to forgive me. I'm sure she will once we're able to sit down and have a conversation, but she's still reeling from the realization that Jonah and I are intimately involved. To be honest, *I'm* still reeling from the realization.

I open her door one more time to check on her before going to my bedroom. She's out cold. I'm sure she'll wake up with a raging hangover, but right now, she looks peaceful.

I kind of hope she does have a hangover. What better way to ensure your child doesn't drink again than for their first time to be an awful experience?

I hear my cell phone ringing, so I leave Clara's door cracked and go to my bedroom. In all the times Jonah has called me, this is the first time I've allowed myself to be excited to hear his voice. I sit down and lean back against the headboard and answer it. "Hi."

"Hey," he says. I can hear the smile in his voice.

It's quiet for a moment, and I realize he probably had no pressing reason to call me other than just to talk. That's a first. It's exhilarating, feeling wanted.

I slide down onto my back. "What are you doing?"

"Staring at Elijah," Jonah says. "It's so weird how fascinating it is just watching a baby sleep."

"It doesn't end. I was just staring at Clara when you called."

"That's good to know. So things were better when you got home?"

I laugh. "Oh, Jonah." I press my hand to my forehead. "She's wasted. She and Lexie drank two and a half bottles of wine while I was at your house."

"No."

"Yes. She's gonna regret it in the morning."

He sighs. "I wish I knew what advice to give you, but I'm at a loss."

"Me too. I'm calling a family therapist in the morning. I should have done it sooner, but I guess it's better late than never."

"Should I expect her in class tomorrow?"

"I don't know that she'll be able to get out of bed."

He laughs, but it's an empathetic laugh. "I hope the years drag by before Elijah is that age."

"They won't. It'll go by in a blink." It's quiet for a moment. I like hearing him breathe. I kind of wish I was there with him right now. I cover myself with my blanket and roll onto my side, resting my phone against my ear.

"You want to know one of my favorite memories of you?" Jonah asks.

I grin. "This sounds fun."

"It was my senior prom. Your junior prom. You remember?"

"Yes. You went with Tiffany Proctor. I spent the whole night trying not to watch the two of you dance. I can admit now that I was insanely jealous."

"Makes two of us," Jonah says. "Anyway, Chris was excited leading up to prom because he'd gotten a hotel for the two of you. I tried not to think about it all night. When it came time for him to leave, he was drunk."

"*So* drunk," I say, laughing.

"Yeah, I had to drive you guys to the hotel. Dropped Tiffany off first, which pissed her off. When we got to the hotel, the two of us had to practically drag Chris up the stairs. When we finally got him on the bed, he passed out in the center of it."

I remember, but I don't know why that's Jonah's favorite memory of me. Before I can ask him what was so special about it, he continues the story.

"You were hungry, so we ordered a pizza. I sat on one side of Chris, and you sat on the other. We watched *Blair Witch Project* until the pizza got there, but we didn't have anywhere to set the pizza so that we could both reach it."

I smile at the memory. "We used Chris as a table."

"Sat the box of pizza right on his back." I hear humor in Jonah's voice. "I don't know why I had so much fun that night. I mean . . . it was prom, and I didn't even get kissed. But I did get to spend the entire night with you, even though Chris was passed out between us."

"That was a good night." I'm still smiling, trying to think of one of my favorite memories with Jonah. "Oh my God. Remember the night you got pulled over?"

"Which time? I got pulled over a lot."

"I don't remember where we were going, or if we were coming from somewhere, but it was late, and the highway was empty. Your car was a piece of shit, so Chris wanted you to see how fast it could go. You got all the way up to ninety when you got pulled over. When the cop came to your window, he said, *'Do you realize how fast you were going?'* You said, *'Yes, sir. Ninety.'* And then the cop said, *'Is there a reason you were driving twenty-five miles over the speed limit?'* You paused for a moment and then said, *'I don't like for things to go to waste.'* The officer looked at you, and you waved toward your dash. *'I have this entire speedometer, and most of the time, I don't even use half of it.'*"

Jonah laughs. Hard. "I can't believe you remember that."

"How could I forget? You pissed the cop off so bad he pulled you out of the car and frisked you."

"I got community service over that ticket. Had to pick up highway trash every Saturday for three months."

"Yeah, but you looked cute in your yellow vest."

"You and Chris used to think it was hilarious to drive by and throw empty soda cans at me."

"All his idea," I say in defense.

"I doubt that," Jonah says.

I sigh, thinking about all the good times. Not just with Jonah but with Chris too. And Jenny. So many with Jenny. "I miss them," I whisper.

"Yeah. Me too."

"I miss you," I say quietly.

"I miss you too."

We both bask in this feeling for a moment, but then I can hear Elijah starting to fuss. It doesn't last long. Jonah must have soothed him back to sleep somehow.

"Do you think you'll ever take a paternity test?" I ask him. I know Elijah looks just like Chris, but it could be a coincidence. I've been wondering if Jonah wants valid proof.

"I thought about it. But honestly, it'd be a waste of a hundred bucks. He's mine, no matter what."

My heart feels like it rolls over in my chest after that comment. "God, I love you, Jonah." My words shock me. I know we said it earlier, but I didn't mean to say it out loud just now. I was just feeling it, and then it came out.

Jonah sighs. "You have no idea how good it feels to hear you say that."

"It felt good to say it. Finally. I love you," I whisper again.

"Can you just say it like fifteen thousand more times before I hang up?"

"No, but I'll say it one more time. I am in love with you, Jonah Sullivan."

He groans. "This is torture. I wish you were here."

"I wish I was too."

Elijah starts to cry again. He doesn't let up this time. "I need to go make him a bottle."

"Okay. Give him a kiss for me."

"Will I see you tomorrow?"

"I don't know," I admit. "We'll play it by ear."

"Okay. Good night, Morgan."

"Good night."

When we end the call, I'm amazed by the ache it leaves in my chest. I successfully fought these feelings for so long, but now that I've opened myself up to him, I want to be near him. I want to be in his arms, in his bed. I want to sleep next to him.

I replay our entire conversation in my head as I try to fall asleep.

A noise startles me, though. The sound came from the direction of Clara's bedroom. I jump out of my bed and rush down the hallway. She's not in her bed, so I open her bathroom door. She's on her knees, gripping the toilet.

Here we go.

I take a washcloth out of the cabinet and wet it, then kneel down next to her. I hold back her hair while she pukes.

I hate that she's experiencing this, but I also love it. I want it to hurt. I want her to remember every terrible second of this hangover.

It's a couple minutes later when she falls against me and says, "I think it's over."

I want to laugh because I know it isn't. I help her back to bed because she's still very drunk. When she lies down, I notice she's just using a sheet to cover up. I go to the spare bedroom, where I put all the things I confiscated. I grab her blanket and her sequined pillow, then grab a trash can and take them all to her.

While I'm tucking her in, she mutters, "I think I have vomit in my nose."

I laugh and hand her a Kleenex. She blows her nose and drops the Kleenex in the trash can. Her eyes are closed, and I'm stroking her hair when she says, "I don't ever want to drink again." Her words are slurred. "I hated the pot too. It smelled so bad. I don't want vomit in my nostrils again, it's the worst."

"I'm glad you hate it," I say.

"I hated sex too. I don't want to do that again for a long, long time. We weren't even ready. He tried to talk me out of it, and I wouldn't listen."

I know she's drunk, but her words surprise me. What does she mean he tried to talk her out of it?

That was *her* idea?

I'm still stroking her hair when she begins to cry. She presses her face into her pillow. I hate that whatever happened between them is making her feel this guilty. "He obviously loves you, Clara. Don't cry."

She shakes her head. "That's not why I'm crying." She lifts her head from the pillow and looks at me. "I'm crying because it was my fault. It's my fault they died, and I try not to think about it, but that's all I think about when my head is on this pillow. Every single night. Except one time I fell asleep wondering why teddy bears are made to be cuddly, when real bears are so mean, but besides that one night, all I can think about is how it's my fault they had the wreck."

"What are you talking about?"

She drops her face back into her pillow. "Go away, Mom." Before I even move, she lifts her head again and says, "No, wait. I want you to stay." She scoots over, patting the bed next to her. "Sing me that song you used to sing to me when I was little."

I'm still trying to catch up to what she said about the wreck being her fault. Why would she think that? I want to ask her about it, but she's too drunk to hold a real conversation right now, so I just climb into bed with her and appease her. "What song?"

"You know, that song you used to sing to me when I was little."

"I sang you a lot of songs. I don't think we had any one particular song."

"Sing something else, then. Do you know any Twenty One Pilots songs? We both like them."

I laugh and pull her against my chest.

"Sing the song about the gold house," she says.

I run my hand soothingly over her head and start to sing quietly.

She's nodding as I sing, letting me know that's the right song.

I continue singing the song, stroking her hair, until the song is over and she's finally asleep.

I gently slip out of her bed and stare down at her. Drunk Clara is kind of funny. I'd prefer to have seen it for the first time when she was twenty-one, but at least it happened here, where I'm the one who gets to make sure she's taken care of.

I tuck her blanket around her and then kiss her good night. "You're driving me crazy right now, Clara . . . but my God, I love you."

CHAPTER
THIRTY-TWO

CLARA

Never in my life have I felt this terrible.

I probably shouldn't have driven to school, because my head hurts so bad I can barely keep my eyes open. But my mother took my phone last night, and I wanted to talk to Miller. I *need* to talk to him. I don't really recall much that happened after Lexie arrived, but I certainly remember everything that happened with Miller before he left. And I regret all of it.

When I see his truck pull into the parking lot, I get out of my car and walk over to it. He turns it off and then unlocks the passenger door. I have no idea if he's still mad at me, so the first thing I do when I'm in his truck is scoot across the seat and wrap my arms around him. "I'm sorry I'm crazy."

Miller hugs me back. "You aren't crazy."

He pushes me away, but only so he can readjust our position. He scoots toward the middle of the seat and pulls me onto his lap so that I'm straddling him and can look him in the eyes. "I felt bad after I left your house, but I was upset. I've wanted to be with you for a while now, but I want our time together to be meaningful to us and not related to or in spite of anyone else."

"I know. I'm sorry. I feel terrible."

Miller pulls me against his chest and rubs a soothing hand over my back. "I don't want you to feel terrible. I get it. You've been through a lot, Clara. I don't want you to stress out even more because of me or us. I just want to be part of everything that makes your life better."

God, I feel like such an asshole. I'm relieved and lucky that he's as understanding as he is. I kiss him on the cheek and look at him. "Does that mean you don't want to break up with me anymore?"

He smiles. "I never did. I was just upset."

"Good." I kiss the inside of his palm. "Because it's really gonna hurt when it happens someday. Just thinking you were breaking up with me for two seconds hurt like hell."

"Maybe we'll never break up," he says, his voice hopeful.

"Sadly, the odds aren't in our favor."

He drags a thumb across my bottom lip. "That's a bummer. I sure will miss kissing you."

I nod. "Yeah. I'm a great kisser. The best you'll ever have."

He laughs, and I drop my head to his shoulder. "What do you think will be the cause of our future breakup?"

"I don't know," he says, entertaining my distracting thoughts. "But it'll have to be way more dramatic than last night because we're in too deep."

"It will be," I say. "It'll be extremely dramatic. You'll probably become a famous musician, and you'll fall in love with the fame and leave me behind."

"I don't even play an instrument, and I can't sing for shit."

"I'll probably become a famous actress, then. And I'll introduce you to one of my costars who is more famous than me, and you'll find her more attractive, and you'll want to touch all her Academy Awards."

"Not possible. That kind of person doesn't exist."

I sit up so I can see his face. "Maybe they'll colonize Mars, and I'll want to move there and you won't."

He shakes his head. "I'll still love you from a different planet."

I pause.

He said, "*I'll* still *love you.*" I know he didn't mean it that way, but I grin teasingly. "Did you just admit that you're in love with me?"

He shrugs, and then his lips spread apart in a shy smile. "Sometimes I feel like I am. I'm sure it's not all that deep yet. We haven't been together that long. We argue a lot more than I'd like. But I feel it. Right below the surface. Tingling. Keeps me awake at night."

"That could just be restless leg syndrome."

He smiles with a slow shake of his head. "Nope."

"This could be the cause of our dramatic breakup. You telling me you might be falling in love with me way too soon."

"You think it's too soon? I kind of thought it was the perfect moment." He leans forward and kisses me softly on the cheek. "I've waited three years to be with you. If falling in love with you too soon will ruin that, then I don't even like you. In fact, I hate you."

I smile. "I hate you too."

He threads our fingers together and smiles. "Seriously, maybe we really won't break up. Ever."

"But heartache builds character. Remember?"

"So does being in love," he says.

What a great point. It's such a good point I kiss him for it. I only give him a peck, though, because I don't think he wants his tongue in my mouth after last night.

"Me and Lexie got drunk after you left. I'm pretty hungover, so I think I'm just gonna go back home. I have a headache the size of Rhode Island."

"Rhode Island is actually pretty small," he says.

"Nebraska, then."

"Oh. Well, in that case, you should definitely go home and go back to bed."

I kiss him again, on the cheek. "I'll give you a better kiss next time I see you. But I've been puking all night."

"When will I see you next?"

I shrug. "I'll be at school tomorrow, but I'm probably grounded for a really long time."

Miller tucks hair behind my ear, hugs me, and then says, "Thank you for coming to see me."

"Thank you for putting up with me."

When we get out of his truck, he gives me one final hug. It's comforting, and on the drive home I think about his hugs. My dad's hugs. Jonah's hugs. They're all great.

But if I'm being honest, nothing really compares to my mother's hugs. Or her kisses. I don't really remember a lot about last night, but I do remember her helping me in the bathroom. And for some weird reason, I remember she was in my bed, singing me a random Twenty One Pilots song.

And I remember her kissing me on the forehead, right before she told me she loved me. Even at seventeen years old, I still feel all the comforts of childhood when I'm sick and my mother takes care of me.

I woke up with my blanket and my sequined pillow. It made me smile, even through the headache. Even through my anger.

I wonder if I can somehow separate the anger from the love. I don't want her actions with Jonah to have an effect on the way I feel about her. She's my mother. I don't want to hate her. But what if I won't be able to forgive her?

But how do I even know that Jenny and my dad aren't happy for my mom and Jonah? What if they somehow set this in motion from wherever they are?

What if my anger is interfering with that somehow?

I have a lot of questions. Most of them I know can't be answered. It's making my head hurt even more.

When I finally walk into the house, my mother is awake. She's sitting on the couch with her laptop. Probably still applying for jobs. She glances up at me as I shut the door.

"You okay?"

I nod. "I thought I could do school, but I was wrong. I have a Nebraska headache." I point toward my room. "I'm gonna go back to bed."

CHAPTER THIRTY-THREE

MORGAN

I googled *Nebraska headache* when Clara got home this morning but couldn't figure out what it meant. I thought maybe it was slang, but if it is, it must be brand-new slang.

I feel fairly productive today. I have a job interview for a secretary position at a real estate firm next week. Not ideal, because the pay is low, but it's a start. I find the idea of selling real estate appealing, so I thought if I could get the job, I might get a taste for it and see if that's what I want to study. I've been looking up ways I can somehow work and go to college at the same time. There are so many more options now than there were when I was eighteen. If I had the opportunity to take night classes and online classes when Clara was younger, I probably would have finished my degree.

I've been feeling sorry for myself, but in reality, this isn't all Chris's fault. I knew he wasn't invincible. I could have easily gone to college part-time to prepare myself if something were to ever happen to him.

And I'm honestly lucky he had a life insurance policy that'll give me time to figure it out.

As I was looking through paperwork in the bedroom, I came across my birthday board, which Clara and I worked on the night before Chris died. I never put it back where I usually keep them because the next day altered everything. It somehow ended up under my bed. It reminded me that we still need to do Clara's. I know she probably doesn't feel like it, but it's tradition, so when I hear her up and showering, I pull out the craft supplies and set them on the table. I make a charcuterie board and set it on the table next to her birthday board because I doubt she'll feel like eating much, but she needs to eat something.

When she finally walks out of her room, I'm at the table on my laptop. She stares at her birthday board. I close my laptop, and surprisingly, she walks to the table and takes a seat without a fuss. She pops a grape into her mouth. We make eye contact, but neither of us speaks. She grabs a blue marker, and I grab a purple one.

She stares at her board—at all the things we've put on it over the years. I like it because her handwriting has evolved throughout the years. Her first goal was written in green crayon, spelled wrong. *"Americun Gurl dol."* It was a want rather than a goal, but she was young. She eventually learned the difference over time.

Clara begins to write something. It's not just one thing. It's several things. When she's finished, I lean forward and read the list.

1. I want my mother to see my boyfriend for who he really is.

2. I want my mother to be honest with me, and I want to be honest with her.

3. I want to be an actress, and I want my mother to support that dream.

Clara puts the lid back on her marker, pops another grape in her mouth, and walks into the kitchen to get a drink.

Her goals make me sigh. I can tackle the first one. I can pretend to tackle the second one. But the third one is tough for me. Maybe I'm too realistic. Too practical.

I follow her into the kitchen, and she's pouring herself a glass of ice water. She pops two aspirin and swallows. "I know you want me to major in something more practical, but at least I'm not running off to Los Angeles without getting a degree first," she says. "And I need to start looking at schools soon. I need to know what we can afford now that Dad is gone."

"What if we compromise? What if you get a degree in something more realistic, like psychology or accounting, and then after you graduate, you can move to Los Angeles and audition for roles while holding a *real* job."

"Acting *is* a real job," she says. She walks back to the table and takes a seat, selecting a piece of cheese to eat. She talks while she chews. "The way I see it, my life is going to go one of three ways."

"Which are?"

She holds up a finger. "I get a BFA in acting from the University of Texas. I try to become an actress. I succeed." She holds up another finger. "Or, I get a BFA in acting from the University of Texas. I try to become an actress. I fail. But at least I followed my dreams and can figure out where to go from there." She holds up a third finger. "Or. I follow *your* dreams, major in something I am absolutely not interested in, and spend the rest of my life blaming you for not encouraging me to follow my dreams."

She drops her hand and leans back in her chair. I stare at her a moment, soaking in everything she just said. I realize as I'm looking at her that something happened. I don't know when or if it was gradual or overnight, but something has changed in her significantly.

Or maybe something has changed in me.

Colleen Hoover

But she's right. The dreams I have for her life aren't nearly as important as the dreams she has for herself. I grab my marker and pull her birthday board toward me. I write, *"My dreams for Clara < Clara's dreams for herself."*

Clara reads it, and it makes her smile. She takes another bite of cheese and starts to get up from the table, but I don't want to be done yet. I feel like I may not get another opportunity to talk like this with her for a while.

"Clara, wait. There's something I want to talk to you about."

She doesn't take her seat. She grips the back of the chair—an indication she doesn't want this conversation to last long.

"Last night, you said something to me, and I want to know what you meant. It might have been the alcohol talking, but . . . you blamed yourself. You said the wreck was your fault." I shake my head in confusion. "Why would you think that?"

I see her swallow. "I said that?"

"You said a lot of things. But that one seemed to really upset you."

Clara's eyes immediately moisten, but she releases the chair and turns away. "I don't know why I said that." Her voice cracks as she walks across the living room, toward her bedroom.

For once, I can tell she's lying.

"Clara." I stand up and follow her. I reach her before she disappears down the hallway. When I spin her around, she's crying. It's heartbreaking, seeing her so upset, so I pull her to me, holding her, attempting to soothe her.

"I was texting Aunt Jenny when they had the wreck," she says. She's clinging to me like she's scared to let go. "I didn't know she was driving. One second, we were chatting, and then the next . . . she stopped responding." Clara's shoulders are shaking against me.

I can't believe she thinks it's her fault.

I pull away from her and hold her face in my hands. "Jenny wasn't even driving, Clara. It wasn't your fault."

She looks at me with shock. Disbelief. She shakes her head. "It was her car. You told me . . . at the hospital, you said she gave Dad a ride."

"I told you that, but I swear it was your father who was driving. He was driving Aunt Jenny's car. I never would have told you that if I knew you would think it was your fault."

Clara takes a step back, swallowed up in confusion. She wipes her eyes. "But why would you tell me that? Why would you say she was driving if she wasn't?"

It hits me that I have no idea how to back up the lie I told her. And I have no excuse for it either. And I'm a terrible liar. *Shit.* I shrug, trying to make it seem like it's less than it is. "I just . . . maybe I was confused? I can't remember." I take a step toward her and squeeze her hands. "But I promise I'm telling you the truth now. Your Aunt Jenny was in the passenger seat. I'll show you the accident report if you don't believe me, but I don't want you thinking this was your fault for another second."

Clara isn't crying anymore. She's looking at me with suspicion in her eyes. "Why was Dad driving Aunt Jenny's car?"

"He had a flat."

"No, he didn't. You're lying."

I shake my head, but I can feel my cheeks reddening. My pulse is racing. *Just let it go, Clara.*

"Why were they together, Mom?"

"They just were. He needed a ride." I turn to go back to the table. Maybe if I start cleaning, I won't start crying, but when I reach the table, my fearful tears begin to pour out. This is the last thing I wanted. The *last* thing.

"Mom, what aren't you telling me?" She's beside me now, demanding answers.

I turn to her, desperate. "Stop asking questions, Clara! *Please.* Just accept it and never ask about it again."

She takes a step back, as if I just slapped her. Her hand goes up to her mouth. "Were they . . ." There's no color left in her face. Not even her lips. She sits down in a chair and stares at the table for a moment. Then, "Where's Dad's car? If it was just a flat, why did we never get it back?"

I don't even know how to answer that.

"Why did you refuse to combine their funerals? They basically had all the same friends and family, so it made more sense, but you seemed so angry and kept demanding they be separate." Clara covers her face with her hands. "Oh my God." When she looks at me again, her eyes are pleading. She's shaking her head back and forth. "Mom?"

She's looking at me with fear.

I reach across the table. I want to shield her from this blow, but she's running toward her bedroom now. She slams her door, and I'll follow her in a second, but I need a moment. I grip the back of the chair and lean forward, trying to breathe slowly—to calm myself. *I knew this would kill her.*

She opens her bedroom door. I look up, and she's rushing back to me, full of more questions. I know exactly how she feels, because I'm still full of questions.

"What about you and Jonah? How long has that been happening?" There's an accusatory tone to her voice.

"We weren't . . . the night you walked in on us. That was the first time we ever even kissed. I swear."

She's crying now. She's pacing, like she doesn't know what to do with all the anger. Who to throw it at.

She clenches her stomach and stops pacing. "No. *Please*, no." She points at the front door. "That's why he left Elijah here? That's why he said he couldn't do it?" Clara is gasping now between tears. I pull her in for a hug, but it doesn't last. She pulls away from me. "Is Dad? Is Jonah not Elijah's father?"

I feel like my throat is so constricted noise can't even slide up it. I just whisper, "Clara. *Sweetie.*"

She sinks to the floor in a heap of tears. I lower myself and put my arms around her. She hugs me back, and as good as it feels to be needed by her right now, I'd give anything for this not to be happening. "Did you know? Before the wreck?"

I shake my head. "No."

"Did Jonah?"

"No."

"How did you . . . when did you find out about them?"

"The day they died."

Clara hugs me even harder. *"Mom."*

She says my name with such a guttural ache it's like she's needing something she knows I can't give her. A comfort I don't even know how to provide.

She pulls away from me and stands up. "I can't do this." She goes to her room and comes back with her purse and her keys.

She's hysterical. I can't let her drive a car like this. I walk over to her and take her keys out of her hand. She tries to snatch them back, but I don't let her have them.

"Mom, *please.*"

"You aren't leaving. Not when you're this upset."

Clara drops her purse in defeat and covers her face with her hands. She just stands there, crying to herself. Then she slides her hands down her face and looks at me with imploring eyes, dropping her arms to her sides. *"Please. I need Miller."*

Those words coupled with that look in her eyes—it all shatters me. It feels like my soul has been stomped on. But somehow, even beneath all the pain, I understand. Right now, I'm not what she needs. I'm not the solace she'll find the most comforting, and even though it feels like the death of a huge part of our relationship, I'm grateful to know there's someone out there who gives her that besides me.

I nod. "Okay. I'll take you to him."

CHAPTER THIRTY-FOUR

CLARA

Miller has a line of customers when I walk into the theater. As soon as he looks at me, I can tell he wants to jump over the counter. He looks worried but helpless. He holds up four fingers, so I nod and walk to theater four.

I sit in the closest seat to the door this time. I'm too tired to walk all the way to the top.

I stare at the blank screen, wondering why Jenny never decided to act. She'd have been good at it. My dad too.

I shake my head, lifting my T-shirt to wipe my eyes. I should feel relieved to know that my text didn't cause the wreck because Aunt Jenny wasn't even driving, but I don't feel any relief at all. I don't even feel anger. I feel like all my anger has been directed at my mother for so long that I don't even have any left. Right now, I just feel disappointed. Defeated.

It's as if all the romance novels I've ever read have turned into dystopian fantasies. My whole life, I thought I had these great examples of love and family and humanity around me, but it was all bullshit. The love I thought my father had for my mother was a lie. And the thing that bothers me the most about it is that half of me is made up of him.

Does that mean I'm capable of being the kind of human he was? The kind to betray your spouse and child while plastering a loving smile on your face for so many years?

I hear the door to the theater open. Miller walks over to me and then leans down to kiss me. I pull away. I don't feel like a kiss right now. Or maybe I don't feel like I deserve a kiss right now. Whatever this is I feel for him, it worries me that it's nothing more than manufactured signals from my brain that'll eventually fade.

Miller steps over me and sits down in the seat to my right. "Did I do something wrong?"

"No," I say, shaking my head. "But you will. I will. Everyone does. Everyone fucks up."

"Hey," he says, touching my cheek, pulling my teary eyes to his. "What happened?"

"My father had an affair with Aunt Jenny. Elijah is his. Not Jonah's."

My confession stuns him. He drops his hand and falls against his seat. "Shit."

It felt weird, saying it out loud.

"Does Jonah know?"

"He didn't know until after the wreck."

Miller lifts an arm and slips it behind me, despite my earlier hesitance to let him kiss me. He begins to gently rub my back. I lean into him, even though right now, I'm convinced that love is stupid and I'll probably break his heart someday.

I shake my head, still in disbelief as I think about it all. "I idolized my dad. I thought he was perfect. And *her*. She was my best friend."

Miller kisses me on top of the head. "How's your mother taking it?"

I don't know how to answer that, because looking back on it, I don't know how my mother even got out of bed after finding something like this out. For the first time since the wreck, I feel this ache for her—for what she went through. What she's still *going* through. "I have no idea how she's still functioning."

It kind of even makes sense now that she and Jonah would lean on each other through this. They had to. They were the only ones who knew, so who else could she have talked to about it besides Jonah?

We're quiet for a while. I'm trying to work through it. I think Miller is just giving me time to process everything. I don't expect him to give me advice. That's not why I'm here. I just needed to be near him. I wanted his arms around me.

It reminds me of all the times growing up, how my father would always comfort my mother. She didn't need it a lot, but sometimes I would see him holding her while she was upset.

Now I realize it was all fake. All those looks of concern he gave her—they weren't real. He was sleeping with her sister. How could he pretend to love her while doing something so incredibly vicious?

I trusted him more than I've ever trusted any man in the world. It makes me doubt everything. Everyone. Myself. Maybe even Miller. I don't even know what Miller's intentions actually were in the beginning.

I face him. "Would you have cheated on Shelby with me?"

He looks thrown off by my question. "No. Why?"

"That day in your truck. I thought maybe you wanted to."

Miller sighs heavily with a look of guilt on his face. "I was confused, Clara. I wanted to talk to you, but when you got in the truck with me, I didn't like how I was feeling. I wouldn't have cheated on her, but I can't say that I didn't have the urge."

"Do you still talk to her?"

He shakes his head, but the shake of his head is coupled with an eye roll. He looks like he's growing frustrated with me. It slams me right in the chest. Every time I'm angry, I find myself involving him somehow. I'd almost rather him break up with me than lose respect for me, but if I keep behaving this way, that's exactly what will happen.

"I'm sorry," I say. "All of this is messing with my head, and I don't know who to be mad at."

Miller brings my hand to his mouth. He kisses the back of it, giving it a reassuring squeeze.

"Remember when you thought I was epic?" I laugh at that. *How could anyone think I'm epic?*

"I still think you're epic," he says. "*Frustratingly* epic."

"Or epically frustrating. You started dating me at the absolute worst moment of my life. I'm sorry you've had to deal with all this shit."

He lifts his hand and gently cups my face. "I'm sorry *you've* had to deal with all this shit."

Sometimes when he says things to me, his words feel like they reach me through my chest rather than through my ears. I love that he's so understanding. So patient. I don't know where he gets it from, but maybe the more I'm around him, the more I'll become like him. "Imagine how great we'll be when I'm finally emotionally stable."

He pulls me into a hug. "You're great now, Clara. Damn near perfect."

"Near?"

"I'd say a nine out of ten."

"What's the reason for the one-point deduction?"

He sighs. "It's that pineapple on pizza, unfortunately."

I laugh, and then I lift the armrest that's separating us to snuggle against him. We're quiet for a while after that. He holds me while I try and work through my thoughts, but I know he can't stay here all night. After a few minutes, he kisses me on top of the head.

"I need to get back to work. It's not even my break right now, and the manager is on duty tonight."

"What time do you get off?"

"Not until nine."

"Can I stay until you get off work? I need a ride home."

"How'd you get here?"

"My mother dropped me off."

"Oh. She doesn't know I work here, huh?"

I nod. "She does. That's why she dropped me off here."

Miller raises an eyebrow. "Do I sense progress?"

"I hope."

He smiles and then kisses me. Twice. "There's a cartoon starting in theater three in about fifteen minutes. Want to go watch it while you wait for me?"

I crinkle up my nose. "A cartoon? I don't know."

He pulls me out of my seat. "You need something light right now. Go watch it, and I'll bring you food."

He holds my hand as we walk out of the theater. He walks me to the showing next door, but before I go in, I kiss him on the cheek. "One of these days, I'm going to be better for you," I say, squeezing his hand. "I promise."

"You're perfect just how you are, Clara."

"No, I'm not. I'm only a nine, apparently."

He's laughing as he backs away from me. "Yeah, but I really only deserve a six."

I find a seat far away from all the little kids, all the way at the top. Miller was wrong. I don't think the cartoon helps, because I can't stop thinking about what happened.

It isn't lost on me that my anger over finding out about my father and Jenny isn't nearly as intense as it was when I thought my mother and Jonah were the ones having the affair.

I contemplate that, and I realize it comes down to one thing. *Selflessness.*

It seems so insignificant, but it's not. My mother was put through the most maddening, painful, tragic event of her life. Yet, as always, she put me first. Before her anger, her grief, the betrayal. She did everything she could to shield me from the truth, even if that meant unfairly taking the blame.

I don't doubt my father's love for me, but I don't know that he would have done the same if the tables were reversed. I'm not sure Jenny would have either.

As devastated as I am to finally know the truth, it actually hurts less than when I thought my mother was the one in the wrong.

Since the day I was born, every decision she's ever made for herself was made in order to benefit me. I've always known that about her. But I'm not sure I appreciated it until tonight.

The cartoon has ended and the theater has cleared out, but I'm still staring hard at the blank screen, wondering how my mother is doing. She's the real victim in all of this, and it makes me sad to know that the two people she's leaned on for most of her life are the same two people who weren't there to catch her when she fell. Hell, they're the ones who made her fall in the first place.

I can't imagine all the invisible bruises she's covered in right now, and I hate that some of them are there because of me.

CHAPTER
THIRTY-FIVE

MORGAN

I called Jonah after I got home from dropping Clara off at the theater. It was ironic, because I needed him in much the same way Clara needed Miller. We talked for a while, but Elijah was already asleep, so he couldn't come over.

I would have gone to him, but I didn't want to be away from the house in case Clara came home.

Two hours have gone by, and I've done nothing but pace the floor and stare at the blank television screen, wondering how she's doing. Wondering if Miller is giving her the reassurance and comfort she needs right now.

Even if he is, I feel this emptiness in me, and it's creating a pull to go find her. After she's been gone for two and a half hours, I finally grab my keys and decide to drive myself back to the theater.

Miller is behind the concession stand when I walk inside. He's helping two customers, but I don't see Clara anywhere. I stand in line and wait until he's free. When he hands the customers their change and they step out of my way, he looks up and stiffens.

I like that I make him nervous, but I also hate it. I don't want to be unapproachable to someone my daughter cares so much about.

"Looking for Clara?" he asks.

I nod. "Yeah. Is she still here?"

He looks at the clock on the wall behind him, then nods. "Yeah, she should be alone in theater three. The movie ended fifteen minutes ago."

"She's . . . alone? Just sitting in a theater by herself?"

Miller smiles and pulls a cup off a stack, filling it with ice. "Don't worry, she likes it." He fills the cup with Sprite and hands it to me. "I've been busy, so I haven't been able to take her a refill. You want anything?"

"I'm good. Thank you."

I start to turn around but stop short when Miller says, "Mrs. Grant?"

He looks to his left, then his right, ensuring our privacy. He leans forward a little, looking me in the eyes. He presses his lips together nervously before he speaks. "I'm really sorry about sneaking into your house the other night. And for . . . all the other stuff. I really do care about her."

I try to see him for the first time without all the preconceived notions Chris had about him. I want to see him as Jonah sees him—like he's a good kid. Good enough to date Clara. I'm still not sure about that yet, but the fact that he's just given me what seems like a very genuine apology is a good start. I nod, giving him a small smile, then head toward theater three.

She's all the way at the top when I walk in. The lights are on, and she's staring straight ahead at the blank movie screen, her feet propped up on the seat in front of her.

She doesn't notice me until I start walking up the stairs toward the top row. When she does lay eyes on me, she sits up straighter and pulls her feet down. When I reach her, I hand her the Sprite and take a seat next to her.

"Miller thought you might need a refill."

She takes the Sprite and sips from it, moving her empty cup to the seat on the other side of her. Then she lifts the armrest between us and leans into me. It takes me by surprise. I wasn't sure what to expect from her. She's been through a lot tonight, and to be honest, I've been waiting for the aftershocks to hit. I take advantage of this rare moment of affection by wrapping my arm around her and pulling her to me.

I don't think either one of us really knows how to start the conversation. A few long seconds go by before Clara says, "Have you ever cheated on Dad?"

She doesn't ask it in an accusatory way. It's almost like she's just working through a thought, so I answer her honestly. "No. Up until Jonah, your father was the only guy I'd ever kissed."

"Are you angry at them? Dad and Jenny?"

I nod. "Yes. It hurts. A lot."

"Do you regret marrying him?"

"No. I got you."

She lifts her head. "I don't mean do you regret ever dating him or getting pregnant with me. But do you regret marrying him?"

I brush her hair from her forehead and smile. "No. I regret the choices he made, but I don't regret the choices *I* made."

She lays her head back down on my shoulder. "I don't want to hate him, but I'm mad that he did that to us. I'm mad that Aunt Jenny would do something like that to us."

"I know, Clara. But you have to understand that their affair had everything to do with us, but also absolutely nothing at all."

"It *feels* like it had everything to do with us."

"Because it did," I say.

"You just said it didn't."

"Because it doesn't," I say.

Clara lets out a short defeated laugh. "You're confusing me."

I urge her off my shoulder and turn in my seat a little so that we're facing each other. I take one of her hands in both of mine. "Your father was a great father to you. But as a husband, he made some shitty choices. No one can be the perfect everything."

"But he just *seemed* so perfect."

The betrayal in her eyes saddens me. I don't want her to go through life with this memory of Chris. I squeeze her hand. "I think that's the problem. Teenagers think their parents should have it all figured out, but the truth is, adults don't really know how to navigate life any better than teenagers do. Your father made some big mistakes, but the things he did wrong in his life shouldn't discredit all the things he did right. Same goes for your aunt Jenny."

A tear spills out of Clara's right eye. She wipes it away quickly. "Most mothers would want their daughters to hate their fathers for doing what Dad did."

"I'm not most mothers."

Clara's head falls back against the red velvet chair, and she looks up toward the ceiling. She laughs as tears continue rolling into her hair. "Thank God for that."

It wasn't a direct compliment, but it makes me feel good, nonetheless.

"If I tell you something, will you promise not to judge me?" she asks.

"Of course."

She tilts her head toward me, and there's a trace of guilt in her expression. "I was sitting in Miller's truck with him after school one day. It was before he broke up with his girlfriend. I wanted him to kiss me so bad, Mom. And I would have let him if he tried, which is what bothers me so much. I knew he had a girlfriend at the time, and I would have let him kiss me anyway. Now that I know what Dad and Aunt Jenny did, it worries me that being capable of an affair is a personality trait, and I got that from Dad. What if it's some kind of inheritable moral weakness?" She looks back up at the ceiling. "What if I cheat on Miller someday and break his heart like Dad and Aunt Jenny broke yours?"

I hate that she thinks this. That she's questioning herself. Sometimes Clara asks questions I can't answer, and I'm scared this may be one of them.

But then I think about Jonah and the connection I had with him when we were younger. Maybe talking to Clara about that is a bad idea, but this parenting shit didn't come with a handbook.

"I had a moment like that once. I was your age, and I was in a pool with Jonah."

Clara suddenly turns her head to look at me, but I keep staring up at the ceiling while I talk.

"We didn't kiss, but I wanted it to happen. I was dating your father at the time, and Jonah and Jenny had their thing, but when I looked at him in that moment, it's like a wall lifted and blocked everything else out. It isn't that I didn't care about Jenny or Chris—it's just that in that moment, I only cared about the way it felt to be looked at like that. The attraction I had for Jonah in that moment left me with blinders on. And I think he felt the same way."

"Is that why he broke up with Jenny and moved away?" Clara asks.

I tilt my head and look at her. "Yes," I say with complete honesty.

"Is that why you were so mad when he was back in Aunt Jenny's life?"

I nod. "Yeah, but I didn't realize it at the time. I never acknowledged I even had feelings for him until recently. I never would have done that to Jenny."

Clara frowns, and I hate seeing that look on her face. The look of realizing that someone so important to her could do something so terrible. The fear that she might be capable of doing the same thing someday.

I sigh and look back up at the ceiling. "I've had more time to mull over all of this than you have, so maybe I can share some of the wisdom that was born from all my anger. Think of it like this. Attraction isn't something that only happens once, with one person. It's part of what drives humans. Our attraction to each other, to art, to food, to entertainment. Attraction is fun. So when you decide to commit to someone, you aren't saying, *'I promise I'll never be attracted to anyone else.'* You're saying, *'I promise to commit to you, despite my potential future attraction to other people.'*" I look at Clara. "Relationships are hard for that very reason. Your body and your heart don't stop finding the beauty and the attraction in other people simply because you've made a commitment to one person. If you ever find yourself in a situation where you're drawn to someone else, it's up to you to remove yourself from that situation before it becomes too hard to fight."

"Like Jonah did?"

I nod. "Yeah. Exactly like that."

Clara stares at me a moment. "Dad couldn't remove himself from the situation with Jenny because she was always around. Maybe that's why it happened."

"Maybe."

"It's still not an excuse, though."

"You're right. It's not."

She lays her head back on my shoulder. I kiss the top of her head, but she doesn't see the tears that begin to roll down my cheeks. It just feels so good to finally have this conversation with her. It feels good to know that my daughter is a lot more emotionally equipped for the truth than I assumed she was.

"All the stuff I've done—it's not Miller's fault. He just tried to be there for me. I don't want you to hate him."

She doesn't need to convince me anymore. When I found out he tried to talk her out of having sex with him, I stopped hating him. And then when he apologized to me tonight, I actually started to like him. "I don't hate him. I actually kind of like him. I'd like him *more* if he never sneaks into your room again. But I do like him."

"He won't," she says. "I swear."

"Mrs. Nettle will tell on you, anyway."

She lifts her head. "Is that how you found out?"

"Sometimes it pays to have the nosiest neighbor alive."

Clara laughs, but when she sees my tears, her smile fades. I wave it off. "They're good tears. I promise."

She shakes her head. "My God. We have been *so* mean to each other."

I nod in agreement. "I didn't think we had it in us."

"You grounded me from reading *books*," she says, laughing.

"You called me predictable."

"Well, you definitely proved me wrong."

Somehow, we're both smiling. I'm appreciative she took the news so well. I realize her feelings could change again tomorrow. She'll go through a lot of emotions, I'm sure. But for right now, I'm grateful to have this moment with her.

Maybe that's something I need to learn to cherish a little more. Our relationship isn't always going to be sunshine and roses, but whenever there's a break in the storm, I need to take advantage of those breaks. No matter what mood I'm in or what's going on in my own life, I need to bask in these moments of sunshine with Clara.

"Can we start with a clean slate? Like . . . can we just forget the weed and the detention and the alcohol and the skipping school? I really want my phone back."

"That's not all you did wrong," I say.

"I know, but I was running out of breath. The list is *really* long."

Despite everything she's gone through, I'm still convinced she needs to be grounded. But she's not the only one who wants to start with a clean slate. I'm not exactly proud of my own behavior.

"I'll tell you what. I'll give you back your phone if you promise to stop making fun of me for preferring cable TV over streaming."

Clara stares at me very seriously. "Oh, man. I don't know . . ."

"Clara!"

She laughs. "Fine. Deal."

CHAPTER THIRTY-SIX

CLARA

My mother and I walk out of the theater holding hands. Miller is at the far end of the hallway, emptying a trash can. My mother doesn't see him, but I do. Right before we turn to walk toward the exit, Miller smiles at me.

This moment isn't even about me and him, but there's something about the way he's looking at me right now that feels like he might have just fallen in love with me.

I smile back at him, knowing I'll remember this three-second silent exchange forever.

CHAPTER THIRTY-SEVEN

MORGAN

This morning when I woke up, it was the first day since the accident that our house wasn't filled with tension. I was up studying real estate terms for my upcoming job interview, and Clara hugged me before she rushed out the door with a Pop-Tart.

After school, she texted and said she was working on her film project with Miller. Whether she's telling the truth, I don't know. But she's seventeen. She has a curfew, so as long as she meets it, I'm not going to press her for details on what she and Miller do when they're together. I already know she's on birth control, and I'm pretty sure they're not actively having sex, thanks to her drunken admission.

I'll bring it up soon, but when the timing is right. I want to ease into this new dynamic we have. If I jar her too much, she might pull back again, and that's the last thing I want.

I invited Jonah over for dinner. It was nice. We sat at the breakfast nook and took turns feeding Elijah, laughing at his excitement over trying new foods.

Elijah is now on a pallet on the living room floor, playing with a couple of baby toys Jonah set out for him.

Jonah and I are on the couch. He's lying against the arm of it, his legs spread out to fit me between them. My back is against his chest, and we're both watching Elijah play on the floor.

Jonah's left arm is draped over my stomach, and every now and then he'll press a kiss against the side of my head as we chat. The more he does it, the more used to it I get and the less guilt I feel. I want him to keep doing it until I finally feel no guilt at all. I think that'll take a few more months, though.

I sigh at that thought, so naturally, Jonah says, "What's wrong?"

"I just worry too much, I think. I worry that their betrayal will cause us to never fully trust each other."

"I'm not worried." He says it with such confidence.

"Why?"

"Because. We've never been with the person we belonged with until now."

I tilt my head back so I can see him. Then I kiss him for that.

He brushes his thumb over my lip and regards me with a serene look. I'm not sure it's a look I've ever seen emanate from Jonah Sullivan. He's spent a long time fighting something he no longer has to fight, and the peace within him shows. "We'll be fine, Morgan. More than fine. I promise."

The front door opens, and Jonah and I both react. Clara wasn't supposed to be home for another hour. I sit up on the couch, and Jonah pulls his legs out from under me.

Clara pauses in the doorway, staring at us. Then she closes the door. "You don't have to pretend anymore." She drops her purse and walks over to the floor. She sits down next to Elijah.

Jonah looks at me, silently asking if they should leave. Clara sees the look he gives me. She reaches for Elijah and picks him up, leaning with her back against the couch opposite from us. "Stay," she says to Jonah while looking at Elijah. "I want to play with him for a little while."

Jonah and I are silent as we watch her. We don't know what mood to expect. Last night was good between us, and so was this morning. But we haven't confronted this thing between me and Jonah with her yet. I'm not sure we're ready to, because Jonah and I haven't even really confronted it.

Clara is holding Elijah, trying to get him to repeat sounds she's making.

"Has he said any words yet?" she asks, looking up at Jonah.

"Not yet. It'll be a few more months before he can do that."

Clara looks down at Elijah and starts making more sounds. "Can you say *Dada*?"

He kicks his legs against her stomach, bouncing and making random noises. Then, to our astonishment, he repeats her. He says it so perfectly that no one moves a muscle because I think we're all doubting what we heard.

Then Jonah says, "Did he just . . ."

Clara nods. "I think he did."

Jonah leaves the couch and sits down next to Clara on the floor. He's too young to be repeating words willingly, but I move closer to them anyway in case he does it again. I sit on the floor on the other side of Clara.

She repeats herself. "Dada?" She tries to get Elijah to mimic the sound again, but he just makes lots of other sounds instead. I know it was a fluke, but the timing couldn't have been more perfect.

Clara tilts Elijah so that he's facing Jonah. "There's your dada, right there," she says.

I don't know if it's hearing Clara refer to Jonah as Elijah's dad that does it, or hearing the word come out of Elijah's mouth, but Jonah's eyes begin to spill over with tears.

As soon as I see the first tear roll down his cheek, *I* start to cry.

Clara looks at Jonah, then looks at me, then back at Jonah. "Great. I thought I was done with the tears."

Now *she's* crying.

I watch Clara, and even though she's crying, she's playing with Elijah with a smile on her face. Then she does something unexpected. She sighs and leans her head on Jonah's shoulder.

It may not seem like much to her, but it means the world to me. The gesture is more than any words could ever be worth.

It's her telling him she's sorry. Sorry for what Chris did to him. Sorry for thinking it was our fault.

That one little move makes me cry even harder. I think it makes Jonah cry harder, too, because as soon as she pulls her head from his shoulder, he's looking the other way, trying to hide it.

Elijah is the only one who isn't crying out of the four of us.

"Wow," Jonah says, blowing out a breath. He uses his shirt to wipe at his eyes. "We're such a mess."

"The messiest," Clara says.

We all sit on the floor like that for a while, playing with Elijah. Laughing at the faces he makes. Laughing when he laughs. Trying to get him to say *Dada* again, but he doesn't.

"What are you going to tell Elijah about all of this?" Clara asks.

"The truth," Jonah says.

Clara nods. "Good. The truth is always the best choice." She kisses Elijah on the cheek. "I've always wanted a little brother. Maybe in a more conventional way, but this will do."

I like that she's mature enough to separate the reason for Elijah's existence from her love for him. Resentment is a heavy load to carry through life.

I've been full of pride these last twenty-four hours. Watching her handle all of this with such grace and maturity makes me so proud of her.

Elijah yawns, so Jonah begins packing up his stuff to leave. I help him, but when we're both standing at the door, prepared to say good night, it's awkward. I want to walk him out, but I don't know what Clara would think of that.

I can tell Jonah wants to kiss me, but he wouldn't do it in front of Clara.

"Good night," he whispers. He winces, like it hurts him to walk away from me without a kiss, since he's had to do that so many times before.

"Oh, come *on*, you guys," Clara says, sensing the awkwardness. "It's weird, but whatever, I'll get used to it."

Relief spreads across both our faces, so I walk Jonah out after we have Clara's permission.

After Jonah has Elijah in the car, he closes the door, wraps his arm around my waist, and spins me so that my back is against his car door. He kisses me on the cheek.

I feel nothing but relief as he holds me. The last few days could have gone wrong in so many more ways, but they didn't. Maybe that's thanks to Clara. Or Jonah. Or all of us. I don't know.

"She's amazing," he says.

"Yeah, she is. I forget how hard it is being a teenager. Especially one in her position. I feel like I continue to diminish the hormones and emotions that come along with being that age."

"You've been incredibly patient with her through all of this."

His compliment makes me laugh. "You think? Because I feel like I lost my mind a few times."

"I can only hope to be half the parent you are, Morgan."

"You're raising a child that isn't biologically yours. That already makes you twice the parent I am."

Jonah pulls back, smiling down on me. "I like it when you compliment my parenting. It's kinda hot."

"Same. Watching you be a good dad is the thing I find most attractive about you."

"We're so weird," he says.

"I know."

Jonah threads his fingers through mine and wraps our hands behind my back, pressing them against his car. He kisses my cheek. "Can I ask you a question?" He feathers his lips across my cheek until they come to rest against my mouth. I nod. He pulls back, but just far enough that we're able to look at each other. "Will you be my girlfriend?"

I stare at him for two seconds before laughter erupts from my chest. "Do guys still do that? Ask people to be their girlfriends?"

He shrugs. "I don't know. But I've been wishing I could ask you that for a hell of a long time now, so it'd be nice if you would just humor me with a yes."

I lean forward, brushing my lips against his. "*Hell*, yes."

He releases my hands, bringing his up to cup my face. "I want to kiss you, but I'm not gonna use tongue because then I won't be able to stop kissing you. I don't want Clara thinking we're out here making out."

"But we are."

"Yeah, but it's still weird for her, I'm sure." He gives me a quick peck. "Go inside and act natural."

I laugh, then wrap my hands around his head and pull him to my mouth. He groans when our tongues meet and pushes me harder against his car. We kiss for an entire minute. Then two.

When he finally pulls back, he shakes his head a little while running his eyes over my features. "It's surreal," he says. "I gave up on the thought of us so long ago."

"And I never even allowed myself to think we were a possibility."

He smiles, but it feels like a sad smile. He slides both his hands down my back. "I'd give it all back if it meant they didn't have to die.

As happy as I am to be with you, I never wanted it to happen this way. I hope you know that."

"Of course I know that. You don't even have to say it."

"I know. I guess I'm still grappling with it all. I'm happy to finally have you, but I also feel guilty because of the way I got you." He pulls my head against his chest. I slide my arms around his waist, and we hold each other like that for a while. "Part of me wonders if you really want this. *Me.* I would understand if you didn't. It's a lot to take on. I don't have the money Chris had, and I also come with an infant. It'd be like starting over for you, and maybe you want time for yourself now. I don't know. But I'd understand. I want you to know that."

I want to shake my head and disagree with him immediately, but I think about what he's saying. If we do this, I'll be raising another child. I'll be committing to a whole new life, right after the only life I've known has been altered so drastically. For most people, they'd need more time to adjust. Especially going from such a long marriage to a brand-new relationship in the span of just a few months. I can see where Jonah might expect some hesitation on my part.

I close my eyes and roll my head until my face is pressed directly against Jonah's chest. I can feel his heart racing.

I slide my hand up his shirt, moving it across his chest until my palm is right over his heart. I keep it there for a moment, paying attention to the extreme rate it's pumping blood through his body. I can tell by the speed and the strength of his heartbeats that he's full of fear right now.

It makes me sad, because if there's one thing Jonah Sullivan shouldn't have to worry about, it's the way I feel about him. But I've never actually expressed to him all the whys.

I lift my head, coming eye to eye with him as I tell him everything he deserves to hear. "When we were teenagers, you're the only one who used to laugh at my jokes. And you used to hide it, like it would give away how you felt about me. I always watched for your reaction, though. And sometimes Chris and I would get into arguments, but I noticed you never used that as an opportunity to try and break us up. You would just listen to me vent, and then you'd remind me of all the great things about him. And when Jenny got pregnant last year, I honestly didn't think you would step up. But you did. And then the night you came back for Elijah after finding out he wasn't biologically yours . . . I think that's when I fell in love with you as a complete person. It was no longer just pieces of you I loved. I loved you as a whole."

I don't want him to feel like he has to follow that up with anything. I already know how he feels about me. How he's felt about me. It's his turn to understand how it feels to know that he's always been someone's first choice.

I pull my hand from his shirt and bring it up to his cheek. "I married Chris because he was the father of my child, and I wanted to make it work. I did love him," I add. "And I'll always love Jenny too. But you're the first and only person in this world I've ever loved without some reasoning or justification behind it. I just love you because I can't help it, and it feels good to love you. The idea of getting to raise Elijah with you makes me happy. And I know before we made love for the first time, I told you I'd regret it, but I've never been more wrong. I didn't regret it that night, and I don't regret it now. I'm confident that I'll never spend a single second of my life regretting you."

I lift up on my toes and kiss him softly on the lips. "I love you, Jonah. So much." I slip around him and walk to my house. When I open my front door, I glance back, and Jonah is standing in the driveway, smiling at me.

It's a beautiful thing.

I close the door, and for the first time in my entire life, my corners are beginning to feel like they're filling up. Jonah already fills all the parts of my life that always felt so empty with Chris.

And I'm proud of Clara and the woman she's turning into. It was a bumpy ride to get here, but she's had a tougher road than most kids her age. My sense of pride as her mother has returned.

I'm still not quite sure what I want to be or what career I want to go into, but the last couple of months of figuring it out have been exciting to me. Getting a job and going back to college is something I've been wanting to do for a while, but for some reason I've always felt it was too late. It's not, though. I'm a work in progress. Maybe I always will be. I'm not sure I'll ever feel like a final draft, and I'm not sure I want to. The search for myself is becoming my favorite part of my new journey.

I recall what I wrote on my birthday board: *Find your passion.* Maybe I don't have just one passion. Maybe I have several, and I've just never made myself and my wants a priority. The idea that I have the rest of my life to figure myself out is exciting. There are so many things I want to try, whether they work out or not. I think finding my passion *is* my passion.

—

After Jonah leaves and Clara goes to bed, I go to my room and pull out all the letters from Jenny that Chris kept locked away in his toolbox. Since the day I found out the truth, so many questions have gone through my head. I used to think I needed the answers, but I no longer need them. I know that I loved the best versions of Jenny and Chris. But they fell in love with the worst versions of each other—the versions capable of betrayal and lies.

I'm always going to have memories of them because they were a huge part of my life. But these letters are not my memories of them. They aren't ones I want to know or keep in any capacity.

One by one, I rip them into tiny shreds without reading them.

I'm content with the direction in which my life is headed, and I know if I obsess over the past, that obsession will only serve to anchor me in a place I am more than ready to move on from.

I toss all the torn pieces of their history into my bathroom trash can. When I look up, I'm met with my reflection in the bathroom mirror.

I'm starting to look happy again. *Truly* happy.

It's a beautiful thing.

CHAPTER THIRTY-EIGHT

CLARA

A few months later

I walk to the back of the living room and slip my hand inside Miller's. We're both nervous. We've worked so hard on this film, and I really want Jonah to like it.

My mother turns out the lights and takes a seat on the couch next to Lexie and Efren. Jonah is seated at the edge of the love seat, anticipating the video more than any of them.

We decided in the end to make a mockumentary. There was way too much seriousness in our lives when we started this film, so I really wanted something fun for a change.

Our time limit for the entire thing is just a few minutes, so it was harder than we thought to execute something with a beginning, middle, and end in such a short amount of time, but I'm hoping we pulled it off. We just don't know if anyone else will appreciate the humor in it.

Miller looks at me, and I can see the nervous energy in him. We smile at each other when the film begins to play.

The screen is black, but then words flash across it in bright-orange letters, revealing the title: *CHROMOPHOBE.*

The scene opens on a character, aged seventeen. The name *KAITLYN* flashes across the screen. Kaitlyn (played by me) is sitting in an empty room on a stool. A light shines on her as she stares off camera, nervously wringing her hands together.

Someone off camera says, "Can you tell us how it all started?"

Kaitlyn glances into the camera with transfixed fear. She nods nervously. "Well . . ." It's obviously hard for her to discuss. "I think I was five, maybe? Six? I don't know exactly . . ." The camera zooms in closer to her face. "But . . . I remember every word of their conversation as if it happened just this morning. My mom and dad . . . they were standing in the living room, staring at the wall. They had all these . . . these . . . plastic paint swatches in their hands. They were trying to decide on a shade of white to paint the walls. And that's when it happened." Kaitlyn swallows but continues, despite her reluctance. "My mother looked at my father. She just . . . *looked* at him like the words about to come out of her mouth weren't about to ruin our family forever." Kaitlyn, obviously disgusted by the memory, wipes away a tear that's sliding down her cheek. She sucks in a deep breath and then continues speaking on the exhale. "My mother looked at him and said, *'How about orange?'"*

Her own recollection causes Kaitlyn to shudder.

The screen fades to black, then cuts to a new character. An elderly man, gaunt and gloomy. The name *PETER* flashes across the screen. This character is played by Gramps.

Peter is sitting in a green midcentury modern chair. He's picking at the chair with his frail fingers, loosening some of the fuzz. It falls to the floor.

Again, a voice somewhere off camera is heard. "Where would you like to begin, Peter?"

Peter glances into the camera with dark almond eyes encased in years of accumulated wrinkles, all different in depths and lengths. The whites of his eyes are bloodshot. "I'll begin at the beginning, I suppose."

The screen cuts to a flashback . . . to a younger version of Peter, in his late teens. He's in an older house, in a bedroom. There's a Beatles poster hanging over the bed. The teen is rummaging through his closet, frustrated. Older Peter's voice begins to narrate the scene.

"I couldn't find my lucky shirt," he says.

The scene playing out on-screen is of the frustrated teen (played by Miller), walking out of his room and then out the back door.

"So . . . I went to find my mother. To ask her if she'd seen it, ya know?"

The mother is standing at a clothesline in the backyard, hanging up a sheet.

"I said, *'Mom? Where's my blue shirt?'*"

The screen is back on the older version of Peter now. He's staring down at his hands, twiddling his thumbs. He blows out a quick breath, bringing his eyes back to the camera. "She looked right at me and said, *'I haven't washed it yet.'*"

The screen now shows the teenage boy again. He's staring at his mother in utter disbelief. He brings his hands to the sides of his head.

"That's when I realized . . . ," Peter's voice-over says. "I was left with only one option."

The camera follows the teenage boy as he stomps back into his house, back to his room, and back to his closet. His hands push apart the clothes in his closet until the camera is focused on a lone shirt, just hanging there, swaying front to back.

"It was the only clean shirt I had."

The camera is back on older Peter. He presses his sweaty palms against his thighs and leans his head back against his old green chair. He stares up at the ceiling in thought.

A voice from off set calls out to him. "Peter? Do you need a break?"

Peter leans forward, shaking his head. "No. No, I just want to get it over with." He releases a puff of air, looking back at the camera. "I did what I had to do," he says with a shrug.

The camera follows the teenage boy as he rips the shirt off the hanger. He yanks the dirty T-shirt he was wearing off and then angrily puts on the clean shirt he just removed from the closet.

"I *had* to wear it." Old Peter is staring at the camera now with a stoic expression. "I couldn't go shirtless. It was the *fifties*." He repeats himself in a whisper. "I had to wear it."

A question comes from off set. "What color was the shirt, Peter?"

Peter shakes his head. The memory is too difficult.

"Peter," the off-camera voice urges. "What color was the shirt?"

Peter blows out a frustrated breath. "Orange. It was *orange*, okay?" He looks away from the camera, ashamed.

The screen fades to black.

The next scene opens on a new character, professional in dress. She has long blonde hair, and she's wearing a crisp white shirt. She's straightening out her shirt when she looks at the camera. "We ready?" she asks.

"Whenever you are," the off-camera voice says.

She nods. "Okay, then. I'll just start?" She's looking at someone else for direction. Then she looks at the screen. "My name is Dr. Esther Bloombilingtington. I am a chromophobia expert."

A voice off camera says, "Can you define that term?"

Dr. Bloombilingtington nods. "Chromophobia is a persistent and irrational fear of color."

"What color, specifically?" the off-camera voice asks.

"Chromophobia presents itself differently in every patient," she says. "Sometimes patients have a fear of blue, or green, or red, or pink, or yellow, or black, or brown, or purple. Even white. No color is off limits, really. Some patients may even find themselves fearing a *number* of colors, or, in more severe cases . . ." She looks deadpan into the camera. "*All* colors."

The off-camera voice poses another question. "But you aren't here to speak about any of those colors today, are you?"

Dr. Bloombilingtington shakes her head, looking back into the camera. "No. Today, I'm here for one reason. One color that has resulted in alarmingly consistent results." She lifts her shoulders with an intake of breath. Her shoulders fall as she begins to speak again. "The results of this study are important, and I feel this needs to be shared with the world."

"What needs to be shared?"

"Based on our findings, we have discovered that the color orange is not *only* the cause of most cases of chromophobia, but our research proves beyond the shadow of a doubt that orange is, by *far*, the absolute worst color of all colors."

The off-camera voice asks, "And what proof do you have of this?"

Dr. Bloombilingtington looks very seriously into the camera. "Aside from several dozen likes on our Twitter research polls and quite a few views on our Instagram stories regarding this subject, we also have . . . the *people*. The people and their stories." She leans forward, narrowing her eyes as slow, dramatic music begins to play. "Just *listen* to their *stories*."

The camera cuts to black.

The next scene opens back up on the first character, Kaitlyn. She's holding Kleenex now as she speaks. "As soon as my mother said those words to my father . . ." She lifts her eyes and looks at the camera. "He . . . he *died*."

She brings the Kleenex to her eyes. "He just . . . he looked at her, shocked that she would even *suggest* orange as a color for the living room walls. As soon as she said it, he dropped all the little plastic color swatches on the floor, and he grasped at his heart and he just . . . he *died*."

Kaitlyn has a look of bewilderment on her face. "The last word he ever heard spoken aloud . . . was *orange*." A sob breaks from her chest.

She shakes her head back and forth. "I'll never be able to forgive my mother. Who suggests *orange* as a *wall* color? It's the last thing he heard. The *last thing*!"

The camera goes black immediately after her outburst.

It opens on a flashback of young Peter, driving in an older blue truck. He's wearing the orange shirt. His face is twisted and contorted with anger.

"I wanted to wear the blue shirt but had no choice," older Peter narrates. "I knew Mary preferred blue. She'd even said it to me the day I asked her out. I told her I liked her yellow dress, and she twirled around for me and said, *'Isn't it pretty?'* I nodded, and then she said, *'I like your shirt, Peter. Blue looks good on you.'*"

The camera is focused on old Peter now, sitting in his green chair. His eyes are even more bloodshot than they were in the beginning. "When I showed up at the theater . . . she was standing out front. Alone. I parked the truck, turned it off, and I just watched her. She looked so pretty, standing there in her yellow dress."

The flashback shows young Peter, sitting in his truck, wearing his orange shirt while he watches a pretty girl waiting, alone, wearing a yellow dress. He winces.

"I just couldn't do it. I couldn't let her see me like that."

Young Peter cranks his truck and begins pulling out of the parking lot.

The camera switches to old Peter now, in his green chair. "*What* was I supposed to *do*?" He's so angry he's rising out of his seat, but he's too old to come to a full stand. "I couldn't just walk up to her in that shirt! Leaving was my *only choice*!"

He falls back into his chair. He shakes his head, obviously regretting a choice that had a profound impact on the rest of his life.

"Peter?"

Peter looks up to the right of the camera, at whoever belongs to the off-set voice.

"Can you tell us what happened to Mary?"

Peter winces, his eyes somehow finding a way to pull in even more wrinkles.

"What happened to Mary, Peter?"

Peter half stands again, angry, throwing an arm out. "She married Dan Stanley! *That's* what happened!" He falls into his seat again, sadness consuming him. "They met that night . . . at the theater. The night I was supposed to take her out in my blue shirt. They fell in love. Ended up having three kids and some goats. Or sheep. Heck, I can't remember. They had a lot of 'em, though. I used to have to drive by their farm on my way to work every day, and them darned animals looked so . . . *healthy*. Like Dan Stanley took real good care of 'em. Just like he took good care of Mary, even though she was supposed to be *mine*."

Peter reaches over to an end table next to his chair. He grabs a Kleenex. Blows his nose. "Now here I am." He waves his hand around the room as if he has nothing to show from his life. "Alone." He wipes his nose again, looking into the camera. It zooms in on his face. There's a long, awkward pause. Then Peter says, "I don't want to talk about this anymore. I'm done."

The screen goes black again.

The next scene opens on Dr. Bloombilingtington, her eyebrows drawn together in concern.

"What do you hope people gain from this documentary?" the off-set voice asks her.

She looks into the camera. "What I hope for . . . the only *thing* I hope for . . . is that everyone watching this comes together in the banning of this atrocious color. Not only does orange ruin lives, but the word doesn't even *rhyme* with anything. People *try* to rhyme words with orange, but . . . there's no perfect rhyme. There just *isn't*." The camera zooms in on her face. Her voice is a serious whisper. "There never *will* be."

The screen goes black.

New words flash across the screen in every color *but* orange. They say, If you or someone you know has ever seen the color orange or spoken the word orange out loud, you could be a sufferer of chromophobia. Please contact a psychiatrist for an official diagnosis. If you would like to donate to or be a part of our campaign efforts in the banning of this color from our language and our world, please email us at TheColorThatShallNotBeNamedCampaign@gmail.com.

The screen goes black.

The credits begin to roll, but there are only three of them, since me, Miller, and his gramps played every role.

Miller held my hand through the whole thing. His palm is sweating. I know the entire video is only five minutes long, but it felt longer. It certainly took a lot longer to make.

The room is quiet. I'm not sure if that's a good or a bad sign. I look over at Jonah, but he's still staring at the television.

Lexie and Efren are staring at the floor.

My mother is the first to speak. "That was . . ." She looks to Jonah for help, but he's still staring at the TV. She continues talking. "That was . . . *unexpected*. The quality was great. And the acting. I mean . . . I don't know. You asked for honesty, so . . . I don't get it. Maybe I'm too old."

Lexie shakes her head. "No, it's not about age, because I am so confused right now."

"It's a *mockumentary*," Miller says defensively. "They're supposed to make fun of documentaries. They're *funny*."

Efren nods. "I laughed."

"No, you didn't," Miller says. He walks over to the light and flips it on.

I'm still waiting for Jonah to say something. He finally looks away from the television, bringing his eyes to the two of us. He just stares for a silent moment.

But then . . . he starts to clap.

It's slow at first, but the clap picks up speed as he stands. He starts to laugh, and I can sense Miller finally begin to ease up with Jonah's reaction. "That was *brilliant!*" Jonah says. He puts his hands on his hips and stares back at the television. "I mean . . . the quality. The acting." He looks back at us. "Who played Peter?"

"That's my grandpa," Miller says.

"*So* good," Jonah says. "I thought it was fantastic. I think you two might have a shot with this one."

"Are you just being nice?" my mom asks Jonah. "I can't tell."

"No. I mean, I think we all went into it thinking it was going to be something a lot more serious. Maybe something more personal. But when I realized it was a mockumentary, I was speechless at how well you pulled it off. You nailed it. Both of you."

Miller and I both sigh with relief. We worked so hard on it. And I know it's silly, but that's the point.

I'm not offended that no one else understood it. We really only cared what Jonah thought, because his name is going on it as the sponsoring teacher.

Miller scoops me up into a hug. I can feel the relief emanating from him as he sighs against my neck. "I'm so glad that's over," he says. "I thought he was going to hate it."

I'm relieved too.

This is good.

Miller goes to the laptop that's hooked up to the TV. "Okay, I have one more video."

I tilt my head, confused. "But we only made the one . . ."

Miller looks at me and grins. "This one's a surprise."

He pulls up a different file, and as soon as the television connects to his computer, Miller rushes to the lights and turns them off.

I don't know what he's up to.

I'm still standing in the back of the living room when Miller wraps his arms around me from behind. He rests his chin on my shoulder.

"What is this?"

"Shh," he says. "Just watch."

The film opens with Miller staring at the camera. He's holding it himself, pointing it at his own face. He waves. "Hey, Clara." He sets the camera down. He's in his bedroom. He takes a seat on his bed and says, "Okay, so I know you said you don't like anything elaborate, but . . . I kind of started this before you told me that. So . . . I hope you like it."

The screen goes black and opens up to footage of the two of us. It's all the B-roll he's taken over the last several months. Clips of us sitting against the tree at the park. Clips of us working on our video submission. Clips of us at school, at his house, at my house.

The montage of clips ends, and in the next scene, it actually has sound. It's Miller, fumbling with the camera. He's at his truck, and he slams the door, pointing the camera at himself. "Hey, Clara. I think you should go to prom with me." He whispers it when he says it, then sets the camera up on the tripod. He points it at me.

It was the first day he had set up the camera, when we were at the food truck. He walks away to go order our sandwiches, and the footage shows me making silly faces at the camera.

The next scene is the day we skipped school. He's setting the camera up, pointing it at the tree. I'm leaning against the tree, staring out at the water. Miller isn't in the shot at first, but then he sticks his face in front of the camera. "Hey, Clara," he whispers in a hurry. "You should go to prom with me." Then he backs away from the camera and slips between me and the tree, like nothing was amiss.

I had no idea he was doing any of this. I turn around to look at him, but he urges me to keep watching the television.

The next three scenes are all from while we've dated, with him sneaking in random promposals while we're together and me having no idea he was doing it.

Then a scene opens up to him standing in line at Starbucks. He points his camera at me. I'm sitting alone in a corner, reading a book.

Oh my God. This is the first day we kissed.

Miller turns the camera back on himself as he's standing in the Starbucks line. "You're so cute, sitting over there reading your book," he whispers. "I think you should go to prom with me."

"Miller," I whisper. I try to turn around and look at him again, but he doesn't want me to take my eyes off the television. I'm just in shock. I wasn't expecting any of the footage to be from before we were dating.

In the next scene, Miller is outside, leaning against a pole. I don't recognize the location at first, but when he wipes away beads of sweat from his forehead and pulls the sucker from his mouth, I realize he's standing in front of the city limit sign. He's looking into his camera when he says, "*So.* Clara Grant. You just drove by, and I know you saw me standing out here on the side of the road. Here's the deal. I have a girlfriend, but I stopped thinking about her when I go to bed at night, and Gramps says that's a bad sign and that I should break up with her. I mean, I have had a thing for you for a long time now, and I feel like I'm running out of opportunity. So I'll make you a deal. If you turn your car around at the bottom of that hill and come back, I'm gonna take that as a sign, finally listen to my gut, break up with my girlfriend, and eventually ask you out. I might even ask you to prom this year. But if you *don't* turn your car around, then I'll assume you and I just weren't meant to—" His eyes flash up, and he catches sight of something. He grins and then looks back down at his phone. "Look at that. You came back."

That portion of the video ends, and now I'm crying.

When the next scene begins, I don't recognize it at all. The camera is pointed at the floor and then at Gramps.

Gramps looks a few years younger in this video. Healthier than he looks now. "Get that out of my face," Gramps says.

Miller turns the camera on himself. He looks younger too. He's skinny, probably about fifteen. "Gramps is excited for the show," Miller says sarcastically into the camera. Then he points his camera toward the stage.

My heart is thundering in my chest when I recognize the set.

My mind also starts to race. Twice, Miller's grandpa tried to tell me about something that happened when they were at the school when Miller was fifteen. And twice, Miller was so embarrassed by it he shut him up.

Miller kisses the side of my head because he knows I've been wanting to know this story since the first day I met Gramps.

The camera cuts off. When it cuts on again, it's the same night, but it's the end of the play. The camera is on me now. I'm fourteen, standing onstage by myself, delivering a monologue. The camera slowly pans away from me and onto Miller.

His gramps must be holding the camera now.

Miller is staring at the stage. He's leaning forward, his hands clasped beneath his chin. The camera zooms in on him as he watches me onstage. The camera stays there for a solid minute. Miller is hanging on to every word I'm saying onstage, completely engrossed. Gramps never once takes the camera off him, but Miller has no idea his gramps is filming him.

The monologue is the end of the play, so when I deliver my last line, everyone in the audience begins to clap.

Miller doesn't.

He's immobile. "Wow," he whispers. "She is incredible. *Epic.*"

That's when he looks at his grandpa and sees the camera pointed in his direction. He tries to snatch the camera out of Gramps's hand, but Gramps pulls it away. He angles the camera so that it's showing both of them. Miller rolls his eyes at his grandpa when he says, "I think you just fell in love."

Miller laughs. "Shut up."

"You did, and I got it on camera." He points the camera at Miller again and says, "What's her name?"

Miller shrugs. "Not sure. Clara, I think?" He opens the playbill and scrolls through it, pausing on my name. "Clara Grant. She played the role of Nora."

His grandpa is still filming him. Miller isn't even denying what his grandpa is saying. Everyone in the audience is now clapping for the actors as they walk out onstage, but Miller is staring at the camera. "You can stop now."

His grandpa laughs. "I think it's cute. Maybe you should ask her out."

Miller laughs. "Yeah, right. She's a ten. I'm like a four. Maybe a five."

Gramps turns the camera on himself. "I'd give him a solid six."

"Turn it *off*," Miller says again.

Gramps smiles at the camera. He points it at Miller one more time. When they announce my name and it's my turn to take a bow onstage, Miller bites his lip, trying to hide his smile.

"You look lovesick," Gramps says. "Damn shame, because she's out of your league."

Miller faces the camera. He laughs and doesn't even try to hide the fact that he seems smitten. He leans forward, closer to the camera, looking directly into it. "One of these days, that girl is gonna notice me. You just wait."

"I'm not immortal," Gramps says. "Neither are you."

Miller looks back at the stage and laughs. "You're the worst grandpa I have."

"I'm the only grandpa you have."

"Thank God," Miller says, laughing.

Then the camera cuts off.

Tears are streaming down my cheeks. I'm shaking my head, in complete shock. Miller still has his arms wrapped around me. He brings his mouth to my ear. "And you said promposals were stupid."

I laugh through my tears. Then I turn around and kiss him. "I'm obviously wrong a lot."

He presses his forehead to mine and smiles.

Someone turns on the lights. We separate, and my mother is wiping her eyes. "Now *that's* what you guys should have submitted."

Lexie is nodding in agreement.

"Doesn't meet the criteria," Jonah says. "It wasn't all filmed this year." He looks at Miller and winks. "It was great, though."

I stare at the blank television in disbelief. And then, something strikes me. "Wait a second." I face Miller. "You said you named your truck after a Beatles song. But Nora was the name of my character in that play."

He smiles.

"Do the Beatles even have a song called 'Nora'?"

He shakes his head, and I can't even believe this guy right now. He's never going to be able to top this.

꘎

An hour later, I'm still on a high. Not a *real* high. A Miller high.

He promised he'd feed me because I'm starving, but he's heading in the opposite direction of town.

"I thought we were going to eat."

"There's something I want to show you at home, first."

I'm sitting in the middle of his truck seat, leaning my head on his shoulder. I'm looking down at my phone when I feel the truck begin to slow down. We pass Miller's driveway, though. He pulls off to the side of the road in the dark.

"What are you doing?"

He opens his truck door and grabs my hand, pulling me out. He walks me a few feet and then points at something. I look up at the city limit sign.

"Notice anything?"

I look down, and it's cemented to the ground. I laugh. "Wow. You did it. You moved the entire city limit."

"I was thinking we could hang at my house and order pizza with Gramps tonight."

"Pepperoni and pineapple?"

Miller shakes his head, drops my hand, and begins walking back to his truck. "So close to a perfect ten, Clara. *So* close."

Five minutes later, me and Gramps are acting like Miller ordering pizza is the most exciting thing we've ever witnessed. We're both sitting on the edge of our chairs. I'm biting my nails. Miller has the phone on speaker, so the room grows tense when the pizza guy says, "I don't think we deliver that far out. Our delivery area is inside the city limit."

"I do live inside the city limit. By about twenty feet," Miller says confidently.

There's silence on the other end of the line before the guy says, "Okay. Got you in the system. We should be there in about forty-five minutes."

When Miller hangs up the phone, we both jump up and high-five. Gramps can't really jump up, so I give him a low five.

"I'm a genius," Miller says. "Five months of hard and very illegal work finally paid off."

"I'm kinda proud of you," Gramps says. "Even though I don't want to condone anything illegal. But I mean . . . it's pizza, so . . ."

Miller laughs. The alarm on Gramps's medication timer goes off, so I walk to the kitchen to get him the pills he needs. I've been helping Miller out with Gramps while he's at work. There's a full-time aide here during the day, but it's getting to where he needs help during all the other hours too.

I like getting to spend time with Gramps. He tells me so many great stories about Miller. About his own life. And even though he still jokes that his wife skipped town, I love hearing him talk about her. They were married for fifty-two years before she died. Hearing the stories of the two of them helps reaffirm my belief in love.

Jonah and my mother help too. It was weird for a while, seeing them together. But they're a good fit. They're taking it slow and have decided to wait before making any big moves, like moving in together. But we have dinner with Jonah and Elijah almost every night.

Jonah is a completely different person with my mother than he was with Aunt Jenny. Not that he wouldn't have been happy living a life with Aunt Jenny and Elijah. But my mother makes him light up in a way I've never seen before. Every time she's near him, he looks at her like she's the greatest thing he's ever seen.

I catch Miller looking at me like that sometimes. Like right now, as I stand in the kitchen, prepping meds for his grandpa.

I take them to the living room and sit next to Miller on the couch.

Gramps swallows his meds, then sets his glass of water on the table next to his chair. "So? I guess you finally saw the video of when Miller fell in love with you?"

I laugh and lean into Miller. "Your grandson is a romantic."

Gramps laughs. "No, my grandson is a nitwit. Took him three years to finally ask you out."

"Patience is a virtue," Miller says.

"Not when you have cancer." Gramps stands up. "I've been waiting to die for seven months now, but it ain't ever gonna happen. Guess I might as well get this over with." He uses his walker to slowly make his way into the kitchen.

"Get what over with?" Miller asks him.

Gramps opens a drawer where he keeps a lot of his paperwork. He rifles through it and then pulls out a folder, bringing it back to the living room with him. He tosses it on the table in front of Miller. "I wanted to wait and have my lawyer tell you about it after I was dead. Thought it'd be funnier that way. But sometimes I think I might never die, and you don't have much time left to apply for college."

Miller pulls the folder toward him. He opens it and begins to read the first page. It looks like a will. Miller scans over it and chuckles. "You actually left me the rights to your air in the will?" Miller asks, looking up from the papers.

Gramps rolls his eyes. "I've been telling you this for ten years, but you keep laughing at me!"

Miller shrugs. "Maybe I'm missing the joke? How can you will someone *air*?"

"They're air *rights*, you dumbass!" Gramps pushes back in his chair. "Bought them when I was thirty, back when me and your grandma lived in New York. Bastards have been trying to get me to sell them for years, but I already told you I was giving them to you, and I don't break my word."

I'm just as confused as Miller, I guess. "What are air rights?"

Gramps rolls his head. "They don't teach you kids anything in school. It's like owning land, but in bigger cities, you can actually own parts of the air so people can't build in front of your building or on top of your building. I own a small chunk of that air in Union Square. Worth about a quarter of a million dollars last time I checked."

Miller chokes on nothing. He keeps choking. Sputtering. I pat his back before he stands up and points down at the folder. "Are you kidding me?"

Gramps shakes his head. "I know how much you want to go to that school down in Austin. My lawyer said it's gonna cost you about a hundred and fifty thousand to get a degree. Plus, you'll have taxes to pay when you sell the rights. I figure you'll have enough left to help with a down payment on a house someday or maybe travel. Or buy some film equipment. I don't know. I ain't making you rich, but it's better than nothing."

Miller looks like he's about to cry. He paces the room, trying not to look at his grandpa. When he does, his eyes are red, but he's laughing. "All this time you kept saying I was inheriting *air*. I thought you were just being you." He walks over to his gramps and hugs him. Then he pulls back. "And what do you mean you've been waiting to die first before telling me about this? Why?"

Gramps shrugs. "I thought it'd be funny. Me getting in one final joke after I'm dead, when you weren't expecting it."

Miller rolls his eyes. Then looks at me, smiling. I can tell we're having the same thought, and nothing makes me happier than knowing we might be in the same city after I graduate next year. At the same school. We might even have some of the same classes.

"You do realize what this means, right?" I ask him.

Miller shrugs.

"The University of Texas? Your school color will be *orange*, Miller."

He laughs. So does his grandpa. But Miller doesn't realize the jokes aren't over. I'm saving one of them for prom.

I bought the perfect dress for our special occasion. It's the most atrocious shade of orange I could find.

ACKNOWLEDGMENTS

First and foremost, I want to thank you for reading this book. I seem to be unable to stick to one genre, so the fact that you guys support whatever I'm in the mood to write is the thing I cherish most about my career.

I tend to always have a huge list of people to thank with each book, but I think I covered almost everyone I know in the acknowledgments for *Verity*. While I could do that again, I'm going to condense these acknowledgments to focus first on a few people who had absolutely nothing to do with the creation of this novel. Kimberly Parker and Tyler Easton, I want to thank you guys for being such an epic example for all parents. The way you both coparent is inspiring and hopeful, and I feel you guys need to be acknowledged. I'd also love to thank Murphy Fennell and Nick Hopkins for the same reason and for being the two best parents my niece could hope for.

Thank you to those who read through this book as I was writing it. Brooke, Murphy, Amber Goleb, Tasara, Talon, Maria, Anjanette, Vannoy, and Lin: I appreciate your honesty and feedback. You all make me want to continue to grow in this career, and that's why I continue to bombard you with first drafts.

A huge thanks to my agent, Jane Dystel, and the entire team. You guys continue to amaze me with your continued support, knowledge, and encouragement.

Thank you to Anh Schluep and everyone at Montlake Romance. This is our first book together, and I have thoroughly enjoyed working with the entire Montlake team. I can't wait to create more stories with you guys!

Thank you to Lindsey Faber for being an absolute delight to work with. I hope I get to keep you forever.

To all of my author friends, readers, bloggers, bookstagrammers, booktubers, industry professionals, and the like. Thank you for being part of this wonderful book world. The creativity inside all of you keeps me inspired.

ABOUT THE AUTHOR

Photo © Julien Poupard

Colleen Hoover is the #1 *New York Times* bestselling author of several novels, including the bestselling women's fiction novel *It Ends with Us* and the bestselling psychological thriller *Verity*. She has won the Goodreads Choice Award for Best Romance three years in a row—for *Confess* (2015), *It Ends with Us* (2016), and *Without Merit* (2017). *Confess* was adapted into a seven-episode online series. In 2015, Hoover and her family founded the Bookworm Box, a bookstore and monthly subscription service that offers signed novels donated by authors. All profits go to various charities each month to help those in need. Hoover lives in Texas with her husband and their three boys. Visit www.colleenhoover.com.